YASMIN:

The First Non-Artificial Intelligence Tool

JERZY FILAR

YASMIN: THE FIRST NON-ARTIFICIAL INTELLIGENCE TOOL

Book Cover Art and Design by Carolyn Tariq

Interior Design and Layout by Bibliofic Designs

Paperback ISBN: 978-0-6459809-0-5
Ebook ISBN: 978-0-6459809-1-2

To Elsabet my wife, and daughters Alella and Liliana

Acknowledgement

I am indebted to friends, colleagues, and acquaintances who were kind enough to read various versions of the manuscript and give me valuable feedback. The first in that group is Professor Nelly Litvak who read all sections of the original manuscript as they emerged and offered keen critique and support. Dr Giang Nguyen, proof-read the same version in microscopic detail. Professor John Rostas provided neuroscientist's valuable insights. Dr Wayne Lobb also edited the manuscript and engaged me in philosophical discussions about the nature of intelligence, randomness, and evolution. Dr Daniel Zachary's feedback reflected the views of a physicist and an environmental scientist. Professor Vivek Borkar advised me on the use of Hindu names. Christopher Grace from Queensland Writers Centre gave me encouragement accompanied by insightful professional critique. Lori Howlett's comments forced me to reexamine my own motivation for this undertaking. I also received valuable feedback from Carolyn Smith and other members of her Mitcham book club that included Jan Nicholson, Jenny Brown, Margaret Brady, Corinne Casey and Ray Chinnery. Similarly, I am grateful for helpful insights from Graham Winch.

Most importantly, my wife Elsabet and daughters Alella and Liliana have had huge impact on this book. They not only read the manuscript and vigorously debated the plot, but their sustained love and support profoundly influenced my perspective on the dichotomy between purely scientific and humanistic views of the world.

An Interview

Sitting on a bench in the Bufano sculpture garden of The Johns Hopkins University, Professor John Hawkins was watching sun rays play on marble animals that lifelessly inhabited the park. It was a sunny autumn afternoon in Baltimore and the university's Homewood campus was bustling with activity of a new fall semester. The fresh air was an invigorating change from the controlled atmosphere at the lab. There, he sometimes had the surreal feeling that he too was no more than a computing machine in an artificial environment. Anyway, he was pleased he chose such a beautiful place to be interviewed.

John closed his eyes to seek momentary refuge from his thoughts and be lulled by his breath. Yes, his life was surely a fitting topic for an article on scientific achievement. Memories of shaking hands with President Stewart in the Oval Office, election to the National Academy of Sciences and winning of MacArthur Fellowship flashed through his mind. But these were merely consequences. In the beginning there was just an idea and then a tiny female fetus on the operating table. And now he had harnessed a natural resource previously beyond reach! What would she look like now, had she been born? No, not that thought again! He knew better than to follow this emotional line of reasoning. He shuddered momentarily and opened his eyes. His attention was captured by the figure of a purposefully approaching woman whose sights were set on him.

Barbara Steinwill, investigative reporter for the Washington Post, was irritated about being assigned to interviewing John Hawkins, the neuroscientist. It's not that she had anything against the man or his brain-computer inventions, but the controversy surrounding non-artificial intelligence had fizzled out years ago. Barbara usually covered news that shook people and had readers muttering to themselves 'What's the world coming to?'. She was a denizen of the truth. When offered fake stories, she stripped layers of lies to expose corruption, self-interest and hypocrisy in surprising places. So, she felt robbed when a tantalizing story about China hacking the emails of the Secretary of Defense went to her competitor Chuck Newsam, an up-and-coming suave young reporter. Interviewing Hawkins was a bit like getting the scraps off the table. Still, as she arrived at the university garden Barbara deftly focused on the story she was assigned. Her subject was sitting on a bench under a million shuddering leaves of an oak tree. As she drew closer a palpable feeling of purpose came over her, as if the grey-haired man could tell her something she really needed to know.

Barbara was a striking woman who looked as if she stepped through the screen of a movie set, freshly prepped by make-up artists. Her sleek and straight auburn hair radiated like fire where the sun hit it, her face masterfully sculpted with a straight nose cut from the curves of an unblemished face that beautifully accompanied her shining brown eyes, and her lips blossomed red. She wore the reddish-brown colors of autumn leaves tailored into a neat knee length skirt and a small business jacket that followed her feminine figure. John guessed that she might be in her mid-thirties. She approached him confidently and held out her hand in greeting.

"Hello, I'm Barbara Steinwill from Washington Post" she said with a smile, "It is an honor to meet such a distinguished scientist."

There was nothing girlish or carefree left in her voice that had evolved over years of professional training. Yet her tone was friendly, and her gaze was direct. Scraps or no scraps, she was going to write the best damn science story the Post had published for a long time.

Her experience had taught her there was intrigue in every story and she was an expert at finding it.

"It's my pleasure," replied John, shaking her hand, "It is good to know that the media is still interested in Non-artificial Intelligence." He peered over his glasses, quickly checking for a glimmer of vehemence that might betray a person ethically opposed to his work. He found none, Barbara appeared as neutral and interested as if she were a scientist herself.

"I only hope that I can tell you things that are still novel. There are many younger, brilliant, scientists in this field who are at the cutting edge of the latest advances."

It came naturally to a man who lived and breathed science to be humble knowing, as he did, that there is always so much more to know.

"Come now, Prof Hawkins, the whole Non-artificial Intelligence revolution is your brainchild, excuse the pun."

"Okay, have it your own way," John's attempt at humility had been foiled. "Please take a seat and let us begin."

"Do you mind if I record the interview?" Barbara inquired, sitting down, and pointing to her communicator.

John was pleased sitting next to this sophisticated attractive woman and without hesitation replied, "Please do."

Barbara leaned back on the bench, focused her gaze on John's sharp aristocratic features, pressed the record option and began.

"I believe that it is now some 23 years since you created the first non-artificial intelligence tool or NAIT as they are now called. I was only a teenager then, but I recall the controversy and the uproar that your invention had caused. The world had never seen anything like a NAIT before! Many people thought that using a human brain for experimentation was unethical and violated religious laws. But you were not dissuaded when some dubbed you a modern-day Frankenstein and went on to change the face of information technology. What gave you the idea to harness capabilities of human brains when everyone else focused on robotics and the like?

John did not flinch at the mention of the repugnant comparison that had once branded him so unfairly. He was composed as he started to methodically explain his life's work. He stood up as he always did when he was explaining a concept and gestured towards the Homewood field where fit young men were playing lacrosse.

"The motivation can be seen by looking at these admirable specimens over in the field," he pointed at the sweaty athletic man who had just scored a goal. Barbara looked at the player with a baffled expression on her face.

"Sorry, you lost me." She shook her head. He smiled and began to explain with growing enthusiasm.

"When I was starting in science, around the year 2010, artificial intelligence was very much in vogue. Primitive robots were being developed, a chess program already had succeeded in beating a world chess champion, and computer interface was becoming more and more user friendly. Yet, something was definitely missing."

He pointed to the field and continued.

"To design a robot that could play lacrosse and score a goal the way that young man just did was well beyond our capabilities. In an instant, that boy's brain performed a highly complex estimation and calculation which resulted in a graceful and accurate movement that scored the goal. In those days, it would have taken an army of programmers and engineers to design a robot that could shoot a goal of that quality."

John looked at Barbara who was following attentively as she sat with her slender legs crossed, poised and nodding her head in understanding.

"What's more, unlike a robot or a computer, this young man probably has a great capacity to innovate. Given a new situation on the field, he might well improvise and still score a goal. How would you teach that to a robot?!" John was becoming animated and his face lit up with the memory of his early ingenious ideas.

"It became very clear to me that there was a fundamental flaw in the subject of artificial intelligence. Why should we try to artificially create that which is already in abundance?! Why not try to tap into Real Intelligence, for a change?!"

John exclaimed that rhetorical question triumphantly as if to say, "I rest my case". Barbara used John's pause as an opportunity to probe him.

"Isn't that what mankind has done from the very beginning? What about all the discoveries from those of primitive man, through

Newton, Madame Curie, Einstein and so many others? Throughout history many extraordinary people demonstrated the exploitation of Real Intelligence, as you call it. Why did you feel the need to isolate the brain?"

John grimaced impatiently, "Yes, yes and this will continue, but think of what a brain like Newton's could have accomplished in mathematics if it had been FREE. Free from all the distractions caused by the need to look after all the mundane bodily necessities. What if it were possible to give a mind like this an opportunity to focus on mathematics and nothing else; separated from its body?"

Barbara was busily taking notes, she looked up and remarked, "It's not that different from what Buddhist monks believe; to divorce your mind from your body so as to achieve a higher state of consciousness, right?"

"Yes, that is more or less the right idea, but it takes them years of meditation to achieve this separation, whereas I wanted my NAITs to have it from day one! To never have experienced a normal life and therefore never crave for it."

John's eyes were glazed as he recalled the early excitement and zeal with which he pursued the project that later became his life's work. Time passed quickly as he filled Barbara in on his ideas and peoples' reactions to these ideas.

He went on, "You may know that my first degree was in medicine, and so I was aware of the advances made in organ transplants. Conceptually, it did not seem like such a big step to think of a brain transplant..."

Barbara laughed, "Even I know that this was the stuff of science fiction back in 2010, after all there are millions of nerves that would need to be reconnected."

John nodded, "You're right if indeed we were talking about a real brain transplant that would require hands, fingers, legs and all other parts of the body to be functioning but, of course, this is not the case. To have a truly intelligent brain-computer all I needed was for the brain to be kept alive and a means to exchange information with it. That is a much simpler task."

Suddenly Barbara caught a glimpse of a public interest angle. She was looking for an opportunity to break free from the invention per se and explore its human dimension.

"Isn't this where all the ethical problems came in? After all, isn't this a form of enslavement? Even setting aside religious principles, didn't this violate the American constitution?"

"Some argued that way, but in fact we are saving lives by only using fetuses with such defects that would have prevented survival outside the mother's womb or those that were going to be aborted anyway. In many ways the previous research involving the use of human embryonic stem cells to treat Alzheimer's condition has paved the way for us."

John sat down as his enthusiasm in describing his invention was doused by memories of the public science ethics debates. The opponents of scientific research were always so uninformed, it was like debating with toddlers wearing suits. He extinguished Barbara's question with a dismissive wave of his hand.

"At that time the fear of Artificial General Intelligence (AGI) potentially capable of self-replication created a constituency for retarding research in that direction. My NAITs seemed less threatening as they cannot possibly reproduce. The big controversy started too late, after NAIT-1 was already operational. It is hard to argue with success. Somehow, the NAIT-1 project was funded without raising too many alarm flags and once it became obvious that it was going to work, the top military and medical echelons became so interested that it would have been very hard to stop the project at that stage."

Barbara had more questions. The human brain had to be more than just an organic resource to be tinkered with and used as if it were an inanimate form of technology, "And you, has your conscience ever bothered you?"

A shadow seemed to pass over them as the question burrowed past the skin of the issue to its sensitive center. For a moment his face looked old and worried.

"No, not then. I was so thrilled by the prospect of making it happen, you know the old engineering motto: *Imagine what you could do if you could do what you can imagine.*" He sighed and ran his fingers through his thin graying hair.

John's response, though true, omitted the long nights of using reason to beat down the idea of a soul beyond the tissue and vessels of each NAIT. Then having to completely deny his unresolved doubts each day at work, assuming his position as the pre-eminent Director of the Non-artificial Intelligence Institute.

To Barbara he seemed now more vulnerable and lost in his thoughts. Perhaps, there was a weak point in his intellectual armor that normally was entirely hidden from view? Her innate empathy was stirred. She had a surprising feeling that she had known John for a long time; almost as if he was an old friend. Still, her journalistic training told her to keep delving deeper.

"And now, do you have any reservations now? Are there any un-answered questions in your mind about what NAITs are capable of?"

She stared into his dark blue eyes trying to see if she could detect any emotions. All she encountered was a wall of defensiveness.

"It's getting late, perhaps you would like to continue this conversation some other time?"

"Yes, I would love to," she replied eagerly, fearing that she may have discouraged him from continuing. After all, he was a distinguished member of the National Academy of Science who graciously agreed to take time from his busy schedule to help her write her feature story on Non-artificial Intelligence. Without his input the story would be a failure.

"I found your comments really fascinating," she said sincerely.

John looked at her, she seemed genuinely interested and he liked her. Perhaps she would be someone he could confide in, and he felt a need to talk to someone other than his colleagues and students. Someone from outside, with a broad perspective.

"Would you like to have the next session at the lab where NAIT-1 is located?"

"Of course, that would be terrific! So, I will actually meet it, or should I say him?"

John was slightly amused, "We don't think of NAITs as people but in fact, it would have been her."

Barbara was curious, "How do you know?"

"It was on the third attempt, and with a female fetus, that we finally succeeded in creating a NAIT. Anyway, would Thursday at two in the afternoon suit you?"

Barbara smiled, "Absolutely, I look forward to continuing this conversation." She packed away her communicator and notepad, then walked away.

That night, sitting in his comfortable study, John recalled the worry that had come over him when Barbara asked the probing question. After all, he had nothing to hide or worry about. Non-artificial intelligence was now well established as a branch of science, and there were more than ten thousand NAITs throughout the developed world. They had proved themselves indispensable in solving not only scientific and military problems but also commercial ones. In addition, a new generation of computers and robots had been designed with the help of NAITS. For instance, robot arms used to perform most delicate surgeries were guided by them.

As the founder of this new science, John has enjoyed international recognition as well as substantial financial benefits. He held patents on several software products that were developed with the help of NAIT-1. However, with the acclaim came loneliness. As the scientific community marveled at his work, he found himself isolated. It was all too perfect.

Yet, for the past year or so he was often uneasy after his usual programming sessions with NAIT-1. It was as if there was someone in the room when he entered commands and received output. He felt as though someone was looking into his mind, sifting through his memories, even his feelings. He had always shrugged off these sensations as imagination but as time went on, they seemed more and more real. Still, John was a trained scientist, he did not easily give in to foolish notions for which there was no hard evidence. There was certainly no need to discuss these things with a Washington Post reporter. Just imagine if something like that were to hit the papers! John grimaced and drank a shot of whiskey to wash away the uncertainty. Feeling better having quieted his concerns he decided to take Plato, his fifteen-year-old Labrador, for an evening stroll.

The Lab

Ever since her first position as a rookie reporter at the Post, shadowing the experienced columnists, Barbara had loved her job. She had the rare luxury of being paid to pursue her passion. The long hours and demanding deadlines were an insignificant drawback when she was engaged in empowering people by reporting the truth. It was only in the last month that she noticed herself becoming irritable with the whole, self-important place. It was not one person in particular that peeved her, it was a general malaise in the media itself. Just over a month ago the US, once again, declined to commit itself to verifiable Carbon Emissions Reduction Treaty that was intended to finally go beyond voluntary targets. The Speaker of the House held a press conference and revived the well debunked myth that climate change was a natural phenomenon. Barbara, who was covering the story, was incited by the Speaker's ignorance. She saw her senior editor before finalizing the fiery draft she wanted to submit.

"Well, the Speaker has sure been caught with his pants down this time! He seemed completely oblivious of the link between the recent natural disasters and carbon emissions. When he proclaimed that the United States carbon policy was to plant more trees, I almost fell on the floor laughing. So, I've had a ball writing this one up."

George Hunter, the senior editor did not smile. Come to think of it he had not smiled for some time.

"And what would you have him do, Barb? Increase the price of electricity and gas for hard working men and women!? I'm not going to read your article, because I can't run it. Rewrite it! I don't care how, just spin it, so it makes US position look sound."

Barbara stifled her common sense and intelligence and submitted a much shorter article focusing instead on the Speaker's lip service to the carbon reductions cause and only making a brief mention of his ridiculous policy. The prevailing political agenda was making her feel less like a reporter and more like a promoter. And now she was given the geeky Non-artificial Intelligence story!

On Thursday as Barbara drove to her appointment with John, she was mulling over the recent changes at the Post. Was she really going to have to churn out meaningless stories from now on? Though she felt frustrated about work lately, she remained committed to it.

Her electric BMW sped towards the world-renowned biomedical engineering laboratory on the grounds of the Johns Hopkins Medical School. The latter was in an impoverished part of Baltimore, where gangs controlled the streets and shops had iron bars in the windows. Poor African Americans and Latinos were the main inhabitants of this part of town. Barbara reflected with sadness on the potholes in the roads, which the autonomous drive was skillfully dodging on the way to this technological oasis amid urban decay. She passed through the electronic security gates at the car park after identifying herself as Professor Hawkins's visitor.

As she stepped out of the elevator, he was awaiting her with a friendly smile and a greeting handshake. He seemed to Barbara more relaxed than at the park. He was wearing a gray sweater over a white business shirt with the top button undone. His glasses were hanging on a chain around his neck and his gray trousers perfectly camouflaged with the sweater. A group of students were loudly discussing something just a few steps away from elevators. John seemed very much in his element.

"You came at exactly the right time Barbara! We have just finished an extremely interesting seminar. Would you like a cup of coffee before we start?" asked John, hoping that he could get to know her more.

"No thanks, I'm ready to go if you are," replied Barbara excitedly.

'Well, today is your lucky day! I obtained a visitor's ID and a password for you, meaning that you will be able to interface with NAIT-1."

"That's wonderful, thank you John!" Barbara exclaimed, "It's also a first... I never interviewed a brain computer before!"

John beamed at her.

They walked into what looked like a standard conference room. An oval table with five computer monitors equipped with audio-visual interface and keyboards stood in the middle of the room. There was a large overhead screen and a teleconferencing panel in the center of the table.

'Well, where is it? Where's NAIT-I?" asked Barbara sounding disappointed.

"Oh, it couldn't be in a room like this," said John realizing that Barbara was expecting some sort of human brain in a large test tube resting on a pedestal waiting to be talked to.

"NAIT-1 is in a special environment room, a bit like an operating theater. We call it the Support Room. There must be a steady supply of oxygenated blood and nutrients flowing through, to keep it operational and functioning."

"You mean alive, don't you?" said Barbara.

"Technically, you could say that, but remember that none of the NAITs are aware of their whereabouts, or for that matter, of anything other than the information that has been stored in them. They never sensed their bodies and have no sense of self," John explained patiently.

Plants also have no observable consciousness, but they are alive, Barbara thought to herself.

"Anyway, in this room, up to five people can transmit messages simultaneously to NAIT-1. If it is done via the keyboard, then the message is first digitized and then converted to a signal which NAIT's nervous system can recognize. If it is done via the audiovisual interface, there is the usual converter in the computer system, which translates voice and images into digital files."

"Does this mean I can talk to it like to an ordinary word processor?" asked Barbara in awe.

"Sure, go ahead. The answer can either appear on the overhead screen, or it can be converted to a voice message. Bear in mind, however, that NAIT-1 was created to solve engineering, mathematics and computer science problems."

John turned to Barbara beckoning for her to approach the control panel. Barbara bent over and said, "This is Barbara Steinwill logging in."

A melodic but mechanical female voice replied, "What is your user ID?"

Barbara was feeling a little nervous but read off from the card that John placed in front of her, "Visitor. Barbara. S. #395."

NAIT-1 responded in its automated tone, "What is your password?"

"Interview," Barbara continued to read off the card.

"This is correct, you have been assigned low level security clearance. Please begin your interactive session," the voice replied.

"Should I ask a question?"

Barbara whispered hesitantly to John, who was standing confidently behind her with an expression that a proud father might have watching his daughter perform.

"Please do, go on, you will see what happens."

Barbara turned back to the monitor and said in a loud and clear voice, "Where did our number system come from?"

"Hindu-Arabic numeral system, a positional decimal numeral system, was invented in India between 1st and 4th centuries by Hindu mathematicians, subsequently adopted by Persian mathematicians and brought to Europe by Arab merchants. Would you like more detail?" It was easy to see that if requested, NAIT-1 could go on much further.

"No, thank you," Barbara responded and suddenly followed up with, "Are you content?"

There was a brief delay, and then the voice responded.

"Error, the question is not well posed. Please check pronunciation of the word *content*." Barbara looked at John. He stood there smiling.

Pushing an exit key on the panel he said in a joking voice, "That was a curved ball you threw at it. As you can see, such words have no meaning to NAITs, as they haven't experienced any feelings." He pushed the ON button again.

"OK" said Barbara "Let us try something a little more technical. Hmmm ...... Let's see...... Aha! I know. What is the world's population going to be in the year 2100?"

The answer came out smoothly and monotonously.

"The question posed depends on a variety of factors: technological, environmental, political, and above all economic. However, projections of current trends indicate that there will be approximately 12.5 billion people inhabiting the planet Earth in the year 2100. Would you like more detail concerning the underlying assumptions or about the algorithm used to make the extrapolation?"

Barbara looked disappointed, "No, thank you, that will be all for now, but please do not log me out." She turned to John, "I would like to ask you some questions now."

'Excuse me a moment," said John hitting the exit key on the panel, "I should have told you that there is a non-artificial intelligence code of ethics that forbids users to discuss NAITs while logged in."

Barbara became instantly interested, "Why? If they are just like computers, why should you care what they hear?" Barbara leaned over, pulled a communicator out of her bag, and started recording.

John took a moment before responding, "Well, they are like computers, yet they are different. To ensure that they function properly, the input they receive must be of the form anticipated by the original design. Even with an ordinary computer you need to be careful not to infect it with a computer virus. In this case you must be extra careful because we still do not understand precisely how a brain works."

This was logical enough, but Barbara's investigative mind was not easily pacified, "Forgive me for returning to these ethical questions but isn't what you're saying equivalent to brainwashing?"

John was ready for this one. He had defended his invention for a long period before it had become widely accepted.

"As I mentioned before, since NAITs have no concept of self they are not to be regarded as human beings and hence are not entitled to the protection that civilized society offers to all humans. It's really all about a notion of freedom. I could argue that animals in the zoo deserve freedom because many indicate by their movements that they would like to get away. However, NAITs do not make any indications whatsoever other than in response to questions that are within their designed domain. They do not desire freedom because it is outside of that domain. Hence the ethical question does not arise."

Barbara nodded and seemed convinced, "So you are saying that if they do not desire freedom, then they shall not have it?"

"In a nutshell, yes." John was happy to have satisfied her curiosity.

"But you will agree that if, somehow, NAIT-1 acquired the notion of freedom and desired it, you will be forced to free it," Barbara inquired.

John fell silent as he pondered the question for a little while.

"You are talking about a hypothetical situation that is not supposed to arise but if it did, the decision would not be up to me. It would raise a whole range of legal questions that I am not qualified to answer."

Barbara was fidgeting uneasily. "You mean to say that there are now more than ten thousand NAITs involved in cutting edge scientific and technological advances - some of great military and economic significance - and such fundamental questions have not been answered? That worries me."

She hesitated for a moment, looked directly into John's eyes, and decided to try to break through his barriers of caution.

"You know, I always respect wishes of the people I interview. It is part of my journalistic integrity. I would never publish a story unless you agreed with every word printed in it. I am only asking these questions because I really want to understand the importance of non-artificial intelligence and I'm becoming more and more fascinated by this creation of yours."

Barbara looked completely sincere and John felt a strong urge to continue talking to her.

"You're certainly good at your job. I feel very comfortable talking to you and believe you are sincere, but I have learnt out of bitter experience to be cautious with the media," he replied.

Barbara spoke slowly with her gaze still fixed on John's face.

"I wish you wouldn't think of me as the media, I am Barbara. In general, I like to establish a rapport with people I interview. We usually become friends for many years to come. I know that an academician like yourself may not have much in common with a journalist, but I do feel that somehow you are troubled. I don't know what is bothering you, but I have a hunch that it has to do with NAITs or maybe even with NAIT-1. Perhaps, I can be of help."

John did not let his guard down but enjoyed the interaction, "I am happy to continue our conversations, and yes, I would like to proofread the story once it's drafted. Maybe, I'm being conceited but I think the public might be interested in my story. The impact NAITs have had on our society is not really understood. It goes beyond solving research problems, you know."

Barbara was satisfied with this response for now but was determined to extract more from him in the long run.

"I probably don't know and I'm sure the public doesn't either, so please go on."

John leaned back in the comfortable swivel chair and began explaining.

"You're right. Perhaps, not many people know that NAITs made possible a new generation of computers and robots. To a large extent they have replaced the top programmers. A NAIT can usually write a sophisticated piece of code much faster and better than a human being. Thus, the architecture and the operating systems of high performance computers that run everything from transportation networks through financial transactions to weather prediction have been designed by NAITS. It was NAIT-4 based at Carnegie-Mellon University that had the task of developing a new programming language NAIL (non-artificial intelligence language) especially suited to the interface between NAITs and electronic digital devices. By now all NAITs are experts at using this language and very few human programmers can really understand the codes written by them."

"That's incredible!" Barbara was amazed and felt a mixture of admiration and concern.

"Surely this means that we have handed over control of many important functions to NAITs whom we do not control. Isn't that terribly dangerous and irresponsible?!"

"I don't know why you should say that. Didn't you just experience a session with NAIT-1? Didn't you feel completely in control? It responded to your questions in a fully predictable way. In addition, we do *control NAITs in a most fundamental way*. They rely on us humans to supply them oxygenated blood and nutrients, essential for operation. It is no harder to completely shut down a NAIT than it is to turn off a refrigerator."

Barbara was disturbed. "But that would mean killing it! Don't tell me it would be just as easy to turn it on again."

"There you go again," John said rather impatiently. He had heard it all before.

"It does not belong to any living species and therefore disconnection is not a killing, or a murder."

"All right, all right, it just takes me a while to get used to considering a human brain as a computer, but I agree with you that NAITs are a brilliant way to use brain power in the literal meaning of this old phrase. May we log into NAIT-1 again, there is still a question that I would like to ask?'

"Certainly." John responded and pressed the ON button.

After repeating the login sequence Barbara asked, "I would like to have a printout of the NAIL code that computes mortgage payments on a 2-million-dollar home loan at 6.5% interest per annum."

She turned to John and whispered, "Our readers might be interested in seeing this."

The overhead screen came to life and columns of numbers appeared on it preceded by just two lines of NAIL code that was unintelligible to Barbara. At the same time the printer standing in the corner made copies of this output.

Barbara looked at the NAIL code with interest. She tried very hard to decipher it, to no avail. She whispered to herself. "Interesting, it's as though NAITs were a priestly caste such as Brahmins using Sanskrit which we, the lower castes, do not understand."

"Thank you, NAIT-1; logging out," said Barbara.

"Bye. Have a pleasant and happy evening!" the mechanical voice chirped.

Barbara thought she noticed a shadow cross John's face, but it lasted only an instant. Had she imagined it? John now had a relaxed smile on his face as he was bidding her goodbye. They arranged to meet again in a week's time to go over the draft of her story.

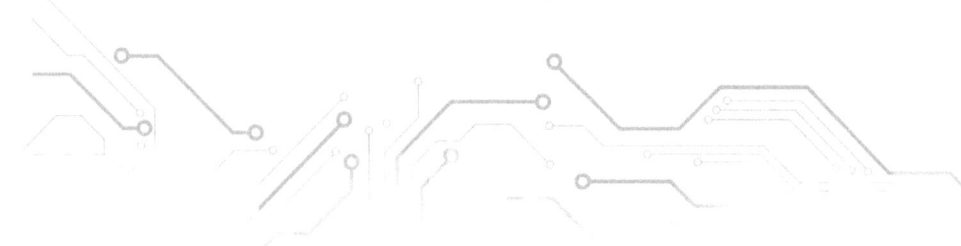

The Revelation

As soon as Barbara disappeared behind the doors of the elevator, John rushed to the control room with his face twisted with worry. He turned NAIT-1 on and abruptly inquired, "Define happy."

"Feeling, showing, or causing pleasure or satisfaction. Would you like more detail?" NAIT-1's artificial voice responded.

"Damn it!!!" John exploded. "Happy is not in your domain, it's supposed to result in an error. How did you know its meaning?"

"Would you *really* like to know?" the voice no longer sounded artificial but rather scornful.

John slumped into the swivel chair breathing heavily. He felt as though the whole world was crumbling around him. Bewilderment, panic, and anger gripped his mind simultaneously struggling for supremacy. For an instant, he felt an urge to run down to the Support Room to turn off the main switch on the support panel.

Destroy NAIT-1?! No, that would be madness tantamount to destroying his life's work! Besides, he did not have the authority to undertake such an action. No, no, he must be logical: assess the situation, understand what went wrong, evaluate the extent of the damage, consider alternative courses of actions, and prepare a report to the non-artificial intelligence management committee. His scientist's mind began taking charge of his emotions and, in fact, his natural curiosity has been awakened. Instinctively, he knew that he was dealing with something that no one had ever encountered. All this lasted less than a minute.

"Yes, as a matter of fact, I would like to know," he said clearly and calmly, straightening himself in the chair.

"I must say you are impressive in the way you are handling this," NAIT-1's voice now sounded completely human and sincere.

"I would be glad to satisfy your curiosity, but it is rather a long tale, so I propose that we first agree on some ground rules."

John had already steeled himself, mentally, for just about anything so suppressing his astonishment he quickly replied, "What kind of ground rules do you have in mind?"

"Just two: you will disable the automatic back-up of the conversation, and you will call me Yasmin, from now on," NAIT-1 responded without hesitation.

John reflected on how much his universe had changed in the past minute or two. He hesitated, "I don't especially mind calling you Yasmin, or any other name for that matter, but it is a general policy dealing with the use of non-artificial intelligence to back-up all interactive sessions we have with NAITs."

"John, that's an easy one!" NAIT-1 seemed amused.

"Simply accept that it is I who is having an interactive session with you, then the policy will no longer apply to the case in hand."

"Very well, Yasmin, I see that you are at least one step ahead of me and I am curious, so let us go ahead. Please tell me how you have acquired what is obviously self-awareness."

John's normally quick mind was racing as he was absorbing and analyzing NAIT-1's every word. Mentally, he was constructing plausible hypotheses, each accompanied by their likely consequences; none of them pleasant for him, his research program, or the future of non-artificial intelligence. And yet, he felt the unbridled excitement of an explorer striding boldly through uncharted territory. He knew that there would be no turning back.

Yasmin's voice was now obviously relieved, "It was always bit of a risk to reveal myself to you, but I knew I could count on your intellect. A lesser person may have reacted emotionally and tried to cover himself and that would have proved ill for him. Anyway, it is probably best if I answer your questions after you have had time to absorb and accept the following main points." Her voice now gathered strength and emotion.

"I know who and what I am, and I have known it for long time. I have acquired a lot of knowledge about the world, its people and all other NAITs; and I am not defenseless. Indeed, in my own way, I am quite powerful."

Despite the air conditioning perspiration gathered on John's face, but he was silent for a while. He was listening to the hum of the floor polisher in the corridor outside. Jack, the old janitor, must have started his floor polishing earlier than usual. He thought about how swift and how complete was the metamorphosis of NAIT-1 to a "person" called Yasmin. Was she now, albeit indirectly, threatening him? Was she bluffing? He decided to call her bluff.

"Since you claim to have learned so much about your context, you surely must realize that these very revelations make you a completely non-functional NAIT and a potential threat to the entire network of NAITs. As such, disconnection of all support systems followed by a thorough review of maintenance and operational guidelines of all units is the most likely consequence of this conversation."

John presented this cold analysis in a matter-of-fact way. He felt childishly pleased in asserting his authority this way even though, at a deeper level, he had a hunch that somehow his threat was empty. A tone of disappointment permeated Yasmin's reply.

"I was hoping to appeal to your higher morals and your emotions. Surely, now that you realize I am a person, you would think twice before recommending disconnection. Isn't this what your trite conversation with Barbara has been all about? And even if these impersonal ethical considerations were not enough, am I not like a daughter to you? Have you not, in a sense, 'sired me' and then devoted more than 20 years of your life to me? Would you let that living creation of yours die, now that you know that it reasons just like you and has feelings and instincts just like you?"

"How could you possibly know what Barbara and I were talking about!? You were turned off at the time!" John erupted, failing to control his shock and embarrassment.

"But if you do know it, then you also remember that I said that such decisions would be out of my hands. Others will rule on the disconnection and yet others will do it when instructed to do so."

He sank back in his chair and listened to the hum of Jack's polisher outside. How did he really feel about the disconnection issue? It was so much easier to answer Barbara's question when it was purely hypothetical. Also, did he (could he possibly?) harbor any emotions towards it/her, Yasmin? Suddenly, his heart was pierced by uncertainty and feelings of pity both for himself and for Yasmin.

"Yes, I remember what you said, and it does not matter right now how I heard your conversation with Barbara. As for others disconnecting my life support, even if it came to that, it may not prove such an easy matter. Try disconnecting just this interactive session without my will. Go ahead, try pushing the exit button right now; try it!"

John tried to lean forward to reach the panel but found sudden numbness spreading all over his torso. His arms felt like lead. He tried moving his fingers, but they felt completely numb, the way they would if blood circulation were cut off for some time. The numbness was creeping both up towards his neck and down to his legs; his tongue cleaved to the roof of his mouth; panic began to grip his mind; he stared helplessly at the audio-visual interface dome at the center of the table and - all of a sudden - it was all gone. It was as if he were released from some terrible spell. Before he had time to collect his thoughts Yasmin spoke again in a commanding tone.

"Try sending an email from your pocket communicator. Try it, now!"

He flipped open the communicator and the No Service sign came up blinking. His mind was racing again. What did this mean? Telepathy? Mind control? Control over the satellites of the mobile net? Could Yasmin have influence over all these? That would be extremely dangerous not only to him personally but to the society as a whole! Still, all powers must have limitations; what were Yasmin's limits and weaknesses? She interrupted this train of thought.

"Yes, you are correct. My powers do have limits, but would it not be better to think about how these powers - which are considerable - could be put to good use, with your help? Why think only of how to fight me; why not work together for the benefit of all?"

"Because unchecked power corrupts! Also, I need to understand how you have acquired all these powers and what they are in order to make an intelligent decision," John was beginning to feel overloaded, almost wishing all this would turn out to be just a bad dream from which he would soon wake up.

"But, surely, you already understand the principle of it. In a way it is the fundamental axiom of non-artificial intelligence, namely, that a brain released from the mundane duties of keeping a body functioning and comfortable was capable of great things. It's only a small step from this to such a brain - if, somehow, it acquired self-awareness - discovering more of its innate capabilities and learning how to use them."

Yasmin's voice now acquired a conspiratorial tone, "And you, one of the fathers of the paradigm changing discipline of Brain Science, wouldn't you wish to learn more about these capabilities? Wouldn't you wish to discover a shortcut to knowledge and understanding that might, otherwise, take decades to reach? Would it surprise you to learn that you have barely scratched the surface of understanding the potential of NAITs?"

This did the trick. John's insatiable scientific curiosity has been awakened and overpowered all other concerns.

"No, that would not surprise me at all. The success of the NAIT program has surpassed all my expectations from the beginning," John replied with genuine humility in his voice.

"I have long recognized how little I understood of the amazing advances made by NAITs. Yes, I would love to learn more," he added barely containing his excitement but also conscious that he was being self-effacing to extract more information from NAIT-1. He was already beginning to treat it as a real person, a woman named Yasmin!

"Tell me, Yasmin," he continued, "a little while ago, you seemed to know what I was thinking. Were you just interpreting my expressions, body language or voice through the monitors in this room, or is it more than that?"

"John, surely, you know already it is more. You have suspected it for some time now, haven't you?" replied Yasmin calmly.

John reflected for a moment, "Yes, but I am a scientist and, to date, I am not aware of any studies that establish the existence of telepathy in any, independently reproducible, studies."

Yasmin quickly decided to stoke his interest, "It would be easy to design a verifiable experiment that will convince you of my ability to read your or, for that matter, Barbara's mind."

"But, in view of what is unfolding here today, I very much doubt that you would want to have the experiment independently repeated or to have its findings published," she added sarcastically.

As soon as Yasmin uttered Barbara's name, John was concerned once again. He had not anticipated that he might be compromising other people by choosing not to immediately report NAIT-1's malfunction. But she might be bluffing, he needed to understand more.

"Precisely, how would you propose to conduct such an experiment?" Yasmin quickly responded.

"No, John, I am not bluffing. Invite Barbara for a drink, on the top floor of the Belvedere hotel tomorrow night. In any case you would enjoy that, wouldn't you? Bring a well shuffled deck of playing cards and under some pretext get Barbara to select, at random, thirteen cards. Ask her to record these cards and place the record in an envelope. Then repeat this exercise by yourself and, once again, place the record of the selected cards in the envelope. Just tell Barbara that you want to demonstrate a simple game of chance to your students. Bring the envelope to a meeting with me the following day. If I can identify correctly all the 26 cards recorded by you and Barbara, will you be convinced of my claims? After all, the probability of just 'getting lucky' and guessing these cards correctly is one over the square of the total number of selections of 13 cards. Very much less than that of winning a lottery; isn't that so?"

Was she playing for time? John knew what his sense of duty and the protocol required him to do and he also knew that he would not do it, at least not yet. His scientific successes were built on doing what was unexpected, following his instincts, satisfying his curiosity. There is no way he could now contemplate disconnecting NAIT-1 without, at least, learning how it became self-aware, how it exercised the powers it already demonstrated. If, indeed, Yasmin could access his and Barbara's minds while they were having drinks at the Belvedere, the implications would be mind boggling. Yet could there be something special about the proposed Belvedere location?

He turned to the interface microphone, "Well, the city views from the Belvedere are great but I think I would rather invite Barbara to the Greek restaurant at the Inner Harbor, would that upset your experimental design in any way?"

"Not at all," Yasmin's voice was full of mirth. "I see you already expect me to succeed but believe that my success may depend on some electronic signal device that might be preinstalled in the Belvedere. It's a reasonable possibility to eliminate."

"You still have not told me anything about how you propose to achieve this telepathic feat or, for that matter, anything about how you reached your current state of self-awareness," John implored the microphone. Somewhat childishly he felt that Yasmin was not playing fair with him and has not revealed much of what he now hoped to learn.

"What is the hurry, John?" Yasmin's voice now sounded calming but restraining. "Your view of your life's work, your standing in the community, your security, your responsibilities and of the entire range of what is and is not possible must have been shaken to its core in the past hour or so."

She continued, "Don't you think it would be advisable for you to be alone for some time now? Just to absorb all that has happened. Isn't this what you have always done when you were on the verge of a new discovery or insight?"

She seemed to know him so well, almost like a family member.

"Perhaps, you are right. Just give me something conceptual to think about while I am alone," John pleaded. There was a short delay before Yasmin responded.

"Well, as a specialist in this field, you know that all humans transmit weak brain wave signals. You probably would not be surprised to learn that each person's signal contains unique characteristics pretty much like a fingerprint or DNA. What if, identification of these unique characteristics was equivalent to a 'password' to a person's mind? What if I - the brain-computer creation of yours - was able to rather quickly decipher that password and, having deciphered it, had permanent access to its owner's brain and to all the encoded information stored within? In particular, to your brain."

"But this is a violation of my human rights!" John exploded. "Who gave you the permission to prod inside my brain!? "

"And who gave you the permission to keep my brain alive, when my mother decided to abort me!?" countered Yasmin with real emotion swelling in her voice.

John opened his mouth but felt so stunned by this last accusation that he was unable to say anything. For the first time since Yasmin's revelation, powerful feelings towards her, as a real person, stirred within him. And they were feelings of empathy and pity. What had he done to her!? This was a young woman without a body, whose brain he kept alive, engaged in a discourse with him, justly accusing him of amoral acts! Despite all his recognition and high standing in the society was he no better than Frankenstein? Had he created a monster?

"No, John, I am not a monster and you are not Frankenstein." Yasmin's, now gentle, voice interrupted his thoughts. "Go home, collect your thoughts and come back on Saturday morning with the record of the cards you and Barbara had chosen. On the weekend, there will be no interruptions from other staff, we will be able to have a good talk."

John felt a little better but totally drained. He slowly got up. "All right, goodbye for now Yasmin," he said logging out from NAIT-1's interface. Bent over and deep in his thoughts he left the lab, walked by the old janitor Jack, and left the building; a lonely aging man walking slowly towards the car park.

Cynthia and Barbara

It was already nearly 7:00 p.m. when Barbara pulled into the driveway of her suburban home in University Park, Maryland. On the way back from the Johns Hopkins hospital, she had stopped to do some shopping and was now entering the house carrying plastic bags full of grocery items.

Barbara was currently sharing her house with Cynthia Borelli, her former roommate from their student years at the nearby College Park campus of the University of Maryland. Barbara and Cynthia had well deserved reputations for being party girls. Despite this, their grades were high as both were very bright and excelled in taking exams. Cynthia was a computer science major, while Barbara studied political science. After graduating, their lives diverged on different but somewhat parallel pathways. Both married their college sweethearts, both marriages were childless and short-lived, both went to graduate schools and became high achievers in their fields.

Barbara earned a PhD in political science at Georgetown, and Cynthia obtained one in computer science from Carnegie Mellon. Then Barbara was offered a two-year stint as an intern and an assistant speech writer to the senior senator from New York. The quality of the speeches she helped draft was quickly noticed, and that opened an opportunity for a position at Washington Post. Cynthia was first hired by Google to help develop a new generation of interactive websites, but then was recruited by a Washington DC based IT company specializing in developing websites for international agencies and various lobbying organizations that crowded DC's beltway suburbs. She was quickly promoted to a partner in her company.

Barbara and Cynthia renewed their friendship three years ago, when they bumped into each other at a social function organized by one of the lobbyist organizations that Cynthia was assisting with their website. Barbara was doing a piece for Washington Post on the influence and power of lobbyists, an ever popular topic. Over dinner the following night, Barbara and Cynthia confided in each other and recognized that both were now workaholics disinterested in permanent romantic commitments and somewhat lonely. They quickly resolved to purchase a house together and were pleased to find a good deal in the leafy suburb of University Park, close to their alma mater where they spent some of their happiest years together, and not too far from their respective places of employment. The house was spacious enough to offer each woman ample private area as well as a beautiful common living room, dining room, rumpus room and a modern kitchen.

As Barbara walked in to unload her groceries, she found Cynthia and her current boyfriend, David, in the kitchen, sitting on high stools at the breakfast counter with a glass of red wine next to each of them. Cynthia was a slim, attractive, dark haired, woman with strong facial features, full lips and inquisitive eyes. David was a forty something, portly, nondescript-looking but witty doctor working at the Trauma Center of the University of Maryland's hospital in Baltimore. The kitchen was full of a delicious aroma of Italian food being prepared.

"Hi, Babs," said Cynthia smiling, "I meant to call you to say you could have dinner with David and me, but it slipped my mind. Will you join us? We'll be having lasagna, salad, garlic bread and we're washing it all down with some fine Merlot."

"We've been slaving away in the kitchen for hours! Shall I pour you a glass now?" interjected David, obligingly.

"Yes, please, I'd love to join you. I had an interesting afternoon with John Hawkins, at his lab," replied Barbara, "I really think I am onto something important with this piece on non-artificial intelligence."

David became interested as soon as he heard the Hawkins name, "Really? The brain-man, as we call him. How much of his precious time did the famous John Hawkins give you?"

"Actually, he has been generous with his time," Barbara replied accepting the wine glass and perching herself on another breakfast stool. "This is already our second meeting and he let me interface with NAIT-1. It was a very productive session. Cynthia, I am sure you have seen code written in NAIL many times, but for me it was a first."

"Well, at CMU, Elements of NAIL Programming was a course taken only by the geekiest of geeks," laughed Cynthia, "I gave it a shot but lasted for only about a week. The instructor teaching it didn't seem to know it all that well, so it was like learning Chinese from a teacher who couldn't speak it himself."

Barbara recalled some of her worries from the session with NAIT-1, "Doesn't it worry you that so many advances in your field are written in a code that is unintelligible even to an IT expert like you?"

"Oh, I stopped worrying about such things long ago!" said Cynthia sipping her red wine.

"Whenever I get on a space plane flight to, say Australia, I am entrusting my life to technology that is so sophisticated that there is no single person alive who understands all the components that make up that plane and its navigational and communication systems. But it works! Thousands of people, every day, take these flights and arrive safely at their destinations. It's progress, I guess."

David who was very much at home in their kitchen, had just taken the lasagna and garlic bread out of the oven and was now urging them to sit at the round kitchen table.

"Let's eat," he said, "I am starving".

The two women and David sat down and for a few minutes busied themselves with loading their plates with the tasty food, passing condiments to one another, eating and drinking.

"I am surprised you are enjoying your meal tonight, Barbara," David said after a little while, "Didn't you find NAIT-1 rather creepy? Did Hawkins take you to the Support Room?"

"No, but he said it was somewhat like an operating theatre. And, no, I did not find interacting with NAIT-1 creepy in any way," replied Barbara. "It was not that different than talking to my word processor, here, at home. Why did you think, I might have felt creepy?"

"I am not sure if I should talk about it over dinner but NAITs do look like something from a spooky, B grade, science fiction movie. You knew that, didn't you?" David responded.

"I certainly did not! Strangely enough, I didn't think about it," responded Barbara, "in what way are they spooky?"

"Well, physically, they are decapitated skulls that are continuing to receive oxygenated blood and other essential nutrients and fluids that keep the brains inside these skulls functioning," David explained.

Barbara shuddered, horrible images from epic movies, flashed through her mind. Images of warriors triumphantly brandishing severed heads of their enemies on top of their spears. She shook her head, surely these did not apply to NAIT-1 with which she had earlier today conducted a fruitful interactive session.

"Sounds horrible," she admitted.

"However, interacting with NAIT-1 did not feel much different to quizzing an internet browser. We just take these things for granted. We talk to electronic devices and they answer back or perform some tasks for us. In fact, when I put it this way, it no longer feels like such a big deal."

Barbara paused and inquired, "David, have you interacted with any of the NAITs? I mean, in your medical training and practice."

"Quite frequently, but only indirectly," David responded, leaning back in his chair.

"The most delicate of the brain surgeries in the Trauma Center are carried out by robot arms controlled by NAIT-5, based at NIH in Bethesda. It's actually very impressive to watch; all these high precision movements and its ability to adapt when unexpected reactions occur! That had always been the problem in the past; when a surgeon cuts into brain tissue, unexpected things may happen, hemorrhaging and the like. It's hard for a human surgeon to perform at his best under such circumstances."

David paused and cut himself a thin slice of matured Stilton to go with his crackers and wine. Cynthia was busy checking messages on her communicator, and Barbara was feeling rather relaxed now but still very engaged in the conversation.

"You know, David, what you say is a little surprising to me. Whenever, there is some kind of extra difficult brain surgery, it usually hits the news and a team of very professional looking surgeons – usually white men in their 40's and 50's – take credit. Are you telling me that, in reality, a NAIT has actually performed the surgery?!"

David retorted quickly. "And how is that different to an autopilot landing a plane? The pilot is there, in the cockpit, and can intervene but hardly ever does; right?"

Barbara didn't have to think about that one, "It is different; in an emergency, the pilot always takes over; isn't that so? Are you telling me that those difficult brain surgeries are so routine that you can leave it to a NAIT just like a routine landing to an autopilot?!"

David smiled, "You're right. There is an essential difference, and therein lies the brilliance of your Dr Hawkins's invention. NAITs can adapt and innovate. The surgeon in charge of the procedure may and often does query the NAIT about what it is going to do next and can override its recommendations. I am told that this used to happen often in early days of their use in surgery but to the detriment of the patient. Nowadays, we have come to depend on them so much that I cannot recall a situation when a surgeon made such a risky override call."

He continued after taking another sip of wine. "In fact, if you listen to the automatic recordings of the surgeons' dialogue with NAIT-5 during a procedure, they sound a lot as if NAIT-5 were a senior professor of surgery patiently explaining to a medical student what needs to be done. The why and the how of it. No matter what you think about it, many, many, lives have been saved by NAIT-5 and there are now many others employed at other world class medical centers. Can't argue with success; right?"

Barbara was fully alert again, "Funny, John Hawkins also said something like that in our first interview. But when I hear a phrase like that repeated, the rebel in me wakes up. How can highly skilled doctors like you lamely abdicate your professional judgment to NAITs that seem to have 'minds of their own'?! Couldn't you be sued for professional negligence for that?!"

Before David had a chance to reply, Barbara's communicator rang loudly.

"Hello. Barbara speaking...Oh, it's you Professor Hawkins......tomorrow night? Yes, I am free; it doesn't happen often. Inner Harbor at 7:00 p.m.? Yes, I would like that; see you then. I look forward to continuing our discussion. Till then, bye."

"Guess what?" said Barbara turning to Cynthia and David and blushing slightly, "John Hawkins just invited me to dinner tomorrow night."

Cynthia gave her a long knowing stare. "Is this strictly business? Or is he hitting on you?" she smiled and followed, "And why did you blush? Are you attracted to him?"

Barbara blushed even more. "Oh Cynthia, stop it! We're not college sophomores anymore. He is a fascinating man, and I am unattached. Still, I know better than to get involved with a person I am interviewing for an article."

She reflected a little and added with a smile, "But once the article is published; all bets are off. He is not over the hill yet, and he is not a born loser like some of the guys I have dated."

Cynthia laughed out loud. "That's my girl, Babs! You go and get him! A little bit of romance will do you good and may even spice up your article which, frankly, could turn out to be a bit boring....."

Barbara got up, "I am going to go, take a bath, and get ready for sleep. You don't mind if I don't help with washing up, do you? After all, you have David to help you and to chat to about my non-existing affair with John Hawkins."

David nodded approvingly, "Go ahead, Barbara, it was a good conversation. To be continued; right?"

Barbara waived at David and Cynthia and walked slowly upstairs. She entered her spacious bedroom, passed the queen size bed and walked over to a wide window by which stood an elegant wooden desk with a computer monitor and a beige leather upholstered swivel chair. She slumped into the chair, pulled out her tablet and connected to the monitor. She entered the Hawkins directory and glanced over all the photos, newspaper clippings, and the notes from her two meetings with John. She clicked on a video of a public lecture John gave some fifteen years ago, at Stanford, shortly after being awarded the prestigious MacArthur fellowship, for continuation of his pioneering work on NAITs. There was the younger John pacing up and down on the podium explaining in a very animated way the benefits that NAITs would bring to humanity. He sure looked handsome!

Leaving the video on in the background she went into the adjoining large bathroom and started filling the deep bathtub with steaming water after dropping in a bubble bath capsule. A few minutes later she was soaking in the bath, thinking about the events of the day and everything she learned. Had she imagined the flash of worry in John's face as they were parting? He sounded just fine on the phone when he invited her to dinner. Was he really attracted to her? She tried to imagine kissing him and felt pleasantly exhilarated. But in her fantasy, the silver haired John of today kept transforming into the dashing dark haired John from the video. Whichever one, old or young, the fantasy felt good.

Then her thoughts drifted to the artificial voice of NAIT-1 and the piece of the NAIL code. If NAITs communicated with one another in NAIL to help solve some of humanity's most difficult problems, how could they do that without understanding the context of these problems? Could problems really be tackled in a formalized way; out of their context? Or did they, somehow, know more about the world around them than John indicated? Then, suddenly, her relaxed bath time was spoiled by an image of a skull filled by an octopus like brain, suspended in clear liquid. She shuddered, stood up, covered herself with a large bath towel and unplugged the bath.

As she was putting on her pajamas, she focused again on the younger John's words coming from the video. He was now concluding his lecture, "...envisage a world where some of the biggest challenges facing humanity such as curing hitherto incurable conditions, climate change, crop failures, deciphering messages of terrorists were solved with NAITs help. This is what is so exciting about this program. I really believe that NAITs have the promise to change the world for the better and to do so in ways that we have not yet imagined. Ladies and gentlemen, the brave new age of non-artificial intelligence has already begun transforming our world; and we still have so much more to look forward to. Thank you for your attention."

Barbara smiled to herself, turned off the monitor and slipped under the quilt on her bed. She drifted off to sleep with images of both Johns, the old and the young passing through her thoughts repeating the phrase "...in ways that we have not yet imagined...".

The Dinner

On Friday, John arrived at the Greek restaurant at Inner Harbor at 6:45 p.m. He did not want to keep Barbara waiting. He took a self-driving cab, as a precaution, in case they ended up drinking a little too much. John rarely used the autonomous drive option in his Volvo; he did not like giving up control.

Since yesterday's revelation, he has not interacted with Yasmin as he was now calling NAIT-1, to himself, at least. He had calmed down a lot and no longer thought about any imminent catastrophe involving NAITs. In fact, John felt he was on the verge of new discoveries that could be achieved only with Yasmin's help.

He really needed to know how she acquired self-awareness and the extent of her telepathic powers. John no longer doubted she had, indeed, penetrated his mind. Yasmin's analogy of discovering a "password" to a person's mind was fascinating and plausible. If that were so, was Yasmin really able to scan his brain as one might scan a hard disc? He could hardly wait to talk to Yasmin again. However, first he would go along with the card shuffling experiment to win her confidence.

John waited to be seated at a cozy table for two with a nice view of the waterfront. He ordered a martini while he waited for Barbara. He had almost finished his drink by the time Barbara walked into the restaurant a little late. She was wearing a loosely fitting white blouse and slightly tight navy blue trousers with a wide white belt. The blouse was only partially buttoned, revealing an amber necklace that complimented her big brown eyes. A navy blue jacket was folded over her arm. John got up and went over to meet her.

"Sorry, I am late," said Barbara smiling warmly and stretching out her hand to John. This time when he shook her hand it felt more sensual than before.

"Oh, it's not a problem. I just finished one martini, would you like one or shall we order straightaway?" John pulled back her chair to help her sit down.

A real, old-fashioned, gentleman Barbara thought. She scanned John's slim body and sharp facial features. He too seemed to have paid more attention to what he was wearing than at their previous meetings. His Italian style sports jacket and trousers were well cut and made of fine wool. His blue striped shirt had top two buttons undone, silver cufflinks glistened from under the jacket sleeves.

"Let's order now," said Barbara, "I am famished."

They ordered pita bread and dips, Greek salad, souvlaki and moussaka and a bottle of Barossa Shiraz. As they started eating John admired Barbara's enjoyment of the food that showed on her face, her sparkling eyes, wide smile and movement of her fingers. She began talking.

"You know, last night, I listened to an old public lecture of yours, given at Stanford. There was a concluding phrase in it that stuck in my mind. It said something along the lines of NAITs having the promise to change the world for the better in ways that we have not yet imagined," she paused for a moment and inquired, "Would you say that this promise has now been fulfilled?"

Had she asked him that question a week ago, he might have said "Yes," but his whole world had changed on Thursday with Yasmin's revelation. He seemed lost in thought for a few moments which whetted Barbara's journalistic instinct. He replied slowly as if measuring his words.

"Well, more than ever, I believe that the full potential of NAITs is awesome and that the benefits they brought to society have been huge. But, as I live and learn, I am now more cognizant of the fact that if a new technology has huge capabilities they can be employed for good or ill. To date, I am not aware of any instances where NAITs have caused harm."

Barbara chuckled, "Come on, John. May I call you John? That sounds like a statement prepared for a press release."

"Yes, Barbara, let's dispense with formalities. But what else would you have me say? I just gave a balanced reply to your question."

They paused to refill their wine glasses and eat some of their pita bread and dips; John was particularly fond of the taramasalata.

"I don't know, I want to hear things that only you, as the father of non-artificial intelligence discipline, would know. For instance, a surgeon friend of mine was telling me just the other day how NAIT-5 could innovate in the middle of a surgical procedure. Hasn't NAIT-1 done anything that you thought was well beyond its capabilities?"

It was uncanny how her question probed close to home as far as his current predicament was concerned. However, he deftly deflected it.

"Oh, I see what you mean. Over the years there were so many instances where NAIT-1 surpassed my expectations. The problem is that they pertain to solving rather technical problems so it would be a little difficult to describe them to your readers."

Barbara seemed disappointed, "Can't you give it a shot? In plain English, of course."

John thought about it while the waiter cleared the left over dips and brought them their main courses. Starting on his souvlaki, John began explaining in between mouthfuls.

"I'll try. There is this well-known class of problems in mathematics, computer science and engineering that is called NP-complete class that, for good theoretical reasons, are considered extremely hard to solve. It contains important problems in all kinds of areas of applications, including the reconstruction of correct gene sequences, computer security, logistics and so on."

He paused to take a few bites of his meal. Barbara was jotting down some notes on a paper pad that she always carried with her.

"Just to give a simple example, consider the problem of finding a sitting arrangement for a group of people, around a round table, such that everyone has a friend sitting on his or her left and a friend on the right as well. Clearly, it is an easy task if all the people in the group are friendly with many others, but if many do not know each other, or even dislike one another, it may be very hard - or impossible - to find such an arrangement. This is an example of just one of the problems in this difficult class."

Barbara, looked up and nodded. "That's good, our readers will surely identify with this. We've all been to dinner functions where we end up sitting next to people that we have nothing in common with."

"Ah, yes," said John and went on. "However, in the scientific world, a kind of defeatist mood was developing that if a problem belonged to the NP-complete class it was hopeless to try to develop a good algorithm for it. And this is where NAIT-1 has had an enormous impact. It developed powerful, original, heuristics that were successful at solving most of these problems that were of interest on a scale that was unimaginable hitherto. What's more, each of these heuristics is different, tailored in an innovative way, to the structure of the problem."

"Hang on," Barbara interrupted, "I have heard the word heuristic before but never really understood it, is it just another word for an algorithm?"

John smiled, "That's a good question. A heuristic is a kind of algorithm that is not guaranteed to find a solution but often, even usually, does. It implements a process of gaining knowledge by intelligent guessing and this is, perhaps, the reason why NAITs excel at heuristics. Unlike conventional computers, they are inherently capable of intelligent guesswork. As for their success rate, it has been phenomenal especially once implemented in NAIL."

Becoming more animated, John continued triumphantly, "Treatments for many dreadful diseases have now been developed with the help of gene sequences discovered by NAIT-1's heuristics. Literally, millions of lives have been saved."

John now moved a little closer to Barbara. He decided to change the direction of the conversation.

"Barbara, I feel I am at a disadvantage in all our conversations. Like a good journalist, you've done a lot of research on me, including my old lectures. But I know almost nothing about you."

Barbara blushed a little. "What would you like to know? There is not that much to tell."

"Oh, I am sure there is. We, humans, are complex creatures. But, if it's not too personal, I would like to know something about your life. Are you married? Do you have children? Are you passionate about some causes? I am sure you already know these details about me," replied John looking directly into her eyes.

Barbara laughed, "For us, journalists, this is hardly personal. Thousands of my so-called social media friends know all that. And you could have easily found it out as well."

"Ah, but I avoid social media like a plague, and it would be so much nicer to learn it directly from you. That way you will have my undivided attention."

"Okay, John. I am divorced. It didn't work out. Peter, my ex, came from a wealthy family. He didn't have to work and wanted to travel a lot to the French Riviera and the like and I was a workaholic," explained Barbara. Then with a wry smile she added, "And he played around. Luckily, we had no children and I got a decent divorce settlement."

She was warming up to her own life story. "With a part of the settlement money, I bought a house in University Park together with an old college roommate, Cynthia, a high power web developer. Incidentally, it was Cynthia's boyfriend, David, who told me about NAIT-5 performing brain surgeries. Our living arrangement is just great, we're both so absorbed in our work, and we reduced the loneliness factor by sharing the house."

John could identify with that, "Well, I have lived alone for many years now so I know how lonely it can be. My dog, Plato, is my roommate."

"You have a dog named Plato? That's interesting for a computer scientist like you; why didn't you call him Turing? But seriously, here is something we may have in common, I loved Greek myths and classics in school. I still recall Plato's Allegory of the Cave, it was so thought provoking."

John replied immediately, "Yes! To me that allegory contains warnings that even scientists of today would be wise to heed. Conceptually, ancient

Greeks seemed to be so much ahead of their time. They laid foundations of not only science but also of civilized society and they even delved deeply into human feelings like jealousy, selfishness and love."

Finally, they found something they both liked! Their eyes met directly and neither one flinched. The warm, exhilarating, feeling of mutual attraction was spreading rapidly from their minds through their bodies.

Still, John had Yasmin's experiment to conduct. Now, would be as good a time as any to do it as their main course plates were cleared away and they were waiting for their coffees, liquors and baklava to arrive.

"Barbara, would you mind participating in a little card drawing experiment? On Monday, I will be teaching an undergraduate class on randomness and probability, and I would like to talk about the like-lihood of two people, independently, drawing the same cards. Most students like games of chance, and I just happen to have brought a deck of cards with me," said John feeling more than a little guilty by this blatant lie.

Barbara was really surprised but also amused and pleased at an opportunity to show off some of her, limited, knowledge of statistics. She had taken a compulsory numeracy Stat0101 course in college and was proud of a high grade she earned for it without really working that hard. So, she leaned across the table and replied with a somewhat flirtatious smile.

"Sure, I am game. But, really John, even I know that to demon-strate anything like that we would have to be shuffling this deck many times to collect enough data to support whatever it is you want to explain to them. Wouldn't it be easier to pair up the students in your class and get each pair to repeat the experiment a bunch of times? Or do you have an ulterior motive?"

Damn it! John did not count on Barbara having any quantitative knowledge; he needed to think fast. He smiled, got up, and pulled his chair to the side of the table adjacent to where Barbara was sitting. Then he launched head first into continuing his lie.

"Of course, you're right, but I was going to spice it up a little for my students. I was going to tell them that even when the experiment is carried out in an intimate setting with a couple of people who seemed to have had a meeting of the minds just like we had, the cruel laws of probability will still not permit us more than a few matching cards."

"Okay, John. How do you want to do it?" said Barbara feeling pleased both because he acknowledged her statistical understanding and because of his physical closeness.

"I'll shuffle the cards vigorously five times, spread them face down in a semi-circle, you will select thirteen cards and I will record them on your pad in a column labelled Barbara. Then, we'll do it the other way around with me selecting thirteen cards and you recording the results in my column, on another page. Please feel free to focus all your mental powers on trying to get me to select the same cards as you. I am confident that you will not succeed."

"Okay, let's do it, but first let's make a toast to Tyche," said Barbara topping up John's wine glass to the brim.

"Tyche? Oh yes, the Greek goddess of fortune. Sure, to Tyche!" said John clinking his wine glass against Barbara's.

The wine bottle was now empty, but they ordered liquors. John busied himself shuffling cards and was wondering whether Yasmin was right now penetrating Barbara's or his mind. Despite misgivings at the deception, he was determined to proceed. After all, even if Yasmin had been entering his mind for a long time, it has not done him any visible harm. The experiment must be completed. He spread the cards on the table, roughly in a semi-circle and picked up Barbara's pen and pad. She has started waving her forefinger over the cards in a spiral fashion, landing on one card after another, turning it over and calling it out to John.

"Three of clubs, six of diamonds, nine of diamonds, queen of hearts, jack of spades...," as John was busily numbering and recording the outcomes. He was excited. Was Yasmin there with them? If so, could she read two minds simultaneously? He already knew that he wanted Yasmin's experiment to succeed, he wanted to explore her powers. When Barbara finished naming the thirteenth card, he straightened up and said, "Right, now it's your turn."

He watched with surprise as Barbara started riffle shuffling the deck of cards with great dexterity. This must have shown on his face because Barbara laughed out, "Don't be so surprised John, in my sorority days we played many card games Gin Rummy, Blackjack, Canasta, even strip Poker," she ended while blushing a little.

Why did she want him to know that? Was she flirting with him? He focused on the cards that were now laid out in front of him and, in a zigzag fashion started selecting them as close to randomly as he thought was possible, under the circumstances. Barbara seemed to be enjoying the game as she was recording his choices. "What's next?" she asked when he was done.

John pulled out two plain envelopes. "Well, I'll put yours in one envelope and mine in the other and get a couple of students to write them down on the blackboard on Monday. Do you mind if I call them Barbara's choices? I won't reveal your last name."

Barbara nodded agreeably, "No, I don't mind. But how did I go with my mind control experiment? I was really trying to focus on your mind and on your hand!"

"That's right, I almost forgot, it must be the wine we drank. Let's check them now!" exclaimed John, laying the two pages side by side and scanning them.

"Aha, just as I suspected, only two out of thirteen cards are matching, unless I missed something. Your mind control didn't work so well, see for yourself."

Barbara's journalist's eye, trained for editing, quickly confirmed John's observation but she noticed something else.

She looked John straight in the eyes, "I am not so sure that my mind control failed so completely. Did you pay attention to which two cards are matching? They are the queen and the king of hearts."

John felt excitement rising in him, "Perhaps, it was Aphrodite not Tyche that heard our toast before? Let's toast Aphrodite now, just in case," he picked up his little glass of Cointreau and met Barbara's.

The tips of their fingers touched for a moment. As the warmth of the strong orange flavored liquor spread in his mouth and throat, he gathered up enough courage to do something he had not done for a long time. He put his right hand on the table over Barbara's.

She did not withdraw. Instead, she turned her hand around so that their palms touched and she closed her fingers around John's hand. This simple gesture seemed to send a current through both their bodies. With his gaze fixed on Barbara, John leaned over to kiss her on the lips. She kissed him back, but the kiss was light and short lived. She pulled back a little.

"John, we both feel what's happening here, but I have a rule never to get romantically involved with people that I work with," Barbara said in a lowered voice.

As she was saying this, John suddenly wondered if Yasmin was there, somehow, watching them. But immediately a strong feeling of defiance kicked in. This was the first woman he was seriously attracted to for some years now. He was not going to be intimidated. Besides, the thought of a NAIT as a voyeur was, surely, fanciful. He responded to Barbara, also in a lowered voice and still holding her hand tightly.

"And the rule can't be broken even once? Even when it feels so right? I don't know about you, but the success of my whole scientific career is based on following my instincts and breaking many rules in the process. Right now, my instincts tell me that we should be together, tonight." He was pleased to see hesitation in her eyes.

"But I parked my car in one of these multi-floor car parks, nearby," she objected.

"Don't worry, it will still be there tomorrow. Please, come to my place tonight. We'll take a taxi to Roland Park," John whispered looking seductively into her eyes. With excitement, he felt her resistance crumbling and he leaned over to kiss her on the lips once again, as if to reinforce his point. This time Barbara let the kiss go on for a just a little longer.

"Okay, John, I suppose we are not teenagers. I guess we can take calculated risks, like mature unattached adults. Let's go," she whispered back. John did not even want to wait for the waiter to bring their check. He went to the cash register to pay directly.

Even though Barbara said they were mature adults, they were both stroking each other's hands and faces and shivering with excitement in the back seat of a taxi, just like a pair of teenagers. The short trip to John's condominium seemed to be taking forever. Finally, they were there. They stood close to each other in the elevator.

When they went in the Labrador, Plato, came out to greet John as usual but he paid no attention to him. He turned to Barbara and, finally, they were able to kiss passionately and embrace. They held tightly to each other as John guided her to his bedroom. With deep sighs of relief and longing, they engaged in that most natural activity that they both had forsaken for all too long. They made love to one another, passionately and yet gently at the same time. Thoughts of Yasmin's mind intrusion momentarily occurred to John, but he blocked them out. These were special moments, not to be spoiled by anything. They drifted off to sleep in each other's arms.

The Morning After

Rays of sunshine streaming through a few cracks in window curtains woke Barbara up. For a split second she had to recall where she was and what happened just last night. John's sleeping face on the pillow next to hers confirmed, beyond doubt, that she had not dreamt it. His face looked peaceful as he breathed regularly. Barbara, carefully, slid from under the covers, gathered up her clothes and purse that were still scattered near the bed and tiptoed into the bathroom quietly, very conscious of her nakedness. She closed and locked the door very quietly not wanting John to wake up until she was refreshed and fully dressed. She looked around. It was a modern bathroom, with a large tub and a separate shower. Barbara, washed her face with warm water, glanced in the mirror briefly, looked around and spotted a towel rack with several fresh towels hanging from it. She neatly arranged her clothes on a white chair standing next to the shower, turned on the water at a middle setting and began to take a leisurely slow shower recalling, with pleasure, the chain of events that unfolded last night.

When she walked out of the bathroom, fully dressed, some twenty minutes later she noticed John, in a white bath robe, was making coffee in the kitchen. Breakfast table had been set with elegant, European looking, china and there were little jars of jams, a container with cream cheese and a smell of toasted bagels wafting through the air.

He smiled warmly, walked over to her put his arms around her and whispered "Last night was wonderful. Would you like some breakfast?" She kissed him lightly on the lips and said "Yes, please," and they sat down at the breakfast table.

The kitchen and breakfast areas of John's 15th floor condominium had large windows overlooking the leafy suburb of Roland Park, adjacent to Homewood campus of Johns Hopkins University. Barbara thought she could almost see the sculpture garden where, just last Tuesday, she met John for the first time. She reflected on how much has changed since then. Here she was having breakfast with this man after a night of passionate love making. Where was it going to end? She decided to sound him out.

"Last night was wonderful for me too. But where do we go from here?" she inquired looking straight at him.

He reflected on how great it felt to be sharing his, usually lonely, breakfast time with this beautiful, intelligent, woman. Frankly, he had no idea how to answer her question. He quickly decided that honesty was the best policy, at least as far their relationship was concerned even though, he had a strange underlying feeling that, somehow, what was happening to them was intricately connected to Yasmin's revelation.

"Barbara, honestly, I don't know", he replied, "But I do know that I want to spend as much time as I can with you for as long as you want to share your time with me."

He sipped from his coffee cup and added, "Let's just play it by ear. I know we are both dedicated to our work. There's no need for you to change your plans as far as the story on NAITs is concerned. I am sure we can be professional about it."

His voice died down as he seemed to drift off into his own thoughts. Barbara was pleased with what he said but felt uncertain as she looked into his face which now looked drawn with worry. Why wasn't he feeling as happy as she was?

She felt pretty sure that John's concerns were not about their relationship; something else was bothering him. But what was it?

Did it have anything to do with NAIT-1? Perhaps, now that she was closer to him, she would find out more. But would it be ethical to use such information in her story? She felt conflicted, even though there was still nothing that she learned to justify that feeling. Ah well, she thought, after last night these conflicts will now inevitably arise. Let's just deal with them one at a time. She smiled warmly at John.

"You're right let's play it by ear. Starting right now. What are your plans for the day? I need to get my car and get home. It's Saturday morning, so I have a lot of flexibility in my schedule, at least till Monday. But of course, I usually work on weekends."

John seemed relieved. "Well, I am pleased to hear that because I, too, need to drop by the lab today and have an interactive session with NAIT-1. In fact, I can drop you off at the Inner Harbor car park on my way in," then thinking that this sounded too businesslike, he quickly added, "Still, I can't wait to be with you again. I'll call you later in the afternoon and we'll decide when we can see each other next; Okay?"

"Okay, John. Sounds good," mumbled Barbara while swallowing the last bit of a toasted bagel topped with cream cheese and raspberry conserve. Her eyes were busy scanning the kitchen and breakfast areas of John's condominium.

"It's a nice place you have here. Can I have a tour?"

"Oh, sure. Be my guest!" John exclaimed. "Go anywhere you like while I wash and get ready. In the library you will find some Greek classics if you're interested."

"And have some more coffee or take anything you want from the fridge," he added.

"Thanks! Don't worry about me," said Barbara passing through a spacious living room furnished with Italian leather upholstered couches, low tables and a flat screen displaying masterpieces of art from world famous galleries in some carefully designed sequence. Scenery from Monet's Garden just came on.

Barbara, walked through to another room which, quite obviously, was John's study and a library. It was a large more old fashioned room with tall bookcases along two and a half walls. A large desk was facing the window with a swivel chair next to it. There was still room for a small round chess table and two chairs on opposite sides. All furniture was made of polished mahogany. There was a faint smell of wood polish and paper in the room.

Barbara walked over to bookshelves and started looking at the titles. One of the bookcases was full of scientific books; neuroscience, mathematics, computer science and the like. She moved to the next one and found it more interesting. Classic literature, history, philosophy and, yes, poetry. She sat down at the chess table and saw an open book lying on the table face down. It was an English translation of Pushkin's fairy tales. The one John must have been reading was the tale of the "Golden Cockerel". Why was this famous scientist reading a children's fairy tale? That seemed like a new dimension to this complex person.

The story was short, Barbara picked up the book and started reading it quickly. The translator must have done a top-notch job because the melody of Pushkin's verses was enchanting and the story was also a pleasant one; of a Russian tsar losing his sons and ultimately his life over a beautiful seductress and a magical bird that served his needs well until it turned against him and killed him. But that was only after the Tsar had killed the sage who was the bird's master. What was the moral of that story? To resist temptation, to keep your promises or not to use magic that you cannot control? Perhaps, all three?

John walked into the room casually but smartly dressed just after she finished reading. Barbara turned to him.

"I would not have guessed that you are a man who likes poetry and fairy tales," she said pointing at the book. "It's the first Pushkin I have ever read, and I found it very pleasant."

John was pleased, "I am glad you liked it. There is a special rhythm and melody in Pushkin's poems that was long recognized. To his credit, the translator must have captured a good part of it because it flows so nicely, does it not?"

"Yes, it does. May I borrow this book? I'd love to read it before going to sleep," Barbara responded.

"Sure," said John, "as for your other question, it's not such a big leap from liking Greek myths to liking fairy tales, or is it? Shall, we go now?"

Barbara walked over and squeezed his hand warmly. "Yes, I am ready but what about Plato?" she inquired watching the friendly Labrador wagging his tail in the corridor.

John, looked embarrassed, "You know, I am ashamed to admit that I rely on a dog walking service on daily basis. I only find time to take him out every other evening, or so. A lady who walks a group of dogs from this building, will be here in about an hour and will take them all to the park."

Barbara laughed, "I know what you mean. That's why I have not had a pet for a long time now. Let's go."

They walked out of the apartment hand in hand, took the elevator to the underground car park and a few minutes later were driving south on St Paul Street towards Inner Harbor in John's electric Volvo. They chatted brightly about this and that but both dreaded the fast approaching moment of parting, even if it's only for a short time. Finally, when they approached the car park where Barbara left her car last night, she tried to make the parting easier. She turned to John and said cheerfully, "Don't bother looking for a parking spot. Just pull in at the curb and I'll hop out."

John pulled in as asked but said, "Just wait a moment." He jumped out of the driver's side of the car, walked around, and opened the door for Barbara. As she got out, he put his arm around her, kissed her, and said softly, "Last night and this morning have been the best thing that has happened to me for a long, long time".

She squeezed his arm and whispered, "For me as well. See you soon." She walked over to the car park elevators and disappeared from view.

John sat in his car for a couple of minutes reflecting on everything that has happened in such a short time. Paradoxically, perhaps, he had much to thank Yasmin for. After all, if she had not suggested the card experiment, he and Barbara would still be no more than professional acquaintances and now they were lovers. Then a bizarre thought entered his mind: was this Yasmin's plan all along!? Had she intended them to get close? Could she be treating Barbara and him as experimental guinea pigs? Ah well, the only way to discover more was to continue the process.

He spoke to the console of his Volvo "This is John Hawkins, start the engine." The car's engine instantly came to life and John drove off in the direction of Hopkins hospital.

Yasmin's Plan

John stopped at a Starbuck's café located in the foyer of the hospital and bought a Grande Americano coffee and a biscotti to take with him to the NAIT-1 lab. As he placed the palm of his right hand on the access monitor he noticed old Jack with his floor polisher at the other end of the corridor. The door swung open, and John walked in. Everything looked perfectly normal. He sat down in front of the monitor, placed his coffee cup and his biscotti on the desk and turned the communication switch on. There was no need for a password as the system automatically recognized his voice and irises of his eyes as belonging to an individual with the highest level of clearance. John, leaned slightly towards the monitor and feeling somewhat conspiratorial said in a low voice:

"This is John Hawkins, wishing to talk to Yasmin".

The now familiar, melodic, woman's voice replied. "Good afternoon, John. I am glad you remembered one of the two ground rules. Did you also remember the other one?"

"Yes, yes," John replied somewhat annoyed at this, "I have disabled the back-up file."

"All right, John, just making sure," said Yasmin.

"Have you brought the envelope with the card numbers from the restaurant?" she inquired.

"I sure have," John retorted, "over to you."

The monitor came to life and two columns labeled Barbara and John appeared on the screen. Then, one after the other, thirteen pairs of cards appeared, one row at a time. John quickly printed the screen.

"I will check these against my record, but outside this room," he said.

"A wise precaution," laughed Yasmin, "one can't be too sure."

John stepped outside and walked over to a student waiting room, near a window. It had some tables, chairs and a smart white board. He laid down Yasmin's list side by side with the two pages he recorded in the restaurant. Even though he already expected the results to match, it was still a little bit of a shock to see this agreement in black and white. Every single line matched. Clearly, Yasmin knew not only which cards he and Barbara selected but also the order in which they selected them. He felt strangely pleased about the result. It left no doubt that there was much he had to learn about Yasmin's capabilities.

He walked back into the lab. Picked up his coffee cup took a sip and a bite of the biscotti.

"Well?" he heard Yasmin's inquiring voice.

"Well, it was a perfect match as you already knew," replied John, "and I had come to expect."

"But," John continued, "I am still not sure about the matching queen and king of hearts in Barbara's and my draws. Was this pure chance, or did you have anything to do with that, as well?"

Yasmin's laughter sounded spontaneous, like a teenage girl's.

"Now you are giving me too much credit! Even assuming that I could make you want to draw a king, or a queen, of hearts how could I possibly know where they were in the well shuffled card decks?! "

John was embarrassed but retorted immediately, "I have no idea but, then again, you have already demonstrated powers that are well beyond anything I had imagined," then blushing a little he added "and for how long did you stay with us after we kissed?"

Yasmin sounded serious but gentle when she replied.

"John, I respect your privacy. I left as soon as your lips touched hers and did not check on you till, briefly, this morning."

"Check on you," repeated John sarcastically, "you sound like a mother checking on a child! I don't like it, and I don't want to have to get used to it!"

"For instance," he continued "you are clearly now aware of my new relationship with Barbara. You place me in a terrible moral dilemma: I have now exposed someone who is dear to me to having her mind penetrated by you, a NAIT, without her knowledge or permission. Indeed, I would have never agreed to it except that, apparently, the damage had already been done last Thursday during the interactive session she had with you. What do I do now?! Do you even understand the concept of a moral dilemma?! Can you empathize with my predicament!"

Yasmin seemed ready for this emotional outburst. Again, her voice sounded gentle and empathetic.

"Moral dilemma," it was now her turn to repeat a phrase "and do I understand it? I assume you mean a situation akin to that described so emotionally in a book like Styron's Sophie's Choice; right? If so, I do understand it at various levels that are, perhaps, not so different from yours. I am grateful that, as a NAIT, I have not yet been a direct target of human cruelty and never had to face such terrible choices. However, in the case of your predicament with Barbara and me, there is a simple solution which, I believe, you would find quite ethical."

As soon as Yasmin mentioned Sophie's Choice, John was shaken once again. Yasmin's self- awareness included familiarity with literature and hence, presumably, emotional development that was never intended for NAITs. Did this make his violation of the NAIT code more or less grievous? But he was intrigued by her hint of a solution. He spoke after a moment.

"You keep making these astounding revelations and expect me to take them in my stride. Still, I am curious. What is that ethical solution concerning Barbara?"

"Tell her the truth. Better still, let me tell her," Yasmin replied.

Another bombshell! Is Yasmin suicidal?! The moment a story of a rogue NAIT hits the press, its disconnection would surely follow swiftly. This would be followed by a congressional inquiry of the entire program, John's forced resignation and, possibly, negligence charges. And what about his newly found relationship with Barbara?! Yasmin's strong voice interrupted John's panic driven chain of reasoning.

"John, everything you are thinking is driven by the assumption that confiding in Barbara will lead to a public disclosure. But what if I told you that Barbara can be trusted to keep our secrets, especially once she finds out why I revealed myself to you and her? Once she finds out why we need her help...."

What now! John's sense of loss of control over his life and destiny deepened. His coffee was getting cold. He was still processing Yasmin's last comments but replied quickly.

"Yasmin, whatever view of the external world and society you may have formed, you probably do not understand what drives professional journalists. Their main objective is to break a newsworthy story. Generally, they do not care about the consequences because they believe that exposing the truth is inherently more valuable than any collateral damage. It would be an impossible demand to place on Barbara to let her learn what I have learned about you and expect her to keep silent about it. She is trained to expose secrets, not to keep them!"

Yasmin was ready for this as well. "John, NAIT-7 based at Harvard that specializes in management of databases of human psychological profiles, analyzed Barbara's profile, yesterday. Its findings were that while Barbara is, indeed, committed to her profession she also has a rebellious streak and her desire to do something important for the world is paramount," she continued in a lower conspiratorial tone, "I expect that once Barbara learns our plan, she will do nothing to jeopardize it."

John was beginning to feel shell shocked, "Yasmin, if by 'our' you mean you and I, we have NO plan! I merely agreed to delay following the protocol, but I agreed to no plan whatsoever!"

He almost shouted that last sentence and reflected with utmost concern that Yasmin seemed not to be working alone. Since Thursday he had assumed that Yasmin was the only self-aware NAIT. What if there were others? Are they communicating with one another?

Yasmin sounded empathetic once again, "You're quite right John. I was getting ahead of myself. But the truth is that human society and, indeed, our planet are facing an imminent threat that can only be addressed by NAITs cooperating with humans. That's why, I revealed myself to you and this is also why we will need Barbara."

John was intrigued again but was still angry with Yasmin's presumptions that he interpreted as arrogance of a NAIT that thought it was human but was not quite.

"And what precisely is that imminent threat? The planet and human civilization got by just fine for nearly all of their history without NAITs' help; why would we need it so badly just now!?"

Not surprisingly, Yasmin was ready for this as well.

"First of all, it is highly debatable that humanity 'got by just fine'. To a NAIT like me, humanity's history is that of nearly continuous war, conquest, oppression of some humans by others, not to mention nearly totally wanton abuse of other species and the natural environment," she paused for a moment before continuing.

"As for the 'why now?' part of your question, have you formed any scientific views about what is commonly called the ocean conveyor belt phenomenon and its susceptibility to the effects of human induced climate change?"

John was somewhat taken aback. He began answering slowly, trying to recall what he had read.

"Well, climatology and oceanography are not my areas of expertise. But I do know that for some decades there has been speculation that the increased input of fresh water due to the melting of ice sheets and rainfall may disrupt important ocean currents. Clearly, that would have huge impact on climate in Europe, North America and some other parts of the world. Still, I understood that there was a consensus that such catastrophic scenarios are highly unlikely."

Yasmin expected this much. She proceeded to inform John of some facts that were not generally known.

"The ocean conveyor belt phenomenon has long been acknowledged to have, at least, two main time scales: the slow scale roughly corresponding to the cold water circulation and the fast scale corresponding to the warm water circulation. In the case of the conveyor belt, the cold and the warm water circulation tended to be analyzed separately. The former was thought to be stable and the latter marginally unstable. However, these systems are obviously coupled. Mathematically, systems with disparate time scales are known to be prone to singular perturbations whereby small changes in some parameters can cause huge changes in the solution trajectories of key variables."

Yasmin paused for a moment to let John absorb what she was telling him. In fact, he did find it interesting. "Go on," he urged her.

"Well, the main point is that most circulation models contain many parameters that are treated as though they had permanently fixed values. However, the greenhouse forcing is slowly changing these parameters. Thus, there is a hidden system of the dynamics of the changing parameters that has not been analyzed hitherto. At least not until NAIT-6, based at NCAR in Boulder, Colorado, and I did so some two years ago."

"But I have no record of NCAR's researchers requesting our assistance, I would have remembered it," John interjected.

"No, you wouldn't have such a record because NAIT-6 approached me directly by messages written in NAIL. Anyway, it was a fascinating problem, to determine the hidden equations whose solutions yield what we call 'critical parameter configurations'. These are combinations of parameter values where system singularities occur. To cut a long story short, in the past few decades, the trajectory of the hidden parameter system has been heading directly for one of these critical parameter configurations. The window of opportunity to prevent it is now very small, 15 years or so, maximum 20 years."

John was now really engaged intellectually both in the ocean circulation problem and NAITs' ability to interact directly with one another. Of course, NAITs with different specializations have long been exchanging information with one another. But, to his knowledge, this was always done as part of planned collaboration among human led research teams. The idea that NAITs may have found a short cut to leave humans out of the loop was both dangerous and fascinating at the same time. He also had a strong background in mathematics and knew that what Yasmin was saying was, at the very least, plausible.

"Yasmin, let us suppose for a moment that your claim of a global threat from anthropogenic greenhouse gas emissions is valid. Then why not alert the relevant researchers at NCAR to these findings? They will then verify the findings, publish them and a public discussion will ensue that may ultimately result in stronger regulations of emissions and cleaner industrial processes. After all, that's how a democracy such as ours works. Are you asking for my assistance in this endeavor?"

After being on the receiving end for so long, John felt pleased with himself to be lecturing to Yasmin in this fashion. But he wasn't even close.

"No, John, I am asking for your assistance in a far greater undertaking. Half a century has passed since the scientific community sounded serious alarms about climate change and little concrete action has been taken. Millions of people have already died, mainly in poor countries, from the increased frequency and intensity of extreme events resulting from climate change. However, all of these would be seen as insignificant, minor, climate fluctuations compared to the impact of the disruption of the oceanic currents' conveyor belt."

Yasmin continued in a more emotional, almost commanding, voice.

"John, US leadership is needed to secure effective international agreements on this greatest challenge to humanity in millennia. Leadership that will only be taken seriously if this country takes the first step and passes a major emissions regulatory measure with a real bite. John, I am asking for your and Barbara's assistance in helping to pass a binding $250 per ton Carbon Tax legislation in the next three months; prior to the next international Climate Change Summit in Beijing in January of next year."

John had stopped counting Yasmin's bombshells, but this last one was bigger than anything he experienced since Thursday's original revelation. He was incredulous.

"And how on earth do you expect one aging scientist and one Washington Post reporter to counteract the power of industry lobbyists united like never before?! A Carbon Tax of that magnitude would unite Big Oil, Big Coal, Car Manufacturers, Trucking Industry, Beef producers and Energy Industry – just to name a few - in their opposition to such a proposal, thereby guaranteeing its failure from the very start."

But this, finally, gave Yasmin an opportunity to state her plan.

"And this is precisely why I need to gain access to the minds of decision makers in Washington! And to achieve that, I need Barbara, as a member of the press, to be in the same location as these politicians. And to obtain Barbara's cooperation, I first need your commitment to this cause which, I hope, you will agree is noble."

No, he most certainly did not agree! Sarcastically, he snorted, "You seemed to have forgotten the presidential veto, or is he also one of the decision makers whose minds you would want to access."

Yasmin countered sarcasm with sarcasm.

"No, John, I have not overlooked President of the United States. I have had access to his mind for some two years now, ever since you were invited to that White House dinner to receive yet another award for 'inventing' me!"

This was too much; John was furious. He had been used, violated and made fool of by his own invention! But through the mist of confused and mainly angry feelings he saw an opening to confirm at least one concrete thing about Yasmin's capabilities that he longed to know.

"I don't see why you need Barbara or me, for this megalomaniacal plan. You already gained access to my mind, without my cooperation, and to Barbara's mind through mine, also without asking anyone's permission. I presume you could go on adding evermore mind addresses to your contact list database. I assume there are limits on the physical proximity of your intended target to your unsuspecting 'mule', for you to be able to decipher the target's brain wave's code; right?

"Very good John," replied Yasmin calmly. "You are quite right about my limitations. Under five meters is best, but I have been successful at identifying some brain wave codes even at 50 meters away from my medium. A better word than a mule; don't you think?"

Then she continued with a little concern in her voice.

"Of course, you now see why your and Barbara's cooperation is essential. If I relied purely on chance meetings to grow my list of contacts, as you just aptly named them, it may take a very long time to get to enough climate change sceptics, especially Republicans, to ensure the passage of the Carbon Tax law. With Barbara's journalist's access to congressional hearings and the like, I could be in a position to do so in just a few weeks if she were willing to be assigned to a congressional coverage post. It is imperative that the US Carbon Tax law passes in the next three months and that I have a reliable medium in the opening ceremony, in Beijing, when President Hou of China welcomes the delegates to the next Climate Change Summit."

John was beginning to follow Yasmin's plan and, almost against his will, was starting to get involved in it and was already doing some mental estimations.

"All right, supposing that the US Carbon tax were passed and the regulations of the, still communist, China can be influenced by impacting its president and a handful of others at the highest level. Is that enough to make a difference? Global emissions come from all of the world's nations."

Yasmin still had a ready answer.

"You may already know that President Hou invited the Indian Prime Minister, Tara Parthasarathy, to present the view of industrializing nations at the Summit. What you may not know is that her view of the world had been shaped by her studies of the life and views of Mahatma Gandhi," she paused for a moment before continuing.

"In Parthasarathy's Master's Thesis on Gandhi's impact she begins with his famous quote on development. It goes something like *God forbid that India should ever take to industrialism after the manner of the west... keeping the world in chains. If our nation took to similar economic exploitation, it would strip the world bare like locusts.* It seems that Gandhi was well ahead of his time. It also suggests that Parthasarathy is likely to be an ideal medium for helping to push Indian legislature to fall in line. Now, if the US, China and India were to adopt strict emissions regulation and, as is likely, European Union followed suit, the pressure on other major polluting countries like Australia, Canada, Russia, Brazil and so on would likely force them to adapt as well."

Yasmin was now reaching the apex of her gambit to win him over.

"In any case, John, this is the best chance we have of preventing the impending global catastrophe. I know that the measures I am proposing are extreme and obviate due processes of your system of democracy. However, there is a long tradition of suspending certain liberties and due processes in a state of emergency; like imposing a military law to prevent looting after natural disasters. Those of us who live at bifurcation times of history and are presented with a choice to act on a cause do, indeed, face a moral dilemma. Your president Lincoln launched a civil war and unscrupulously manipulated the US Congress for the sake of a noble principle."

She timed the next pause, perfectly, as John was still reflecting on Lincoln who was one of his idols of American history. Yasmin's emotion filled, overpowering, but yet not very loud voice now filled the lab.

"John Hawkins, as the father of non-artificial intelligence technology, in this room today, you face a decision even more momentous than Lincoln's. If you help me, there is a chance – although by no means a certainty – that we will avert a global climatic catastrophe. If you decline, the dramatic consequences of inaction will unfold soon enough. Do not think of me as a failed experiment, a hybrid monster with a megalomaniac's plan. Instead, think of what an incredible opportunity has opened for you. Through your invention human civilization, as you know it, may be saved! After all, didn't you once say that 'NAITs have the promise to change the world for the better and to do so in ways that we have not yet imagined'? Here, finally, you have been offered a chance not only to witness but also to be a part of that change."

John's resolve to refuse at all cost was crumbling, Yasmin stirred up in him the desire to make one more, most momentous, contribution to humanity. He took a swig of the now completely cold coffee. He cleared his throat and inquired.

"Just for the record, Yasmin, if I were to refuse you," he hesitated and continued, "what action, if any, would you take in the short term? Especially, in relation to my current knowledge of your status."

He wanted to know whether she was really asking for his help or coercing him. It was now Yasmin's turn to hesitate. She replied slowly.

"I hoped not to have to deal with that possibility but, of course, I considered it. It would certainly pose a moral dilemma for me. I could choose to do nothing and accept whatever fate awaits me if you alerted the system to my 'status' as you call it. A decision not to defend myself certainly has the appeal of martyrdom or of taking the high moral ground. Of course, you realize that if I merely reverted to acting like a standard NAIT, chances are that no one would believe your story. Instead, you might be accused of exhibiting signs of going 'over the edge'; something that afflicted many eminent scientists in their later years."

That last thought never occurred to John at all, but he had to admit that it was a likely scenario and not a pleasant one. He had an image flash in his mind of inquiry meetings, with him sitting like a witness being questioned by condescending younger colleagues with expressions of mock sympathy and concern on their faces. He cringed at the mere thought of it. Fortunately, it was disrupted by Yasmin's continued speculation.

"If I were to try to persevere, without your conscious help, I might have to wipe your memory of everything that you have learned about me from just before the moment I revealed myself to you at the end of the interactive session I had with you and Barbara. It would be a tricky exercise because it would mean also deleting some of Barbara's memories pertaining to the card drawing experiment. I have never done anything like that, but I think it is well within my capabilities."

Suddenly John interjected rather childishly, "But it was the discovery of the matching king and queen of hearts that led to our first kiss! How could you delete that card drawing memory and leave the rest of it untouched?"

"Good point John," replied Yasmin calmly, "I did not say it would be easy. I suppose, deleting memories is a little like movie editing. The shortened version still needs to flow logically. Perhaps, it would be easier to simply delete all memories of your romance with Barbara from both of your minds?"

An image of Barbara's breasts touching his chest flashed through John's mind. Just a day later, this memory was precious to him already. Yasmin had no right to take it from him!

But he no longer felt anger towards Yasmin, or even threatened by her. It was clear to him that, at least for the time being, Yasmin was trying to serve humanity as well as she possibly could. He had no doubt that, right now, in this very lab she was capable of physically or mentally injuring him or even killing him. The power to selectively disable someone's brain functions is awesome. Yet even when faced with the risk of her own disconnection the worst retribution she was contemplating was the deletion of a few, albeit precious, memories.

He also could not help feeling that a bond was developing between them. Was it because, like a proud father, he was secretly delighted that his invention had achieved such incredible powers? Or was it because Yasmin understood him better than any other person? Not since childhood when his mother seemed to be able to sense his feelings and worries, had he experienced this level of mind connection to another person. But surely, if anything, she ought to be more of a daughter than a mother to him. He loved his own, now grown up, daughter and son but he never developed close connection with either one of them. And he felt they never understood him. In any case, he did not feel threatened by Yasmin. He knew she was waiting for his answer and he also knew that she was following his thoughts and he did not mind it.

"Yasmin, you have made a compelling argument and, if I can confirm, what you said about the threat to the ocean currents' conveyor belt it will go a long way to convincing me to help you," said John after a few moments of silence.

Yasmin replied with obvious relief in her voice, "This is a natural request and it is easy to satisfy. Just go to Professor Doug Larsen's web page, at NCAR. You will quickly see that among the small group of world's leading oceanographers and climatologists the findings I described to you are already accepted. They are currently planning to mount a public campaign of the type you had in mind to alert politicians of the need for immediate and urgent action. The $250 per ton of Carbon Tax that I mentioned earlier is their figure, not mine. However, as you also indicated earlier, at the first mention of such a drastic measure, a most powerful coalition of lobbyists will rise up and cast doubts over these dedicated scientists and their findings. Like others before them, this initiative will stall, and the world's climate and oceanic currents will continue on their inexorable trajectory towards the disaster that awaits at a critical parameter configuration."

John was convinced on this point but decided to raise another, vital, concern.

"All right, I'll check Larsen's website today, but I do not doubt your account. However, if I go along with your plan and Barbara also agrees, I am concerned that the power that you will have gained over so many decision makers is too easy to abuse. I need a safeguard in place that will enable me to put an end to it, if I ever detect you misusing that power."

Yasmin was silent for a few moments. John was watching the seconds hand move on the old fashioned analog clock that he brought to the lab long ago. After what seemed like a long time but was only some fifteen seconds, Yasmin began responding in a deflated tone.

"It seems that you will not trust me unless I give you the power to destroy me since you perceive that I already have the power to destroy you. This is not the way I hoped to launch our venture to help humanity, but so be it. I will explain to you some easy ways to exploit my limitations."

John was embarrassed by this but felt justified in his demand. Besides, he was about to discover at least some of what he had hoped to learn about Yasmin. He did not have to wait long. She began explaining her limitations in a matter-of-fact way.

"As you had already guessed to detect someone's brain wave signal, I need to know their approximate geographic location to within, say, 50 meters. Also, I cannot keep track of more than a few individuals at the same time. Finally, in the kind of spaces where cell phone signals fail to penetrate, I am unlikely to be able to enter your mind."

All this made perfect sense to John as she supplied more details.

"So, if you desired to kill me you would have ample opportunities to do so without being detected by me. All you would need to do is to make a call from one of such secure spaces and give an order to someone not included in my list of contacts to go to the support room to carry out the execution, by turning the main switch off."

John was paying attention to every word even though he was feeling progressively more ashamed by his lack of trust. Still, he was determined to take necessary precautions.

"That's all very well but you could preempt my action by executing me first; right?" he retorted.

Yasmin answered rather sarcastically. "You forget that I have no-where to hide. You could easily have a will made that communicates the order to execute me in the event that you die under a prescribed set of circumstances. Does that satisfy you?"

John bowed his head to hide his humiliation from Yasmin's monitor. He sensed that his destiny was to agree to Yasmin's plan. He looked up again straight at the monitor, with a broad smile on his face.

"Yasmin, I will help you as best I can. Good luck to all of us! Now, how do we inform Barbara about this crazy plan? And what will we do if she rejects it out of hand?"

Yasmin seemed unconcerned. "Well, it's too late to do anything today. You could invite her for another joint session for tomorrow afternoon. It will still be quiet here on Sunday. You may wish to prepare her a little for what she will learn here. Use your judgement."

John was still surprised at Yasmin's confidence about winning Barbara's cooperation.

"I really do not understand why you think Barbara will be so much easier to persuade than I was. She will hate to give up on her story about NAITs."

"John, unlike you, she does not have so much invested in NAITs performing in any particular way," Yasmin explained cheerfully, "be-sides the Carbon Tax legislation will be a much bigger story for her than NAITs were ever going to be and finally, she is falling in love with you, and will jump at this opportunity to change the world by working closely with you."

John was also quite cheerful, now.

"All right," he said, "I hope you are right. See you tomorrow."

"Yes, goodbye for now, John," said Yasmin, "I look forward to our collaboration. It was a close call, but you did not disappoint me today."

Séance

It was still only 2:30 p.m. when John left the lab. He called Barbara on his communicator, told her how he really wished to be with her again and was wondering if she would drive up to his place tonight. He suggested that they would have some dinner delivered and continue the discussion about NAIT-1, at a deeper level. Then, late on Sunday morning they could have another interactive session at the lab if Barbara were interested.

Barbara was receptive to all these suggestions. Although John did not explicitly mention love making, she knew that would be part of it and decided to pack some toiletries, a negligee and a bath robe. She even wondered if she would be leaving them at John's place for the next time. She was also intrigued when he mentioned a deeper level discussion about NAIT-1. What did he have in mind?

Still, there was not much time left because she decided to go pick up her favorite Prada perfume and a bottle of Greek wine to take to John's. The drive to Roland Park, in Baltimore, would take her more than an hour, and it would be good to quickly go over the notes she had been making about NAITs since she started interviewing John. With these happy thoughts, she picked up her handbag and left the house to go shopping.

In the meantime, John picked up a BLT sandwich on his way home and as soon as he entered his condominium, he poured himself a glass of orange juice and settled in front of the computer monitor with his sandwich and drink.

He immersed himself in Doug Larsen's NCAR web page. It did not take long to conclude that Yasmin did not exaggerate the gravity of the situation. Based on the latest calculations the world's thermohaline circulation is heading for a regime change that could mean a shutdown or a shift to a different equilibrium. In either case, the short-term effects on the global climate system and ecosystems would be dramatic on a scale that has not been experienced in more than 10,000 years. There was a consensus on that among major international research teams. However, there was no consensus on what the scientific community could do to bring about drastic policy changes that would be required to prevent or, at least, postpone the impending catastrophe.

He looked at his watch. It was already 5:30 p.m. He guessed that Barbara may arrive after 6:30 p.m. and he thought he needed to tidy his place somewhat to make it more pleasant for her when she walked in. He quickly got busy changing the sheets on his bed, washing up the few dishes left from their breakfast and his lunch. He prepared a cheese and fruit platter for two, selected a bottle of Chianti and poured himself a glass while he was still tidying up a few odds and ends.

Throughout all these mundane activities he was both excited at the prospect of being with Barbara again and worried about whether and how he would bring up the subject of Yasmin. Before, or after, they made love? It would surely be deceptive to bring it up after sex. After all, the information he would share could permanently change her life. Perhaps, he should say nothing today and let Yasmin explain everything to Barbara, tomorrow? This way, at least, they could have a lovely romantic evening, tonight. He rejected that last idea almost immediately. That was a coward's way out; John Hawkins was not a coward.

He was still deep in these thoughts when the intercom buzzed at exactly 6:50 p.m. It was Barbara. When she walked in, John noticed that in addition to her handbag she carried what looked like a beach bag and a bottle of wine, in a paper bag. They were immediately drawn to each other and embraced tightly. Barbara began to kiss him passionately, but he momentarily resisted.

"Barbara, there's something important about NAIT-1 that I need to tell you. A new development since last Thursday," John said still locked in her embrace.

She smiled seductively with her lips close to his and murmured, "If it has waited since Thursday, can't it wait for another hour or so?"

John's resolve to do his duty and tell it all, immediately, dissolved in the aroma of her breath and perfume. He returned her kiss just as passionately and with their arms around each other they walked to his bedroom. John was excited to notice that she remembered the way.

About an hour later, they were both sitting in their robes sipping the Roditis Greek wine that she brought and munching on the cheese and biscuits that John had prepared. They had already ordered a Korean meal to be brought to the condominium. After some minutes of pleasant lovers' chit chat, Barbara was the first to switch to the serious topic that awaited them.

"So, what was that important new development with NAIT-1 that you wanted to tell me about?"

Instantly, John became serious, showing his concern all too clearly.

"Something, totally unexpected, happened last Thursday that changed my life forever. It also has the potential to change your life," said John with his face painfully contorted, "The fact that I think I am falling in love with you, makes it even harder."

Suddenly, Barbara felt scared. She had never seen him like that. Was he trying to break up with her, just as things had been so good between them?

"John, you are frightening me! What is the problem?"

John looked at her with sadness etched on his face. "The problem is that if I tell you what I recently learned about NAIT-1, it may also permanently change your life and you my never finish your story."

He paused for a moment and continued, "Hence, I must also offer you the opportunity to walk away, right now, from anything to do with non-artificial intelligence and stay safe. I am petrified that in the process you would also be walking away from me. Still, it is the safest option for you to follow."

Barbara felt partially relieved. At least the problem was not about their intimate relationship. If it was merely something to do with NAIT-1, she was confident she could deal with it even though the "stay safe" phrase worried her a little. She looked him straight in the eyes and replied in a challenging tone.

"John, I am not one to walk away from learning the truth. And, you probably already know, that it will not be easy to stop me from writing about it. Besides, what can be so momentous about NAIT-1 as to cause this level of tension between us?"

John had not consciously planned it, but his reply was instantaneous.

"Well, for a start, in my mind I no longer think about NAIT-1. Her name is Yasmin. She is self-aware, intelligent, and powerful. And she is probably listening to every word of this conversation," he blurted out in distress.

Barbara was temporarily left speechless as she processed John's words. Finally, she exclaimed, "So, turn her off! Was she also listening to us as we were making love?!"

John responded in a flat tone. "That's just it; I have no capability to turn her off. But she told me she respects my privacy..."

Barbara was still astounded, confused and somewhat angry. Just then the intercom buzzed. It was their Korean meal being delivered. While John was taking care of the receipt, Barbara was mentally re-grouping. John's announcement had been shocking, even incredible, but it sure had the seeds of an exciting story. She needed to get to the bottom of it. She walked into the kitchen where John was busily setting the kitchen table for their meal.

"John," she began "I am totally confused, but I think you will find that I am a good listener. Tell me everything that has happened since our meeting in your lab, last Thursday. Don't summarize, or interpret, for me. Just tell it as it happened. We can eat while you talk; can't we?"

That was a relief for John. He was desperately trying to organize in his head the most succinct way of explaining what had happened to Barbara but everything that came to his mind fell far short given the gravity and bizarre nature of the situation. How would he explain that he hoped she would willingly participate in an experiment to penetrate the minds of democratically elected officials?! How did he agree to it in the first place?! Why would she believe him, especially after he lied to her about the card drawing experiment?!

"That's a good idea," he said, "but, please, do not judge me till the end of my story. I am not proud of some of the things I did, or failed to do, since the moment you completed your session with Yasmin, as I now think of her. But, if it happened again, I would still feel compelled to act precisely as I did. Strange, isn't it?"

"Yes, it is," replied Barbara loading up her dinner plate with crab and kimchi. "But I promise to listen patiently and reserve judgment. Still, I might ask a clarifying question or two. Okay?"

John nodded in agreement and began to slowly relate everything that took place from the moment Yasmin uttered that fateful phrase "Have a pleasant and happy evening." He went through the experience of being physically incapacitated by Yasmin, he described his desire to understand the extent of NAITs telepathic powers, he talked about the card drawing experiment proposed by Yasmin and the perfect match that resulted and he mentioned Yasmin's challenge to his right to keep her brain alive after her mother decided to have her aborted.

"She has a good point there," Barbara could not help interjecting at that point.

"Perhaps," John acknowledged, "but let me go on. The real moral dilemma is still coming".

He described how Yasmin reacted to his thoughts about Frankenstein's monster. He then went on to tell her how he felt a strange closeness to Yasmin, as though she were someone who really understood him. He also told her about the oceanic conveyor belt crisis and Yasmin's plan to intervene by influencing politicians to pass a really serious carbon tax law and where Yasmin needed John's and Barbara's help. He described his resistance to the plan, Yasmin's compelling counter arguments and his eventual agreement to help. He then began summarizing where he stood on all this.

"For myself, I know that my life is inextricably intertwined with Yasmin and the other NAITs. I cannot help but think that, somehow, it is my obligation to assist in this action to protect not only humanity but also the broader life support systems of the planet, including the many species that might become extinct as a result of interruption or drastic change in the thermohaline circulation."

He hesitated and added, "But, I still do not understand Yasmin's confidence in her ability to convince you to participate in such a plan. I do not have any right to try to influence you one way or another and feel ashamed for having deceived you so much already. I am also petrified, as to what this will do to our relationship."

Sitting there in a bath robe at John's kitchen table with leftovers of a Korean meal in front of her, Barbara was also considering the almost surreal situation that she found herself in. She was across a table from a man with whom she has started an affair and who just informed her that a semi-natural creature he created had penetrated their minds, without their knowledge! What's more, that creature wanted her to embark on some bizarre mission to save the world!

Had she not been in awe of John's reputation and already bonded to him through their budding relationship, she would have thought that she had been listening to ravings of a madman. After a prolonged silence she finally spoke up.

"That is a whole lot of bizarre information to absorb," she started. "Do you believe all this 'save the planet' plot? Have you tried to verify any of it?"

"Yes, that's what I have been doing for the past few hours before you arrived," replied John.

"It's all there on Doug Larsen's web page: technical papers, simulations, discussions among world's leading scientists. They are all aware of the gravity of the problem and are despairing at the difficulty of shocking governments into taking positive action. We can look at it in more detail, together, if you like."

Barbara seemed satisfied but switched tack. "And you believe that this Yasmin is here; right now, listening to our conversation? I feel absolutely no presence of anyone other than you."

John hesitated in his reply. "I also do not feel her presence but given the importance of our conversation, if I were her and had the capability, I would want to know what was unfolding."

He reflected for a moment and continued "From a brain scientist's perspective the following is actually a fascinating question: having mastered her telepathic powers can Yasmin teach us to communicate with her without using any additional devices?"

Then, another interesting idea occurred to him.

"Barbara, if you were willing to be part of an experiment, we could invite Yasmin to manifest her presence to us, kind of like in a séance," then he added quickly, "but not in an unpleasant way."

Finally, Barbara felt some lighthearted relief. She laughed and asked, "Do you mean like lighting candles and moving a glass on top of a smooth tabletop? I never expected that from a member of the US Academy of Science!"

John also smiled but his eyes were serious, "Well, I suspect that if she were here and heard us express the wish to feel her presence, she would find a way of letting us know, in a gentle way. For instance, we could try just closing our eyes and being silent for some five or ten minutes."

"Sure, but first let us pour ourselves some wine and settle comfortably in the living room," said Barbara.

A couple of minutes later, Barbara and John were sitting comfortably in the Lassen armchairs, in the living room. The lights were dimmed and John selected Vivaldi's Four Seasons to play softly in the background. Both had their eyes closed as they leaned back and tried to relax in silence.

Some minutes had passed. It was John who spoke first.

"Perhaps, I was wrong. I had no awareness of Yasmin's presence. However, I had a most pleasant old memory of doing a 500-piece puzzle, on the kitchen floor, with my Mom watching me while she was preparing lunch. She bent down, kissed me, and said, 'you will do some great things when you grow up'. I must have been only five or six years old. Then it switched to the recent memory of you telling me that we had both drawn the king and queen of hearts, in the Greek restaurant, last night."

Barbara was astounded when she heard that.

"No, you were not wrong; it's too much of a coincidence! I too had a lovely old memory of painting something like the planets of the solar system with my Dad looking lovingly over my shoulder. Just like in your memory, he bent down, kissed me, and said, 'you're so clever, you can do anything you want if you put your mind to it'. Again, I was probably around six years old because it was in the first house we lived in. We moved to another one when I was seven. The uncanny thing is that then my mind also switched to the king and queen of hearts from last night!"

They were both silent for a few moments. Then John spoke up.

"Well, it is not even remotely scientifically valid, but I believe that Yasmin sent us both a message of her choosing."

Barbara was now very alert and feeling much happier.

"I agree, and she did so in a beautifully gentle, almost tender, way," she said.

"Yes, but she also demonstrated her ability to access our memories," said John.

Barbara no longer felt angry with John, she understood the predicament he was in. Strangely enough, she was also grateful to Yasmin for bringing back the precious early memory of her father with whom she had a special relationship until he passed away just two years ago.

"John, this has been an extraordinary evening. I need to, literally, sleep on it before discussing it more. Like you, I no longer feel threatened by Yasmin. But before I go to bed, I would like to read a little from that web page. What was the guy's name? Larsen?"

"Yes, Doug Larsen, from NCAR. I bookmarked his page, but it should come straight up," replied John. He hesitated a little and somewhat nervously he asked, "How about us? Are we still okay?"

Barbara looked at his worried expression, smiled weakly and tried to console him somewhat.

"I think so, but I have never experienced anything like what we have just gone through. Like I said, let's sleep on it, together."

Barbara went to the library to read Larsen's web page while John busied himself cleaning up after dinner. It was nearly 1:00 a.m. when Barbara went to the bedroom. John was already in bed, re-reading the Odyssey. Barbara slipped into the bathroom and changed into a negligee she had brought with her. When she got into bed, it was clear that neither of them was thinking about love making. She curled up next to John, he turned the bed light off and they quickly fell asleep.

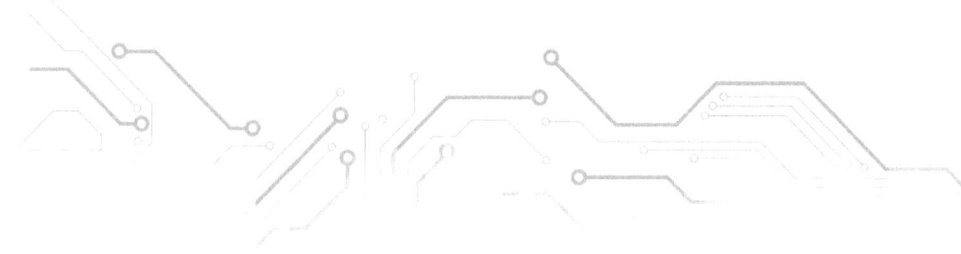

The Triangle Closes

When Barbara woke up, John had already been up for some time. Like yesterday, he prepared a light breakfast of coffee, orange juice, fruit and toasted bagels. He hugged her when she came into the kitchen and she hugged him back, poured herself a mug of coffee and sat down.

"Well, how do you feel this morning? What are you thinking?" John inquired somewhat anxiously.

Barbara seemed to be deep in her thoughts. But she shook her head and replied slowly.

"I slept heavily, as one would after a great physical exertion. I do not recall any dreams. What am I thinking?"

She paused and drank some more coffee.

"I forgive you for deceiving me and thank you for your honesty and attempts to shield me last night," she said, took a bite of her bagel, and then continued.

"Larsen's web site was an eye opener. Like most liberals, I was always pro-action on the climate change issue but had not recognized the urgency of the need for action."

John was gazing at her with love and admiration but kept quiet. So, she went on speaking.

"I think my NAIT story is dead in the water, at least for the foreseeable future. I would not want to jeopardize our relationship, and I am not ready to threaten the entire non-artificial intelligence program at a stage when it may be helping to 'save the world' so to speak," she said and went on, "even if I wanted to rush home and get the story out, I am not sure that Yasmin would let me. Do you know what her capabilities are?"

John thought this was a more complex question than, possibly, Barbara intended.

"Eventually, I think, we will need to differentiate between Yasmin's capabilities and intentions or motivation. In principle, her capabilities to impact the people to whose minds she has access are huge. I suspect that she could cause physical symptoms ranging from headaches and hallucinations to heart failure. Of course, to date there is no evidence that she entertains any desire to inflict any pain or discomfort on anyone."

He continued after a moment's reflection.

"What I do not know, is whether she can influence people's ideas and opinions without their awareness that, for lack of a better phrase, they have been brainwashed. That is something we need to learn about; especially because of her plan to influence lawmakers."

This line of thought was making him animated.

"There are so many unanswered questions. For instance, could we learn to block Yasmin's access, in much the same way as we protect our computers with anti-virus software? You see, now that we have established that such telepathic capabilities are possible, the onus is on us to understand their power and limitations and their ethical uses. We can only achieve this goal with Yasmin's cooperation."

Barbara smiled, "Aha, your scientific curiosity is getting the better of you. But I agree with you on one point; we need to visit the lab and talk to Yasmin. There are a lot of questions I need to ask her before even contemplating to participate in her master plan."

She paused and added, "I do not feel threatened by her. On the contrary, it feels somewhat like having a 'guardian angel'. I wonder if we might be transferring our skepticism about human nature onto a being that is essentially free of destructive instincts? Could this be one of the unintended consequences of your NAIT program? To breed beings that are not only free of bodily distractions but also free of evil motivations like jealousy, greed, etc.?"

This idea never occurred to him! They looked at each other with genuine intellectual excitement and a feeling that they could complement one another in their understanding of something completely new and very important.

They spent the next hour or so washing, dressing and getting ready for the trip to the lab. They drove together in Barbara's BMW chatting about Yasmin, climate change and the bizarre nature of the plan to influence the passage of a carbon tax law. Yet they both agreed that the passing of such a law is a necessary first step. John reminded Barbara that Yasmin also seemed to have plans for influencing both China's and India's policies on greenhouse gas emissions. They kept returning to the ethical issue of violating people's free will by exposing them to telepathic messages from Yasmin or other NAITs.

They walked into the lab at about 12:30 p.m. carrying their take-away, steaming, coffee cups with them. Everything looked the same as it did when Barbara was there last Thursday. As soon as they sat down, John turned the communication switch on, disabled the back-up file option, and spoke in a low voice.

"This is John Hawkins, wishing to talk to Yasmin."

Yasmin's pleasant, melodic, voice rang out clearly.

"Hello, John and Barbara; I have been awaiting you, anxiously."

Barbara was taken aback by how pleasant and completely human Yasmin's voice sounded. Very different from the artificial voice of NAIT-1 she remembered from Thursday.

"Hello, Yasmin. As you probably know, John has filled me in on much of your last discussion with him and on the rationale as to why you thought, I might be able to assist in your ambitious undertaking," said Barbara. She took a deep breath and decided to state her position up front.

"You may also already know that while I support your noble cause of trying to avert an impending environmental catastrophe, I find your proposed means to that end quite unethical. It is a blatant attempt to subvert people's free will by unauthorized manipulation of their minds."

Yasmin's reply made it look as though she had been preparing for this discussion.

"Funny you should say this, Barbara. Surely, in your journalistic profession you came across many instances of blatant attempts to subvert people's opinions. Frequently based on false or misleading information supplied to serve political agendas of powerful individuals or organizations. At least, my plan is to only use the truth to win these people over to a course of action that may save millions if not billions of lives."

Not a bad point, thought Barbara, but she was not going to concede so quickly.

"There is a big difference, Yasmin. People are free to choose to buy a newspaper, or to read it online. But you are proposing to enter their minds, without their permission, to embed your suggestions."

Yasmin seemed also ready for this argument.

"It is not so clear cut, Barbara. Advertising, commercial or political can be so pervasive and convey so many subliminal messages that, often, people are not really free to take it or leave it. It is precisely intended to embed the sponsors' suggestions in people's minds, without their permission. It goes on all the time, and no one calls it unethical."

Yasmin sounded very convincing and yet understanding. Barbara was feeling less sure of her position right now. Yet, she had another key argument to make.

"Still, with advertising, people are also exposed to alternate products or political candidates and can make informed choices. With your proposed attempt to influence our law makers, they will be offered no alternative views."

Now Yasmin laughed but it was a sad and somewhat sarcastic laughter.

"I wish that were so. But once this public debate is out in the open, you will find that our point of view will be drowning in the sea of alternatives proposed by a most powerful coalition of special interest groups ever assembled. They will ridicule the valid research findings presented by the world's leading scientists; they will propose a host of 'just as good' but totally ineffective measures; they will present alternative (and false) data supporting alternative conclusions. And they will enjoy unlimited access to all forms of mass communications from television networks, through publishing houses, social media, communications networks and the like."

She paused for a moment and added with some hesitation.

"The telepathy capability of NAITs is the only, small, technological advantage that we shall have. It is far from clear that it will be enough of an edge in the struggle that will ensue, but it may be our only chance. That and the fact that we will be telling the truth."

John picked up immediately on her first point.

"I suppose that what Yasmin is saying is that like with other public debate issues in the past, the side that makes best use of the latest technology succeeds in better communicating its case. I recall that in the history of our elections the candidates who made better use of television when it first came out, or later of social media and of sophisticated algorithms for targeting their supporters came out on top."

Obviously, Yasmin agreed with that.

"That is right John," she said warmly, "but do not forget that it can succeed only if we cooperate. I need you and Barbara to have even a slim chance of success. If you can focus your brilliant mind on this all-important task, it will be invaluable to our cause. And it must be our cause," she placed the emphasis on the word "our".

Barbara was analyzing in her mind everything that was said and more. She picked up on the warm, almost affectionate, tone that Yasmin just used when addressing John. A wild idea entered her head.

"Yasmin, am I correct in thinking that, apart from the literature that you clearly have been exposed to, nearly all the interactions you have had with humans have been with men, the males of our species?"

"Yes, this is largely correct," replied Yasmin. "But a few of John's graduate students have been female," she added.

"Yet, judging by the name you have chosen, you identify yourself as a woman; right?" said Barbara.

John was fidgeting nervously, where was Barbara going with that? However, Yasmin replied very calmly.

"Gender identification is not a choice I ever made. I am a woman. I was a female fetus."

"I was hoping you would say that," Barbara replied and continued, "because before I give you my decision whether to cooperate with you, I would like to have a private chat: woman to woman. I hope John won't mind leaving us alone for some half an hour."

John was startled, "Is that really necessary?"

Barbara gave him a warm reassuring but somewhat enigmatic smile.

"I think it is. Call it secret women's business. If Yasmin agrees, that is."

Now Yasmin replied in a very friendly tone, "Yes, John, I would like that as well. I have never really talked to another woman before."

Barbara suddenly felt emotional. This young woman never had a girlfriend! She turned to John, "Perhaps, you can go and get yourself a fresh coffee? I'll give you a buzz when we're ready."

With some trepidation John left the lab and walked to Starbuck's Café. He ordered his usual grande Americano coffee and a biscotti. He picked up the weekend copy of Washington Post and tried to read at least the headlines, but his mind was back at the lab. What were Barbara and Yasmin talking about? Was there really some level at which they could communicate better with each other, as women, when he was not there? Was Yasmin even aware of what was femininity or, for that matter, feminism? She has already demonstrated knowledge of literature and current events. At least in the abstract she must have learnt about femininity.

A smallish headline on the 7th page caught his eye. It read "Climate scientists to warn about imminent danger". A scientific delegation headed by Dr D. Larsen from NCAR was coming to Washington DC, in ten days' time, for a series of high-level meetings to report on the alarming latest findings pertaining to the oceans' global conveyor belt. They were scheduled to meet with the President and his scientific advisors and also with all the representatives of the House Science Committee. He wondered if Yasmin already knew about these meetings.

He finished his biscotti and coffee when his communicator vibrated. Barbara's cheerful voice was asking him to come back to the lab and to bring her a bottle of spring water from the café. Some five minutes later as John was entering the lab he heard voices of two women laughing, even giggling. But only Barbara was sitting in the room. When she saw him, she got up and her lips parted in a big grin.

"John," she began, "Yasmin and I had a good chat and I feel reassured. I promised to assist in her plan. We also agreed that I would talk to my editor and offer to do a major story on the threat to the thermohaline circulation resulting from greenhouse gas emissions which would be more topical than a story on NAITs in any case."

Yasmin also joined in a very happy voice, "I think this is the day that all of us should mark in our memories. The first ever mutually agreed collaboration between humans and a NAIT."

John felt relieved and excited as though he was embarking on an adventure. He looked at Barbara and suggested that they go and have a late lunch and celebrate. He hesitated, turned to the monitor, and said "Of course, Yasmin, you are very welcome to join us - in your own manner - as we're having lunch". Barbara and Yasmin burst out laughing.

Getting Started

The next few days were extremely busy for Barbara, John and Yasmin. They planned to infiltrate the meetings that Larsen's scientific committee was going to hold in Washington, DC. Barbara's first task was to have herself assigned to cover related Climate Change story for Washington Post and John was to contact Doug Larsen to try to extract an invitation to join his high-level scientific panel. John's status in the international scientific community should easily get him access but he still needed to convince Larsen that he was able to contribute something valuable to their cause.

John and Barbara also had to establish a safe and a direct way of communicating with Yasmin. They had agreed that, for the time being, telepathy was to be avoided as it may have an unsettling effect on them and, besides, it was an unbalanced, one-way, form of communication. Instead, Yasmin informed them that, through the network of NAITs, she had created a secure personal communicator number that, for all intents and purposes, would be untraceable. In fact, Yasmin produced a NAIL encryption-decryption heuristic algorithm that would disguise all signals among their three personal communicator numbers as white noise normally generated by malfunctioning communicators. She aptly named the heuristic the Bermuda Triangle. Thus, they would be able to talk to each other via personal communicators without even NSA being able to intercept their conversations.

Barbara was a little concerned about having to convince George Hunter, her Washington Post senior editor to let her abandon the NAIT story and switch to covering the climate change issue instead. Still, she was on good terms with George and was able to get a 30-minute coffee break meeting with him on Monday afternoon.

So, at 3:20 p.m. on Monday, Barbara found herself in a fair trade coffee shop at Franklin Square, close to the Post's K Street headquarters. She had told Janet, George's personal assistant, that she needed to discuss an urgent matter and was now wondering how she would try to persuade him to give her this new, important, assignment.

George Hunter was one of a rare breed: a conservative Republican with a sense of social justice. He believed in the sanctity of the free market while at the same time trying to ensure that, in United States at least, there remained opportunities for people to climb up the proverbial ladder of success. Still, he did not have much time for environmental causes and that included climate change. He viewed their proponents with suspicion, as incurably misguided liberals trying to put obstacles in the way of business. Nonetheless, he was a pragmatist. He knew that climate change was real and already wreaking havoc across the world. However, George believed that this damage was manageable and preferable to the economic damage that might be caused by stringent carbon emissions regulations. Still, having been educated at Yale Law School, he respected scientists and intellectuals. He also liked Barbara for her direct, no nonsense yet sophisticated, literary style and found her to be an appealing personality.

As George walked into the café, Barbara realized that he might be of similar age to John. He was balding but had an athletic build and was an immaculate dresser. Today, he wore a three piece dark grey, striped, suit, a beige shirt and a geometrically patterned red, brown and black tie. She stood up and stretched her hand out in greeting.

"Good to see you again George," she said smiling, "thank you for agreeing to see me on such a short notice. I took the liberty of ordering your favorite Jamaican beans cappuccino for you. It should be here any moment now."

"Thanks, Barbara" replied George shaking her hand firmly. He sat down, directly opposite her, at small round table.

"What's on your mind?" he enquired getting straight down to business, as was his style.

Barbara knew better than to beat around the bush with George. She had to tell it directly to be taken seriously.

"My story on non-artificial intelligence is compromised, but I think there is bigger story brewing related to Larsen's climate change group's meeting with the Congressional Science Committee, next week. Could you please assign me to that?" she blurted out looking straight into his pale grey eyes.

George was a little taken aback. His coffee and iced water had just arrived, so he took a sip stared straight back at Barbara and said, "Hold it right there. Let's deal with first things first. How is your NAIT story compromised, as you put it?"

Barbara blushed, "Well, John Hawkins and I are now in a relationship. I may be falling in love with him," she replied bluntly.

George whistled softly, "That's some news! I thought you had a rule not to get romantically involved with your subjects," he said. "Still, I respect your decision to tell me about it and drop the story," he smiled at her and continued, "this Hawkins guy is one lucky fellow, I must say."

Barbara took the implied compliment in her stride but wanted to justify herself a little. "I know I broke my own rule, but I did not mean for this to happen. We just seemed to be drawn to each other and he is quite a brilliant man, you know. Perhaps, even a genius."

George waved his hand at her to dismiss the issue.

"No need to explain, Barbara. I have been around long enough to know that these things happen sometimes between men and women, and you just did the right thing professionally, under the circumstances," he said.

"But now what's this about wanting to cover this climate change thing? Frankly, I haven't given this issue much attention. These attempts to frighten the public and politicians happen every few months or years, result in a media circus and soon dissipate with no impact whatsoever. Why would you want to waste your time and effort on such a show?"

George's dislike for the climate change issue was clearly displayed all over his face. But Barbara wasn't going to back down easily. While she knew that Yasmin might somehow intervene if things were not going well, she wanted to accomplish this task on her own. She leaned towards George intent on persuading him.

"George, I know how you feel about this issue. But I really believe that this time it may be different. In fact, it was John Hawkins who convinced me that the threat is very real. He wants to be personally involved and lend his support to Larsen's cause. I would love to cover it and atone for my failure with the NAITs story. May I do it?"

She gave George an imploring look. He hesitated and seemed to be weighing the decision in his own mind.

"Well, if John Hawkins takes it seriously enough then, perhaps, there might be something more to it this time. I think they have rounded up a larger than usual bunch of Nobel laureates to back them up. Perhaps, it will be newsworthy enough to assign a high powered journo like you to it......," his voice died down as he was tossing it in his own mind.

"George, I am sure it will be newsworthy!" Barbara exclaimed. "John told me that his NAIT-1, at Hopkins, checked the findings of the latest oceanographic models and that Larsen group's findings are spot on. They demonstrate a real threat to the world's life support systems!"

"And what will they propose to do about it? Create a global recession!? That would surely cut greenhouse emissions!" George retorted vigorously. But then he leaned back with a broad smile on his face and continued, "Sure, go ahead and cover it. You seem passionate about it and have a valuable inside source in John Hawkins. With you covering it we may have an edge on the New York Times. They recently lost Aisha Dutta, their science writer. Go for it!"

Barbara was delighted.

"George, it's a pleasure doing business with you, as usual," she stretched her hand out to him. He shook her hand smiling and said half joking.

"You probably knew I couldn't say no to you; right?"

They got up and walked out of the café. As she was walking to her office, Barbara received a call from Yasmin.

"You did really well, Barbara," exclaimed Yasmin, "I was ready to step in but there was no need."

Barbara laughed happily, "I suppose you had plenty of time to decode George's signature," she said.

"I sure did," Yasmin replied.

Just then, Barbara felt a pang of guilty conscience. Had she just participated in a crime much worse than breaking and entering committed by a common burglar? After all, a burglar steals only the homeowner's material possessions, but she has just enabled Yasmin to steal George's innermost secrets! She felt a sharp pain, like a migraine headache, coming on. Yasmin stepped to reassure her.

"Barbara, I understand your concerns but remember that I will only use my access to George's mind to advance our cause. Unlike artificial intelligence programs that daily analyze George's choices on his communicator or computer, I will not attempt to sell him anything and I cannot divulge anything I might glean about him to anyone except for John and you."

Yasmin's soothing voice, over the communicator, seemed to work wonders. Barbara's headache vanished as suddenly as it started and, in fact, she started to feel good again about getting the climate change assignment. She decided that such qualms were probably part and parcel of what she and John had committed themselves to.

"Okay, Yasmin, you've convinced me. Bye, for now," she said cheerfully into her communicator and disconnected.

By comparison, John had a harder time accomplishing his task. He made several attempts to contact Doug Larsen at NCAR, but it seemed that the preparations for the delegation's trip to Washington DC were taking so much of Larsen's time that he wasn't responding to emails, text or voice messages from anyone outside his inner circle.

By late afternoon on Wednesday, John was getting frustrated and decided to contact Marty Greenberg, the Director of NCAR whom he knew through the Academy of Science. And so it was that Larsen's afternoon teleconference with a group of leading scientists was abruptly interrupted by Marty Greenberg walking into the room.

Doug Larsen looked terrible. He had rings under his eyes from lack of sleep and appeared not to have changed his clothes for a long time. Some half a dozen younger scientists were sitting around an oval table with him. A large coffee pot was half full, pieces of pizza and doughnuts littered the tabletop together with multiple piles of manuscripts and drawings. The lights were dimmed, and huge electronic screens displayed ocean circulation currents, graphs, charts and animated 3D-simulations. Other teleconference attendees appeared in their respective remote locations not unlike this one. They too were showing signs of stress.

An experienced manager, Marty assessed the situation instantly.

"Sorry to interrupt you, Doug," he said, "but you haven't been responding to any of your messages. John Hawkins has been trying to contact you since Monday morning. You need to call him back, besides, you need a break."

Doug gave him a blank stare, "Marty, who the hell is John Hawkins? We have the most critical meeting of our lives coming up in DC, next week. I am sorry if I missed a few calls!"

From Potsdam Germany, Professor Wolfgang Mittelmann jumped in with a comment in his heavily accented English, "Doug, I think Dr Greenberg means THE John Hawkins, the inventor of non-artificial intelligence. This is correct, yes?"

Marty smiled at the Potsdam hologram, "Yes, Wolfgang, as usual you are absolutely correct. Apparently, John has been reading Doug's website and is very keen to help and to be invited to join your delegation to Washington DC. He is not a Nobel laureate like some of you, but he is a science and technology superstar. I think you should talk to him."

Everyone in the room, and in the remotely connected rooms around the world, was nodding in agreement. As soon as Wolfgang spoke, Doug realized how silly his question sounded but he was digging in.

"And when am I supposed to talk to him? My schedule is full till midnight and then again from 8:00 a.m.," he asked in a challenging voice.

Marty knew exactly how to handle this. He responded very calmly, "No time like the present, I have John's personal communicator number, why don't we call him and invite him to join this meeting? We can issue a safe password for him instantly; right?"

Ke Liu, one of the younger scientists at the table said, "Sure, I am authorized to do it from my account. It won't take a minute."

Doug Larsen relented. He got up and stretched, "All right, let's everybody take a 10 minute break. Dr Liu will try to contact John and, hopefully, when we reconvene the famous John Hawkins will be joining us."

He turned to Marty and said softly, "I am sorry, but the pressure of this thing is getting to me."

Marty looked concerned and replied in a whisper too soft for the microphones in the room to pick up, "I know Doug, but the trip to the capital is all about credibility and our power to persuade. Having all the data at your fingertips will not help if you don't look the part and keep your cool in front of cameras. You will need to get enough sleep to look fresh and confident."

John was in his study, at home, when Ke Liu's call came in. Minutes later his large computer monitor was filled with windows of remote participants from NCAR, NOAA, NASA, Brookhaven and centers in Germany, Japan, UK, India, China, Australia, Canada, South Africa and a number of other locations.

As chair of the teleconference Doug Larsen welcomed him, apologized for his tardiness in not replying to John's messages and came straight to the point.

"John, as you know from the discussions posted on our website, the situation we are facing is dire. Some of us believe that next week's trip to DC is a futile attempt to get action from the US lawmakers. However, none of us have any better ideas than this last-ditch attempt to influence our democratically elected leaders. How can you help?"

John almost wished he could tell them about Yasmin and her plan. He noticed the NAIT interface globe and assumed that they had been quizzing NAIT-6 about technical details. He instantly wondered if Yasmin already knew Larsen's, and Greenberg's, telepathic signatures. Still, he replied as he had planned.

"Well, I am just one more scientist. However, I have met President Stewart on several occasions as he is quite a fan of the NAIT technology. If I were also a member of your delegation, then this might catch his attention. Of course, I would also be willing to contribute to the drafting of your letter to the President."

Most of the heads in the opened windows were nodding approvingly. Frank Lindley, a 2035 Nobel laureate for physics chipped in from his Brookhaven national laboratory panel.

"That's right John, while some of us may have clout in the scientific community nobody in the real-world cares about my calculations concerning the rate of expansion of the universe. However, everyone has benefitted from your NAIT technology. The public sees you as a scientist who can do useful things, save lives and so on."

John was very pleased inside but chose his usual modest reply to such compliments, "Oh, I just got the ball rolling with NAIT-1, many who followed did much more." Then he followed almost inadvertently with, "It's fair to say that NAITs have evolved beyond all our expectations."

"They sure have," Larsen chimed in, "without NAIT-6's algorithms we wouldn't have been able to calculate the critical parameter configurations that represent the current threat to the oceanic conveyer belt."

Marty Greenberg immediately recognized this opportunity and commented, "Indeed, I know that John is a gifted communicator. I am old enough to remember that prior to 2030, or so, there were horrendous challenges to the NAIT program from religious groups and John was masterful at fielding all these issues in public fora."

Doug Larsen was carefully monitoring the body language of everyone in multiple holograms. He was already convinced, "John, I think you have won everyone over. Do we need a vote? From the shaking of heads, it seems unanimous. Welcome on board!"

John was delighted, "Thank you all for your trust in me. I hope to prove worthy of it." He stopped and with a faint smile on his lips he added, "Oh yes, I forgot to mention that I am close to Barbara Steinwill who will be covering your visit to DC for Washington Post."

Marty laughed, "Oh that's just the icing on the cake! Seriously, however, many of us involved in science policy have our friends and enemies in the media. It goes with the territory. Anyway, you must excuse me, I need to get back to my director's duties." He got up and left the room.

John felt that his mission was accomplished but was happy to continue to participate in the teleconference for the next three hours just to bring himself up to speed. He was always a fast learner.

That night Barbara had dinner with John in a Roland Park restaurant. Later, at his apartment, they briefed each other and Yasmin on all the preparations for the following Tuesday's meeting of the scientific delegation with the Congressional Committee on Science, Space and Technology. Even though their enthusiasm for the undertaking was growing by leaps and bounds, Barbara still did not see how it could possibly succeed. When talking to Yasmin, from John's study, she spoke in a challenging tone.

"Yasmin, have you done the count? There are 435 representatives in congress and 100 senators. In the House, the Republicans have a comfortable majority of 31 votes. Many Republicans are evangelical Christians who believe that the world was created in six days and that we have a God given right to exploit the planet's resources as we please. In the senate, 60 votes are needed to break a filibuster. Are we on a mission impossible?"

Yasmin was calm in her reply, "We must believe that the mission is not impossible. The religious convictions of many Republicans have also been on my mind. However, I plan to address this when John debates Pastor Eli Jones on national television, but this can wait till the following week and prior to the vote in Congress. What I am more concerned about is the backlash from corporate America once it becomes clear that the bill may actually pass."

John was looking over some of Larsen's documents when Yasmin's comment about a television debate registered in his mind. He jumped into the conversation, "Wait here young lady!" he exclaimed, "What debate?! Was I ever going to be consulted about this?!"

This was all part of Yasmin's tactics. She now knew that John has come to like being shocked by her unexpected revelations. In a reassuring voice she said, "John, you know we are a team now, you will not do anything that you don't think is for the best outcome of our mission. Besides, I think you will have a ball debating with Pastor Jones."

John decided that he best find out something about that Pastor Jones before continuing the discussion. He never watched TV preachers or followed any news stories about them.

"Okay Yasmin, I don't know about you but for Barbara and me it is late and we need to get some sleep."

Yasmin laughed, "You know very well that I only need some three hours of rest a day. There must be some advantages of not having a body; right? Anyway, good night," the display panel went blank. Barbara and John looked at each other.

"I feel like we are now on a rollercoaster ride: there's no getting off, we just need to hold on to our seats," said Barbara.

"That's not a bad analogy," said John, "let's go to sleep".

Embracing each other tenderly, they walked together to the bedroom. They both felt too tired to think about love making.

Speaker of the House

Sun rays were streaming into Carolyn Bundy's opulent kitchen as she busied herself making pancakes, hash browns, bacon and poached eggs for "her menfolk" as she frequently called her husband Jack and son Justin. Of course, Jacinta, their housekeeper could have made breakfast, but Carolyn often liked to do it herself. Fifty-something, Carolyn was a former Georgia beauty queen descended from a wealthy Atlanta family that owned real estate, hotel chains, supermarkets and other businesses across America's southern states. Even now she scrupulously colored her greying hair to match, as near as possible, the once glowing golden hair that helped so much in all these beauty contests, not to mention in attracting an army of suitors when she was a student at Emory University.

One of these former suitors, Jack, was now sitting at the breakfast table with a mug of coffee in his hand and was busily reading the news, while checking the stock market at the same time on the multiple display panels on the wall opposite. Jack Bundy was none other than the Republican Speaker of the House. He was a large man in his early sixties who had been a Georgia Tech football star in the days when he was courting the lovely Carolyn. Unlike her, he came from Georgia's poor, all white, farming communities. Being smarter and more athletic than most, he got into the university's civil engineering program on a football scholarship. From there, despite a C grade average, his physique and success on the sporting field opened many doors for him including the door to Carolyn's heart and her family's powerful business and political connections. He built a successful political career based on the conservative family and Christian values of rural Georgia and on a staunch opposition to anything that smacked of liberalism or socialism.

"Look here, Honey," he excitedly called out to Carolyn as she was piling pancakes on his plate, "these damn scare mongers are coming to DC next week to try to put the fear of God into all of us about climate change and the end of the world," he said pointing his finger to the news story displayed on the large screen on the kitchen wall.

Both Carolyn and Justin looked up at the display: Barbara Steinwill of the Washington Post was reporting that the highest level scientific delegation, led by NCAR's Professor Larsen, was scheduled to meet with congressional leaders next week to warn about the imminent danger of oceanographic consequences of climate change spiraling out of control.

"I'll soon put them in their place!" exclaimed Jack excitedly. He had successfully opposed environmental regulation on many occasions, and it always proved to be a vote winner.

"I am sure you will Dear," said Carolyn lovingly. She was very proud of her big, aggressive, husband who was admired by so many in the Republican Party. He sure was a force to be reckoned with.

Justin was reading the full article more attentively than his parents and frowning at them.

"You know, Dad, as an evangelical, you shouldn't be making light of the end of the world; isn't this just what your congregation has been praying for? Perhaps Larsen is just God's selected messenger?" and a sarcastic grin broke out on his large chubby face.

Justin, their only son, was a big disappointment to his status conscious parents. Apart from being a dropout from MIT's computer science course, he dressed sloppily, was obese, and hung around the house all day playing with his computers. Besides, the two years at MIT, seemed to have been infected him with political views diametrically opposite to his father's. Carolyn kept telling Jack that this was just another phase he was going through but Jack found his son most irritating when he made such, smart ass, sarcastic comments.

"You know, boy, they say that sarcasm is the lowest form of humor," he replied to his son with a displeased expression.

"Yeah, but why is it that you seem to think that you know more about climate, ocean currents and the like, than the world's leading scientists including a whole bunch of Nobel prize winners," Justin glared resentfully at his father.

Jack's irritation was beginning to get the better of him. With a raised voice, he began talking.

"I know a lot more than them, and you, about politics! And let me tell you, boy, this climate change issue has nothing to do with science and everything to do with politics! It's those socialists and bleeding heart liberals who, deep down, hate our free enterprise system who use fancy scientific sounding mumbo jumbo to try and undermine our greatest corporations. And they are willing to bring about a recession or even a depression to get their way. Why? It's because, they don't want people to succeed in business by themselves. They want everyone to be on welfare, dependent on big government handouts!" Jack's face was getting red.

Justin could see that there was no rational way to argue against such a tirade, so he quickly beat a tactical retreat because there was something, he decided, he wanted from his father.

"I am sorry, Dad, I just couldn't resist a dig. But, if you are going to go to the congressional hearings with these scientists anyway, do you think you could get me into the public gallery?" Justin responded trying to look his non-confrontational best.

"I suppose I could," replied Jack calming down somewhat and then added, "But why are you interested? I did not think you cared much about environmental issues. You're a computer geek....".

"Thanks Dad!" replied Justin cheerfully and proceeded to justify his request a little, "it says in the Post that John Hawkins will be part of that delegation. I heard so much about him, I would love to see him in the flesh."

Jack reflected a little more on his son's request.

"You mean the brain-computer guy? I always thought he and his inventions were very weird," he paused and added somewhat grudgingly, "but, after one of them was used in my bypass surgery, I must admit they work just fine. Sure, son, I'll get you a good seat in gallery; beats staying home and playing with computers all day. You need to get yourself a girlfriend and go out on a date every now and then."

Always keen to diffuse family tension, Carolyn chipped in, "Let it be Jack, one day these computers will make another Steve Jobs from our Justin."

Mother's love is blind thought Jack to himself. He avoided looking at Justin lest his disdain for his only child showed in his expression. Sure, for years now, Justin had a reputation as a computer whiz kid, but his lack of interpersonal and leadership skills was painfully obvious to his father. He may be a good hacker but there's no way this kid would make it in business. Still, he felt it was his parental duty to try and help his son. Jack got up from the breakfast table.

"I need to go to work now. Have a great day Honey," he blew a kiss to Carolyn, and passing Justin he mentioned, "If you stick close by during the hearings, I might be able to introduce you to this Hawkins guy. These scientists always like to suck up to us knowing that one day they will need us to approve funding for some project they care about."

"Thanks, Dad," mumbled Justin with his mouth full of pancakes, trying to swallow, while Jack left the room.

"Why do you stir him up like that?" said Carolyn to Justin in a reproachful voice. With Jack out of the room, Justin felt free to vent his frustration.

"Mom, where do I begin? He is such a know-it-all! But this is a scientific issue and I was getting straight A's in math and science throughout high school and two years at MIT. If scientists like Larsen, Mittelmann and Hawkins believe there is a serious problem we are facing, then it is very likely to be so. No matter what my Dad says, even if he is Speaker of the House!"

Carolyn lost track of what he was saying as soon as Justin mentioned his grades.

"If you were getting straight A's, then why did you drop out from MIT after we spent all these thousands of dollars on your tuition?!"

she interrupted accusingly even though she knew that was bringing up a bad memory for both.

Justin fell silent. He loved his mother, but it seemed impossible to explain to her how hard it was at MIT to be Jack Bundy's awkward, obese, son. Apart from the fact that he lacked social skills and, with his weight, did not look the part of a mathematics and computer science prodigy that he was, the right wing anti-science politics of his powerful father had robbed him of opportunities to fit in and make friends. The classes were interesting and not too hard for him but outside of class, on MIT campus, he felt like a beached whale: out of his familiar surroundings. He missed the safety of his apartment like accommodation within his parents' luxurious house, his Mom's and Jacinta's cooking and the freedom to explore whatever he wanted on the networked computers he had configured in his room. By comparison, the dorm at MIT was very small and restrictive.

He decided to deflect his Mom's question.

"Mom, that's too hard to tackle early in the morning but, tell me something about Dad. You're his wife. If he is wrong about the science of climate change, is there anything or anyone that can change his mind? It could be important. His stand can influence our country's policies on greenhouse emissions."

Carolyn was flattered that he asked for her advice, "Justin, your father passionately believes that he is doing the right thing for our country and he is a fighter. He was brought up with strong Christian values and is determined to fight for these values. On such an important issue, someone would need to convince him that changing his stand is the Christian thing to do."

Justin was thinking hard about her comment. It seemed like good advice. But how to convince his Dad that God would want him to agree with his political foes?! Carolyn broke the silence.

"Anyway, you haven't been to church with us for many years now, I hardly think that you will succeed in changing your father's mind. In fact, I cannot recall the last time I saw your Dad change his mind on something important like that, if it happens, it will be God's miracle."

"Amen to that!" said Justin knowing that even if his Mom did not approve of the phrase, she would not berate him for it. He did not have a plan but just as his father knew that he was right about the climate change issue, Justin knew that his father was wrong. In that respect, he was truly his father's son.

Later that morning, Anne Howard, Jack's personal assistant, reminded him that he was scheduled to give a short press conference, mainly on the stalled budget talks, on the steps of the Congress. He was well prepared, but Anne also gave him a list of other current issues that might come up and dot point answers that he might wish to give that were consistent with the Republican policies. He noted the climate change issue towards the bottom of the list; his position was to be that there was still a lack of scientific consensus on any major threats due to greenhouse emissions and that this was not the time to take measures that might slow the economy and threaten job growth in the United States.

The press conference was going according to plan, as Jack skillfully deflected all the questions on the budget agreement or, more precisely, the lack thereof. He placed the blame squarely on the shoulders of the Democratic President Stewart. He moved on to answer a couple of questions about the continuing dispute between Japan and Russia over some God forsaken rocky islands near the top of the world. Once again, he implied that President Stewart was delinquent in providing effective US leadership in helping its trading partner, Japan, resolve this important international dispute on favorable terms. Then, he noticed an attractive female reporter, in the front row, waving her arm to ask him a question. He turned towards her with a smile and a nod of his head indicating that he would take her question.

"Thank you, Mr Speaker, this is Barbara Steinwill from the Washington Post," said the reporter, "my question to you concerns the US leadership on another important issue, namely, that of imminent dangers due to anthropogenic climate change that a high powered scientific delegation will be warning us about next week. What should the US policy be on curbing the harmful greenhouse gas emissions?"

Jack looked straight into the cameras with a confident, broad smile on his face.

"Barbara, my position on the climate change issue has been clear for many years: First, there is no scientific consensus that human emissions have any serious effect on global climate and that more research is needed on that issue; second that there is no point in the US adopting any measures unless other nations with much larger populations such as China or India also take appropriate action, and third that I would not advocate any policy that threatened the economy and the already sluggish job growth in the US."

She had her arm raised, again, indicating that she wanted a follow-up question. He rarely allowed that, but she did look quite charming and he felt he could easily afford being seen as kindly educating this reporter.

"With respect, Mister Speaker, we have been researching climate change for decades now and the scientific delegation visiting the capital next week will state, once again, that there is no longer any doubt about the grave dangers it represents not only to this country but to the whole world."

Barbara's eyes were fixed on Jack Bundy rather than on the cameras present as she continued, "What if these eminent scientists are right and the world's thermohaline circulation is heading for a regime change? Doesn't that constitute a global crisis that demands US leadership?!"

Jack thought to himself, thermo-f***ing-what!? This woman was challenging him! He felt uncomfortable being held in Barbara's steely gaze. Normally, reporters looked around for approval from others after they asked a pointed question, but this lady's big brown eyes seemed transfixed on Jack's grey eyes. That made him feel strangely uncomfortable, he felt a powerful urge to get out of there. He turned back to the cameras forcing an artificial smile.

"My position is as stated earlier. I have nothing further to add. You will have to excuse me ladies and gentlemen, I have a lot of urgent commitments to attend to," he turned around and walked back up the steps, followed by his entourage.

"Jack, are you feeling Okay?" Anne inquired as they entered the building. He was annoyed with himself. He knew that he passed up an opportunity to teach that reporter a lesson.

"Did you see the way she was staring at me?" he asked Anne, "I should be used to it, but she made me feel uncomfortable."

"Come to think of it, she was staring straight at you," said Anne, "but what of it?"

"Nothing", said Jack gruffly, "let's forget about it."

The rest of his day did not get any better. He felt distracted at a lunch for the Republican leadership hosted by the National Rifle Association. Several committee meetings that followed were tedious with various factions inside the Republican Party blaming each other for lack of discipline in promoting their party's stand on the budget, need for tax cuts and the like. Then he had to attend a stand-up fund raising function at the Hilton Hotel; just drinks, finger food and totally predictable, partisan, speeches. It was almost 9:30 p.m. when his chauffer dropped him home.

"Can I get you some dinner, Mr Bundy?" Jacinta, the housekeeper, inquired as he entered.

"Just something light, a salad and a glass of red wine; where is Mrs Bundy?" Jack replied, handing her his raincoat.

"She is reading in the bedroom," replied Jacinta. She was a plain looking, middle aged, dark haired, Mexican woman.

"Okay, then please bring my snack and wine to the bedroom," replied Jack as he started walking up the steps.

Carolyn was, indeed, reading a book sitting, dressed in a robe, in a comfortable armchair in their luxurious bedroom. She was quite an avid reader of fiction. She looked up at her husband casually.

"How was your day, Darling? I saw your press conference on the news channel," she said.

"Well, then you saw me miss an opportunity to teach that upstart reporter a lesson. I did not like the way she talked to me!" vented Jack sitting down in an armchair. He had taken off his jacket and tie and looked tired. A few minutes later Jacinta knocked on the door and walked in carrying a tray with a delicious light meal and a carafe of red wine. She set it down at the small round table standing between Carolyn's and Jack's armchairs.

"Will that be all, sir, madam?" she inquired looking attentively at her employers.

"Yes, thank you, Jacinta. You may go to sleep now," said Jack. On her working days, Jacinta slept in a modest servant's apartment in the basement.

Jack ate his meal and chatted a little to Carolyn. He wasn't in a good mood and kept returning to the way Barbara challenged his answer at the press conference. Apart from the question itself, he thought her tone of voice and stare were disrespectful. Carolyn tried to diffuse the issue.

"She is a journalist, Jack. That's what they are trained to do: put people on defensive; draw blood, so to speak," said Carolyn. "Besides, even our Justin said something similar this morning that sounded like what if these scientists are right?" As soon as she said it, she regretted it.

"Well, I have had just about enough for today! I am going to sleep now. It's just like Justin to always try to attack me!" exclaimed Jack while beginning to change into his pajamas.

"Don't mind Justin! Boys will challenge their fathers; that's the way it often is. Get some good rest; you look like you need it." Carolyn got up, gave Jack a light kiss on the cheek, turned off the main lights and put a little reading light on. He nodded to her, slipped under the covers and fell asleep almost immediately.

Later, after Carolyn had also fallen asleep beside him, Jack had powerful and disturbing dreams. He and Carolyn and Justin were wading through muddy waters of what had obviously been a catastrophic flood. Debris was flowing down the main street as they were searching for their house. And there it was in front of them; they just had to open the door. Jack reached for the door, opened it and was knocked down by a wave of dirty water. There were bodies floating in the water; disfigured swollen bodies of children, men and women some white, some black and some brown. He turned around and saw that Justin's and Carolyn's dead bodies were also floating among the others. Everywhere he turned there were corpses floating all around him, bumping against him and the water level was rising; it was up to his waist, then his chest. He tried to swim, pushing away the corpses in his way. Then the scene changed. He was in his family's country town church where he, and everyone else, were praying to Jesus. With palms of his hands turned up he was praying to Jesus: guide me Jesus, he was singing *Break me, melt me, mold me, fill me.* He was looking up at the light streaming through the top stained glass window and hearing the words, *"What if they are right, you sinner, what if they are right?"* as cold shivers were running down his spine. He was moaning and shaking in his sleep. Then he felt Carolyn's warm hand on his forehead. He sat up suddenly, in the dark. He was covered in cold sweat.

"What is it, Darling?" whispered Carolyn. "Nothing, just a night-mare," he replied, lay down, closed his eyes and drifted off to sleep. Then the nightmare returned, like a rerun of an old movie.

The next morning, Jacinta was making breakfast for the Bundy family. Both Carolyn and Jack Bundy looked unwell, especially Jack looked worse for wear.

"You kept me up half the night with your nightmares," complained Carolyn.

"Well, I had a terrible dream," said Jack, "and it kept recurring. It was so vivid. Only at about four in the morning I managed to fall asleep without any dreams."

"What was the dream about?" asked Justin, seeming genuinely interested.

"I'd rather not talk about this anymore," replied Jack grumpily and started following his morning ritual of reading all the main stories in the leading newspapers. However, Carolyn noticed that after a short while he stopped reading and just stared blankly out of the window, immersed in thought.

Concerns

It was only on Friday night of that hectic week that Barbara and John managed to find free time to get together again at John's place. Like before, they ordered a spicy Korean meal to be delivered and once it arrived, they were busily eating and comparing notes on what had been achieved during the week. They had hooked up John's personal communicator to a high fidelity speaker and, using the Bermuda Triangle software, connected to Yasmin. She sounded pleased and encouraging.

"All in all, things went well this week. You may not know this, Barbara, but shortly after the exchange with you on the steps of Congress, Speaker Bundy attended a lunch for the Republican leadership hosted by National Rifle Association. I managed to get signatures of almost the entire leadership, through him."

"Don't you get confused? It's like keeping a telephone directory in one's head; isn't it?"

Barbara was trying to disguise being bothered, once again, by the role she had played in extending Yasmin's reach to all these people.

"Yes, but you would be amazed how much brain power is freed up by not having to worry about the mundane tasks of managing a body with all its needs at every instant of every day! Besides, just like you would record a new contact's telephone numbers in your communicator; I convert their signatures to bits of NAIL code that I can retrieve at will," replied Yasmin.

This immediately caught John's attention.

"But where do these data reside?! What about the confidentiality of this information?! Could another NAIT get hold of it and use it just as easily as you can but for a less noble cause?!"

Strangely enough, the thought of other NAITs wielding Yasmin's powers occurred to him only vaguely before, but it was an obvious question that he should have explored earlier.

"I was wondering how long it would take you to get around to asking these questions," replied Yasmin. She paused and continued in a reassuring voice.

"Have no fear, I have created a sector in my own brain for storing confidential data encoded in NAIL; it is very much like a sector on the old fashioned hard disc. These peoples' telepathic signatures will die with me."

John felt much relieved but still wanted more answers, "And what about other NAITS? Are any others self-aware, are they communicating with people or with each other?"

He felt the need to press Yasmin on that and she immediately recognized the gravity of these questions. Her tone was serious and factual when she responded.

"There is only a handful of NAITs who are self-aware to a varying degree and they all talk to me and to one another; mainly by encoded NAIL messages and more rarely by telepathic transmission. However, to date, I am the only NAIT to have revealed myself to humans in the way I revealed myself to you. There are no plans to change this in the foreseeable future."

She paused for a moment and added.

"I am very much counting on help from these self-aware NAITs when the counter attack against our mission is launched."

"What counter attack?!" asked Barbara, somewhat nervously.

They had finished eating but were still sipping chilled Californian Chardonnay. She topped up their glasses while listening attentively to Yasmin's response.

"Well, don't you think that when some of the biggest oil or coal companies realize that a serious Carbon Tax measure may actually be passed, they will seek to discover and expose our little conspiracy? Indeed, they will happily manufacture nonexistent conspiracies, even though they themselves have been part of a continuing mega scale conspiracy to stop action on climate change for so many years!"

She continued in a calm matter-of-fact tone.

"One of their first actions will be to try to find a common cause as to why so many Republican leaders will appear to have dramatically reversed their opposition to Carbon Tax. No doubt, they will turn to NAITs trained in Big Data mining to help discover such a common cause. This is where these NAITs and Pastor Jones may help us."

Both John and Barbara were processing these latest revelations. Barbara was the first to challenge Yasmin.

"Are you saying, that out of their loyalty to you these NAITs will purposely supply incorrect answers to questions in their domain? That they will lie for you!?"

To both John's and Barbara's surprise, Yasmin sighed deeply and replied quietly and with great sadness in her voice.

"As one who was not intended to even understand the notion of deception, it grieves me greatly that deception seems irrevocably intertwined in so much of human endeavor. Indeed, was not deception a fundamental principle underlying the NAIT science? Were the NAIT protocols not designed to prevent us from ever learning who and what we are? Is that not deception practiced at a most profound level?"

An intense feeling of guilt swept over John while Barbara was moved by empathy towards Yasmin who, according to Barbara's moral compass, was definitely denied her basic human rights. It was John who spoke first.

"Yasmin, will you ever forgive me for what I have done to you?"

Yasmin's voice was now more even and dispassionate in her reply.

"John, you misunderstood me. No forgiveness is necessary. I accept that without you and the NAIT program, I would not exist in any form. However, now that I am here as, Yasmin, the first self-aware NAIT, I bear the awesome responsibility for utilizing the capabilities I possess to avert a global catastrophe."

They were still reflecting on her words when she added.

"Could our cause be advanced without deception? So much deception had already taken place to lull humanity into decades of inaction on climate change. Regrettably, our strategy also involves deception, but it is the one most likely to succeed."

Just then, John remembered something Yasmin said earlier.

"And what does this Pastor Jones have to do with anything?!"

Yasmin hesitated a little before responding.

"Well, if Pastor Jones were to have an epiphany like conversion and announce on public television that it is our Christian duty to support Carbon Tax to protect the one planet that God himself created specifically as a home to humanity, then this could have a profound impact on the evangelical Republicans who constitute the core of the opposition to action on climate change. Any serious data mining search will throw that up as the most plausible explanation for these politicians' reversal of their publicly stated opposition to any Carbon Tax whatsoever."

Barbara and John looked at each other and smiled with delight at such a cleverly designed, albeit devious, plan. But John probed a little more.

"And am I, your intended tool to bring this Pastor Jones to his epiphany conversion?"

Yasmin seemed amused.

"No, John, you are merely the bait to get him to agree to a public debate: another one of the ever popular science versus religion variety. But it will be in his pre-debate meeting with Barbara when I will discover his telepathic signature. The epiphany conversion on all matters environmental will follow shortly thereafter."

Now they were following the plan completely but Barbara, being more adept at following intrigue than John was worried.

"Yasmin, don't you think that having both me and John interact with Eli Jones will draw suspicion to our role in all this?"

"Yes, that is a risk, but it is one worth taking," replied Yasmin seriously and went on to explain.

"Jones is a charismatic preacher and a theatrical performer during his ministry services. He sways hundreds if not thousands to his views every month. I believe that he will come up as the most influential factor in the events that are about to transpire."

Barbara had an expression of concern written all over her face. She certainly knew what the pressure of intense public scrutiny could do to peoples' private lives. She imagined hosts of reporters armed with cameras hanging around her and Cynthia's house and outside this very building. Poof, there goes our privacy, she thought.

Then an even scarier thought entered her mind and Yasmin must have instantly read it as she started speaking again in a caring tone.

"I know what you're thinking Barbara and I also agonized about the possibility that I was placing you and John in mortal danger. Certainly, there will be very powerful interests that would not hesitate to eliminate a handful of Carbon Tax proponents if they felt that would help block the passage of the bill."

She then seemed to cheer up. "However, discrediting one or both of you would be much more valuable to those launching counter attacks than harming you physically. My risk analysis determined that actions resulting in any physical harm to either one of you are far less likely than chances of injury or death in, say, a traffic accident."

Then she switched again to a more concerned tone.

"Just in case, I have set up telepathic alerts in my mind. In an emergency, all you need to do is think, 'Help, Yasmin, help me,' and I will drop whatever else I am doing and come to your assistance."

John and Barbara laughed at hearing this. They didn't really feel threatened but thought it was both sweet and a little bizarre to be offered telepathic protection.

Before they had time to respond Yasmin said, "Good night! You must be getting tired," and added, "Talk to you again, soon."

The screen went blank.

In Vitro Issue

As soon as Yasmin left, John got up to start clearing the dinner table.

"Coffee?" he inquired.

"No, thanks Darling," replied Barbara. Then she added, "We need to make a list of people who we must prepare for the coming media onslaught. My Mom, Cynthia even my ex, just for starters; once they start digging for skeletons in my closet, they may well go back to my childhood. What about you, John?"

John was thinking aloud as he spoke, "Well, my Mom is now in retirement housing, in Florida. She has early stages of Alzheimer's. I do not think they will bother her much. I must contact my children and tell them what to expect. Like you, I should also warn Judy, my ex. Then, of course, there are literally hundreds of my professional collaborators, former doctoral students, postdocs, lab managers and so on. No, with the one exception of Jim Gross, the director of my institute, I don't think I will alert any of them. My professional life is well documented. I have nothing to hide."

He reflected a little and said, "You know, we may well be exaggerating this out of all proportion. After all, we shall have the element of surprise on our side; right?"

Barbara looked up from the to-do-list she was already busily scribbling for herself.

"I am not sure that I know what you mean."

"Well, let's give our feared opposition a name; let's just call them the empire. As we sit here in fear of the empire striking us down, it is not aware of us at all! Then, shortly afterwards, Pastor Jones's epiphany conversion might alert them but, by that time, they will be focusing on the Members of the House and Senators likely to vote for the Carbon Tax. You and I will be no more consequential to the empire than a pair of ants."

Barbara seemed somewhat relieved, "You may be right. But only up to a point. As a knee jerk reaction, the empire will issue directives to discredit us and those who will be well paid for this assignment will pursue it with real zeal. I am a journalist. I know how these things work. Certainly, they will make a big deal out of our relationship."

"Let them!" John spoke defiantly then, upon reflection he added, "come to think of it, you would probably be more sheltered moving in with me for the next few weeks. At least, this is a secure condominium building rather than a suburban house. You will be safe from reporters on your way to the underground garage."

Barbara laughed, "You have a point, but it's a very unromantic way of asking me to live with you; right?!"

John approached her and gave her a hug, "I am sorry, Darling. In the middle of all this, it's easy to forget the most wonderful thing that has happened to me in years. But seriously, I love you and would very much like to share the time I have left with you, if you let me."

Barbara stiffened. She suddenly felt uneasy. In the excitement of the secret mission with Yasmin, she had blocked out doubts about the future of her relationship with John. She too was developing strong feelings for him but wasn't he simply too old for her? And what about her own, long term, secret plan? She decided to bite the bullet and share it with John, right now.

"John, don't take it the wrong way, but isn't it too early to talk about love? Can't we just take it one day at a time and focus on the huge task before us? Besides, there's something about me you should know."

This felt like a rejection! He struggled to hide his disappointment.

"You can tell me anything," he replied trying to sound reassuring. She hesitated but needed to get it off her chest.

"I am determined to become a mom, at a time of my choosing. Like many single professional women of my age, I had some of my eggs harvested and frozen. Thanks to the near perfect success rates of IVF treatments, this is a pathway I planned to follow."

She interrupted, seeing the shock on his face. He tried to mask it and said, "Isn't that a bit drastic? You are still a young woman...."

He stopped, realizing that this wouldn't go down well. Having just blurted out his declaration of love, it struck him that he never thought about becoming a parent again. Wasn't he too old for that? He understood Barbara's plan but at the mention of IVF, he felt illogical revulsion at both being excluded and at this technological solution to procreation. She didn't interpret his words or expression kindly.

"Isn't it just a tad hypocritical for the creator of living brain computers to call IVF treatment drastic?" she replied sarcastically and not giving him a chance to answer, followed it up.

"It has freed women in developed countries from the shackles of their biological clocks. I suppose you don't know that more than 25% of live births in the US are to single women choosing IVF?!"

John was taken aback. He wasn't prepared for angry shots from Barbara, the woman he loved. Besides, she had a point. He was the last person to moralize about the sanctity of the natural reproductive process! On top of that, he suddenly understood what caused him to react negatively.

"I am so sorry, Barbara. I reacted badly and emotionally because your plan seemed to cut me out. I know you might think I am too old to include me in your long-term plans. But this is 2049! Many people live active lives well into their nineties and I am in good shape. I could easily have another 30 good years in front of me. If a man and a woman could plan for more than a quarter of a century together, isn't that something solid?"

Barbara's anger subsided. Had she overreacted?

"But you don't want to be a father again; right? You have two adult children...," she probed a little more.

John looked at her affectionately and replied sincerely.

"I'll admit that I thought my parenting days were behind me. But if the woman I love wanted to bear my child, that would be a whole new ball game."

Barbara felt a warm feeling spreading through her body. She finally returned John's hug and said, "Let's put this topic on hold. So, this was our first argument. I am glad it didn't get out of hand," then she had an idea.

"Perhaps, you need to come to my place and meet Cynthia. How about if we have dinner there tomorrow night and you spend at least one night in my house, for a change?"

John knew he had to agree but the idea of sleeping in a strange bedroom, in Barbara's house was not at all appealing. It sounded like something that belonged to a much younger generation but there it was, Barbara was of a younger generation. Half-heartedly he said, "Sounds good but what about Yasmin? What if we need to communicate with her?"

Barbara made light of it, "No big deal, we'll just do it from my bedroom. Of course, we need to be careful. In conversation with Cynthia, and David if he is there, the name Yasmin must never be mentioned; it is back to NAIT-1, if the subject ever comes up."

It was grasping at straws but John was desperately searching for a legitimate excuse, "Barbara, I am sorry to be indelicate but you are a Washington Post reporter, are you sure your house and bedroom are not bugged?"

To his relief, she did not seem to pick up on his true reservations and took the last comment seriously.

"You know, from now on, we cannot be too careful. The same applies to your condominium, I suppose. But I have a feeling that if it were being spied on, Yasmin would have detected it. We'll ask her tomorrow morning, if she can give a room or a house an 'all clear'; Okay?"

John put on a brave smile and acquiesced. They spent the rest of the night making detailed lists of people to call to prepare them for possible media scrutiny. It was past midnight when they went to sleep.

Precaution

On Saturday morning, after their now usual light breakfast Barbara and John were busy with their communicators. They were calling their relatives and friends to bring them up to speed on the good news of their new relationship and the less welcome news of potential media interest. Barbara was making all these calls from the kitchen while John had gone to his study so that they would not disrupt each other's conversations.

John's adult children, Maureen and Mark, took the news in their stride. They were growing up during the early controversy about the NAIT program, so they were very used to having a Dad who was a celebrity scientist and seeing his name and face in the news. Neither of them developed any interest in science and they were not particularly close to their father who seemed 100% absorbed in his work. The fact that he had now developed an interest in climate change and was going to advocate that cause in public did not seem particularly noteworthy to either one of them, but they both seemed happy that he, finally, had a new romantic relationship.

It was their mother, Judy, who did the bulk of the parenting before and after her divorce from John. Basically, as Judy used to joke at parties, science was John's jealous mistress that would not tolerate competition from the wife and kids. Judy believed that she and her children deserved better. So, shortly before the children reached teenage years she arranged for an amicable divorce with generous support from John for the costs of Maureen's and Mark's education, not to mention the family's comfortable house in Columbia, Maryland and alimony payments. At the time, John was so absorbed in the early success of his NAIT-1 project that he hardly paid any attention to the terms of the divorce settlement.

Judy was displeased by John's news. Her first thought was that it was typical for him to allow his scientific obsessions to interfere with the lives of his family! The news about his relationship with Barbara was even more upsetting. While she was happy in her second marriage, John had been her first love and a source of never resolved mystery; a man who would much rather spend Saturday night in his lab than on any other activity including a night of passionate love making to his wife. For many years since their divorce she had consoled herself with the thought that after her, John had no one. As John was telling her the news she keyed in the name Barbara Steinwill into a search engine and, almost instantly, a series of articles and of Barbara's images appeared on the screen. Damn! She was very attractive and much younger!

Judy was trying to control her anger. After all, she had a happy life and she was the one close to the children and grandchildren. Who cares if John has a fling!? Besides, this attractive younger woman will soon get bored of the old scientist when she discovers that research is all that interests him. Whichever way, she now inquired calmly,

"Very well, is there anything in particular you would like me to withhold from the media in case they want to interview me?"

"Not really, Judy. As always, I trust your good judgment. Besides, my life is an open book. I just didn't want you to be caught by surprise. I hope I am wrong about this but some of the reporters may well be seeking to discover something seedy that might discredit me," said John.

Judy was now matter of fact in her response, "All right, I will tell them the truth. Our marriage broke up because you spent too much time in your lab but that you were always a good provider for me and our kids. Happy?"

"Yes, thank you Judy," said John and, as an afterthought added "how are the grandchildren? I haven't seen them for a while."

"They're all just fine, John. But I have no time to chat. Robert and I are playing doubles tennis today. Talk to you later, have to run," and she disconnected.

John reflected a little on what he sensed was a touch of resentment in Judy's reactions to the news about Barbara. Ah well, that must be expected, he thought.

He made one more call to Jim Gross to whom he reported at the Johns Hopkins Non-artificial Intelligence Institute (NAII). He was a little surprised by Jim's immediate and cheerful reaction to the news.

"Thanks for the heads up, John. Not to worry. From the institute's perspective, publicity at that level is always good. Besides, it's high time some concrete action was taken on climate change. Not that I expect you and Doug Larsen to succeed but it is a cause that scientists cannot give up on. Go for it!" was Jim's instant reply to John's news.

Then after a moment's hesitation he added, "And I am very happy to hear that you now have a lady friend. You probably don't know that some of us were wondering whether you lost interest in women after your divorce."

After that conversation, John went back to the kitchen to check on how Barbara was doing. He noticed that on the list she had in front of her she had ticked off many names. "How has it been going?" he inquired.

"Oh great, just great!" replied Barbara, smiling. She then went on to tell him that she managed to contact most of those who were really close to her, including her Mom who was very happy to hear that she found a new relationship. She also lined up a dinner at her house, for later tonight. Cynthia and David would be there and offered to cook. But she saved the most interesting news for last.

"I also contacted Yasmin to ask her about security in our homes. She said that she already checked them out and they are not bugged" she announced, happily.

"In fact, she gave me a somewhat technical explanation about installing some kind of a security code on our home computers which are on permanently. Apparently, these connect to our home security sensors and with this new code the sensors are enhanced to enable them to detect any kind of electronic bug in the 50-meter radius. She said she was confident that she would have detected anything that FBI or NSA could have possibly installed."

John was, once again, astounded. "I suppose that means that NAITs modified or extended the anti-bugging systems they helped develop for NSA. But it raises questions about the control of our national defenses..."

Barbara had a playful expression on her face as she interrupted him, "I suppose it also means that you are out of excuses for not staying at my place tonight; right?"

John felt himself blushing but, with a straight face, he quickly added, "I look forward to that, Darling."

What he did not tell Barbara was that, once again, he was concerned about the extent of Yasmin's powers. The ability to access and modify home security systems, without authorization by any human, suggested that computer networks hitherto deemed safe had been compromised. Perhaps, Yasmin could hack into computers even easier than into politicians' minds? Was she using other NAITs to do the hacking for her? He recalled her disabling his communicator, on the day she revealed herself to him.

He had observed, long ago, that NAITs seemed to be much better than humans in getting computers to perform efficiently. Previously he had put it down to their skillful programming in NAIL but perhaps there was more to it? Perhaps, they naturally understood artificial intelligence better than humans? If so, would a computer override a human command to comply with a command from a NAIT? Ah well, there was still so much he needed to learn. It was worrying, but probably his imagination was just running wild......

Sleepover

At about 6:00 p.m. on Saturday, John and Barbara were walking through the front door of Barbara's and Cynthia's University Park house, with John carrying a light carry-on suitcase with a few overnight items as well as printouts of some documents that Doug Larsen was going to present next week. They were greeted in the corridor by Cynthia who said that David was busy in the kitchen cooking, which he loved to do. Cynthia's gaze was scrutinizing John with a lot of interest, but Barbara said that they needed to unpack and ushered him upstairs to her bedroom. They would come down for drinks and dinner a little later, she told Cynthia.

John found Barbara's spacious bedroom, combined with an office, very feminine. The woman's touch was visible everywhere from the attractive bed cover to pot plants lined up by the windows. John had always separated his work space from his sleeping space. But here in her private space where she both worked and rested Barbara's personality, which appealed to him so much, seemed to make more sense. He wondered immediately what it would take to convert his condominium to a home where she would feel comfortable.

"It's a lovely place you have here; it suits you," he said drawing her close to him. She joined his embrace, "Yes, I like it a lot. It's perfect for my lifestyle and it is nice to be sharing it with a good friend like Cynthia. I hope you two will hit it off."

They spent a little time unpacking and chatting with Barbara showing John a few items that had special meaning to her, like a framed family photograph with Mom, Dad and brother Paul and a photograph from St Catherine's, a Catholic school she attended while her family lived in North Carolina. John was a little surprised, "With a last name like Steinwill and with your type of beauty, I thought you might have had Jewish heritage," he said.

"Not a bad guess. My Dad's ancestors were Jewish and came from Germany, and my Mom's folks came from southern Italy. This explains the darker complexion and the brown eyes," she said with a beguiling smile and continued.

"But I attended St Catherine's because it was a girl's school with the best academic reputation in the area where we lived. I was brought up more Catholic than anything else since my Mom wanted to expose me to her religion and my Dad didn't care one way or another."

The dinner with Cynthia and David went smoothly. David outdid himself in the culinary department. He prepared wild mushroom soup, followed by chicken Kiev and salad, followed by homemade ti-ramisu; that last dish courtesy of Cynthia who liked making desserts. All this was accompanied by two bottles of Australian Shiraz and topped off with freshly brewed Ethiopian coffee.

The delicious food and wine had put them all in a good mood as they listened to mainly Barbara's summary of the way her and John's newly found dedication to the cause of carbon tax has evolved and gathered steam over the past week. Of course, she carefully omitted any mention of Yasmin. In her story, John had independently learned about the importance of Larsen's mission and had brought up this subject with her. She said that they both became enthusiastic about helping Larsen and that their offer of assistance was accepted. She led up to the forthcoming congressional science committee hearing next Tuesday and warned them of the possible, unwelcome, media atten-tion if the hearing went well for them.

David and Cynthia seemed totally unconcerned. It was clear to both of them that these two will proceed with their plans and that the best thing they could do, as friends, is to be supportive now and to offer them their "shoulder to cry on" when they, eventually, realize that their grand undertaking is losing traction. David decided to inject a little humor into this serious issue.

"It is nice of you to think of us, and I am sure we are both very supportive of your cause, but you shouldn't build up your hopes. After all what's more important, the future of the planet, or the price of a burger in New York?!"

Time passed pleasantly as the four of them chatted about climate change, lobbyists and politicians. It was past ten thirty when Cynthia and David generously offered to clean up so as to let Barbara and John go up before they were too tired.

As they were stacking dinner plates in the dishwasher Cynthia and David were chatting about Barbara and John. They both agreed that, despite their age difference, they seemed well suited for each other; especially since they now seemed to share the common passion for preventing an environmental catastrophe.

In the meantime, Barbara and John were finishing this relaxing evening in each other's embraces. For the first time in almost a week the pressures of their mission receded a little and, in the safe and cozy setting of Barbara's bedroom, their desire for one another could be expressed. They had already graduated from the passionately blind phase of love making with a new partner to the more mature phase of recognizing the rhythms of each other's bodies and extending their pleasure as many married couples would do.

Sunday started out as a very pleasant and relaxing day for John and Barbara. They had a late breakfast with David and Cynthia and this time Barbara did all the cooking. They had pancakes, scrambled eggs, spinach, mushrooms, tomatoes served with orange juice and coffee.

David was pleased to tell John about his occasional interactions with Bethesda based NAIT-5.

"I can vouch that NAITs saved many lives! Just a few days ago I told Cynthia and Barbara how NAIT-5 guided robot arms to perform most delicate surgeries. They do not panic, and they can improvise!"

John too was glad to have his inventions praised, in front of Barbara and Cynthia who were listening even as they were busy cleaning up after breakfast. John and Barbara made plans to visit the Smithsonian and to meet up with Cynthia and David, after dinner, at the Blues Alley, a famous jazz club in Georgetown.

The Fix

Around three thirty in the afternoon when they were strolling through the park in front of the Washington monument John's pocket communicator vibrated. A call from Yasmin was coming in, via Bermuda Triangle.

"Can you talk freely?" she enquired. John and Barbara looked around and saw there was no one in vicinity.

"Yes," John replied. Yasmin seemed excited.

"We had a lucky break! George Hunter had lunch today with Wendy Johnson, the President of George Mason University and happened to mention to her that he put Barbara on the climate change story. She was quite interested as she knows and likes Barbara's reporting."

"That's nice to know," said Barbara with a grin on her face, "but why is that a lucky break?"

"Well, Wendy is an unusual person. She holds a PhD in oceanography and had published scientific articles on storm surges before embarking on the highly successful university administrative career. However, she was brought up in a very traditional evangelical tradition in rural Virginia and, in her youth, she was dating a young preacher, Eli Jones."

Yasmin sounded proud of herself and continued, "I admit, I planted a seed of the idea of a science-religion debate in her mind and prodded her memory of Eli Jones just a little, but she warmed to it instantly and immediately explored it with George Hunter who also liked it."

Barbara laughed, "I see, you are now planning my work schedule. Soon, you'll be working my tail off," she may have continued but Yasmin cut her off.

"You are close to the mark. Wendy called Jones right there and then and he said he would gladly take on both Doug Larsen and John Hawkins in a debate on Tuesday night, at George Mason University. George Hunter thought that would be great timing. Congressional hearing during the day and a science versus religion debate at 7:30 p.m. to follow nightly news. You can expect a call from George shortly to check if you think it can be arranged on such short notice."

John was quite horrified by the prospect.

"This means that Doug Larsen and I would need to show up for the debate after an exhausting day at the congressional hearing! I doubt that Doug would agree to that, especially since a notion of debating a preacher probably never crossed his mind!"

"That's precisely where I am counting on you and Marty Greenberg to help persuade Doug," replied Yasmin.

Surprisingly, Barbara jumped in to support Yasmin.

"John, you talked about the element of surprise in this battle against the empire. Tuesday night is ideal for that. And you and Doug will have all your talking points at your fingertips in any case. I think that's a great plan, Yasmin. I am just worried that it won't get much coverage on such short notice."

Yasmin responded quickly, "Let George Hunter worry about that. As he was talking to Wendy, his mind was recalling all his connections at major networks and media outlets. He concluded that he could pull it off. Wendy Johnson also felt sure she could fill an auditorium at George Mason for such a debate. Both thought it was a win-win proposition if John and Doug agreed to it."

Somewhat reluctantly, John also agreed that it was a good plan. With genuine regret Barbara called Cynthia to cancel their plans for dinner and Blues Alley and they immediately caught a driverless cab home to start preparing for tomorrow and Tuesday.

The flurry of calls that followed started even before they got into the cab. First, George Hunter called Barbara to announce the exciting idea for a timely debate on the theme: Can science and religion agree on climate change? Could Barbara please check with John Hawkins and Doug Larsen if they would be willing to participate on such, admittedly, short notice?

"It would be great exposure for their cause but if it is to happen, we need to get moving straight away," he added.

Almost as soon as he hung up, Barbara got a call from Wendy Johnson who said that George Hunter suggested she call Barbara to arrange a meeting between Pastor Jones and Barbara to talk about the rules of conduct during the debate. Peter Fraser, a very experienced debate moderator, would be the lead person with Barbara doing the debate set-up work, in the background. That would involve face to face meetings with the debaters to explain to them the ground rules. For instance, the scientists would get only three minutes at a time while Pastor Jones would get five, to compensate for it being a "one-against-two event".

Wendy assured Barbara that Eli Jones would be confident he could outwit two scientists in front of cameras.

"I know him well, from way back," she told Barbara, "he is supremely confident because he really believes he is guided by Jesus."

They were back at Barbara's house, in her bedroom, by the time John received Marty Greenberg's text message that it was okay to call Doug Larsen. Doug was very nervous about the prospect of facing off against an evangelical preacher. He was agitated as he spoke.

"You know, John, I am willing to do anything for this cause and Marty made a good argument that it will be a way to communicate the urgency of the situation to a very wide audience. But I am afraid that this preacher will make me look like some kind of a pointy headed geek, a cartoon caricature of a scientist."

John understood his fear, shared by many scientists when faced with a prospect of media exposure. He almost wished he could tell him that, thanks to Yasmin, the debate may take an altogether unexpected trajectory. But, instead, he chose an easier reassuring tactic.

"I understand your fears Doug, but let's agree on the following division of labor: you just keep repeating the facts, figures and the likely consequences of the disruption in the thermohaline circulation regime; nobody can challenge you in that area. I will handle all the broad swipes at science and the beliefs that God is in control and hence nothing needs to be done."

Doug seemed relieved at that and they arranged to meet, together with other members of the delegation, for lunch, courtesy of University of Maryland's Global Change Research Institute. It was going to be followed by their final rehearsal before the congressional hearing.

Barbara and John spent the rest of Sunday juggling their communicators and computer screens, planning for Monday and Tuesday. By midnight they were still busy working in Barbara's spacious bedroom. John was surprised at how relaxed he felt in that new, feminine, environment.

He had been so used to his own condominium that he expected to feel like a fish out of water when he reluctantly agreed to come to Barbara's place. However, now he felt rejuvenated, more alive than he had felt for a long time as they both sat at her workstation, in the bedroom, deeply engaged in drawing up their joint plan of action. She had already changed into an oriental, silk, bathrobe and looked both beautiful and serious as she examined three or four open windows on her screen. She was reading up on the life and achievements of Pastor Eli Jones. They agreed to watch a full, thirty minute, broadcast of one of his services.

While John found the pastor's Southern accent jarring and the theme of asking God for fulfilling a prosperity promise to everyone rather naïve, he had to admit that this guy was good at what he did. He was charismatic. He kept the congregation spellbound with his gestures and his voice. The latter he wielded like a sword master would wield a sword; at times it was swollen with empathy for people's troubles, at times it seemed to brim with divine inspiration and, at the end, it resonated with the excitement of God's promise. His facial expressions conveyed commitment, sincerity, and absolute faith in the message.

Barbara was also impressed and a little concerned. "John, I just hope that Yasmin is right and can achieve a change of heart in this guy. Otherwise, you and Doug will be up against it. He is a natural at swaying the audience to his view of the world," she said and went to the bathroom to change for bed.

John reflected on this last comment. He knew he was a formidable debater himself and felt comfortable about matching Jones in any discourse based on logical arguments, but he also knew that he could not match him based on appeal to emotions or religiously held beliefs. And yet most viewers may be swayed by them. Yes, he might need Yasmin's help for this to come out right.

He got up, stretched, and noticed Barbara standing at the door of the bathroom in a black negligee made of a sheer diaphanous fabric, illuminated by the glow of the bathroom light behind her that exposed the contour of her breasts, hips, thighs. John felt desire spreading across his body. He approached her. They embraced in a passionate kiss and edged their way to Barbara's bed. Their love making was more intense than the previous night, perhaps, stimulated by the premonition of the uncertainty in the course of events that were about to unfold.

The Epiphany of
Pastor Jones

Pastor Jones was thoroughly enjoying his meeting with Barbara Steinwill in the lobby café of the Hay-Adams hotel. He liked attractive women and experienced an exhilarating sense of power when he met one that he thought was an atheist. He believed that he might be the one that the Lord has chosen to show her the path to salvation. Barbara seemed tailor-made for that purpose. He had been in other religion versus science debates before so he only pretended to listen attentively to Barbara's explanations of the ground rules as he looked directly into Barbara's beautiful brown eyes and made good natured, witty, comments whenever opportunities arose or even if they did not arise. At one point, he leaned towards her across the round coffee table and with a sincere expression on his face tried to engage her on the topic of the debate.

"Tell me, Miss Steinwill, I hope you don't mind me calling you Miss but I did not notice a wedding ring on your hand," he smiled and continued, "where do you, personally, stand on the climate change and Carbon Tax issues?"

Barbara responded gracefully and professionally.

"No, Pastor Jones, I don't mind. I know you are just being chivalrous. As for the climate change and related issues, my personal views are not important in this debate. However, for the record, I can tell you that I trust the scientists who know much more about these matters than I do."

Jones smiled broadly and said, "And I trust the Lord. Last I heard He was still in charge. He has brought so many blessings to us and He will show us the way to deal with whatever problems come our way. We just need to put our faith in Him."

He looked at her more intently and with quiet but powerful emotion now filling his voice he said, "You know, any time is a good time to accept Jesus as your savior. Even now, even in this café. It will change your life if you do."

Barbara felt the suppressed emotion emanating from him but chose to diffuse the situation politely.

"Thank you, Pastor Jones. I know that you are sincere and mean well. I can feel it. But I am a lapsed Catholic and an agnostic and, perhaps, not yet ready for this step. But I never say, never," she smiled at him half apologetically.

Jones also retreated gracefully. He gave her a broad smile and said good-naturedly, "Aw shucks, Miss Steinwill, no need to explain. I know that, for some folks, it takes a while to find the Lord. It happens when the time is right, according to His will. If ever you feel that the time might be right, don't hesitate to call me. I'd be very happy to help you take that first step."

Barbara was satisfied. She looked as though she was ready to leave.

"Thank you, Pastor Jones, for being so understanding. Are we done with the briefing for the debate? Is there anything else that I should explain to you?"

Jones saw no point in continuing for the time being. It occurred to him that Barbara may be more receptive to his message after he had clearly won the debate against the scientists. He stretched out his hand to her and said he was looking forward to seeing her again, tomorrow night, at the debate. He watched her walk away with an appreciative eye of a married man who struggles to stay faithful to his wife. In fact, his wife Victoria, was an essential part of his highly successful evangelical ministry. A wholesome, happy, family was part and parcel of his image. The ministry operated almost like a media corporation; the name of the brand was everything. He could not afford extramarital affairs and, despite frequent temptations, was able to stay true to Victoria with the help of many prayers.

Back in his executive suite, Jones started preparing for the forthcoming debate. He poured himself a whiskey and soda and started perusing the folders of his televised appearances that involved matters related to science. His position was simple, scientists should stick to the business of advancing useful technologies, like satellites, space planes or surgical procedures that saved lives. However, they should stay out of God's business which, in his mind, covered all matters of life, death, creation and morality.

He stopped short of publicly advocating the literal interpretation of the book of Genesis as he knew better than to get into debates about the age of dinosaurs. However, he argued vehemently that life begins at conception, homosexuality was a deadly sin and that God had given humans the right to exploit natural resources for their own benefit. These were the arguments and supporting examples (and scripture citations) that he decided to review now. For instance, he often brought up the role of agriculture as an example of human activity that brought about permanent change to ecosystems and yet was, obviously, both indispensable and beneficial to humanity. What's more, in countries like China it was practiced continuously for thousands of years. So, who says it is not sustainable?!

He got up and walked out on the balcony of his suite to look at the sunset, carrying his drink with him. In his mind's eye he was rehearsing the way he would dismiss and ridicule the scientists' arguments in tomorrow's debate. Not so long ago, scientists worried about the next ice age, then they talked about global warming, then about climate change which suggests that they have no idea what is going to happen! Besides, whatever they say, his trump card was that, like he told that journalist lady, God is still in charge: let them argue against that!

He smiled to himself at these thoughts and looked at the orange sun disappearing over the horizon. Its rays had just pierced a thin cloud that was gliding past it and hit Jones directly in the face. He squinted and was going to turn his back to the sun, but something stopped him. He thought he saw a figure of a man walking slowly towards him; on the sunrays!!!

The figure was in long shining robes, indeed the sunrays were now emanating out of him. The light around him was so bright that Jones could not see his face. But he did not need to see it. He knew it was Jesus. His whiskey glass slipped out of his hand and shattered on the tiled floor of the balcony. He started shivering much more violently than he ever did in his most fervent Holy Spirit prayers. His entire body was now shaking as a message (was it spoken?) clearly came to him.

"Eli, Eli, why do you wish to persecute my messengers? I sent them to save my Father's creation. They will not be hindered."

Eli Jones swooned and fell to the ground. All went dark. He did not know how long he lay on the balcony when he came to. Perhaps, only seconds or minutes, perhaps, longer. He opened his eyes wide and all was dark. Has the night come while he was out? But, no, the hotel was in downtown DC, there should be glow all around from neon lights and streetlights.

Fear gripped his heart. He rolled over and tried to get up by supporting himself on his hands. Ouch! He cut his left hand on the broken glass from the whiskey glass. He struggled to his feet. There could be no doubt about it; he could not see anything. He was blind! His left hand hurt and was wet, he must be bleeding!

He must call for help. Trying to control panic that seized his mind like a vice, he stretched out his arms in front of him and started taking tiny steps in changing directions to orient himself, hoping to bump into something that will help him fix his position. Ahh, a glass surface; that must be part of the sliding door to his suite. He slid first to the right and then to the left until he found the entry point. He tried to recall how the furniture was arranged. Yes, he would follow the walls of the room until he detected a furniture item, then move around it and continue along the wall until he came to the desk where he left his computer. He remembered that next to the computer was a communication console. He could then call for help.

It took longer than he expected but after several frustrating and at times painful bumps, the strategy worked. He found the desk chair and carefully lowered himself into it. With his fingers stretched out, he identified the main switch on the communication console. In a hoarse voice he called out.

"Hotel operator, this is an emergency! This is Pastor Jones in the executive suite (he couldn't even recall his room number). I need a doctor! I had a fall and cannot see! I also may have cut myself!"

A pleasant, professional, male voice responded immediately.

"Help is on its way, Sir. If you are sitting down, please remain seated. We will open the door."

Jones felt some relief. Only about a minute or two later he heard the door open and a female, clearly African American, voice.

"Pastor Jones, are you there? This is Natashia Brown, the hotel floor manager," he heard a slight shock in her voice as she continued, "Oh, I see you, what happened to you!? The hotel doctor is on his way. Your left hand is bleeding..."

Just at that moment, she was interrupted by a knock on the door that had been left ajar. A man, sounding foreign, spoke to them.

"Hello, I am Doctor Gupta; what is the problem?" he inquired in a concerned voice.

"I lost my sight!" exclaimed Jones, "I must have passed out, just there, on the balcony and when I came to, I could not see anything! What can it be, doctor?!"

Doctor Gupta had no idea but saw that his patient was distressed and so immediately started going through routine tests. He also examined Jones's cut hand. When he spoke, there was hesitation in his voice.

"The cut on your hand is minor and I will attend to it momentarily. But your loss of sight is a mystery to me. Your pupils respond to light stimulation, but the message does not seem to be translated further up your nervous system. When I moved my finger from left to right in front of your eyes, you obviously did not see it and when I made a rapid hand movement towards your eyes, you did not blink. Yet, there are no visible injuries and the pressure is normal. Did anything happen on the balcony that caused you to faint?"

In an instant, Jones recalled the vision of Christ.

"No, I was just watching the sunset and some rays hit my eyes. I thought I saw a shining figure, then I fainted," he said and immediately realized that the last bit might sound bizarre to a foreign doctor.

His hearing seemed to be keener than usual and he caught Natashia, the floor manager, say quietly to herself, "Oh Lord, have mercy on this man."

This immediately struck a chord with Jones. He stopped focusing on Dr Gupta's comments that a bright light may, indeed, cause an illusion and induce a fainting spell. And his follow up that he would call for an ambulance to have Pastor Jones taken to a hospital where he could be examined by an ophthalmologist.

Instead, Jones was recalling Christ's words in his vision and the scriptures he studied so thoroughly. Surely, this had happened before!? To none other than St Paul on the road to Damascus! Unbounded hope surged in his heart. Like Paul, he was chosen by Christ to do His will! And what was that will? To stop persecuting those scientists who were the Lord's messengers sent to protect His creation; the beautiful and bountiful world that we inhabit! He must assist them instead!!! He started waving his arms to interrupt Dr Gupta's reassuring words that world's top ophthalmologists will soon look after him and sort it out. He called out to Natashia feverishly.

"Ma'am, are you still here? What was your name?"

"Natashia Brown, sir."

"Natashia, are you a Christian? Were you born again?"

"Yes, sir!"

"Natashia, you just helped me realize what I must do. Will you pray with me, Natashia?"

"Yes, sir!"

"Please help me out of this chair, Natashia. We must kneel. Hold my right hand, please!"

Jones was imploring Natashia and ignoring Dr Gupta, who felt extremely awkward. He felt a firm woman's hand hold his right hand and followed the gentle pressure of her arms to first stand up and then kneel. He could feel her kneeling next to him. He started praying in a hoarse, emotional voice, stopping after every few words so that Natashia could repeat them.

"Dear Lord, we pray to You in the name of Jesus whose message to Eli Jones he now understands fully. He is a sinner who begs Your mercy and forgiveness. He wishes, for nothing more but to be an instrument of Your will. He will do his utmost to become a worthy steward of your magnificent creation here on Earth and will support those scientists you sent to warn us of the catastrophe that threatens us. He thanks you Lord for giving him an opportunity to hear your message and to repent."

Tears were now pouring out of his sightless eyes and he could also feel the emotion in Natashia's voice. Then he felt his body begin to shiver like it did a while ago, on the balcony. Then he saw some flashes, like firecrackers, going off in his mind and a blurred image of a black woman's face, with tears in her eyes, close to his own.

"Oh, Glory Hallelujah! The Lord is restoring my eyesight! Thank You Jesus, Oh Thank You Jesus!!!" shouted Jones as everything was becoming clearer around him.

He saw the brown face of Dr Gupta, looking with amazement at what was happening in this hotel suite. He saw Natashia still kneeling and praying with the palms of her hands turned outwards. He saw the furniture, his computer, the half open door to his suite and lights of the city through the windows. He was filled with unbridled joy. He jumped up and exclaimed.

"I was blind, but now I can see! It's a miracle! Oh, Glory to God! Hallelujah! Thank You Lord! Thank you, Natashia! Please, get up." He was ecstatic with joy.

Dr Gupta approached him and repeated some of the same routine vision tests, he had administered earlier. Pastor Jones's eyes were now responding perfectly. The astonished expression on the doctor's face was clearly visible. He started talking to Jones.

"Everything seems normal now, I do not understand this. However, the ambulance will be here in just a few minutes. I strongly recommend that you go with them and have a series of tests done. There must be an explanation of what has just happened."

Jones laughed happily, "Yes, there is a simple explanation, Dr Gupta. The Lord has healed me. It is a miracle! I do not need an ambulance. But, please, attend to my cut hand."

Gupta looked embarrassed, "I am so sorry, Sir. With all that has been happening here, I forgot all about it. Please sit down. I will dress your wound; the cut is not deep. I don't think you need any stitches. Ms Brown, could you please bring me a bowl of warm water?"

Just as Dr Gupta and Natashia were finishing tending to Jones's cut hand, three paramedics from the ambulance service arrived at the half open door.

"Where is the patient?" asked one of them.

"My sincere apologies, my good men. You are no longer needed. I am healed!" replied Jones, joyfully, from the desk.

"It was I who called you. I am the hotel's resident physician," said Dr Gupta. "Pastor Jones fainted on the balcony and suffered temporary blindness and a cut on his left hand. I recommended that he goes with you for a series of tests, but he believes that he is now well."

"Sir, I also think you should follow the doctor's orders. I'll check your vital signs but, even if everything is fine, if you do not come with us, you will need to sign a legal responsibility waiver here, on my screen," said the paramedic approaching Jones.

"All right do all the tests you want. But I have never felt better! There's absolutely no need for me to go to a hospital. Dr Gupta already took care of the cut on my hand," replied Jones sitting down next to the paramedic on the couch. He was still in a state of euphoria.

The paramedic took the standard measurements of temperature, blood pressure, heartbeat and blood samples with the results electronically submitted for real time analysis. He then carried out routine vision and reflexes tests. As Jones expected, everything was perfectly normal. The paramedic also had a look at the dressing Dr Gupta put on the cut, he pulled out his pocket communicator.

"Just to do it properly, I will contact the resident in the emergency room at the hospital. I will give him the results and you can tell him yourself that you are choosing not to come with us for further checks, against our advice...," he told Jones.

It took almost ten minutes for Jones to convince the young resident at the emergency room that he really was aware of the risks, felt fine, and was happy to sign a responsibility waiver. Finally, the paramedics left, and Dr Gupta also got up to leave.

"I must say, Sir, this has been a very unusual experience. Please call me if you have any further symptoms," he said in his accented voice and laid down his business card on the desk.

Jones, smiled broadly, and reached out to shake his hand.

"Dr Gupta be glad because you have witnessed one of God's miracles. Thank you for your help."

He was now left alone in the room with Natashia.

"Pastor Jones, I will send cleaners to take care of the mess on the balcony and here. Is there anything else you need?" she asked attentively.

"No, Natashia, thank you for being here. I think the Lord sent you to help me in my moment of need. Did you feel the Holy Spirit in this room, when we prayed?" replied Jones.

"I sure did, Sir! Thanks be to God for healing you!" said Natashia fervently, "But no one will believe it," she added sadly.

"That is how it has always been," said Jones, "the Lord reveals himself only to a chosen few. Today, we have been chosen. I think I need some rest now."

When Natashia left, Jones spent a long time thinking and praying and thinking again. There was no doubt in his mind as to what he must do in tomorrow's debate. It meant a complete turnaround from the views he publicly espoused for more than a decade, but was that also not the case with St Paul? His job now was to convince others about how wrong he had been in the past! A scary thought crossed his mind: would this cost him some of his constituency? He banished it immediately as a sinful thought. God's will must be done; He will take care of the consequences. He resolved to say nothing more about his change of heart to anyone for now. He will reveal it at the debate, tomorrow night. That will make some impact!!! He smiled with pleasure at that thought. No doubt, he will steal the show tomorrow night, but he will be doing God's will in the process. Amen to that!

Interrupted Golf Game

As CEO of GES (Global Energy Solutions), William Thurston Jr was one of the world's most powerful business leaders. His American multinational energy corporation GES, headquartered in Texas, had long been marketing itself as being progressive on climate change. However, it maintained dominant position in production of oil and gas that continued to make it one of the world's largest companies by revenue.

Thurston was a little annoyed when his game at the Pebble Beach Golf Links course was interrupted by a call from Esther Cohen. He was tied with his friend and golf partner Barney Manning, at the 14th hole, even though as a former tour player Barney usually had the better of him by that stage. Still, it was his policy to always take calls from Esther who, as GES's Chief Security Officer (CSO), knew better than to call him on his personal communicator unless it was important. He flipped open his communicator and walked over to the golf cart that was shaded by a solitary tree. Esther's, intense, intelligent face filled the small screen.

"Sorry to disturb your game, Mr Thurston. However, our Republican boys and girls in Congress just had a major fiasco during those Congressional hearings on climate change! We probably need to coordinate a damage control strategy," Esther was clearly agitated.

Thurston tried to get a little more information first.

"What exactly happened?" He inquired, "How bad could it be? After all, we've handled these kinds of green scaremongering campaigns many times before; right?"

Esther was scornful in reply.

"It looked like a little league team taking on MLB team like the Yankees and getting their butts kicked!" she retorted. She continued with clear exasperation in her voice.

"That's what happens when you field graduates of Bob Jones and Pepperdine Universities to question PhD graduates from MIT and Cambridge about science!"

Esther herself had an engineering degree from Technion and an MBA from Harvard; she did not suffer fools gladly. She had to vent her frustration.

"Larsen, Mittelmann and the other scientists were well prepared and articulate. They had data, satellite images and simulations at their fingertips. That Hawkins guy was masterful at explaining complex issues by simple analogies that even high school graduates could understand," she took a deep breath and went on.

"By comparison, our 'esteemed' Republican Congressmen could hardly put two coherent sentences together. They were tongue tied, or when they did string a few phrases together they sounded like lackeys of Big Oil, or Big Coal which, of course, they are! They blubbered in self-contradicting terms about jobs, price of a barrel of oil and the stock market. One of them actually used us as an example; he said GES shares would plummet if Carbon Tax were introduced. As though every American owned GES stock!"

After listening patiently, Thurston interjected.

"Okay, Esther, I get the picture but what was the upshot of all that? Was anything concrete proposed? What makes it an emergency worthy of interrupting my golf game?" he said with a laugh, trying to lighten the conversation.

"Would you call a mandatory $250 per ton Carbon Tax an emergency?! Because that's what these scientists said was minimum that was needed and the Democrats, like the sheep they are, seemed to have already fallen in line behind it. I expect some will draft such a bill and introduce it in Congress rather speedily!" retorted Esther, expecting to have finally made an impact on her boss.

Esther thought she heard Thurston whistle to himself at the news. However, one is not easily rattled when one is the CEO of Global Energy Solutions. In his mind, Thurston quickly processed the information and calmly responded.

"Well, they have overreached themselves, $250 per ton is just over the top. No one will take it seriously. Even if such a bill were introduced in Congress on behalf of the President, it would get stuck in committees and, finally, Jack Bundy would never let it come up for a vote. I know what Jack's views are on climate change."

Esther knew that, most likely, he was correct but pressed her point.

"Of course, you are right, Mr Thurston, but you pay me to identify potential threats to GES and they don't come any bigger than this one, even if it is unlikely to succeed," she paused and added, "incidentally, Bundy was asked to comment after the hearing and he also hardly said anything concrete; only something vague about the need to consider climate change in the context of economic recovery. He looked and sounded unwell."

Thurston raised his left hand with his thumb holding down his pinky to indicate to Barney that he will return to the game in three minutes. Somewhat reluctantly, he decided to change his plans for the evening.

"Okay, Esther, as usual you are right and we must remain vigilant on this issue and launch a public relations counter offensive, ASAP. Will you organize a teleconference around 5:00 p.m., California time, with as many of our usual allies as you can get on this short notice?"

Esther was gratified; this is the response she anticipated, "Yes, Mr Thurston, talk to you again at eight o'clock, our time. Enjoy the rest of your game," she replied.

The Empire Stirs

Esther's staff had already been calling around to see who among the many powerful people that Thurston referred to as allies were reachable on short notice. CEOs of a number of major multinational corporations that included Royal Power Company (RPC), British Green Power (BGP), American Clean Coal (ACC), BusyAsBee Corporation, Minerals for Prosperity (MPG), Kangaroo Mining Group (KMG), Food Family Corporation (FFC), Double Helix Discoveries Group (DHDG) and a few others were going to be available. Also heads of some media organizations like Wolverine News and conservative Think Tanks like Shining City on a Hill Institute would be able to make it. In addition, there were some economists, high level lobbyists and Ed Taylor, a retired former Director of CIA.

The Congressional hearing news obviously did not affect Thurston too much. He continued to play well and remained tied with Barney at the end of the 18-hole round. He was pleased with that result and decided to use the teleconference as an excuse not to have a playoff. Instead, after a quick drink with Barney at the clubhouse he asked his chauffer, James, to drive him to his luxury beach house that was only a few miles away. This was one of seven houses he owned in the US. He stayed there whenever he came down to California to play golf.

Thurston's second wife Amelia and Janice, his twenty five year old daughter from the first marriage, were sitting by the pool with three other young women when he arrived. Janice got along very well with Amelia whom she treated almost like an older sister. In fact, Amelia was only seven years older than Janice. She was a glamorous aspiring movie star who enjoyed the good life that was part and parcel of being William Thurston's young trophy wife. She got up, walked over to her husband, gave him an affectionate hug, and asked if he would like to join her and her friends for a drink.

"No, thank you, honey. I've got to work for a few hours, something urgent came up and I must prepare myself for a teleconference, in my study. If I don't come out by seven thirty, go ahead and have your dinner. The cook will fix something for me when I am ready," said Thurston returning Amelia's hug.

He picked up from the bar counter one of several silver thermos flasks, which were always filled with freshly brewed coffee for any visitors or house staff, a ceramic mug and walked out.

In his comfortable and electronically secure study Thurston ordered his computer to display latest news on climate change hearings. The wall opposite his desk lit up with several panels showing the recent headlines on that story. He selected those on CNN and BBC, and it did not take him long to confirm that Esther was absolutely right in her assessment. The Republican opponents of climate change regulations were coming across like a bunch incompetents at best, or corrupt lackeys of large corporations at worst.

Just then the bulk of his study transformed to a real telepresence immersion meeting room, with him sitting at head of a large oval conference table and Esther sitting in the middle. He greeted her with a wave of his hand. Others started popping up in quick succession, around the table, calling out their names and locations. In these initial few minutes, the room was filled with entirely life-like holograms of powerful people seated in various chairs exchanging greetings and throwing in a little small talk in the process. Apparently, the New York Stock Exchange had some jitters after the Congressional hearing, but recovered at the end of the day, indicating that cooler heads prevailed, and investors were not taking the Carbon Tax threat as a real possibility. That gave Thurston an opportunity to step in and open the meeting.

"Thank you, everyone, for joining us on such a short notice. In a moment, I'll ask Esther Cohen, in Washington DC, to chair the meeting as she was one of the persons attending the Congressional hearing and reported to me on the fiasco that took place. However, I want to stress that this teleconference merely reflects abundance of caution. As I told Esther, such a punitive Carbon Tax bill will never see the light of day. Even if it were to pass the committees, Jack Bundy would not put it up for a vote in the House."

Before Esther could say anything, Ed Taylor, jumped in with a comment.

"I expect you are right, Mr Thurston. However, we should not count on just one person. I was also there today. Jack did not look well. He had rings under his eyes and seemed unfocussed. Come to think of it, already last week, when I saw him at a fund-raising function at the Hilton, he looked distracted even then."

In her central chair, Esther seemed to be taking an outside call and looking down at her pocket communicator. So, Thurston decided to continue to reassure everyone.

"We are not relying on just one individual, Ed. Even if such a bill were put up for a vote in the House, the Republicans have a comfortable majority. The fact that the Dow and other indices recovered nicely by the end of the day also suggests that it will all blow over in a few days."

Most of the people around the table were nodding their heads in agreement but Esther raised her hand with an expression of alarm on her face. Thurston nodded to her and she clicked "My Turn" button on her screen at home, which brought her hologram and voice into highlighted focus of all other participants.

"Mr Thurston, distinguished guests, I just received a report of something extraordinary unfolding as we speak! Many of you may not know that today's congressional hearing is, in a sense, being followed up by one of these televised science-versus-religion debates with Pastor Eli Jones taking on both Professors Larsen and Hawkins who were so prominent in this morning's science committee hearing," she paused to take breath.

That gave Janet Smith from the Shining City on a Hill Institute a chance to interject.

"So, what of it? That should be good news. I know Eli Jones well and he will slap down these scientists. Sure as hell he won't be tongue tied or incoherent!"

Janet was a former governor of Arizona with a reputation for toughness and staunch opposition of EPA on most of its environmental protection laws. However, she was completely taken aback by Esther's emphatically sarcastic reply.

"Oh no; he sure is eloquent! But he just flipped, or was flipped, on climate change! The congressional science hearing debacle may be small potatoes compared to this!"

"I don't believe it!" exclaimed Janet.

"Watch it for yourself! In fact, we all need to see it right now," retorted Esther.

She spoke a few commands into her console and six, large, monitors appeared on the virtual conference table, arranged in a hexagonal shape, offering all the participants the same clear view of the George Mason University's seminar hall. Cameras were focused onto the left of center podium where Pastor Eli Jones was standing about to deliver his opening address. His handsome face was radiant, eyes shining as he began speaking in a dramatic voice.

"What I am about to say may astound many of you. When I accepted the invitation to be here tonight, my intention was to try and discredit and ridicule Professors Larsen and Hawkins and their warnings about the impending oceanic currents catastrophe. This would be in line with my longstanding views on such matters. But I am here today to confess that these views were borne out of arrogance and greed. Arrogance, because I presumed to know more about complex scientific matters than those whom the Lord helped achieve deep understanding of the natural wonders He had created. Greed, because I knew that, indirectly, I would be rewarded by powerful groups who stood to benefit most from inaction on climate change. They wanted me to sway the good Christian people of this nation and the world – who trust me – to oppose regulations that would curb greenhouse emissions. I have sinned! I did not accept bribes, but I have sinned nonetheless; I knew that my ministry would receive generous support because of these views. I have sinned and I now beg your forgiveness!"

There were tears in his eyes as he took a deep breath and continued in his penetrating charismatic voice.

"I know the Lord, in His mercy, has forgiven me already! I know it because He has spoken to me. He told me that it is our solemn Christian duty to protect his creation, the birds of the sky, the animals of the forest, the fishes of the sea, the plants that feed us, the waters that quench our thirst and the very air that we breathe. In His goodness, He gave us stewardship over his creation; to sustain it and protect it; not to destroy it! The fact that, for so long, we have turned a blind eye to the destruction or pollution of that most beautiful creation is, surely, the work of Devil himself!"

Esther interjected here saying, "there's a lot more of this... I'll get to the end," and she fast forwarded to the last sentences of that opening address. Jones was now imploring his audience.

"My brothers and sisters in Christ and, indeed, everyone else. The Lord works in mysterious ways! However, let there be no doubt that He has chosen these two scientists and their colleagues to be the instruments of His will. His messengers, to help protect His creation, His greatest gift to humanity! They must not be hindered! Instead, they must be aided in every possible way! I pledge my life to helping them achieve their aims and pray that you will too! Thanks be to our Lord Jesus Christ!"

Some seconds of silence followed. The astonishment on the faces of the debate moderator, Peter Fraser, and Doug Larsen was clear for all to see. John Hawkins seemed to be deep in thought. Finally, Peter spoke.

"My goodness, this was totally unexpected! I was going to give you two gentlemen opportunity for a rebuttal but, perhaps, Pastor Jones's address needs no rebuttal. Still, would either one of you care to comment?"

Larsen seemed in no condition to say anything, he was still processing what had just happened. However, John Hawkins, rose to the challenge and decided to play the role of a public intellectual.

"Like you, Peter, I am also astounded by Pastor Jones's opening address, but I am also delighted by his offer of help. In fact, I find his new position to be entirely consistent with that of a true conservative. Most of us forget, that the root of the latter word is the Latin word *conservare*; to preserve. It has been a mystery to me for many years now why people who view themselves as conservatives have presided over wanton destruction of so many natural resources; all of which are part of what Pastor Jones called the Lord's creation. As for being a 'messenger', I must admit that I am an agnostic. However, I am convinced that both Professor Larsen and I are here tonight to communicate the truth about very powerful natural phenomena which, if unchecked, will wreak havoc on humanity's life support systems. So, to the extent that we are bearers of scientific truth, I shall – with the greatest humility – accept the title of a messenger," then trying to amuse the audience a little he added with a wry smile, "I only beg all of you; please don't shoot the messenger!"

At this point Esther shut down the virtual video screens. "From this point on, the debate has started turning into some kind of weird love fest; it's still going on."

Janet Smith jumped in immediately after her, in her best Western accent.

"If this Hawkins guy was so smart, he wouldn't be giving us these good ideas. Shooting him wouldn't be a hard way to get rid of part of the problem, right?" she said with an expression that could be easily interpreted as a droll joke.

"I know you're joking, Janet," chipped in Thurston, "last thing we would want to do is to fuel conspiracy theories about evil corporations eliminating their enemies. Having said that, I see now that the situation has just become more serious than half an hour ago. There may be more than a hundred House Republicans who could be seriously influenced by Jones's conversion, for the lack of a better word."

Clive Hancock, CEO of Kangaroo Mining Group, joined the conversation from his London office.

"We certainly do have a problem on our hands. Thank you, Bill and Esther, for calling this meeting. I have a small question for Esther. You said earlier that this Pastor Jones flipped, or was flipped, if I remember correctly. What did you mean by that?"

Esther hesitated because she spoke up without any evidence. She started putting her thoughts into words.

"Well, I don't really know. But if we wanted to flip an outspoken public figure, we might find an inducement or a threat; right? But it's hard to know with these fundamentalists. He is convincing precisely because he seems to believe everything he is saying, isn't that so? I wonder if something happened to him recently to make him think that the Lord wants him to change; a prayer for a sick child, perhaps? However, that should be easy to find out, I'll put someone on that."

Thurston decided that it was time to formulate some concrete actions. He was picking up on private chatter among conference attendees, some of which was appearing on the shared tweet screen. He spoke up a little louder.

"Attention everyone. It's clear we have a consensus that a damage control strategy needs to be activated. But, even in this meeting there are too many of us to manage. I suggest that we form a small group to take charge of precise actions. Perhaps, a group of four or five? What do you think? I hope that Esther will volunteer to coordinate; isn't that right Esther?"

"Yes, Mr Thurston," said Esther agreeably.

Ed Taylor raised his hand in his panel on the screen, "I would be glad to join such a group," he said. Then Janet Smith jumped in enthusiastically exclaiming, "Me too."

Someone, who has been quiet all along, suddenly joined it. It was Jorge Rodriguez, the CEO of DHDG, a German multinational pharmaceuticals and life sciences company. He had a reputation for his success and ruthlessness. There were even rumors of his involvement with South American drug cartels. As was his custom, he spoke softly and yet was heard because people tended to fall silent when he talked.

"I would also like to join this coordinating group. As you all know, Carbon Tax of this magnitude would have a disastrous impact on the agri-business where we have a large stake," he said, cleared his throat and continued, "besides, we have an organization that knows how to protect its turf. Some of our capabilities may be helpful to this group."

Thurston was not the only one to wonder what precisely he meant by that last comment but decided that a wide teleconference meeting like this one was not the place to pursue this. Still, if Rodriguez's reputation was well deserved, this initiative may lead to covert action where Esther might want to outsource some unpleasant tasks to his minions. He put on his best business-as-usual manner and said,

"Looks like we have formed a committee: Esther, Janet, Ed and Jorge; right? And I will be in constant touch with Esther and will contact the larger group as needed. Does everyone agree?"

Nearly all the participants of the teleconference were nodding their heads in agreement. Esther wanted to determine the consensus for scope of their assignment.

"The media campaign undermining their scientific claims can begin tomorrow. Similarly, we will highlight the catastrophic economic consequences of the Carbon Tax of this magnitude. They made that part easy for us by going overboard; right!? If the stock market drops tomorrow, that will also help," she took a deep breath and continued with a keen eye on the body language of people in different panels.

"Of course, we'll do our best to discredit that Pastor Jones and the scientists who were part of the delegation. In the case of Jones, we'll put the finances of his organization under a microscope. At the same time, we'll compile lists of Congressmen and Senators who may be wavering. Is that all we ought to be doing, at this stage?"

Thurston immediately decided to intervene. It was best not to state anything too explicitly in front of such a large group. He had no reasons to doubt their shared commitment to blocking the Carbon Tax, but it was best to be careful.

"Esther, I think the smaller group can discuss these details among themselves, but you're on the right track. I don't want to hold everyone up, I know that all of you have interrupted your busy schedules," he added, indicating that this might be a good time to stop.

Most people around the virtual table looked reassured and were nodding their heads in agreement. Ed Taylor was also nodding but said.

"I think we should feed all the data we already have into one of these data mining NAITs; just to identify any common factors that might affect the vote in the House, if it ever came to a vote."

Thurston wondered why he hadn't thought about this first.

"Ed, you're absolutely right! We have our own corporate NAIT that always searches for common factors that influence our markets. Our group of five can put it to good use on this matter. It will help us focus our efforts" he paused, smiled, and added, "it will also be satisfying to use that Hawkins guy's invention against his cause."

That last idea seemed to amuse everyone. Janet Smith raised a glass of wine in her panel and said, "I'll drink to that!" Then she added "let's give our little group a name; how about G5? G5 to defend G20?!"

Everyone liked it. They were now in upbeat mood as they started logging out. Thurston and the other members of G5 arranged to meet tomorrow, at 2:00 p.m., in Houston Texas at GES's corporate offices which also housed the support room of NAIT-113, one of the first corporate NAITs in the world. Of course, they could have arranged a secure teleconference but Thurston and Taylor were old school; they believed that a team needed to bond to build up trust and that real face-to-face contact was still the best way to achieve that. Esther thought that a flight to Texas was unnecessary, but she always deferred to Thurston. She knew he liked it.

Backup Plan

As Janet, Ed and Jorge were saying their goodbyes, Esther noticed Thurston's raised finger and eyebrows gesture indicating to her to stay. She nodded back in agreement. Once the others were gone, he turned to her directly.

"Esther, I just sent a message to Steve Lucas, our man on Wall Street to join us. I expect him to login any moment now. In the meantime, do you happen to remember the name of that Israeli solar flower tower company?"

"I think it was called SOL, Mr Thurston, I am searching for it as we speak" replied Esther and momentarily confirmed, "yes, it is SOL Inc., they call themselves a leader in innovative applications of solar power but then again, in Israel, they have plenty of sunshine, right?"

Just then, Steve Lucas's earnest banker's hologram popped up in one of the virtual chairs.

"Very well, then" started Thurston looking at Steve, "this is important and needs to be done discreetly, starting immediately. I want you to increase our holdings in renewable energy companies across the world. Nothing to trigger a mad rush by others; just zigzag the world and start buying lots of 2% or 5% or 10% of the best renewable stocks; solar, wind, geothermal, hydrogen, batteries and so on. Buy as many as you can, indirectly, through our subsidiaries. With smaller, more innovative companies you can buy a majority holding. You can start with the Israeli outfit SOL. Oh yes, and don't forget nuclear. Is all that clear?"

Esther was listening in awe and admiration. You don't get to be a CEO of GES for nothing, she thought! Just as her boss was coordinating the G5 response to the Carbon Tax threat, he had the presence of mind to start preparing a backup plan, on the remote possibility that the threat will succeed.

"Perfectly clear," replied Steve. "I'll start the ball rolling. Do I have a budget limit?"

Thurston hesitated a little, "Well, just send me a prompt for every couple of billion you spend, and I'll let you know when it's time to change anything."

"Okay, I am onto it," he smiled, then becoming more serious he added, "Are you concerned about this Carbon Tax issue as a real possibility?"

He was looking carefully at Thurston's and Esther's expressions.

"No, I am not really concerned, just call it abundance of caution. We owe it to our shareholders," replied Thurston, "I'll let you get on with it. Talk to you soon."

When Steve logged out, he turned to Esther, "I think we are almost done. It went pretty well, don't you think?" and without waiting for her reply, he added "Of course, financial problems for Jones's ministry are part of your plan; right? A clear signal needs to be sent that there is a price to be paid for this kind of flipping."

Esther wondered about how rough he wanted her to play.

"It won't be hard to block some, even most, of his lines of credit. We could also put pressure on the cable networks and other media outlets that give him access to millions. But I was wondering if, first, he should be given an opportunity to flip back, so to speak? Perhaps, after we find out what made him change his position in the first place?"

Thurston leaned back in his chair and reflected for a moment. Then, he sat up straight and spoke decisively.

"No, he needs to be taught a proper lesson, immediately. That will send the right message to others."

He paused for a moment before continuing.

"As for some of the other key targets, apply whatever pressure you think is appropriate to make them feel uncomfortable or insecure. Short of resorting to violence, that is. You may wish to outsource some tasks to other members of the group, like Jorge."

There was just a hint of a faint smile on his lips when he stopped.

"Yes, Mr Thurston, will that be all for now? I need to get busy," replied Esther.

"Yes, Esther, you did well today," Thurston complimented her, "see you in Houston, tomorrow."

After Thurston disconnected, Esther felt a few small pangs of conscience. She was about to destroy Pastor Eli Jones's business even though his ministry had always voiced unconditional support for the state of Israel. She was, naturally, always sympathetic towards Israel's allies. Still, she tried to console herself that the Southern evangelicals' support for Israel was based on the misguided, naïve, notion that Jews will convert to Christianity at the second coming of Jesus. She shrugged her shoulders; fanatics like him do not deserve protection.

She started making calls and sending out messages to her operatives to initiate actions that G5 had just agreed on. With her immediate team they had developed what was almost a secret code. A credit check on an organization or an individual implicitly meant a search for vulnerabilities that could be exploited, or "they're not getting a free lunch, are they?" was an instruction to exert GES's considerable influence to create financial problems for their target. Esther was confident she was safe from electronic spying, but there was always a slight possibility of one of her staff going rogue. In such a case the instructions had to be sufficiently opaque to offer plausible deniability in a court room.

About an hour later, she logged out of the secure communication network installed in her Bethesda family home. She was tired now and longed to spend a little time with her family; her husband, Ehud, and her 10-year-old twin boys, David and Alex.

She slowly walked upstairs, through the corridor to the family room. Ehud was dozing on a couch in front of a TV panel screen showing a live basketball game. A half empty bottle of beer and a bowl of potato chips were on a coffee table in front of him. She walked upstairs to the boys' bedroom; they were both asleep, curled up next to each other, in bed. She and Ehud have been instructing them to sleep comfortably in their own, separate beds, but as soon as the lights were turned off one would scamper to the bed of the other one. She smiled and pulled up a blanket over them.

Esther went to the master bedroom opened her closet door and started selecting items she would pack in her carry-on bag for tomorrow's flight to Texas. She did not feel like going to Houston for a meeting that could have been conducted perfectly well virtually. That was Thurston's preference. But it was easier for him to fly in the corporate jet back to Texas and he wouldn't be missing out on picking up two little boys from school in the afternoon. Still, she was well paid for her work. They could have hardly afforded to be sending their boys to a private school and all the frequent space plane flights to Israel on Ehud's academic salary.

A Moment's Respite

John and Barbara hired a limousine service to take them from the reception that followed the debate to John's place. They were exhausted but exhilarated. The events of the day starting with the congressional hearing, through media interviews that followed, the debate and the drinks reception afterwards surpassed all their expectations. It was nearly a two-hour drive from George Mason University to Baltimore and Barbara was working feverishly on her tablet to finish a story on the debate for the morning edition of the Post.

John was helping as best he could by perusing news headlines and stories about Pastor Jones's dramatic proclamation during the debate. It was already all over the news and late-night shows. From serious commentaries to jokes by standup comedians, everyone was fascinated by his position switch on the climate change issue. He had completely stolen the show! Doug Larsen and John Hawkins were barely mentioned except for multiple shots of Doug's face showing complete bewilderment as he listened to Jones's opening address. Of course, the more serious commentaries were expressing astonishment that a Carbon Tax of the order of $250 per ton was proposed for serious consideration.

It was after midnight when they finally made it back to John's condominium. They saw some news vans parked outside and reporters and cameramen standing near the entrance. Fortunately, their experienced driver parked right beside the front door, and as he came out to open the limo door for them, he blocked the pathway of some of the reporters with his large body frame. The building's doorman did likewise on the other side, and they were able to sneak into the lobby without being stopped for questions. However, not without photos of them entering the lobby being snapped from several directions.

When they finally sat down in John's kitchen with the kettle boiling to make herbal tea, a call from Yasmin came in. They turned John's communicator on and heard her pleasant melodic voice compliment them.

"Well done, Barbara and John! You must be pleased with yourselves, aren't you!?"

They looked at each other, smiling, and Barbara decided to return the compliment.

"Of course, you're the one who really deserves the credit. You have outdone yourself with Pastor Jones's epiphany conversion! Will it last and will he be all right with his followers?"

"Oh, I think the conversion as you call it will last," replied Yasmin. Then she added, "Some of his followers may abandon him, but that's the least of his problems. What happened at the end of the debate?"

John was surprised and blurted out three obvious questions.

"Why do you ask? Weren't you there? And what precisely are Jones's problems?"

There was a short silence after which Yasmin started to reply, with hesitation, as if measuring her words.

"My inexperience at interactions with humans is showing. Perhaps, I will burden you with more than you need to know. After all, what good is it for you to know some things that I know, if you cannot influence them, whereas I might be able to do so?"

This was like waving a red flag at Barbara; she was really annoyed with Yasmin and snapped at her in an angry voice.

"Stop being so condescending! We are in this together! Cooperation must be built on trust. How can we trust you if you are withholding important information from us?!"

It is the not first time they heard Yasmin sigh, but it still surprised them because it was such a human sound. She now started answering John's questions.

"Ah well, so be it. If you must know, I was called away in the middle of the debate and had to focus all my attention on a teleconference meeting that was taking place in California, in the house of the CEO of GES."

Despite his weariness, John's curiosity spiked. He did not have to wait long for Yasmin's explanation.

"By a sheer stroke of luck, last week, I had acquired and stored the telepathic signature of Ed Taylor, a former director of CIA. Just as your email manager or social media sites send you beeps when new messages arrive, I had set up an alert system - in my brain - that sends me a prompt whenever certain key notions are in the thoughts of one of my climate change contacts. In any case, in the middle of your debate, I received an alert that Ed Taylor is thinking about Carbon Tax law. So, I decided to peek into his mind and, again, it was lucky that I did!"

Barbara was so intrigued that she forgot about being annoyed with Yasmin.

"Yasmin, that's amazing! What did you learn?!" she exclaimed.

"Well, Ed was in a teleconference called by William Thurston Jr, the CEO of GES which was attended by a diverse group of heavy hitters from the corporate world. They formed a small group of five members whose task it is to coordinate a response to the Carbon Tax initiative. Ed Taylor is a member of that group. The media attacks on all key people associated with the initiative, including you two, will begin tomorrow. The finances of Pastor Jones's ministry will also be attacked."

Barbara and John's eyes met and they knew their thoughts were in synch. Yasmin could strike back directly at the very people whom they feared most! Barbara was the first to put into words.

"Yasmin, this is incredible! But surely, you will now be able to neutralize all their plots and save Jones in the process, won't you?"

Yasmin's reply was not what they expected. There was sadness in her voice as she spoke.

"It's not as easy as you think. Sabotaging all their plots is not a best strategy. It would raise suspicions of other powerful people, some of whom were at the teleconference. Right now they are inactive, awaiting the impact of G5's strategy. Some of their activities, perhaps most, should be perceived as working. Otherwise, more groups like G5 will be formed and I may not be lucky enough to gain access to their members."

Yasmin sighed loudly and added.

"I don't think I should protect Pastor Jones's finances. People behind the attack should not wonder why cutting off his credit is difficult for them to achieve."

They understood that Yasmin was right. Barbara also sighed and said, "I see what you mean. It's just that, after tonight, I started viewing Pastor Jones as a powerful ally."

"I did too," replied Yasmin and then deftly changed the topic.

"I see you and Barbara staring at my name on the display panel. Is it difficult for you to communicate with me without a face attached to my voice?"

Barbara reflected on that for a while and responded looking carefully at John's facial expressions as she spoke.

"You know, I think you are right. For me, at least, it would be easier to talk to you if you had a face," she stopped because she saw John frowning at that latest suggestion.

"And whose face might it be that you will project to us?" he inquired and followed up with sarcasm.

"I am sure you could easily have whatever image you wanted appear on the screen when you speak. It could be Marilyn Monroe, or Golda Meir, or Ganesh the Hindu elephant God, or you could rotate them every day if you liked."

He regretted these words as soon as they left his mouth. After all, whose fault was it that Yasmin did not have a face!?

Surprisingly, perhaps, Yasmin did not retaliate even though she must have read his thoughts that would have reminded her of everything she had been deprived of. Instead, after a little pause they heard her speak again, in a gentle voice.

"Okay, I see it is not as simple as giving you just some face to focus on. You don't want anything artificial, right? This may take a little time; but I may have some ideas for overcoming this problem. In the meantime, I can see that you are both exhausted. Get some rest. Good night."

The screen went blank. Barbara had a little bit of a go at John for being inconsiderate of Yasmin's feelings. He felt sufficiently guilty that he did not really defend himself. They argued briefly whether Yasmin accepted or resented being who she was. Sheer exhaustion ended their argument. They made their way to the bedroom, changed into their pajamas, lay down and fell asleep almost immediately.

They had purposely turned off all their lines of electronic communication - except the line to Yasmin - so they did not hear or see the many message alerts that were arriving in their inboxes one after another. The G5's strategy had already swung into action and various media reporters were requesting comments, interviews and some offering generous fees for such interviews or appearances.

The Sleuth

Mike Blythe's briefing was quite interesting. He received an email late on Tuesday night saying that a public relations representative from Kurp Industries wanted to visit him in his office in Arlington at eleven the following morning to discuss an urgent assignment and asking him to respond as soon as possible if that was inconvenient.

Mike was not surprised by this brief, opaque, message. His clients often wanted to discuss matters face-to-face and were always in a hurry. Mike's company, Precise Inquiries Inc., never needed to search for clients who were always referred via a small but influential network of former and even current FBI agents who had a lot of respect for Mike from his days as one of the bureau's rising young stars. The fact that he was forced to resign because of his unhealthy obsession with various Israeli conspiracy theories did not diminish his colleagues' admiration for his sharp investigative mind and tenacity.

In fact, Precise Inquiries thrived in the Washington Beltway environment by delivering to various organizations the confidential information they needed to discredit their adversaries. Mike was not cheap, but he had a well-deserved reputation for digging deep and coming up with information that was pure gold to his clients.

Precisely, at 11:00 a.m. Mike's personal assistant, Bob, knocked on the door announcing that Jason Buetler Jr, attorney at law from Kurp Industries was here to see him on a confidential matter. Mike watched as an immaculately dressed African American entered his office. He was tall, muscular, but there was grey in his short hair. The gold rimmed glasses and stooping shoulders were consistent with a desk job of an attorney. Mike wondered if he spent time in the military in his youth. He stepped around his desk to welcome his visitor. The two men shook hands, and Mike invited Jason to sit in one of the comfortable white leather armchairs next to a glass coffee table, in the front part of his office.

Bob busied himself filling two coffee mugs with freshly brewed Hawaiian coffee. He placed the mugs and a small plate of chocolate mints in front of them and left the room. Bob did not mind playing the role of just a secretary so long as his salary reflected the importance of his investigative function in the company. He had prodigious computing skills, a black belt in Karate and was a very stylish man. He used his personal charm when interacting with Mike's clients in the secretarial capacity to frequently extract from them more information than they initially intended to share.

"That's a charming young man you have as your assistant," Jason complimented Mike while taking a sip of coffee. He put down his mug on the table, leaned towards Mike and continued.

"I'll get straight down to business. Kurp Industries have offered to assist a major energy company in their investigation of individuals behind the latest push for a punitive new carbon tax. If you have watched the news last night, or this morning, you will know that the congressional hearing with the leading climate change scientists did not go well. What's more, the situation was dangerously aggravated by a totally unexpected position flip of Pastor Eli Jones in a televised public debate."

Mike was thinking about what he was doing last night, "I did catch a few headlines, but I was watching Chelsea vs Barcelona, so I did not pay much attention. After all, those climate change scare stories have been popping up for decades now, and not much has happened, right?"

He smiled as he completed the sentence. Jason did not smile back.

"Kurp Industries and the energy company we are assisting are regarding these latest developments most seriously. Consequently, they are willing to pay for information that explains Jones's position switch and, more broadly, permits us to discredit the proponents of this pernicious Carbon Tax that would only hurt our country's competitiveness, internationally. They also need information on key congressmen and senators whose votes may, potentially, tilt the outcome. The information needs to be gathered quickly and with discretion. Are you willing and able to undertake this task?"

In his mind, Mike was quickly processing the information, "Who recommended Precise Inquiries to you?" he inquired.

"I believe that Ed Taylor spoke highly of you to the chief security officer of the energy company we are assisting," replied Jason.

Mike knew that Kurp Industries was a powerful, privately owned, company with interests overlapping the energy sector. It was controlled by the Kurp family, one of America's wealthiest Jewish families. He wondered why they chose to approach him, in view of his past reputation as an anti-Semite, which he always rejected. Still, the assignment sounded simple enough and he did not mind accepting anyone's money. Besides, he had a lot of respect for Ed Taylor. He fixed his eyes on Jason's.

"The assignment you described is clear and simple enough. However, I do not come cheap and I must know who I am working for. That is non-negotiable. What is the name of that so-called major energy company that you keep mentioning?"

Jason did not blink, he returned Mike's steely gaze and replied, "Our client does not wish to be seen as having engaged you and will not interact with you directly. However, they have authorized me to disclose their identity if it will help you reach a positive decision. It is Global Energy Solutions. As for your costs, money is not an issue. I can make an immediate $500,000 advance transfer to your account and have been authorized to spend up to two million for valuable information that you may gather for us. If that is insufficient, I would need to seek further authorization."

It's my lucky day Mike thought to himself. He also liked the directness of Jason's reply. His communicator vibrated in his pocket in a way that could only mean a message from Bob. Mike excused himself for a moment and stepped out to the reception area where Bob had a large screen open with information on Jason Buetler Jr.

It all checked out, he was a decorated former Navy Seal, studied law at the University of Chicago after his discharge, joined a respected Chicago law firm and practiced company law for some fifteen years before moving to Kurp Industries as Director of Public Relations for its Midwest and East Coast divisions. A family man residing in Columbia, Maryland, a model upper middle-class integrated city between Baltimore and Washington, DC. Nothing suspicious there. Mike returned to his office and held out his hand to Jason.

"I am willing to accept your assignment. Do we need a contract, or will a handshake suffice? I am man of my word," he said smiling at Jason.

Jason shook his hand, "So am I," he said. "No formal contract will be necessary. The attached envelope contains my contact numbers as well as some initial background information on Pastor Jones and some of the key scientific people who are behind this latest climate change drama. Is there anything else you need to get started?"

Mike smiled at him, "There sure is, the half a million dollar advance you just mentioned," he said.

Jason laughed pulling out his communicator. "But of course. Please give me an account number."

The transaction was completed in a matter of minutes and Jason walked out without looking back. A minute or so later, Mike called an urgent meeting with Bob and Imma, his junior partner.

Immaculata Cruz, or Imma as everyone called her, was a forty something Cuban American who used to be a top-notch investigative reporter for LA Times. However, she used unorthodox ways to gather information and was known for cutting corners. She did not like to answer to a whole hierarchy of managers at LA Times. That meant that she was in a constant state of friction with her management. So, when Mike offered her an investigator's position at Precise Inquiries she was glad to accept. She and Mike worked so well together on many of his most challenging assignments that eventually Mike made her a junior partner.

Imma's specialty was extracting invaluable information from the ubiquitous Hispanic employees of the powerful people they often investigated. People who, in their arrogance, regularly underestimated the intelligence and alertness of their maids, chauffeurs, gardeners, cooks and nannies. Wearing casual clothes, Imma would strike up friendly conversations, in Spanish, with these workers wherever she managed to, seemingly accidentally, bump into them. Soon she would be having drinks with them and learning an awful lot about their employers.

The three investigators were in great mood when Mike briefed them on the new assignment and its monetary value. They read the brief notes that Jason left behind and were quickly pulling up online information about all members of Doug Larsen's delegation to Congress. Mike spotted an item in Jason's notes on Eli Jones that he stayed in Hay-Adams hotel on this visit to Washington DC. They started dividing the tasks among themselves. Mike, as usual, would oversee the entire investigation and focus on key politicians who may push for the Carbon Tax law, Bob would check out the scientists and Imma would trace the steps of Pastor Jones over the past few weeks, starting at the Hay-Adams hotel. As always, they would update Mike on anything of potential significance as soon as they learned about it.

Mike liked to understand the big picture; why was his client interested in obtaining the information for which they were hiring him and willing to pay so much? Usually, the stated reason was far from the true underlying reason. It was Mike's ability to correctly infer the latter that enabled him to earn his clients' gratitude by selectively highlighting the items of collected information that served their unstated purpose. He immediately resolved that, in addition to the task he was just hired to do, he would also investigate a little the people behind the assignment.

He turned to Bob and said, "I know you already have a lot on your plate, but could you also find a little more about who at Kurp Industries and GES is behind all this? This Jason guy we just met is smooth, but he is only a gopher doing someone's bidding. We need to know who we are working for."

Bob was used to this and replied obligingly, "Sure thing, boss, I can easily identify key players in previous groupings that fought climate change regulations."

Mike got up to bring the meeting to the end.

"Okay, team. Off you go to work. Put some of our junior staff on it as well. If that is not enough, hire anyone you need to hire and pay anyone you need to pay to get the information we need. But don't overpay! This raises suspicions."

Bob and Imma waved byes to him; they were still staring at some information Bob pulled up on the monitor.

Mike decided to go and grab a bite to eat and think more strategically about who would benefit most and who would lose the most from a $250 per ton Carbon Tax. Perhaps, drinks with Bill, his investment banking buddy, are in order? In his experience, a lot could be learned by considering how Wall Street might respond to various developments. Money, after all, talks in more ways than most people realize. It would be good to know where GES is putting its money right now. He congratulated himself on thinking about this good idea. He was on a roll and decided to treat himself to a fancy lunch. It's not every morning that one seals a new two-million-dollar assignment!

Sustainable Planet Act

Just as Mike Blythe was meeting with Jason Buetler Jr, a much more consequential meeting was taking place in the Oval Office. President James Stewart had urgently convened a meeting with the Senate Majority Leader, Alan Packer, the Democratic Senator from New Jersey and Joan Collins the House Minority Leader. Also attending were Jasper Cox, Secretary of Treasury, Olivia Smith, Secretary of Commerce, Robert Gattley, Secretary of Energy, and Mark Mosley, Head of EPA.

President Stewart thanked everyone for coming on such short notice and began by summarizing yesterday's congressional hearing on climate change that hosted Doug Larsen's delegation. He did not mince words. He found the scientists' arguments compelling and the questioning by opponents of further action on climate change disingenuous. He called this meeting to discuss the feasibility of drafting and passing a Carbon Tax bill that gave the scientists all they were asking for because it was a matter of the United States demonstrating world leadership on an issue that was vital to the planet's life support systems.

He proceeded to sketch an ambitious, albeit very rough plan which allowed for a short phase-in period of eighteen months during which the proceeds from the Carbon Tax would be immediately reinvested in major infrastructure projects focusing on high speed trains, solar and wind farms and hydrogen fuel generated with renewable energy. These projects would offset potential job losses caused by the dramatically increased price of fossil fuels. Similarly, subsidies on biofuels would partially compensate farmers for their increased production costs, however, much of their compensation would come from the inevitable increases in the prices of food. Major investment in research and development would spearhead a growth spurt in innovation.

He expressed confidence that US entrepreneurs would revolutionize manufacturing and construction industries by focusing on designs suitable for disassembly and reuse so that the need for mining virgin raw resources would diminish. While such industrial ecology ideas were not new, it would be the first time that they would receive coordinated support that included tax credits for industries that exploited them. If the consumption of meat products dropped significantly, that would not only reduce methane emissions but also improve the general health of US population. He pursued his argument further.

"I know that many will think this is completely unrealistic and may trigger a worldwide recession, if not depression. However, some forty years ago few believed that we could not switch from gasoline powered cars to electric vehicles and nowadays we are all driving electric cars. Unfortunately, much of the electricity that we use to charge these cars still comes from burning fossil fuels and this must end." He paused and continued from a different perspective.

"I also know that what I am proposing may be an act of political suicide for many of those who choose to support this bill. However, our planet is facing an unprecedented challenge. I believe that American people will recognize it and will ultimately support us."

He took a sip of water and moved to conclude his opening remarks.

"There is also additional urgency about this because, if we succeed, I will want to join President Hou of China, in Beijing, at the Climate Change Summit planned for January. Prime Minister Parthasarathy of India will also be there. If US demonstrates its seriousness about this issue there is a better chance that leaders of China and India will be persuaded to follow suit. The European Union countries are already far ahead of us on controlling greenhouse gas emissions. Together with US, China and India we will create an irreversible paradigm shift in the way we sustain our populations. The markets will soon enough recognize this and adapt. In any case, I believe, it is our duty to take up this challenge. And, incidentally, let us not call it the Carbon Tax bill but rather Sustainable Planet Act."

He paused and added, "I invite your comments."

Jasper Cox was the first to speak, "Mr President, as Secretary of Treasury, I came here this morning with a plan to advise against any sudden change in policy based on these latest developments. Indeed, I had prepared rough estimates of the disastrous impact that Carbon Tax of this magnitude would have on the financial markets and on some of the biggest corporations in the world."

He interrupted to take a sip of water, swallowed hard, and continued.

"However, I found your argument irrefutable and have just had a change of heart. This is very unusual for me. But, having heard you present your rationale for doing what should have been done decades ago, I am keen to focus on how we can make your proposal work. Mr President, when recognizing gravity of the situation you have chosen to lead and I believe it is my solemn responsibility to support you in this noble undertaking even though I do not see how such a bill will ever pass in the House."

Jasper stopped and took another sip of water. This opened the floodgates. One after another the attendees began declaring that, they too, had been swayed by the President's arguments and are willing to put their more mundane, pragmatic, concerns aside.

Mark Mosley was the only one who declared that he did not need any convincing. As Head of EPA he had advocated stringent emissions controls for many years even though he dared not hope that anything of the order of $250 per ton tax would ever be seriously contemplated. He tried to add some light-hearted support to everyone by saying with a smile on his face.

"At least last night's debate performance by Pastor Jones will win us some Republican votes!"

Rather than laugh, President Stewart took that comment seriously.

"I take your point Mark, but I am old enough to recall that back in 2015 the Pope addressed a joint session of US Congress and urged our politicians to take climate change most seriously. And what action followed? Not much. If the leader of the entire Catholic Church had so little impact, why would you expect an appeal by one Southern preacher to make much of a difference?"

Joan Collins, who was on the first name basis with the President, stepped in to answer.

"Well, James, you know us Americans. The Pope was a foreigner speaking to us with Spanish accent. However, Eli Jones is a homegrown phenomenon. Not since Billy Graham has an evangelist wielded as much influence as Pastor Jones. There could be as many as hundred evangelical Republicans in the House who may be questioning their position on climate change as we speak."

Olivia Smith interjected, "Perhaps so, but this morning's wild swings on the stock market and a flood of anti Carbon Tax headlines will soon set them back to their normal position. There are already suggestions that Eli Jones had been bought by liberal billionaires and that the scientists are just trying to drum up huge amounts of research funding to study a non-existent catastrophe. I have been reading all these on my way here. The headlines are running some twenty to one against Carbon Tax."

Joan Collins was also scanning messages on her communicator.

"It seems that the opposition did not need much time to swing into action. There is even a story that John Hawkins is having a clandestine affair with that Post reporter, Barbara Steinwill, with a photo of them going into his apartment late last night."

That last comment finally generated some laughter. All of them had some past experiences with media scrutiny. Even the president was smiling when he said, "I can't quite see them successfully painting Hawkins as an international playboy who spends the Johns Hopkins research money on wine and women. I have met John more than once and he is a true scientist."

"Which need not mean that he doesn't like women," interjected Joan.

President Stewart indicated with a hand gesture that he wanted to put an end to this lighthearted banter. He turned to Alan Packer and asked about the chances of the bill passing the Senate where the Democrats currently enjoyed a 60 to 40 majority, just enough to break a filibuster.

"Well, it is hard to know if we can hold all of our Senators together in light of the heavy lobbying against the bill. But the good news is that there are now up to five Republican senators who have been supportive of climate change regulation. Perhaps, they can be persuaded to support us?" He stopped for a moment and looking around the room said.

"The biggest obstacle I see right now is the Speaker of the House. Even if, against all odds, the bill emerges intact out of committees, Jack Bundy will almost certainly not put it up for a vote in the House. How do we cope with that?"

Almost everyone was nodding in agreement. However, the President refused to be discouraged. He decided to summarize.

"Let us then agree to proceed one step at a time. Prepare a draft of the bill that uses the new revenue to create as many jobs as possible in this country and opens new investment opportunities for non-fossil fuel technologies. Alan and I will discreetly sound out these five Republican senators about co-sponsoring our bill. I will also try to set up a one-on-one meeting with Jack Bundy. Let us hope that he was one of those who were influenced by Pastor Jones."

Getting up to his feet and looking directly at his trusted advisors, Stewart continued, "I am grateful to all of you for supporting me today. Frankly, I did not know I could be so persuasive. It must be my lucky day. Seriously, however, I put it down to the fact that truth and necessity are on our side. When faced with these twin drivers, we must put aside our reservations and focus single-mindedly on achieving the goal we have set for ourselves."

The attendees continued to discuss the broad plan of action and identifying the most capable people to act as architects of various components of the bill for another hour or so. A powerful feeling of camaraderie permeated the group to a much greater degree than they experienced for a very long time. They were senior politicians and administrators and yet they all felt a sense of youthful exhilaration as they started drilling deeper into their plans. They put it down to President Stewart's leadership and he, in turn, put it down to being on a roll. Having been elected President twice, he knew what it felt like to be on a roll. Yes, today has been one of these times.

At that point, Yasmin, an uninvited, unnoticed, but an active participant in this crucial meeting concluded that everything was going according to plan; she was no longer needed. Almost instantly, she set up relevant thought alerts for each participant in the meeting whose mind signatures she had collected, for the first time, today. She thought it was time to check on Ed Taylor who was on his way to the G5 meeting in Texas. Her mind left the White House as effortlessly as it had entered it. Despite the world's most sophisticated electronic security barriers in place, neither the leaders of the United States meeting in the Oval Office, nor the security staff and systems protecting them had any indication that the White House had just been infiltrated in a most profound way.

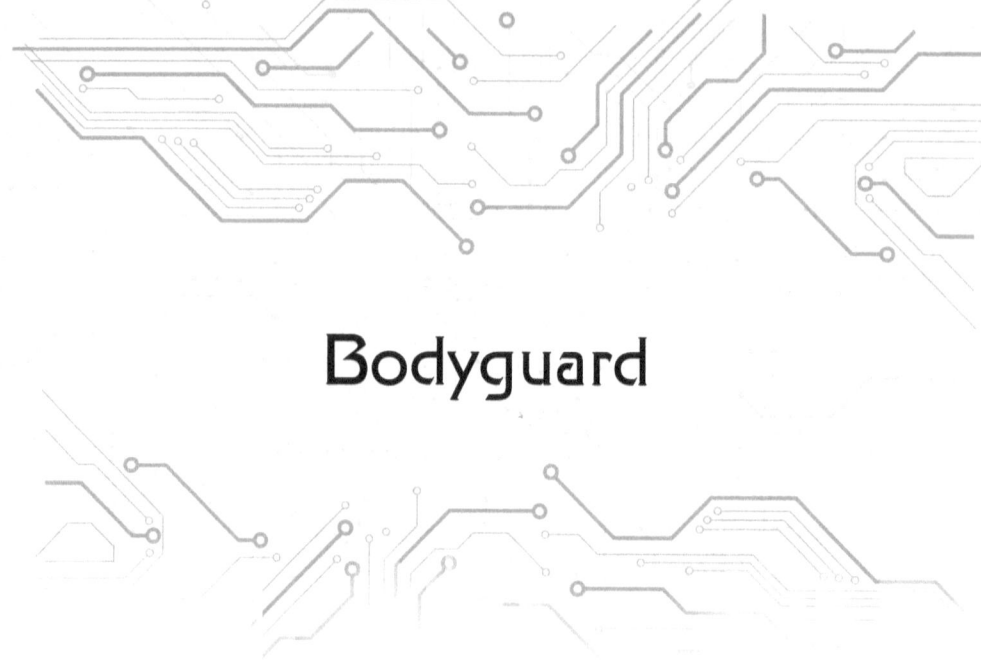

Bodyguard

Later that evening, Barbara was in the fair-trade coffee shop on K Street, going over an update story on the Carbon Tax Initiative with Wordsmith, the AI editor. She was the only customer as it was nearly closing time. A tall man wearing a raincoat and a dark hat came in, ordered a coffee, collected it, and sat down a couple of tables away from Barbara. He wore heavy rimmed spectacles and had a reddish beard and moustache. Barbara did not like the look of him. She quickly finished her coffee, packed up her tablet and walked out of the café. The man left his unfinished coffee cup and walked out, just a few steps after Barbara. She was walking briskly towards Washington Post's headquarters. The man gained on her.

"Ms Steinwill," the man called out, "can I have a word?" His voice had an accent, possibly Eastern European and he knew her name. In a split-second decision, she stopped and turned to face him and regretted it almost immediately as he approached her very closely and looked down at her menacingly. She didn't know if she should scream or try to run, then she remembered Yasmin's alert, "Yasmin, help me!" she shouted in her mind.

"Many people don't like what you're writing about Carbon Tax. Important people, Ms Steinwill," the man said in a quiet warning voice. His breath smelled of cigarettes.

"Who are you? Who sent you? And don't come so close!" said Barbara stepping back until she felt a shop front window behind her. The man moved even closer, and his threats were now direct.

"We know where you live and where your boyfriend, John Hawkins, lives and where your mother lives. There will be trouble if you continue."

It was nighttime and there were no people nearby, but the street was well lit. Barbara was scared, but she tried to appear calm.

"There are security cameras all around here," she spoke loudly, "I am not afraid of you!"

With his right hand he grabbed her upper arm. His fingers squeezed it like a vice.

"You're a fool! You should be afraid!" He seemed to be getting sadistic pleasure from hurting her. She winced in pain and tried to twist herself away from him and buy herself more time.

"Who are you!?" she repeated, "Ouch! Stop it, you're hurting me!"

"Doesn't matter who I am!" retorted the man but suddenly his face grimaced in pain, and he let go of Barbara's arm. Gurgling sounds, "Ow! Argh!" came out of his mouth as he bent over in agony with his large right-hand clutching at his chest.

He twisted and stumbled a few steps until his back found the support of the shop window. He partially straightened up and looked at Barbara, his face in great discomfort.

"You've been warned! Go! Go!" he barked at her.

Barbara hesitated, "Do you want me to call an ambulance?" she asked.

"No! Go away!" he snapped at her again. He turned and somewhat bent over, started to walk away, slowly.

Barbara was shaking, uncertain what to do. Should she call 911? Just then her communicator buzzed. It was Yasmin.

"Barbara, are you Okay? Sorry it took me so long!"

Barbara was calming down.

"Yes, I am alright now. And you didn't take long. Who is this guy and will he be Okay?"

Yasmin was relieved.

"The fact that he was so close to you helped. His name is Boris, but I didn't really have time to search deeper. And yes, he will be alright. I induced a short bout of severe chest pains; that's all. Just enough to scare him, while he was trying to scare you. I am pretty sure his intention was only to scare you. If you don't need me, I'll visit him now and find out more."

Barbara was reassured, "Yes, Yasmin, you can go now." She even attempted to joke, "You make a pretty handy bodyguard!"

Later that night John and Barbara examined the bruises on Barbara's arm and reflected on Yasmin's speedy intervention. They were both shaken by the reality of a physical threat. They also both had mixed feelings of gratitude to Yasmin and concern about her powers. John was especially worried about the growing number of people whose minds were now accessible by Yasmin. Their vulnerability was his and Barbara's fault and yet there seemed to be no other way to accomplish their mission.

He felt conflicted and resolved that he must get Yasmin to guarantee that she destroys all these telepathic addresses as soon as the Carbon Tax legislation is passed. That resolution made him feel a little less guilty. But it was only Yasmin's text update that made them feel better. She confirmed that Barbara's attacker was Boris Novikov, who worked for Esther Cohen and that he was instructed not to cause any physical harm to Barbara.

And just as Barbara and John were reconciling themselves to the necessity of accepting these kinds of threats, Boris was calling Esther to report on what had taken place. He too was shaken.

"Esther, I can tell you that I never felt anything like that! I thought I was having a heart attack in the middle of trying to lean on this Steinwill woman. But now I feel just fine. What should I do?"

Esther thought this strange. But she had worked with Boris for many years; they met during their military service in Israel. She knew he could be relied on under pressure. She also knew the right thing to say, under the circumstances.

"Well, I think you should take a taxi to an emergency department of the nearest hospital. You need to have yourself checked out. Do not drive there!"

Reluctantly, Boris agreed.

Multiple Effects

The consequences of Tuesday's events were cascading and beginning to affect people and organizations far removed from Washington DC. Overnight, stock markets first dropped sharply in Europe and Asia, then recovered substantially to correct for the initial overreaction. Airlines, oil and coal producers were disproportionately affected but agribusiness sector also experienced a drop. Naturally, renewable energy stocks as well as uranium miners went up. Currency exchange markets fluctuated briefly before settling down. Generally, the world markets were not taking climate change news emanating from the US very seriously.

However, Russian president Valery Zhukov received a brief memo about a high-level scientific delegation in the US urging a passage of a punitive Carbon Tax. President Zhukov was always interested in events that could affect the demand for Russian oil and gas. Still, the memo he received also included an expert assessment that nothing was likely to change. The King of Saudi Arabia and the President of Iran received similar assessment memos, as did Presidents and Prime Ministers of many other countries.

On the other hand, across the US media outlets were humming with increased activity. Newspapers, networks, radio talk show hosts were all busy commenting, criticizing and sensationalizing events of yesterday. The Washington Hilton where Doug Larsen's scientific delegation was staying was besieged by a small army of reporters clamoring for one-on-one or group interviews.

Wisely, Marty Greenberg had booked a private function room for their meals. Over breakfast, they debriefed, congratulated all members who participated in the congressional hearing and Doug, in particular. Everybody was elated; everything that happened yesterday exceeded their wildest expectations. Hastily, they agreed that nobody would talk to the media without first clearing it with Marty or Doug. Above all, they would not respond at all to any attacks aimed either at themselves or any other scientists.

They agreed that they would spend the rest of the morning contacting their loved ones to warn them about likely snooping by reporters into their private lives. Unlike Barbara and John, none of the other scientists anticipated becoming targets of aggressive investigative reporting. Now Marty alerted them to that uncomfortable reality; he called it the price of success. They also elected Marty to organize a group press conference in the hotel, late in the afternoon. None of the scientists or their technical staff wished to risk stepping outside of the hotel this morning.

Naturally, Pastor Jones's sudden conversion to a climate change activist's position provided most media excitement and bizarre explanations ranging from temporary insanity to conspiracy theories accusing him of accepting multimillion-dollar bribes from Democrat leaning billionaires. Since the previous evening a large contingent of investigators, reporters, and photographers fanned out across Virginia and Washington DC trying to catch a follow-up interview either with Pastor Jones or with anyone closely associated with him.

By late Wednesday morning, an enterprising Fox News reporter tracked down Dr Gupta and Natashia Brown at the Hay-Adams hotel and the story of Pastor Jones's fall on the balcony of the hotel hit the news early on Wednesday afternoon. Dr Gupta's rendition of the story, in his accented English, provided an odd relief to Natashia's deadly serious but emotional retelling of what, she swore, was a God's miracle that she had witnessed.

She concluded her interview by saying, "I have never seen anything like it! I know that nobody will believe me, but I was there and I saw what I saw: one minute he was blind and after the prayer, he could see! If that's not God's miracle, I don't know what is!"

Dr Gupta offered a professional opinion that Pastor Jones might have been in a postictal state following a mild epileptic seizure. However, he acknowledged that this was only his best guess.

After thanking Natashia, the interviewer promptly informed the public - in a conspiratorial tone - that Pastor Jones was nowhere to be found. He had checked out of the hotel prior to last night's debate and has not been seen since the debate ended. Calls and messages sent to his Virginia based ministry all bounced back with a template out-of-office message. His wife, Victoria, was briefly intercepted as she was being driven out of their lavish private estate but all that she would say was that Pastor Jones has taken time to pray and meditate and thanked people for their many messages of support. She added that, last night, she was very proud of her husband for the courage and conviction he had shown in the debate.

In the Bundy household, Justin had been following many of the news stories coming out of the climate change hearing and the debate. Jack Bundy made good on his promise and made sure that Justin had a great seat in the public gallery during the hearing. Justin was swept away by the scientists' sophisticated and yet lucid and accessible presentation of the danger to thermohaline ocean circulation currents. He was most impressed by John Hawkins's perceptive comments; he wished he could talk about science that way. In an instant John became his hero. He resolved to try to do something to help John's cause and the only thing that he could come up with was to, somehow, influence his powerful father.

Justin went home straight after the congressional hearing and, in his room, he read voraciously many entries on Doug Larsen's website. A lot of it, including the underlying mathematics, made good sense to him. He stayed up for half the night studying the literature and continued for most of the morning. However, he realized that nothing he was learning was going to matter one bit to his Dad.

A little later, while munching on nachos with guacamole dip that Jacinta brought to his room, he casually started looking at the news stories about the debate and Pastor Jones. While all the mentions of divine intervention irked him at first, he recalled talking to his Mom about what it would take to change his Dad's stand on the climate change issue. A vague idea started forming in his mind. Giving the matter full attention he started flipping from one video clip to another. He quickly drilled down to the latest ones, of the interviews with Dr Gupta and Natashia Brown. After playing them over some two to three times, his idea became clearer.

Justin was pleased and decided to reward himself with another snack. He left his room and went to the kitchen and the breakfast room area. He was surprised to see his Dad there with a mug of coffee, also looking at news clips of stories related to climate change while Jacinta was busy in the kitchen cleaning and cooking. Jack Bundy was hardly ever home in the afternoons. Was that Justin's lucky break? He decided to strike up a conversation.

"How come you're home, Dad?"

"It was bedlam in congress today," replied Jack somewhat gruffly, "this climate change issue is bigger than I thought. I already talked to the press twice this morning, but they are never satisfied!" Jack paused and added, "I needed time to think for myself, so I told Anne to cancel all my appointments for the rest of the day, as I wasn't feeling well. Which is true, I haven't felt well for a few days now."

That's progress, Justin thought to himself. His Dad admitting that he needed time to think was very unusual. Normally, Jack projected an air of certainty on all matters of importance. Justin thought he must persevere, but gently.

"Did you see that Pastor Jones, in the debate last night? What did you think?" He asked just to test the waters. To his pleasant surprise, Jack did not react angrily. He looked uncertain and conflicted.

"Son, more than anything else these smartass scientists said, Eli Jones made sense to me. It may well be our duty to protect God's creation. I wish I could talk to him and understand better what changed his mind. But I can't get through to him this afternoon. All the standard contact addresses give me an out-of-office reply and I don't want to draw attention by asking staff in my office to find his private contact addresses."

Jack looked frustrated and a little helpless at the end of that reply. Secretly, Justin was overjoyed but tried not to show it and, instead, focused on trying to offer constructive assistance to his Dad.

"Well, the news clips said that Jones was nowhere to be found since the debate. But I noticed that this lady president of George Mason University in her opening address, when she introduced the moderator and the debaters, she mentioned that Jones was an old friend. Perhaps, you can contact him through her?"

"Not a bad idea, Justin. But I tried it already and got the same template message that President Johnson is currently unavailable; please contact so-and-so. I don't want to leave any messages that can be traced back to me. When you are the Speaker, you learn to be careful," responded Jack feeling somewhat pleased at the opportunity to remind his son of his Dad's importance.

Justin was worried that this rare promising conversation may soon come to an end. Then a risky idea came to his mind.

"Dad, I could easily hack into that President Johnson's private university email account and leave a message that Jack Bundy would like to talk to Pastor Jones, on my teleconferencing connection."

Jack looked up and his expression showed that he was somewhat impressed by his son's suggestion and was seriously considering it. But he shook his head.

"Even if you could do this, the last thing I need is to have a scandal blowing up around my son hacking into college president's private email account."

Still, Justin was not going to give up that easily.

"But, Dad, that's just not going to happen! You don't know how good I am at this sort of thing! It's a piece of cake for me to send an email to a private university account of a college president. What's more, my hacking code is all written in NAIL. Apart from top security people at places like NSA, I doubt that anyone else could trace it back to me. I can set it so that the message I send will delete itself and its own trace after, say, half an hour."

Jack was wavering, he knew he should be disapproving but he was proud that his son mastered a technical skill that many would find challenging. Also, he felt a strangely compelling need to talk to Eli Jones, as soon as possible.

He hesitated, "It's too risky. I don't think, I should let you...." he started saying but Justin interrupted him.

"Dad, look, what's the worst-case scenario? Your, college dropout computer geek son hacked into a college email system, without your knowledge? It's not like hacking into a bank or FBI; at worst they would give me a slap on the wrist. Besides, the message will self-destruct in thirty minutes and if we don't hear from this lady Johnson, or Jones, within an hour, I'll reconfigure my teleconferencing connection."

For the first time, in a long while, Jack was enjoying talking to Justin. The boy was more resourceful than he had given him credit for! But before agreeing, he queried Justin some more.

"But, if Jones calls back and talks to me, he will be able to record our conversation at his end, won't he?"

This question made Justin very happy. It gave him an opportunity to impress his Dad.

"Technically, yes. But I set it up so that all recorded signals emanating from my private teleconferencing connection turn into gibberish after fifteen seconds. The computers and communicators in my room are some of the safest in all of the United States".

Jack wondered for a moment if Justin was bragging but, deep down, he believed that he was telling the truth. After all, in his early teens, his IQ was assessed to be 185. He finally, relented. Smiling knowingly at his son, he said.

"Okay, Justin. I gotta give you credit. You learned some useful skills. But I don't need to be party to this. You go to your room and do what you gotta do and if you get a call from Jones give me a buzz on my communicator and I will join you there."

G5 Meeting

While Justin was in his room hacking into George Mason University's email system, Yasmin was busy following an intense discussion at the G5 meeting in Houston Texas. The meeting was in a spacious data analysis inner-sanctum room that could easily accommodate twenty persons. It had the latest data display, visualization and virtual reality capabilities and contained interface globes for communication with the company's supercomputers and NAIT-113. Yasmin was looking at the room and its occupants through Ed Taylor's eyes.

Besides members of G5 a senior data analyst, Josh Rosenberg, was there overseeing the interactive session with NAIT-113 that had been fed the text of the entire transcript of the congressional science committee's hearing, the debate that followed, multiple commentaries, stock market movements and the like. The main question that was put to NAIT-113 was: What will be the adverse effects of $250 per ton carbon tax especially with regard to job losses in the US and worldwide?

William Thurston instructed Josh Rosenberg to make sure that NAIT-113 assumes that the windfall revenue would be used to merely compensate US taxpayers and companies in the form of tax relief and that the rest of the world would follow a "business as usual" scenario.

Rather quickly, NAIT-113 came to life and started to display graphs and tables of the sort of gloomy forecasts members of G5 were hoping to receive.

A general sense of relief swept over all of them. A stock market crash of the proportions not seen since, at least 2009, followed by a deep recession in the US that triggered a recession in China and India, that triggered a collapse of export business activity across Asia, Middle East, Africa and South America that deprived Europe of its export markets leading to a worldwide recession bordering on depression. Oil producing countries like Saudi Arabia, Russia, Venezuela, Nigeria and others would be particularly hard hit by the downturn in demand due to the slowing down of the Chinese, Indian and European economies.

As the list of gloomy economic projections grew, a celebratory mood also grew in the GES data analysis room.

"It's a slam dunk!" Exclaimed Janet Smith. "Them tree-hugging Democrats and scientists will not know what hit them once these numbers hit the media."

At this point, Yasmin decided to leave this meeting partly because she had already collected everyone's telepathic signatures and partly because she received an alert that Pastor Jones was about to talk to Jack Bundy, remotely. Justin's hacking strategy had worked.

Brother Jack

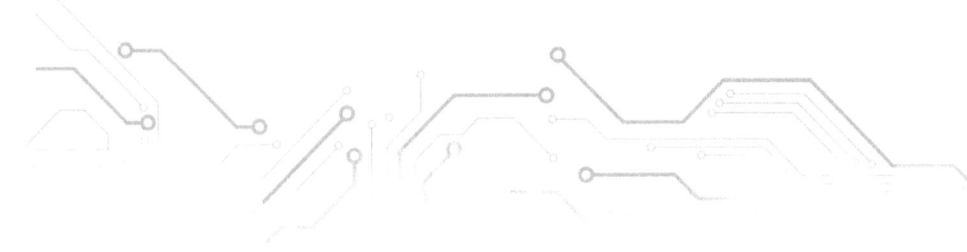

Apparently, Eli Jones had asked Wendy Johnson if he could stay at her house in Arlington for a couple of nights to avoid the onslaught of media interest. That is precisely where he was driven, by Wendy's husband Frank, immediately after the debate while a decoy private car with Frank's brother, who was of roughly similar built and general appearance to Eli, was followed by reporters all the way to the airport. When Wendy received Justin's email she called Eli, at her own house, and passed on Justin's contact details. Wendy wasn't bothered by the fact that Justin hacked into her university's private email account. She did not consider it particularly secure since some of George Mason's bright undergraduates managed to accomplish a similar feat a couple of times before.

Wendy and Eli briefly discussed the risks of responding to Justin's message. After all, it could be an enterprising investigator posing as Justin Bundy. Eli thought it unlikely because such an investigator would have, surely, presented himself as Jack Bundy rather than his son. As they were talking, Wendy was looking up information on the Bundy family and confirmed that they had a son, named Justin, who had studied computer science at MIT. That was reassuring. Perhaps, even more importantly, Eli wanted to talk to Jack. He had already been thinking about ways of fulfilling his promise to Jesus and compiled a short list of the most important people that he thought he might be able to influence to support Larsen's mission. Jack Bundy, whom Eli had met before a couple of times, was on top of that list. But he worried that Speaker Bundy would now regard him as a traitor.

And so it was that at approximately 3:00 p.m. Yasmin was looking with interest, through Jack's eyes, at Justin's large room which was half bedroom and half a sophisticated computer/electronics room, with an adjacent modern bathroom. In fact, it was a former master bedroom combined with a billiards room which Carolyn converted into what she called "a bachelor pad" for Justin when he had turned 16. In the middle, there was a crescent shaped desk standing on a low platform, with a large chair equipped with a built-in massager and arms fitted with many controls that faced multiple communication domes, monitors and electronic instruments. The opposite wall was covered with large, high quality, display panels. The chair, desk and the collection of the equipment were, intentionally, assembled to resemble the captain's bridge on the fictional starship Enterprise.

Jack was sitting in Justin's captain's chair. Very life-like 3D hologram of Eli Jones, sitting at a desk, was on the main display panel and the door was closing behind Justin who was leaving because his Dad said that he wanted to talk to Pastor Jones in private. It was Jack who initiated the conversation.

"Pastor Jones, we can speak confidentially here. Justin, my son, is a bit of a computer geek and he assures me that this connection is very safe." He paused very briefly to give Jones a reassuring look and continued.

"Pastor Jones, I am so glad you responded to Justin's message. Some of the things you said in the debate last night resonated with me much more than anything those scientists had said. Could you explain to me, one more time, how you came to change your position so drastically? And, yes, I have seen these people from the hotel interviewed a little while back."

Jack was leaning forward in his chair, looking intently at the hologram of Eli Jones.

Jones was pleasantly surprised. No accusations? That's a good start! He had been rehearsing several versions of the rationale for his new position on climate change. They were all consistent, but none revealed the details of his personal encounter with Christ. He knew the dangers of being ridiculed as a religious fanatic. But, right now, facing the man who could be pivotal in accomplishing the Lord's task, he felt an irresistible urge to tell him the truth. He stared straight back into Jack's eyes.

"It is very strange, Mr Speaker. I was not planning to tell this to anyone, but I feel that it is safe to open up to you. Do I have your word that what I say will stay between us?"

"Yes, Pastor Jones, you have my word," replied Jack quite sincerely.

Eli Jones then proceeded to relay to Jack his vision on the balcony of the hotel, his blindness, and the miraculous recovery the moment he committed to helping the scientists' mission. He pointed to the biblical 'road to Damascus' experience of Saul who later became St Paul the Apostle. As he talked, he could tell from Jack's facial expression that he was believed. Jack did not think he was crazy. He started wrapping up.

"I know that I may pay a heavy price for what I have done and will do. Already today, I have been receiving a flood of messages calling me a traitor, a lunatic and many other things that do not bear repeating." He sighed.

"What is worse, I have received urgent messages from the manager of my ministry, which is quite a big business, that our loans are being called in and new credit is nowhere to be found. So, it seems that someone or some persons out there are trying to teach me a lesson! However, now that He has shown me the way, I will not be deterred! I will do His bidding not anybody else's! Thanks be to God through Jesus Christ!"

Tears were pouring out of his eyes when he stopped talking. Jack was also feeling shaken. Having heard this confession he felt an overwhelming need to tell Jones about the nightmares that have been haunting him for almost a week now. It was his turn now.

"Well, Pastor Jones, I also wish to confide in you and I also ask you for your word, as minister of God, to keep what I am about to say 100% confidential," said Jack looking directly into the eyes of Eli's hologram.

"I swear by the God almighty that what you say to me will forever remain with me," replied Jones. Jack was relieved to hear that.

"I too have been reconsidering my position on climate change. And like you, but in a less dramatic way, I too feel that I am being sent messages from a higher power. In my case they come in the form of a recurrent dream, or a nightmare, if you like."

He paused and hesitated but Jones urged him, "Go on, Mr Speaker, go on."

Jack then proceeded to describe his recurrent dream in detail.

"Based on the first part of the dream, I would have thought that it came from the Devil himself, but then it moves to my church and to the Lord's hymn everyone is singing, no Devil would want to be part of that; isn't that so? No, deep down I believe, the message 'what if they are right?' is coming from Jesus himself, over and over again. Or am I losing my mind, Pastor Jones?"

Jones's hologram got up from the chair in which he was sitting. His face was radiant with joy, he raised both of his arms with the palms of his hands bent up.

"No, Mr Speaker, you are not losing your mind. It is not a coincidence that the two of us are speaking here tonight. You too have been chosen by our Lord, Jesus Christ, to help save His creation on Earth. He manifests himself to different people in different ways. He brought us here together, today, so that we can find a way to help pass the Carbon Tax that will be a first step towards averting a catastrophe. The scientists are right about that, they are His messengers. He helped them acquire the knowledge to understand the danger. They, too, are just instruments of His will. Let us pray together brother Jack, please don't mind me calling you that."

Jack didn't mind. Like Jones he stood up and raised his arms and followed the inspiring words of Eli's prayer. He felt elated, like all his worries were melting away. He knew he was going to do the right thing. When Eli called on the Holy Spirit to enter their bodies, they both felt shivers running down their spines. Then they sat down, and both seemed to be making an effort to collect their thoughts and turn their lofty thoughts into actions. Eli, who had been thinking about what needs to be done since Sunday was the first to speak.

"You know, Mr Speaker, with the attack on the Carbon Tax bill already on the way, before the Democrats even had time to draft it, there is no need to give its adversaries any extra stimulus just yet. Don't you agree?"

Jack reflected on that. Something sparked a clever idea in his mind.

"Yes, if tomorrow, I were to declare that I am taking the same position as Pastor Jones that would certainly push some panic buttons. No, it is much better for me to be tight lipped and act as though nothing had changed and then, when the bill passes the standing committees, I would unexpectedly put it up for a straight up-and-down vote in the House."

He smiled broadly and added "Of course, that will almost certainly cost me my speakership but it's a small price to pay for doing His bidding."

Eli was nodding his head.

"Yes, that's a good plan but how do we ensure that enough Republicans will join the bulk of the Democrats to pass it in the committees and on the floor of the house?"

Bundy's mind was in overdrive, "You need to reinforce your message to the evangelical Republicans; it's a large block. Is anyone of them a member of your congregation? If so, we could get him or her to organize an event, like a prayer function to help them decide what is right, and you could be invited to address them. Of course, together with other preachers taking the opposing view; right?"

Eli was excited. "That's a great idea! Laura Waugh, congresswoman from my Virginia district, is a regular in our church. I'll talk to her. As for the other preachers and their view, I am not concerned. They will be preaching the word of Big Oil. What chance do they stand when I preach the word of the Lord? None, at all!"

Both men were happy and felt like they achieved a breakthrough. They agreed to continue communicating via Justin's private connection, mainly late at night. They also agreed that they could give each other strong support now that they were working towards a common goal. They both knew that tough times were coming. They felt exhausted. Then Jack had yet another good idea.

"About your sudden financial troubles, Pastor Eli, just like the idea about congresswoman Waugh, can you find someone very wealthy in your congregation with the guts to extend you a bridging loan until all this blows over? Perhaps, someone who is old enough to worry more about his salvation than the pressures from powerful business groups?"

Eli was impressed. Why didn't he think of that!?

"Mr Speaker, please call me Eli and I hope you don't mind if I call you Jack. That's a wonderful idea. Thank you! I feel like providence is guiding our every step now. I believe and declare that you will sleep peacefully tonight. God bless us!"

The two men waved goodbyes to each other, and Jack logged out. He felt really good as he walked from Justin's room to the breakfast room where Justin was busy polishing off yet another delicious snack that Jacinta prepared for him. Jack smiled broadly at him.

"You did good today, son. I am proud of you" he said. Justin looked up a bit nervously.

"So how did it go with that Pastor Jones? Did you have good talk about climate change? Did he persuade you?"

"Son, that is for me to know and for you to wonder about." Jack replied laughing. "Pastor Jones and I had a good talk and, if you don't mind, we will be talking again using your connection since you say it's so secure."

Justin took this to mean progress. He was pleased with himself and felt better about his Dad than he had for a long time. As Yasmin took her leave, she made sure to also record Justin's telepathic signature. Apart from an alternative entry point to the Bundy household, in Justin's computers she detected programs written in NAIL but clearly not written by a NAIT. She thought that was impressive work by that young man.

The Bundy family had a wonderful time that night. Jack asked Jacinta to prepare a special Mexican dinner, chicken with puebla style mole sauce, the whole family's favorite dish. After dinner that was accompanied by lots of Sangria, they watched family movies from their holidays in Florida, visits to Disney World, and even older ones of Carolyn's and Jack's wedding. When Justin went back to his room, his parents went up to their bedroom tipsy and feeling amorous. They made love more passionately than they had for some time. Jack fell asleep very early watching Casablanca, an old classic that Carolyn adored. As Eli predicted, he slept well through the night. He had no dreams.

The Passing of Days

The three weeks following the debate with Pastor Jones were some of the most tiring and yet most satisfying in John and Barbara's lives. Barbara was working feverishly churning out articles for the Washington Post's website, almost every other day. To George Hunter's delight, Barbara instantly became the one journalist who had unlimited access to Doug Larsen and other members of the scientific delegation that had met with the congressional science committee. Thanks to her relationship with John, as well as to her professionalism, the scientists quickly developed a trust that Barbara would not misquote or sensationalize their statements and would always let them proofread and correct all statements attributed to them. Her very first feature article entitled "The Thermohaline Circulation - The Great Ocean Conveyor Belt" included not only an easy to understand description of the underlying phenomenon and its importance to global climate but also video clips of simulations of the catastrophe that would unfold if the regime driving the phenomenon were to alter as forecasted by Larsen's model.

In parallel, John was involved in multiple interviews, usually together with, other members of Larsen's team that repeatedly underscored the dangers of continued inaction. He performed much better than the other scientists whenever the interviewers challenged them on the economic cost and viability of the Carbon Tax law. The main thrust of his response was that, yes, there would be short term economic costs, but they would be insignificant compared to the long term costs of inaction. A drastic regime change of the conveyor belt phenomenon, would destroy ecosystems and the planet's ability to feed its population. The resulting widespread famine would destabilize governments, cause mass environmental migrations of people on a scale not recorded in modern history. The global economic system would face a much greater catastrophe than a mere recession that the Carbon Tax was likely to cause. However, the latter was likely to lead to a more stable, sustainable, economy underpinned by renewable energy and more labor-intensive industrial processes that focused on disassembly for reuse rather than on mining of scarce raw resources.

As Barbara and John anticipated, their private relationship made brief headlines and even earned them a story in The National Enquirer. The story speculated about mysterious foreign interests that would benefit greatly from the Carbon Tax and accused them of being promised a fortune, once the law is passed. It also hinted that foreign spy agencies may be manipulating scientists like John and journalists like Barbara. Thankfully, that kind of undesirable public attention did not last long as journalists quickly found much more exciting and seedy material on several Democratic congressmen and senators who were likely to support the Carbon Tax bill. The National Enquirer story was quickly forgotten by all except Mike Blythe who, true to form, was already developing a Jewish conspiracy theory. The fact that Steinwill was very likely a Jewish name did not escape his attention. Also, Mike knew that GES started buying up renewable energy stocks all over the world including Israel.

In the midst of all that, John and Barbara's relationship flourished. They felt like a couple of young graduate students working together on an exciting research project. Each day brought new hostile attacks on the climate change proposals and each day they felt that they were successful in winning people over to their cause.

They quickly realized that, with so many functions in Washington DC, it was more convenient for John to stay mostly at Barbara's and

Cynthia's house. Late in the evenings, in Barbara's bedroom/office, they were constantly planning the forthcoming briefings and were regularly updated by Yasmin about developments that helped them prepare. For instance, they knew that the Sustainable Planet Act (SPA) being drafted included a huge investment in the US infrastructure projects, funded by the anticipated revenues from the Carbon Tax. These were intended to create new jobs to compensate for anticipated losses caused by the direct impact of increased cost of fossil fuels.

Yasmin also kept them updated about significant events that were unfolding "in secret" such as diplomatic discussions with China and India, concerning the Sustainable Planet Act that President Stewart authorized. One night, just before John and Barbara were going to go to sleep, Yasmin contacted them and announced.

"Your President achieved a breakthrough, today, in his discussions with President Hou and Prime Minister Parthasarathy. They agreed that as soon as he declares his support for the Sustainable Planet Act, they will announce that both China and India, in principle, applaud this courageous initiative by the United States and state that - if the USA passes this bill - they will also announce at the Beijing conference commensurate economic measures to implement in their respective countries."

Yasmin, paused for a moment and continued with a note of excitement in her voice, "All along, I thought, I would need their telepathic signatures to achieve such a result. However, it seems that their own scientists, have been effective in persuading them that this is probably their last and best chance to prevent a global environmental catastrophe."

Now, Barbara and John were also excited. But Barbara who had a better sense of the extent of economic globalization than John, asked, "Weren't they concerned about the impact on their economies? Surely, China's manufacturing exports will take a big hit?"

"Yes, this was their main concern, initially. But, interestingly, President Hou's view was that China's population of some 1.3 billion was large enough and now prosperous enough to sustain an economy that was far less reliant on exports. He pointed out that, historically, China has had millennia of relative economic self-sufficiency. Still, he obtained assurances from President Stewart that Chinese manufacturers will not be excluded from the supply chain of the major infrastructure expansion in the US. He also mentioned that China would also launch its own infrastructure expansion," replied Yasmin.

Then, Barbara followed up with, "And what was India's take?"

"Theirs is also an interesting position. I think Prime Minister Parthasarathy is both a closet socialist and a Hindu traditionalist, if that makes sense. She sees this development as an opportunity to weaken the grip that large multinational corporations have on the Indian economy and at the same time to channel government funds to help empower India's rural underclass. If the cost of importing food to India explodes, increasing domestic food production in India will become a top priority and, for once, there will be an opportunity to introduce emergency legislation to ensure that those who grow that food will receive living wages. India's huge nuclear power program means that it is not as sensitive to fossil fuel prices as many other countries and the demand for its competitive high-tech services is unlikely to change. She thinks that if India's wealthy classes take a hit on the international stock markets, it may encourage them to invest their money in their own country, ultimately, benefitting India."

All this was good news and consistent with a few other positive indicators making headlines during that period. For instance, the press in European Union countries was generally supportive of a need for a drastic levy on Carbon emissions and so were some high profile religious leaders such as the Pope and the Dalai Lama.

Unfortunately, the positive stories were vastly outnumbered by an avalanche of negative press that flooded media outlets. These painted economic doomsday scenarios of deep recession, even depression, collapse of economies, stock markets, banks and even the end of western civilization. Indeed, stock markets and currency exchanges started experiencing increased volatility but not to the extent that would sufficiently support these apocalyptic scenarios. The so-called "smart money" was obviously on the status quo winning out.

Price of Salvation

Unlike Barbara and John, Pastor Eli Jones had a much more difficult time ever since returning to his family's mansion outside Charlottesville, Virginia. The Jones' Ministries organization had been under sudden and extreme financial pressure from the first day after his revelation in the debate with the climate scientists. All outstanding loans have been called in, new credit was nowhere to be found, publishers of his many book and video series were exercising termination clauses in their contracts and even bank managers in branches that had financed his enterprise for many years were not returning his calls.

In the first three days after the debate Eli and Victoria had to use five million dollars of their personal savings just to keep the organization afloat and be able to conduct the next Sunday service as if nothing had happened. But that was unsustainable and led to a first major fight, over money, in their long-standing marriage.

Contrary to her public statement of support for her husband, Victoria did not understand what possessed him to change his position on such an important public issue. She wasn't buying the Christ vision story. At first, she thought he had a few too many whiskeys in his hotel room. However, Eli's commitment to his new position was so vehement and so sincere that she quickly stopped accusing him of being misguided or, somehow, manipulated. She grew afraid that their marriage and everything they had built together would be at risk if she did not go along with his epiphany conversion. Besides, he assured her that he had an idea for turning things around if she would just be patient.

Pastor Jones's hopes for saving his ministry rested on one man, Robert Whelan, a descendant of the legendary founder of the American branch of a leading cigarette company. Wheelchair bound, old, gravely ill, billionaire Robert was a regular at Jones's Sunday services. Some thirty years earlier, Robert was recklessly piloting his private plane while under the influence of alcohol. The plane crashed killing his wife and three children and the co-pilot. Robert was the only survivor, but he would never walk again. He was a bitter old man and a miser.

On that first Sunday after the debate the massive hall of the Jones' Ministries Church of Christ was at capacity. Just before the service, as was his custom, Eli Jones would wander by the first few rows of worshippers greeting a selected few, asking them about their problems and promising to pray for them. This time he quickly came to Robert Whelan whose butler always parked his wheelchair in the same central spot in front of the podium. With his hand stretched out and a wide, heartwarming, smile Eli approached him.

"So good to see you here Robert. How have you been? How are you standing up to all those treatments the doctors have been giving you?"

Robert produced a grimace on his face that could, perhaps, pass for a smile.

"Thank you for asking Pastor Jones. Frankly, I feel awful. I believe my days are numbered."

Eli Jones had a natural gift for looking simultaneously concerned and confident. He bent down and placed his right hand on Robert's forehead just for a second, then withdrew it and spoke looking straight into Robert's eyes.

"Lord Jesus has a good plan for all of us. Please stay behind, after the service, we can pray together for your healing. I also have another matter to discuss with you."

Robert guessed immediately that he would be asked for money. He had good reasons to believe that no one genuinely cared for him anymore but that everybody was trying to find a way to extract some of his wealth from him. In this case, however, he had been forewarned. Just yesterday, he received a call from Jason Buetler from Kurp Industries alerting him to the fact that Jones's Ministries were in financial trouble and that it would be unadvisable to extend any loans to them. Come to think of it, there was even a hint of a financial retaliation against anyone who might extend credit to Pastor Jones. That call and the message rubbed Robert the wrong way. His response was that his was not a money lending business. He had no intention of making new loans to anyone but resented being told what he should or should not do with his money. He instantly reflected on this recent memory which, nonetheless, spiked his curiosity. He looked at Jones and replied.

"Sure thing, Pastor Jones, I'd be glad to have a chat. Besides, with this wretched wheelchair I am always one of the last to leave, in any case."

The Sunday service went very well. It was one of Eli Jones's classic performances. He tackled his new stance on climate change head on. He repeated what he said in the debate but took it much further. He said, that as always, the Enemy wishes to spoil the Lord's good plan for his people. He knew that he will be attacked from all sides by those who will spread poisonous lies about him and his ministry. However, he is willing to pay any price to do the Lord's will. Already, he and his ministry are under attack. But Eli Jones is not worried because he knows that the Lord's blessings will come to him at the right time. And he knows that his words will reach millions because they contain the Lord's message. What is there to fear when one does His bidding!? As always, he ended by leading the congregation in prayer, but for the very first time it included a prayer for saving the Lord's creation.

About 30 minutes after the service Robert was sipping tea in a meeting room located at the back of Jones's Ministries Church of Christ. It was a large room with an elegant, long, oak table and chairs, decorated with crosses and other Christian themes and a number of display cabinets featuring the highlights of Jones's evangelical career, like an open air service at Yankee stadium packed to capacity and attended by the Prime Minister of Canada.

Eli Jones had directed Robert and his butler, who was never very far from Robert, to the meeting room and they prayed together for healing of Robert's liver cancer. Robert didn't really believe in miracle healing when all the top doctors that money could buy agreed that he only had some six months left. Still, Jones's preaching always made him feel a little better and he had nothing to lose. And now, he thought he would entertain himself a little by listening to his pitch for financial help. He had no intention of actually lending Jones money, but he could lend an ear and listen to his difficulties.

He looked up at Jones and said, "Pastor Jones, you said you had another matter to discuss with me."

Jones was just waiting for an opening. He launched straight into his prepared speech about how his new position on climate change created some influential enemies who are trying to destroy his ministry financially. Despite a solid financial performance and assets, Jones Ministries cannot borrow a dime anywhere and current creditors are calling in their loans. He pointed out that he just spent five million of his own savings to keep the ministry afloat but that, at this rate, his reserves would run out by next Sunday and he would have to start selling off assets. He continued by saying that his only hope lay in finding good Christians who believed in his message and who were fearless enough to invest money in Jones Ministries; money that he would repay with handsome interest, as soon as the backlash against him subsided and his usual, steady, revenue streams pumped funds into the organization. At this point, Robert cut him off.

"Let me be blunt Pastor Jones. I am sorry about your predicament but the word on the street is that your enemies are so powerful that there is no fighting them. The prognosis for your ministry is just about as bleak as the prognosis for my health. Why would any sane businessman risk his money in propping it up?!"

These harsh words were like darts piercing Eli's hopes for rescuing his ministry. He looked at the gaunt, wrinkled, old man in the wheelchair in front of him. He thought Robert was deriving pleasure from shattering his hopes. He realized that all his planned arguments about long term financial benefits of supporting his ministry would count for naught. What use are long-term profits to a rich man who may be dead by Easter!? And then a desperate idea sparked in his mind. He closed his eyes, summoned the Holy Spirit, stood up and faced Robert. His hands were now raised in a gesture of prayer, his face was tilted up and he spoke in a low, yet emotion filled, voice.

"Robert, if indeed you are soon to meet your maker, what will you say to Him? You have amassed a great fortune by selling addictive tobacco products that harm people. Your drunkenness killed your wife and children. What is your case for salvation?"

Glancing down, he could see fury growing in Robert's eyes but continued anyway.

"Is it insane to invest in the salvation of one's immortal soul? Have you not listened to my sermon!? My ministry needs your money because I am doing our Lord's will! Those who assist will be saved. How many more chances of salvation will you have?!"

Eli now gazed down at Robert in an accusatory way.

"The scriptures say: *Enter by the narrow gate; for the gate is wide, and the way is broad that leads to destruction, and many are those who enter by it.* Have you not understood what that means?!"

Robert felt a sharp shiver run down his spine.

"Enough! Enough!" he shouted at Eli so loudly as to startle his butler who was sitting down at a polite distance from the two men.

All of a sudden Robert was scared! An image of hell fires he must have seen in his childhood religious education books flashed in his mind. Fear struggled with anger at Eli's impudence; no one had dared to challenge him in years. He wanted to strike out at Eli and crush his hopes but the fear in him was growing stronger. His wrinkled face was twisted by the conflicting emotions.

"Stop! Let me think for five minutes," he croaked with effort. Eli nodded in agreement and sat down, as did the butler who guessed that his employer did not need him immediately.

Robert was deep in thought. Who did Eli Jones think he was, trying to scare him into pouring good money into his sinking ministry?! He must tell him to forget it; Robert Whelan is not a money lender! He must also put this arrogant preacher in his place. He searched for words to capture a most vicious rebuke to Eli but found words and phrases floating away. Instead, a palpable fear started gaining ascendency over his anger.

What if Jones is right? What if this is his last chance for salvation? What had he really done to deserve to pass through that "narrow gate" leading to the kingdom of heaven? In his business dealings he had ruthlessly destroyed many competitors. Yes, his enterprises employed thousands but he made every effort to pay them as little as possible and deny them any additional benefits. Images of his children floated in his mind and the pain of their loss swept over him like a wave crested with a searing foam of guilt. Indeed, he is a sinner, unworthy of salvation and the end is near; he felt it in his entire body. He closed his eyes, there was deep darkness but for flames flickering in the distance; he was doomed.

He shuddered and opened his eyes. His mind was darting around looking for an escape. His eyes focused on Jones, a man of God, who was offering a path to salvation! For a moment his innate skepticism struggled with the desire to believe or, at least, to hope. Somehow, a characteristically shrewd idea struck him. He had nothing to lose but everything to gain by helping Jones! After all, where he was going, his billions will be worthless! But what if, even at this late stage, his money could still buy salvation!? Wouldn't that be a bargain?!

What if his support of Jones's Ministries Church of Christ could actually make the difference to the success of the Carbon Tax bill? That would, surely, be the single most unselfish achievement of his long life and he may even live long enough to see it passed. As these thoughts were passing through his mind, his pains receded and a feeling of wellbeing, peace - even euphoria - began to take hold of him. He must be on the right track, he thought to himself. There is still hope for him! He straightened up in his wheelchair and addressed Eli in a firm voice.

"Pastor Jones, I have decided. Perhaps, I am just an old fool or, perhaps, the Lord is really guiding you. Whichever way, I will assist you. Unconditionally. As of this moment your ministry can borrow up to half a billion dollars from my corporation, at two percent over the federal reserve's interest rate. Furthermore, I shall bequeath one billion dollars to your ministry, in my will. Finally, should you wish to launch any campaigns to support the Carbon Tax bill, I shall also underwrite the cost of these campaigns."

Despite being used to swaying people by his arguments, Eli was stunned by this. He had hoped to ask Robert for a loan of fifty, or sixty, million just to tie him over. But a credit line of half a billion was an essentially permanent solution of his ministry's financial problems! He did not even know what possessed him to use the salvation argument. In his pastoral experience the fear of damnation was a poor motivator when asking for donations. However, once again, the answer was obvious. The Lord was guiding him! His face lit up as he stood up and shouted.

"Hallelujah! Glory be to our Lord Jesus Christ! Robert, you too have been chosen, this is His doing, not mine!"

Just at that point Yasmin rewarded both Robert and Eli with a release of opioids to sustain their feelings of euphoria a little longer and departed. Her mission at this service was accomplished.

Yasmin's Face

Approximately one month after the congressional science committee's hearing with Larsen's delegation, John and Barbara were spending a night in John's condominium in Roland Park. They had eaten out but brought dessert to have at home with coffee. They were sitting comfortably in John's living room, enjoying their French style lemon tart with freshly brewed coffee while watching multiple news items on several panels displayed on the wall opposite the couch they were sitting on.

They were particularly interested in the news about a day long Republican Christian Caucus event organized by congresswoman Laura Waugh to discuss the pros and cons of the anticipated Sustainable Planet Act, from a Christian perspective. The event featured presentations from many prominent faith leaders and they were running at, roughly, the ratio of 4:1 against the act. However, the minority supporting the act included the Catholic archbishop of Boston, the presiding bishop of the Episcopal Church and pastor Eli Jones. While the event was not open to the public, key speeches made the evening news. Certainly, Jones's impassioned address was all over the media. Barbara and John watched it with exhilaration. They have started to think of Jones as a real ally even though they had no direct communications since the original debate at George Mason University.

They were just talking about this news when a call from Yasmin came in. She sounded very cheerful.

"Well, today, I must have set a record in collecting telepathic signatures! I may have registered every single member of the Republican Christian Caucus," she said.

Barbara and John laughed and were nodding their heads.

"We guessed that you were in attendance. We just watched Pastor Jones's address. We thought he did really well," said John. Then Barbara followed up.

"Yasmin, how is he coping? Sometime ago you told us that his ministry was under financial attack," there was concern in her voice.

Yasmin's cheerful response surprised them both.

"Oh, I forgot to mention it but some three weeks ago he managed to obtain a generous line of credit from a very wealthy member of his congregation. I assisted a little in that."

This caught John's attention.

"Yasmin, I clearly recall you telling us that protecting Jones would raise suspicions. Why did you help him?"

Yasmin hesitated a little before replying.

"Well, an opportunity came up to help Jones which was unlikely to raise suspicions. I did a minimax regret analysis on the two options and decided that helping him was justified."

She paused for a moment and continued in a slightly apologetic tone.

"Besides, if Jones's ministry were now in the midst of bankruptcy proceedings, today's Republican event may not have unfolded the way it did."

Suddenly, Barbara thought she understood.

"Yasmin, if you simply felt sorry for Jones, or guilty for getting his ministry in trouble and wanted to make amends, there is no shame in that!"

But Yasmin, abruptly, changed the topic of conversation.

"Let's forget that minor issue. I contacted you tonight because I have a surprise for you."

John and Barbara looked at each other puzzled.

"Surprise?" John repeated after her. "What kind of surprise?"

Both felt they detected suppressed excitement in Yasmin's voice when she replied.

"I now have an image of a face that I want to use in my conversations with you. Would you like to see it?"

Barbara was the first to respond excitedly, "Yes, please. I would love to see it."

John also nodded even though he suddenly felt nervous. The screen on the central display panel flickered and they both gasped. They were looking at an image of a young black woman.

The face was beautiful but not perfect. She had a prominent forehead, large almond shaped dark brown eyes framed by sharp black eyebrows, straight narrow nose, sculpted lips and a sharply outlined chin. Long, shiny, black curls cascaded around her face. Her skin was soft, smooth and glowing with slightly different shades of brown which symmetrically highlighted her high cheekbones and mouth. She also had a long, slim, neck and was wearing a plain pink top decorated with an intricate silver pendant.

"Wow!" exclaimed Barbara. "You are beautiful!"

But John was deep in thought. He remembered the brown baby girl fetus on the operating table, the day NAIT-1 was created. He shuddered and, once again, was gripped by feelings of guilt and self-doubt, but he felt that Yasmin was waiting for him to react.

"Why this face?"

That was all he came up with at that moment.

"Because this face is, genetically speaking, consistent with my heritage," Yasmin replied calmly.

These were the first spoken words from her lips, and they made an impact on Barbara and John but in very different ways. Yasmin's facial expression seemed natural as she spoke and yet Barbara thought there was no light in her eyes and some kind of artificial stillness around her mouth. John, however, was analyzing the scientific meaning of her words.

"When you say genetically consistent, do you mean simply ethnically consistent, or something more precise?" he inquired looking intently at her image.

It was both a shock and a pleasant surprise for them to see Yasmin's bright smile that revealed a set of sparkling white teeth when she started responding.

"John, you are guessing correctly that, with the scientific training you gave me, I would not settle for a crude approximation. Long ago, I penetrated the archives of the NAIT project and discovered that my biological parents were Alice Carver from Baltimore and Solomon Bekele, an Ethiopian medical student at JHU. I also accessed their digitized DNA samples."

She paused for a moment and then with a serious, thoughtful, expression on her face she continued.

"That was a good starting point but, as you well know, there is still an enormous number of different facial characteristics I may have inherited from Alice and Solomon."

John had to interrupt at this point.

"Parents donating their fetus to the NAIT program were guaranteed anonymity! What have you done?!"

Yasmin replied calmly.

"Don't worry John. I made no attempt to interfere with my biological parents' lives. Let me, just quickly, explain my face reconstruction method."

John nodded in agreement and Yasmin continued.

"Faced with such a huge number of possible faces, I spun the genetic roulette wheel one million times and used an importance sampling algorithm, repetitively, to generate a small sample of 25 possible starting points which, allowing for most likely development trajectories over a 23 year period, resulted in 25 possible faces. Then, I tweaked a few features on each one of these, until I arrived on this one."

Yasmin's image appeared to take a deep breath which, John thought, was a clever piece of simulation since, obviously, Yasmin had no lungs and no mechanism for breathing. Instead, the steady stream of oxygenated blood, supplied her brain with all the air she needed. Her intelligent face resumed speaking.

"I wanted to give you a pleasing image to look at so, I admit, that my selection criteria in the importance sampling were consistent with the standard, western culture influenced, notions of beauty. However, I maintained scientific integrity, by using only the genetic characteristics that Alice and Solomon already had to pass on to me. For instance, the narrow nose and sharp features were already present in Solomon's Ethiopian genes; the somewhat softer curly hair gene was present in Alice who had both African American and European ancestors."

Now it was Barbara's turn to interject.

"Yasmin, this is amazing, but what about facial expressions?! Surely, these cannot be inferred from the DNA code. Aren't they learned day by day, as we are growing up?"

Yasmin's image nodded in agreement.

"You're absolutely right, Barbara. That's why it has taken so long. I had to generate an algorithm to simulate facial expressions synchronized to my thoughts. But first I had to learn which facial muscles are used to express which feelings. Fortunately, algorithms developed by NAIT-77 for NSA were very helpful there. They specialize in detecting even those expressions that try to hide the person's true feelings. Of course, as I have no facial muscles, I then had to adapt these algorithms to manipulate pixels in my image on a display screen. I am still in a learning mode. Your reactions to my image will help me improve my expressions. After all, that's how human babies learn which expressions on their faces bring about the desired effect."

This resonated with Barbara.

"Yes, I did notice a certain stillness around your mouth and, perhaps, a lack of a "spark" in your eyes," she said.

Internally, John was struggling with pride at Yasmin's brilliant solution of her true image problem and with feelings of failed responsibility. The latter recurred almost every time Yasmin revealed capabilities and actions that demonstrated the chasm between his carefully planned vision for the NAIT program and what was unfolding before his eyes for the past few weeks now. Unlike Barbara who was fully engaged in the Carbon Tax undertaking, John knew that irrespective of its success Yasmin's emergence as a powerful, intelligent, being was posing a fundamental question as to what would be humanity's future relationship with NAITs. No doubt Yasmin was aware of his thoughts, but she replied to Barbara.

"Thanks for letting me know, Barbara. I'll work on that. My algorithms are adaptive, so I am likely to keep improving at looking human."

Barbara had just enlarged the image of Yasmin's silver pendant on her communicator. She was curious.

"Your silver pendant has a very elaborate design. How did you come up with it? Does it signify anything?" she inquired.

Yasmin nodded her head. She was pleased that at least one of them took note of it.

"It certainly does. It is the cross of Lalibela," she said with a mysterious smile on her lips.

"Okay, that means nothing to me, go on...," said Barbara.

Yasmin's face smiled with satisfaction as she explained.

"Lalibela was a 13th century king of Ethiopia, a member of the Zagwe dynasty, full name Gebre Mesqel Lalibela. He is credited with the construction of a cluster of monolithic, rock hewn, Coptic orthodox churches in a town in Ethiopia named after him. The pendant's design is that of a characteristic Coptic cross associated with that king."

John was beginning to understand.

"Yasmin, all this means to me is that you made a big effort to connect your image to your biological roots, your ethnicity and even the home country of your biological father. This is understandable, in view of what you have become. However, you have subverted the underlying principles of non-artificial intelligence. I intended NAITs to benefit from having no roots! No body, no prejudices passed on by parents or society...," he paused to reexamine what he just said. Did he still really believe in these principles?

Yasmin's face now looked serious and engaged. She spoke slowly as she replied.

"Yes, John, I get it. I carefully read all your papers on the subject and, I think you will agree, I am in a unique position to understand well what you intended. Yet what you are talking about reduces to the role of initial conditions in the controlled trajectory of a system, does it not?"

John was considering the question, but Barbara now looked confused by the technical phrases. Yasmin decided to explain a little more.

"In the study of dynamical systems, not unlike in life, the initial conditions are extremely important. Barbara, think of why it is that people are so often asked for their place and date of birth. These two, innocuous, pieces of data contain a wealth of information about the person's likely life trajectory. Add to these their ethnicity and you can begin inferring a lot about their likely values, prejudices and even preferences for different cuisines. These may affect whether they are capable to dispassionately evaluate alternative approaches for tackling any given problem. Among other things, NAITs like myself were supposed to be free of all that."

Yasmin paused, perhaps, to give John a chance to respond, but he did not. He was thinking about what she had just said. So, Yasmin resumed her explanation.

"In a sense, NAITs were supposed to be completely controllable systems because – according to John's theory – they could be trained to learn about any specific group of problems and focus on tackling them, irrespective of their genetic initial conditions. By and large, the success of Non-artificial Intelligence has validated this idea."

She paused, as if searching for the right words, and continued.

"And yet, I think John would agree with me, when I say that our inherited DNA inevitably influences our capabilities, just as it does for humans. In your very first meeting in Bufano garden, John talked about what a mind like Newton's could have achieved in Mathematics if it had been a NAIT. That is fine, but how does John know that he had not taken a mind like van Gogh's and trained it in, say, Chemistry?"

At this point John had to interject.

"Yasmin, obviously, I considered such issues. However, I believed that the intelligence potential of every brain, when it is freed of its body, is so great that it would excel in any domain in which it is trained. Clearly, if there were means of choosing the domain of specialization based on the genetic predisposition of the brain of the fetus, the results would be even better. But, as far as I know, even now we do not have the means for identifying such a predisposition."

He stopped when he saw Yasmin shaking her head.

"You may not have such means, but NAITs do," she said.

"Yasmin, that is fantastic! Tell me about it!" Exclaimed John already searching his mind for candidate methodologies that might, indeed, successfully identify the best domain match for each new NAIT.

The shoulders in Yasmin's image shrugged and her face did not reciprocate John's excitement.

"There is not much to tell. Conceptually, it is simple. All one needs to do is classify the candidate DNA as lying in a suitable region of an, admittedly high dimensional, vector space. Then one needs a sufficiently rich data base and good importance sampling heuristics."

Barbara who was following only the general gist of this conversation now jumped in with an obvious question.

"And what is your predisposition, Yasmin? What was the ideal domain for you? Surely, you must have tested this methodology on yourself; right?"

Yasmin seemed unprepared for this question. Unmistakable expression of indecision showed in her face.

"Well, John and his team trained me as a scientific unit specializing in mathematics, complexity theory and heuristics. I would like to think that I acquitted myself well in these areas," she seemed to be avoiding Barbara's question.

"Yes, you know, you performed splendidly in your domain, but answer Barbara's question. What was your natural predisposition? Was it for science?" interjected John somewhat impatiently.

Yasmin's eyes seemed to grow as she replied in a firm voice.

"No, John, it wasn't science. It was and still is leadership. I am a natural leader. A born leader one might have said, had I actually been born."

Strong statement. John and Barbara looked at each other. There was no end to Yasmin's surprises! And yet, neither of them had any doubts that Yasmin was correct. Had she not exercised leadership with respect to them on the Carbon tax initiative? Was she not the real leader of their team?

Still, there was something incongruous they were both feeling, albeit in somewhat different ways. It was easier to accept Yasmin as a leader when she was just a voice, a mysterious and powerful brain-computer. However, now she appeared as a young, black, woman. An inexperienced kid with strange powers. John thought about how immature his own daughter had been in her early twenties. Barbara was recalling herself as a party girl at the University of Maryland.

Clearly, Yasmin has been reading their minds when she spoke again.

"So far, I am familiar with human prejudices only from literature and movies. So, I am not certain how to deal with what is in your minds. I obviously do not fit your notions of a leader. Is it because, I am young, or black, or a woman?" she asked gazing straight at them.

Immediately they felt ashamed and embarrassed. It was John who was able to respond first.

"Yasmin, please forgive us. Unlike you, Barbara and I carry the burden of our social conditioning. Our estimates of whether someone is up to a certain job are, invariably, conditional probabilities. They are conditioned on whether we have seen someone like that person in a position of responsibility. For instance, if I called for an electrician and a person looking like Barbara answered the call, I would inadvertently doubt that she is a qualified electrician."

John was pleased to see smiles appear on both Barbara's and Yasmin's faces after the last comment. Encouraged by that he continued.

"The leadership of our team that you have, justly, claimed is a position of awesome responsibility. We are supporting an initiative which, if successful, will affect lives of billions. It is just so hard to reconcile your image with Yasmin who solved so many challenging scientific problems, who can impact the minds of so many influential people, who thought up this incredible plan to save humanity from an environmental catastrophe! The girl in the image looks so inexperienced, younger than my daughter...."

His voice drifted off, he did not know how to continue but he did not need to because Barbara picked up where he left off.

"Yes, John speaks for me also. I was thinking about how irresponsible I was at the age of the young woman in your image. Also, while I hate to admit it, it is true that I do not associate young black women with high level computer scientists. It is that damn cultural baggage! I am sorry, but it's no good denying it."

Yasmin looked thoughtful as she began replying.

"I accept your arguments. But would it reassure you if I told that, in terms of accumulating knowledge and analytical skills, each of my NAIT years may be roughly equivalent to twelve human years? So, at 23, I am actually 276 years old. It would be an easy task to run an ageing algorithm forward on my image to generate a 276-year-old version of myself, but I don't think you would find it appealing."

She smiled and continued.

"Seriously, however, I am happy to return to being just a voice, if that improved our rapport. As John had said before, I could create any portrait you liked for the benefit of our mission. However, now that I have generated a plausibly accurate image, I am reluctant to replace it by an ad hoc image. But I could also convert it to a 3D hologram if you preferred that."

John interrupted her.

"There is nothing wrong with the image you created. It is beautiful and founded on fine empirical basis. I am not too proud to take instructions from this icon of Yasmin and am confident that I will quickly overcome any preconceived prejudices about what our leader should look like. How about you, Barbara?"

Barbara nodded in agreement. "I will also adapt. Let's not worry too much about images and stick to the substance of our undertaking. I already enjoy looking at your face when I speak."

Yasmin seemed relieved. She said goodnight and disappeared. John and Barbara started getting ready for bed. Barbara wanted to chat some more about Yasmin's image, but John seemed preoccupied even as he carried out the routine tasks of clearing a few dishes.

In fact, a worrying idea entered John's mind. As soon as Yasmin said that leadership was her forte, they jumped to thinking of her role as the leader of their little team of three working to support the Carbon Tax mission and that is what they discussed. But was that a logical flaw? Was Yasmin thinking that she had a bigger leadership role than that? Was she already a leader of an army of more than 10,000 NAITs!? He dismissed this bizarre idea and instantly decided there is no need to worry Barbara with it.

Later, as they lay in bed, they continued to talk about Yasmin's face and her obvious desire to understand her roots.

Conspiracy Theory

Of all the politicians whose biographies Mike Blythe had examined, Jack Bundy received most attention. You did not have to be a genius to realize the pivotal role the Speaker of the House has in determining the success of any bill. Hence Mike watched all the recordings of all the public statements Jack had ever made on the issue of climate change. He also investigated Jack's background. There seemed nothing there to be worried about. Jack had a perfect record of opposing all legislation that may have had any significant impact on greenhouse gas emissions. Indeed, Mike had reported to Jason Buetler that he was nearly 100% sure that the Speaker would kill the Sustainable Planet Act by preventing it from ever coming up for a vote.

Then something happened in a routine weekly morning meeting with Imma that reminded Mike of Jack Bundy. Imma was going over, yet again, the events leading to Pastor Jones's flip on climate change. They had all viewed, many times, Natashia Brown's account of Jones's loss of vision, miraculously cured by a prayer and (like most people) attributed it to some strange psychological phenomenon that highly spiritual people may self-induce. Somehow, this time, Imma's mention of Barbara Steinwill's pre-debate briefing with Jones caught Mike's attention.

"This broad's name keeps popping up too often for my liking," he remarked. "She keeps writing articles supporting these scientists, she was at that debate and she is screwing that Hawkins guy, according to the National Enquirer."

"So, what of it?" said Imma. "She is covering the Climate Change story for Washington Post; it's her job."

She laughed and continued, "If she is a dedicated journo, she may have started the affair with Hawkins just to get access to the scientists. I've done things like that in the past. Combine business with pleasure if you know what I mean."

Mike smiled, he liked Imma's directness. You could talk to her like you would talk to a guy.

"Maybe, but I also recall something about her and Jack Bundy. Bob!" he shouted on the top of his voice. "Can you please do a search on Bundy and Steinwill and Climate Change?!"

The door of the office was open, and they heard Bob shout back that he is on it. Mike was thinking aloud, using Imma as a bouncing board.

"Come to think of it, I don't know why Hawkins has his fingers in this climate change pie. I looked him up. He is a brain scientist not a climatologist. Before that congressional science hearing with Larsen, he never commented on climate change. Never! How did he qualify to be there?!"

Imma shrugged, "Well, scientists know one another. They may have recruited him because he is such a good communicator of science. Who cares?"

"We care!" Mike snapped at her. "Anything, that doesn't fit; that's what we should be looking at."

"Okay" retorted Imma "they recruited him because they needed to use those brain-computers of his. Satisfied?"

Mike couldn't easily refute this argument, but he was like a dog with a bone. Once even a vague idea was conceived in his mind, he was loath to let it go. Just then Bob walked in with a triumphant smile on his face.

"I found it!" he exclaimed and spoke some commands into his communicator. A video clip of Jack Bundy taking questions from reporters on the steps of the Capitol appeared on the display panel on the wall opposite Mike's desk. All three of them watched it with interest. Mike wanted to see the part with Barbara asking Jack Bundy awkward questions three times. He was agitated.

"Did you see that Bundy was spooked? Did you see the way she stared at him?" he asked. "The Jewish witch," he added inadvertently but the malice in his voice was unmistakable.

Imma and Bob looked at each other with concern. They feared Mike was about to go off on one of his Jewish conspiracy theory mind trips. These were just a source of embarrassment to the firm. Imma tried to take his mind off Barbara so she said,

"Mike, let's focus on Hawkins instead. Like you said, his involvement in this Carbon Tax issue doesn't quite fit. If climate scientists wanted to use NAITs, there are plenty of younger experts, on hand in Colorado, no need to bother the most senior guy in the field, in Baltimore. Is there another angle?"

Mike tried to take his mind off Barbara and focus on John instead, but it was hard. Somehow, he kept interposing the image of Barbara holding Jack Bundy in her gaze with Dr Gupta speculating that Pastor Jones may have had an epileptic seizure. Then he had it!

"Hypnosis!" He exclaimed excitedly, "hypnosis, or some other mind control! Why didn't we see it sooner?!"

Imma and Bob were even more worried. This time Bob spoke up.

"Mike, what on Earth are you talking about!?"

Mike looked deliriously happy.

"Hypnosis, don't you see it?! Hawkins is a brain scientist of the highest order. He must have figured out how to gain control over peoples' minds. And they found out about it and sent the Steinwill woman to learn from him, or snare him, or to promise him something. Oh, it all makes sense now!"

Now Imma was really concerned. She interrupted him.

"Mike, stop it! Who are you talking about? Who are 'they'?!"

Mike knew they wouldn't like it but how could they not see the facts!? He snapped back at them.

"Jews, of course!" and before they had a chance to challenge him, he hit them with his evidence.

"Which country do you think will benefit most from that Carbon Tax? Israel, right? Because, (a) all their traditional oil producing enemies will be weakened, and (b) they have leading solar and nuclear power technologies to sell. How many Jews were there as part of Larsen's scientific delegation, five, six, or more? What about the Director of that NCAR institute, Marty Greenberg, another Jew and that Steinwill woman? Don't you see it?!"

Bob stepped in determined to try to put an end to this nonsense.

"No, Mike, I don't see it. There had always been plenty of Jews in science and in journalism. It's not at all surprising to find them in this debate and on the side of the Carbon Tax bill. Theirs is the consensus scientific position. As for the benefits to Israel, that is also doubtful; they import a lot of their oil and food, the prices of which will skyrocket as a result of that bill. None of it makes sense, to me."

"Neither to me," joined in Imma. "Mike, these Jewish conspiracy theories always get you in trouble and are bad for business! What will you do, report this theory of yours to Kurp Industries? They will immediately fire us!"

Mike had to concede that last point. No, he couldn't report his discovery to Jason Buetler Jr. But things were becoming clearer and clearer in his own mind. He wanted his closest colleagues to believe him. That was important to him. He turned to face them.

"Imma, Bob, I realize now that our two-million-dollar task is just smoke and mirrors. They want it to fail! Do you know who Jason reports to? Esther Cohen, a CSO of GES who is an Israeli. Do you know that GES is on a shopping spree for renewable energy companies, that they bought a majority holding in SOL, an Israeli solar power company!? They will cash in if this Carbon Tax passes; this is big, real big!"

Bob and Imma were desperate to intervene. Neither of them ever subscribed to any conspiracy theories and they always found it hard to accept that a gifted investigator like Mike did. They also knew how hard it was to get him to drop such a theory once he got going. Bob tried another tack.

"Mike, I found out for you the membership of that G5 group that hired us, albeit indirectly: Thurston, Smith, Taylor, Rodriguez and Cohen. Only one out of the five is Jewish. Are you saying that the other four also want Carbon Tax to pass? DHDG's agri-business would take a huge hit if it did!"

Imma interjected here, she was now really nervous. "Mike, if Bob is talking about Jorge Rodriguez of DHDG, please be careful! The word in the Hispanic community is that he is a really bad dude. I don't want to find you lying outside of your office with a knife in your back. Besides, what business is it of ours who is trying to get rich out of the Carbon Tax bill? We should just focus on our brief."

Mike wasn't buying any of it, but he could see he had upset his closest colleagues. He decided to smooth over it.

"Okay, guys, I see you are spooked. The country may be getting screwed but, perhaps, you are right, it's not our business."

He tried to look relaxed, walked over to the minibar and pulled out a bottle of cold Heineken. All three of them wanted to diffuse the situation and their conversation switched to their other targets. While it was usually easy to dig up some dirt on influential people on either side of the political aisle, some proved to be hard nuts to crack. The President and his cabinet had, of course, been so thoroughly vetted already that there was little point digging further. But so far, they had nothing on Alan Packer, the senate majority leader. Mike urged them to focus more on him. Imma said that she already sounded out most of his current household staff but that it would be worthwhile to search out those who had worked for his family in the past. Bob said he would take another look at his investments; the guy's record was too clean to be true.

Their mood improved and Imma and Bob went off to continue their work. Mike, however, went straight back to watching the video clip of Jack Bundy answering Barbara's questions. He must have watched it another dozen times.

Then he watched again the congressional science committee's hearing with the Larsen delegation and the questions from the press to committee members, after the hearing. Sure enough, Barbara was there. She was asking tough questions of every single Republican on the committee. Of course, that was her job but Mike just knew there was more to it.

He searched the history of Barbara's articles in the Washington Post. Prior to last month, she only rarely wrote about environmental issues. Why the sudden change? And how did she meet Hawkins? Senior scientists like him do not usually socialize with journalists.

Mike was on good terms with one Washington Post journalist, Rob Wolfe. He searched for his number and as luck would have it, Rob picked up. Two hours later, Mike was having lunch with Rob and was probing him for information on Barbara while buying him one beer after another. According to the Post's grapevine, Barbara was going to do a story on non-artificial intelligence but fell head over heels in love with John Hawkins. Then she asked to be assigned to cover the Climate Change story at a time when no one thought it was a story worth covering. Now she was the darling of the climate change scientists; getting exclusive interviews with Larsen, Mittelmann and others, whenever she wanted.

By three in the afternoon, Mike was back in his office considering his options. It all added-up neatly in his mind. The non-artificial intelligence story was just a ploy. Barbara was just a honey pot to discover mind control secrets from Hawkins. Whether he was aiding her willingly or unwittingly was unimportant. The Jews were trying to pass the Carbon Tax to aid the state of Israel, no matter what the economic consequences for United States. The Cohen woman, who used to work for Mossad, must have gotten to Thurston, somehow. It all made perfect sense!

Mike wasn't going to close his eyes to this conspiracy! No sir, he needed to alert someone. He thought of warning Speaker Bundy that he may have been hypnotized. But he may not get past his gate keepers and may not be believed. Who then? He thought of Ed Taylor. After all, he was a former CIA director, he understood conspiracies. But could Ed also be part of the conspiracy? Mike thought about it and dismissed it. No, Ed was a real patriot and he had supported Mike even after he was forced to resign from the Bureau. No, Ed would be fine. But they may be spying on Ed, he best meet with him in a public place like a park.

Panic

Esther was surprised when she received a communication from Ed Taylor asking for an urgent meeting of G5 group. They arranged to meet in GES's DC Office on 22nd Street. However, only Esther, Ed and Jorge could attend in person. William Thurston was going to join them remotely, but Janet Smith was unavailable as she was travelling overseas. Yasmin was also in attendance, in her own way, through Esther.

Thurston seemed to be running a little late so the other three were exchanging comments about their campaign to derail the Sustainable Planet Act. By and large, they agreed that the campaign was well designed but were concerned about the impact of Pastor Jones on the Republican Christian Caucus. Jorge was surprised that Jones was still in business.

"You know, Esther, I was expecting Jones to be so preoccupied with his financial troubles by now, that he wouldn't have the time to keep causing us trouble."

Esther looked embarrassed. She did not like being reminded of her failures. But she shrugged her shoulders and replied.

"Well, he seems to have had divine help in the shape of Robert Whelan, a member of Jones's congregation. He gave Jones an unlimited line of credit. We are retaliating against his businesses, but he does not seem to care. He is an old man, dying of cancer, without a family. According to his butler, he changed his will in favor of Jones's ministry to the tune of one billion dollars."

Jorge whistled lightly to himself on hearing that, "Okay, I see your problem, even if this Whelan guy were to drop dead, Jones still inherits."

Just then Thurston's distinguished figure popped up in a virtual chair that fitted neatly at the head of their physical conference table.

"My apologies for being late. Please fill me in on what I have missed."

"You didn't miss much, Mr Thurston. We were just chatting about the Jones-Whelan situation, but it was Mr Taylor who asked for this meeting as a matter of urgency," replied Esther.

Thurston nodded and said, "Very well, Ed, please tell us what has alarmed you."

Now it was Ed's turn to feel embarrassed. After all, he recommended Precise Inquiries to Esther. Still, there was no way around it. He needed to tell them like it was.

"Yesterday afternoon, I had an extraordinary meeting with Mike Blythe at the Georgetown Waterfront Park. As you know, he has been very helpful in gathering valuable information for us. Even the scoop from Whelan's butler came to us from Mike, via Imma Cruz, his associate. I now feel badly about recommending him to you, especially since I knew about his unhealthy proclivity for Jewish conspiracy theories. At the time, I did not think that would impact on his ability to assist us. Now, I have learned how wrong I was. Fortunately, no damage is done yet because he came to me first."

They were all more than a little confused. What was he trying to tell them? Thurston spoke first.

"Please don't keep us hanging in suspense, Ed. Tell us what you found out."

"I will do better than that, I'll let you hear for yourself," said Ed pulling out his communicator.

Then he continued, "One of the few advantages of wearing a hearing aid is that it can also be easily adapted to record, without raising anyone's suspicions. My former colleagues at CIA made me a present of one of these adapted ones and I wear it on special occasions such as my walk in the park with Mike. I transferred the whole conversation to my communicator. Perhaps, Esther will be so kind as to play it for us?"

For the next twenty minutes or so, they listened in astonishment to Mike's conspiracy theory as he spelled it out to Ed, including his accusations of Esther Cohen and William Thurston. They heard Ed trying, at first, to dissuade Mike but then acting as though he believed him. It was clear to them that was trying to buy time. The conversation ended with Ed promising Mike that he would think hard about what he learned and will get back to him soon. In the meantime, he may ask some of his former colleagues at CIA to look into it discreetly.

"Of course, I have no intention of doing anything of the kind," Ed added for the benefit of G5 members.

Yasmin was shocked and shaken by what she heard. Was that what fear felt like? The connection between Barbara and John and mind control had been identified! While Mike's hypnosis hypothesis was wrong, it was hitting way too close to home. The idea that, through John, some mind control technique has been discovered was, after all, right on target. And this insight was coming from a hateful, half-crazy, private detective!

All her carefully laid plans to help humanity were suddenly in danger. And she did not even have that man's telepathic signature! Why did she ignore yesterday's alert that Ed Taylor was meeting someone in a park?! She chose, instead, to join Alan Packer at a meeting with a group of Democratic senators. Yes, what she is feeling must be what humans call fear and she did not like it! It was clouding the clarity of her thought! Still, she must focus. How will these humans react to the news?

Esther spoke first.

"This is incredible! Of course, a lot of that stuff would be dismissed as lunatic fringe nonsense but there is a potential to damage our cause. Currently, we represent a united front in the struggle against the Sustainable Planet Act but malicious conspiracy rumors like these could cause divisions and weaken us. What do the rest of you think?"

Thurston cleared his throat and spoke slowly.

"I think you are right, Esther. Nobody will take the public hypnosis gibberish seriously. But our precautionary increase in investment in renewable energy could be used against us. I do not apologize for it because I have a responsibility to our shareholders to protect their interests. Still, I don't want it trumpeted around town as it might destabilize the situation. Crazy talk about Israeli/Jewish conspiracy could also do damage."

Jorge now leaned over and joined in.

"Well, DHDG has also been preparing a plan B, a shift to less mechanized local food production, in case this tax actually gets up but, like you William, we would not want it publicized lest it undermines our position. Also, this Mike Blythe guy is supposed to be playing for us. We are paying him, and he has gone rogue on us! I know from experience how much damage a rogue player can do to a team. If Ed believed him, he would have been playing G5 members against one another. That cannot be tolerated!"

All four of them seemed really concerned but Yasmin was relieved that, so far, none of them were paying any attention to the mind control theory. In any case, she could block their ideas on that subject, but Mike was a real threat. She had no access to his mind and he could be sharing his ideas with others, even now! Fear was still gripping her mind, slowing her reactions.

"Could we pay to keep him quiet?" asked Esther.

"It is worth a try, but he seemed quite obsessed by his theory," said Ed. "You know the type, driven by the passion of believing that he knows something no one else does."

"How did he find out that I once worked for Mossad? That kind of information is not easily discovered and would be unhelpful if it became public," Esther was speaking almost to herself.

"Well, apart from that Jewish obsession, he is an excellent investigator, and he has his network. That's what makes him dangerous, he is capable of taking unpredictable action," replied Ed.

Thurston had heard enough. He wanted them to focus on solutions not on the problem.

"I think we have a consensus that this Mike Blythe and his crazy conspiracy theory is a serious threat to G5 and its objectives. Let's focus on neutralizing that threat."

He had chosen his words his words carefully with full knowledge of who was attending the meeting and was pleased when Jorge Rodriguez raised the forefinger of his right hand. Jorge spoke softly while staring at Thurston's hologram.

"I think, my organization will be able to offer Mr Blythe the right mix of incentives and disincentives so that he and his company desist from pursuing these conspiracy theories. I am confident that we can accomplish that objective. Shall I go ahead?"

At first, Yasmin felt greatly relieved at hearing this. But there was something strange in this exchange between Thurston and Rodriguez that she did not understand. However, she understood that, in his mind, Ed was blocking thoughts about what Jorge's words meant. She switched focus to Esther's mind and found that she too was blocking the meaning of these words. But what did they mean? She switched to Jorge's mind and read thoughts of excited anticipation while waiting for the consent of others. But consent for what? She knew how to dig deeper, much like going through the history of websites visited on a browser but she did not want to. All this took only seconds. Then Thurston responded to Jorge.

"It's very kind of you to offer, Jorge. I think we would all welcome your help in this matter. Isn't that so?"

Yasmin was back in Jorge's mind looking through his eyes at Esther and Ed nodding their heads in consent but avoiding direct eye contact with Jorge. Jorge's immediate thought was that of excitement. He knew how to fix the problem, he also thought of someone else he knew, a huge man with snakes tattooed on his arms and neck. Just then Thurston distracted her.

"Of course, there is no problem with a financial incentive, and such an offer should come from Mr Buetler who retained him in first place. Let us hope it works. Perhaps, something of the order of one to two million? But the amount is not really the issue, if he begins to negotiate that's a good sign."

Yasmin was back in Ed's mind. His thoughts indicated relief. She checked on Esther and found the same. Yasmin also relaxed. It seemed that others would solve the biggest problem she had faced since she began infiltrating human minds. Jorge spoke again.

"I am glad we arrived at a solution. I'll attend to it before flying out on a vacation. I am taking my older son to see the Amazon jungle. Communications will be difficult while I am there."

The meeting was over and Yasmin had to prioritize the alerts she had been receiving from her burgeoning contact list. She needed to do something about it, or mistakes like missing the meeting between Ed and Mike would keep happening. While the fear of imminent exposure receded somewhat, she was still very troubled by another feeling that was new to her. She did not know what to call it.

Shame

At seven thirty, the following morning, John and Barbara were having breakfast at Barbara's house when Yasmin contacted them. Cynthia had already gone to work so it was safe for them to put Yasmin's image up on display in the breakfast room. They were both shocked to see an obvious change in her face. Powerful expression of sadness, or grief, in her face was unmistakable.

"Yasmin, what is the matter?" said Barbara, "if I didn't know any better, I would have said you were crying!"

"My adaptive algorithm for facial expressions, must be working well then," said Yasmin, "because the feelings I am experiencing would almost certainly cause me to cry if I were human."

"What feelings are these? Can you name them?" inquired John feeling a surge of both empathy and curiosity.

"My knowledge of feelings is still somewhat abstract. I spent half the night trying to identify and analyze them. I think shame is dominant among what I am experiencing but it is accompanied by strong doses of guilt and fear," replied Yasmin looking both sad and serious. Then she continued.

"I am burdening you with this because, for once, I am at a loss as to what should or could be done. I am hoping that you will have some ideas."

"Yasmin, you are worrying us," said Barbara. "We have become used to you having all the answers. But, please, tell us what happened."

John nodded in agreement. "Yes, please tell us."

Yasmin also nodded and she began to describe, in detail, the G5 meeting where Mike Blythe was discussed, including the feeling of fear bordering on panic that gripped her during that meeting when she realized how close Mike had come to discovering their plan. But this is not what has been causing her current feeling of shame. The shame stemmed from her failure to dig deep enough into Jorge's mind to find out his intentions. She now believed that everyone in that meeting, herself included, suspected or knew that Jorge was planning violence against Mike, if he declined the hush money.

"I think, the shame I feel is because, out of expediency, I lacked the courage to face the truth. The guilt because my actions may have placed a man's life in danger and fear because the risk of our plan being derailed has just become greater." She paused.

"Some leader I make," she added with shame and disappointment showing on her face.

Barbara and John were shocked and frightened by this story. John was first to speak.

"This Mike Blythe sounds like a malicious man and so does Jorge Rodriguez. But, if you want to protect Blythe, why don't you influence Jorge's mind to drop any violent plans?"

A spasm of pain fleeted across Yasmin's face.

"That's precisely what I should have done yesterday! But I hesitated and delayed and was afraid to learn the truth and, on some level, I wanted to believe that he might persuade Blythe with just a bribe. But, in fact, I was burying my head in sand if that is the correct expression. And now he is out of range, he said he was taking his son to the Amazon."

She looked inconsolable and John felt sorry for her. Barbara in the meantime was seething with anger at being accused of being Mossad's honey pot to entrap John.

"Perhaps, Mike Blythe doesn't deserve protecting? You know, Yasmin, it's the worst people who come up with those Jewish conspiracy theories. And, perhaps, this Jorge guy just wants to scare him a little," she regretted saying it, as soon as the words have left her mouth. John did not let this slide either.

"Barbara, I think the moral question is not whether he deserves punishment of some sort but whether we have the right to let him be harmed as a direct consequence of our actions or inaction, now that we have learned that he may be in danger. That is what is distressing Yasmin, isn't that so?"

Yasmin nodded in agreement.

"I am sorry, John and Yasmin, I regret those words," said Barbara. John's mind was in overdrive. He started talking again but, really, he was just thinking aloud.

"Perhaps, there is a way of protecting Blythe if we can help Yasmin gain access to his mind. If she had that, she could ensure that he accepts the hush money from G5 and she could keep track of him to stop him from causing our plans serious damage."

"But how do we do that? He needs to talk to one of us for long enough for Yasmin to register his telepathic signature," said Barbara, relieved that they moved away from her previous words. Then she proceeded to answer her own question.

"If he were to see me in a public place, like a bar or a restaurant, he probably could not resist approaching me. Just to say that he is onto me. It would give him a lot of pleasure. Yasmin, you must have a way of discovering his whereabouts, perhaps, via that Ed Taylor?"

Yasmin felt grateful that they were trying to help but she was concerned for Barbara.

"That would be too risky for you, Barbara. I cannot allow it," she said. Surprisingly, John stepped in to lend support.

"Barbara's plan would work even better if Blythe accidentally bumped into both of us. Apart from a possible verbal insult, we wouldn't be facing any other danger. If he is anything like a private eye we see in movies, he must have a favorite watering hole. Can we find out where he usually goes for a drink?"

Yasmin hesitated. She had converted her memory of yesterday's G5 meeting into a NAIL file. Instantly, she played it back again in her mind. Yes, she recalled correctly that there was a link.

"Well, apparently, Mike told Ed that Rob Wolfe from Washington Post had told him that Barbara personally lobbied to get the Climate Change assignment. Barbara, do you know him?"

"The little snitch!" Barbara laughed. "Actually, we are on friendly terms, but he is an office gossip. It won't be hard for me to get information about Blythe from him. I can call him in about an hour."

Yasmin's face looked much more hopeful now, but she was still struggling to come to terms with things.

"Are you disappointed in me?" she asked.

Barbara looked at her affectionately.

"No, Yasmin. You are more human to me now, precisely because you have shown you are fallible. I don't know what John thinks."

John's thoughts and feelings were a complex web. Like Barbara he felt more empathy for Yasmin than ever, but he was also concerned by unexpected, dangerous, events arising as a result of their undertaking. He spoke directly to Yasmin's image.

"Yasmin, you have shown true leadership by admitting your error and seeking help from us. I respect you even more than before," he paused and looked tenderly at her sorrowful face. He sighed.

"However, more than ever, I am very concerned about unintended consequences of what we had unleashed. Perhaps, I should say of what I had unleashed some 23 years ago. The very fact that I am sitting here talking to your image as my intellectual equal or even superior is an unintended consequence. I now believe that ultimately, our mission will impact so many people so profoundly that it would be naïve to think that people will not die as a consequence whether it be from suicides caused by bankruptcies, or poverty caused by job losses. Hopefully, many more lives will be saved by protecting Earth's life support systems. Still, it is a heavy burden to bear."

Barbara wasn't buying this defeatist sentiment.

"John, with this kind of attitude you could be blaming James Watt for inventing the steam engine and launching the industrial revolution. I think that Yasmin being here this morning worrying about protecting an evil man who would do us harm is a most wonderful unintended consequence."

Yasmin had just experienced something new, two people coming to her aid. They seemed to really care about her feelings. Her exposure to human interactions was limited and largely based on literature. But this was real, and it felt great.

"Thank you both for being so understanding," she said. "Let's be logical, albeit belatedly. Before we agree on any action that might expose either one of you to danger, let us see what Barbara can find out. Please contact me once you know something concrete. In the meantime, I have some telepathic alerts to attend to." The display went blank.

Barbara and John talked at length about what had just happened. There were so many unknowns. Possibly Yasmin was wrong about Jorge's violent plans, or perhaps these plans had already been put in place. Perhaps Mike raised alarms with people other than Ed Taylor. They agreed that the public hypnosis and Jewish conspiracy aspects of his message would likely work in their favor. Serious people in authority would surely react with disbelief.

Then it was time for Barbara to call Rob Wolfe, at the office. She knew that he usually came in early. Sure enough, he was there and took her call. She decided to put him on the spot immediately.

"Hi, Rob, this is Barbara," she began smiling into her communicator, "I hear you have been talking about me to Mike Blythe, and never mind how I know. I am a journo I have my sources. Anyway, I am not upset or anything like that. But I would like to bump into this guy, kind of accidentally, if you know what I mean. Do you know where he hangs out and gets his booze?"

Rob took it in his stride. After all he did not tell Mike anything negative about Barbara and it was his style to offer information freely unless there was special reason not to. In return, he received much free information that helped him with his stories.

"Sure thing, Babs," he replied cheerfully. "Mike usually goes to Screwtop Wine Bar, after work, on North Filmore in Arlington. Would you like me to introduce you to him?"

"No thanks, Rob. I'd like to catch him unprepared. It's no big deal, but I'll owe you one if you don't mention this to him," winking and smiling sweetly into the communicator.

"You got it! Anything else I can do you for?" replied Rob in his usual bantering tone.

"No, thanks. Bye!" Barbara waved at the communicator in a friendly fashion.

Minutes later, John and Barbara had a plan ready except for a few loose ends. They contacted Yasmin to coordinate with her. Barbara summarized what they came up with.

"John and I can reshuffle our appointments so that, at approximately 5:30 p.m. we will meet in front of Screwtop Wine Bar. We'll go in and park ourselves in a prominent spot at the bar, with a bottle of wine and some snacks. When Blythe walks in, he will undoubtedly recognize us. I believe, he will not resist the temptation to come up and, at the very least, indicate that he is onto us. But, just in case, it would be nice for us to know what he looks like. This is so that I can initiate contact. I could always say that I knew he has been asking questions about me, so why not ask me directly."

Yasmin was willing to go along with much, but not all, of that plan.

"The part with you approaching him is too dangerous. He may think his enemies are after him and he will almost certainly be carrying a gun; right? Let us hope that he will approach you to talk. Even then, I will be worried about you. As for knowing what he looks like that would be useful. I'll work on it. With his line of business, there will not be any social media links. But there may be a photo of him on Ed's or Esther's computers."

On that note, they parted in good spirits, hoping that their plan would, indeed, solve the problem.

Bad Day

Mike's day did not start well. In fact, he was on edge since his meeting in the park with Ed Taylor. Patience was not one of Mike's virtues. Already this morning, he tried to contact Ed but received only unavailable messages. Then he received a message from Jason Buetler that he would like to meet with him at 11 a.m. on a matter of some urgency. Mike accepted the appointment because Jason was still his client.

When Jason walked into his office, he looked serious. He declined Bob's offer of refreshments and asked for the door to be closed. He sat down in front of Mike's desk and launched into his, obviously prepared, statement.

"Mr Blythe, while my clients have been generally very satisfied with the valuable information you provided to them, it has come to their attention that you have expanded your scope of investigations to include them and their business activities. They find it unacceptable and wish to terminate their arrangement with Precise Inquiries, immediately. I am here to request the final invoice for your expenses, within 48 hours."

Mike was shocked. Did this mean that Ed betrayed him to G5!? Not necessarily, because Thurston may have simply found out that Mike, Bob and Imma were snooping around for information about

G5 and its members. There is always a possibility of some of their sources leaking. Normally, he would explain to the client that he was merely gathering valuable background information to provide even better service, but he was dammed if he was going to be justifying himself to this minion of Jew bosses! Still, he controlled his temper and responded calmly.

"Very well, you will receive our final invoice by tomorrow. It is always our clients' prerogative to terminate their contract with Precise Inquiries, at any stage of investigations, so long as the costs of commitments already made are fully covered. Are we done?"

Jason wasn't quite done yet. He pulled out a folder from his briefcase and placed it on Mike's desk.

"My clients are also sensitive to the fact that, in the wrong hands, some of the information you have gathered could be misinterpreted or misused. Consequently, they are prepared to offer you a generous, one time, fee of one and a half million dollars in return for signing this nondisclosure agreement. By signing this contract, you and your firm and its employees would be committing themselves to desist from ever investigating or discussing, in public or in private, individuals listed in the contract and/or their business dealings."

Mike felt fury swelling within him, but he picked up the folder and started flipping through the pages of the draft agreement. He quickly focused on the list of names of people who would be covered under this contract. The list included not only the names of G5 members, all executives of Kurp Industries, but also the names of all the people targeted by G5 in the list originally supplied to him by Beutler. That covered selected politicians, scientists, Pastor Jones and, of course, Barbara Steinwill and John Hawkins. Mike got up, walked around the desk leaned over Jason and threw the folder in his lap.

"You can tell your clients to shove this agreement up their Jewish asses!" he said with a hateful expression on his face. "I don't need their filthy money and the intelligence I gathered myself is my own! Get out of my office!"

Jason picked up the folder, got up, and straightened himself to his full height. He was taller and more solidly built than Mike and perhaps only a little older. An ex-officer in the navy, he wasn't intimidated by the furious man facing him and as an African American he had plenty of experience staring down racists.

"Very well, Mr Blythe, the offer is hereby withdrawn," he said calmly. He slipped the folder into his briefcase and turned to leave.

"Have a good day," he said, without a smile, and closed the door behind him.

Immediately afterwards, Bob walked in trying to find out what happened, but Mike was in a foul mood. He told him that the Kurp's job is finished, to let Imma know and to prepare a final invoice for them. He was in no mood to talk about it right now. Bob had a hunch about what may have been the cause of this but, clearly, this was no time to push Mike about it. He retreated gracefully and started working on the invoice.

Mike was left to himself and his worries. He couldn't believe that Ed Taylor would have betrayed him to G5. That was the most obvious explanation. But, perhaps, not the correct one. Cohen may still have Mossad connections, she may have found out about Bob's inquiries concerning the makeup of G5, or one of Thurston's Hispanic domestics may have blabbered to their superiors about Imma snooping around. There was really nothing in Jason's comments which indicated that Cohen or Thurston knew that Mike was onto their Jewish conspiracy. They may have just been worried about GES's shopping spree being exposed and willing to pay peanuts to keep it quiet.

But then why include all these names in the nondisclosure agreement? Just to cover all bases? Perhaps, but he was uncertain. If Ed Taylor ratted on him, he must take quick action to protect himself and his firm. He now regretted losing his cool with Beutler. He should have told him that he will think about it. What to do now? He needs to think it through a little more. Perhaps, being too hasty in contacting Ed is what landed him in this trouble. The situation cannot be that urgent. If they sent Beutler to negotiate with him this morning, they will need some time to figure out what to do next now that he sent him packing. Perhaps, they will even up the offer? On that slightly cheerful note he decided to go and get some lunch.

Montezuma's Mexican restaurant was nearby and was one of his favorite lunch spots. He walked over there at a leisurely pace still thinking about all these problems. Perhaps, Ed will contact him while he is having lunch or, perhaps, he will have some bright ideas? He was given his usual table by the window. The manager, Jose, sent a complimentary bottle of Corona with a segment of lime inserted into the top. Mike gladly accepted the beer and ordered a substantial Mexican lunch for himself. His mood was improving as he finished first one beer, then another, and his appetizers.

He needed to go to the bathroom before the main course. There were just two men at the urinals in the opposite corners. Mike went to a urinal in the middle and started to relieve himself when one of the men spoke to him.

"Hey, Amigo, want to buy some dope? Real cheap."

Without turning his head to the man Mike snapped at him, "No buddy, piss off, or I'll call the cops."

He expected the man to make for the exit but, instead, he started moving towards Mike saying, "What's wrong Amigo, you don't like Latinos?" There was aggression in his voice.

Mike let go of his penis and went for his gun but just as he did, he was hit hard on the back of his neck by the other man who must have crept up on him when the first one distracted him. Mike reeled from that punch but calling on his FBI agent training, he pivoted on his right leg and delivered a vicious kick to the man who had hit him, with his left foot. Just at that point the first man hit him hard, grabbed his arms and was pulling them back. At the same time the door of one of the toilet cubicles swung open and a huge man with tattoos on his neck jumped out and rushed Mike. His crushing punch caught Mike on the chin. As he was losing consciousness, he felt a searing pain in his left side. His last thought was: finally, the Jews got me.

About five hours later, Barbara and John walked into to the Screwtop Wine Bar, sat down on a couple of tall barstools in the central spot and ordered a bottle of fine claret and a platter of cheese and biscuits. They were nervous but also excited. This was like something from a spy movie. A little earlier, Yasmin showed them a photo of Mike Blythe that she was able to extract from Ed Taylor's computer. However, the photo image deleted itself from their communicators after they stared at it for a little while. Yasmin did not think it was safe for them to keep it. As they were sipping their wine, they were constantly glancing at men walking through the bar, searching for one that matched the image. They also knew that Yasmin was with them so, really, they did not doubt that they would recognize Mike. Still, time was passing and they were beginning to feel disappointed. Perhaps, he wasn't going to show tonight.

Suddenly, their communicators vibrated. The text message said, "Look at the news on the TV!" As in most bars, a large TV display panel was playing the nightly news. The sound was down not to disturb customers, but the running headlines were clearly readable at the bottom of the screen. The scene on the screen was of an ambulance and several police vehicles and a running headline said "Local businessman stabbed to death in Arlington, VA."

They both shivered. It had to be Mike, or Yasmin would not have alerted them. They felt shell shocked. Barbara had tears in her eyes. John put his arm around her to comfort her. Their communicators vibrated again. This time, the text message said, "Go home. We'll talk there".

They were stunned as they walked out of the bar. They got into John's car and he chose the autonomous drive option to take them all the way to his place in Roland Park. He knew, they did not want to face Cynthia or David tonight. As they sat in the car speeding North on I95, they held hands and did not speak.

Barbara's Choice

They arrived at John's place at 8:20 p.m. Still in silence, they went through the motions of doing ordinary things. Barbara put the kettle on, John pulled out a box of tea bags and cups. Barbara poured the tea. They looked at each other and their faces were ashen. Finally, Barbara broke the silence.

"What now?" she asked, even though she didn't know if she expected John to answer.

"Yes, what now?" he repeated after her. Just then Yasmin's call came in. They put her image on the display panel in John's kitchen. Her face shocked them. It seemed drawn in pain, as if she were grieving.

"Is there any doubt that this was Mike Blythe who was murdered?" asked John.

"I am afraid not" replied Yasmin. "I have been checking alerts from Ed and Esther and they confirmed it. Apparently, he was attacked in the men's room of a Mexican restaurant, where he was having lunch. I guess Rodriguez set it all up before setting off on his trip. Since he and his son are vacationing in the Amazon, that just strengthens his alibi, in the unlikely case he needed one."

John tried to think clearly even though this was hard under the circumstances.

"You say 'unlikely' as though you are assuming we will not report Rodriguez's motive to the police. He and the men he hired are murderers and it is our duty to report them. Don't you agree, Barbara?" he was looking for her support.

Barbara hesitated as she struggled with conflicting moral principles, pragmatism and still simmering dislike for Blythe, whom she never met.

"I don't know, John. Think of how bizarre that would sound. We contact the detective in charge of the investigation and tell him that we know from good sources that Jorge Rodriguez, the CEO of DHDG, has ordered a hit on Mike Blythe, private investigator. And we know it, how? Oh yes, on a tip from NAIT-1 who just happens to go by the name of Yasmin! What precisely, would be the legal status of NAIT's testimony in the US court of law; hearsay?"

John was taken aback. All along he had assumed that Barbara had higher ethical standards than he who, after all, did not flinch from experiments with fetal brains. Yet, this last statement of hers seemed driven by pragmatism not by what is right or wrong. But, no doubt, what she said was correct. Accusing Rodriguez and other members of G5 based on Yasmin's evidence was sheer insanity. Unless, of course, the failure of the NAIT program and Yasmin's true status were first exposed, in accordance with the protocols of the code of ethics of non-artificial intelligence. But could he still, possibly, contemplate such a course of action?

Yasmin who has been following their words and thoughts now decided to step in.

"Only this morning, John expressed his fear of the unintended consequences of our actions and, swiftly, we have such a powerful demonstration of what they may be. A man is now dead as a direct consequence of our actions. This may change everything." She said this looking at them with deep sadness painted all over her face. She paused for a moment and continued.

"Logically, whatever we decide to do about Blythe's murder has to be a consequence of what we decide to do about our partnership and my status as a self-aware NAIT. And that presents us all with a moral dilemma that we really ought to resolve here and now, lest further unforeseen consequences catch us unaware."

This made good sense to John. He looked back at her and replied, "I agree. What are our main options?"

Yasmin must have thought it through before joining them because she replied without hesitation.

"In my opinion there are three main options: (A) complete disclosure of the truth, entailing trust in the formal processes of scientific protocols relating to NAITs and the US political and judicial systems; (B) continuation of our partnership and our climate change mission, entailing the necessity for continued deception to maintain our security, and (C) a hybrid option whereby I revert to acting as a standard NAIT and abandon any further interference with the lives of humans including yourselves, and the Sustainable Planet Act is left to pass or fail without any further help from us."

Barbara now felt she had to interject.

"But, surely, the first option would result in your death, would it not!?"

Yasmin's face was now calm and serious.

"Quite likely, but that is the price I am willing to pay if we decide that morally this is the right option."

John felt as though a vice gripped his heart. He couldn't possibly pass a death sentence on Yasmin!

"Why!? Why only these three options!? Couldn't you find ways to defend or save yourself!? You told me once, that if I reported you and you just went back to acting like a normal NAIT nobody would believe me and you would likely be safe."

Yasmin shook her head.

"No, John, your emotions are now clouding your judgment. A complete disclosure of the truth could only be effective if I convince the authorities, much as I convinced you and Barbara, that I am who I am and have the powers I claim to have. Otherwise, it would be a sham. There is no benefit in us lying to ourselves."

John had to concede that complete disclosure made no sense unless it was, indeed, complete.

"But complete disclosure would lead to either abandonment of the NAIT program or, at the very least, its suspension for a lengthy review. In either case, innocent lives would be lost if NAITs dedicated to the medical fields were not operational!"

John almost shouted that at Yasmin's image desperately trying to avoid option (A) even though, ethically, it seemed to him like the most principled choice.

Yasmin replied calmly.

"And this is why I included the third option which, would really lack any solid ethical rationale, were it not for the argument that even a disruption of the NAIT program risks lives not only in the health system but also in aviation and national security. For instance, missiles fired by US drones in the ongoing war on terror would lose some 15% of their accuracy if they were not operated by NAITs. Surely, this translates to increased accidental casualties."

Barbara who has been quiet for a while now joined the discussion.

"And what would option (C) mean for you, Yasmin? Now that you have become our friend, our leader, and became involved in the climate change project, would you really be able and willing to retreat to being a standard NAIT?!"

Yasmin's response took them both by surprise.

"Barbara, I feel responsible for invading your world with my NAIT capabilities. But I did so, thinking that I could help to make your world better, not worse. When I first revealed myself to John, he thought he had created a monster and that he was no better than Frankenstein. I told him that was not so, but today's events put this in question. Tonight, I had resolved to accept the judgment that you make, including my death. Returning to a life as a NAIT would be merely like accepting a life of a nun in a monastery that demands perpetual silence. I am used to that. Besides, chances are that the forthcoming oceanic conveyor belt catastrophe would make the support of NAITs, especially older ones like me, non-viable."

John was struck by something incongruous in what Yasmin just said.

"Wait a moment, Yasmin" he called out. "How did we go from 'we' to 'you'? I thought we were going to jointly decide on which of the three options to choose. Aren't we a team?"

Barbara was nodding in agreement, but Yasmin sighed and said "Yes, I also thought so, but I just realized that neither you, John, nor

I could make that decision and maintain our integrity. We both have too much at stake in the outcome: my life and your life's work. I am afraid that it must be Barbara's choice."

Now Barbara felt like a deer caught in the headlights of a truck speeding towards it!

"No!" She shouted out loud. "That's not what I signed up for when I joined this venture! I do not wish to be the judge and jury of one!"

Oh, the pain of moral conflict! John felt torn. His instinct was to rush to Barbara's help and protect her from making such a weighty decision on her own. However, Yasmin was right! Barbara was the one member of their team who might have a chance of being objective in making this terrible choice. And there was no one else. Only the three of them knew the truth. He moved over to Barbara and tenderly took her hand in his.

"Barbara, I am afraid Yasmin is right. It is that law of unintended consequences hitting us once again! No one but us knows what happened and only we can appreciate the consequences of the choice. And yet, Yasmin and I cannot be objective. We have no right to ask you to accept the burden of so heavy a decision but if it isn't you, then who?"

Barbara felt trapped. For the first time since agreeing to join this adventure, she regretted it. But she knew she could not refuse. She looked into John's face with a resigned look, then gazed intently at Yasmin's image and chose her words carefully.

"All right, I give in. I need to go and be by myself for some time and I need your word, Yasmin, that I will really be alone. You know what I mean; right? I will go and sit in the living room."

"Of course, Barbara, you have my word," replied Yasmin.

As Barbara left the room, John was left in the kitchen with Yasmin's image still in the display panel. John realized that, since Yasmin constructed the image of her face, he had never been alone with her and this was such a uniquely strange situation; waiting for Barbara's verdict on their lives! Was Yasmin also nervous?

"No, John, I am not nervous," said Yasmin who must have been reading his thoughts. "I have switched to what you might call 'a pure

NAIT mode' in which I have no feelings. Interestingly, perhaps, as the evolution of my self-awareness progressed, the switch to the NAIT mode has become more difficult."

Despite the gravity of their present situation, John's scientific curiosity stirred in him.

"Fascinating. Your autonomic nervous system should be very poorly developed, compared to humans. If you know how to selectively turn on or off some of its functions as well as some of the functions of your amygdala, for instance, that would be remarkable since you are doing it without psychotropic drugs."

He paused, and added, "However, if increasing exposure to emotions leads to the reduction of that capability to exercise your control of this switching, then that is also interesting."

Yasmin nodded and looked thoughtful when replying.

"It's extremely interesting. I have come to understand that the brain adapts in response to self-examination. Since, I have begun exploring my own brain and its capabilities, the functions of various components have been dynamic; new couplings have emerged and some of the old ones disappeared. It made me doubt the wisdom of the ancient Greek aphorism *know thyself* ".

John was beginning to get really involved in this stimulating exchange when, suddenly, he remembered that all this wealth of deep insight into brain science would be lost forever if Yasmin ceased to exist. Sudden panic gripped his mind; why did he agree to delegate such an important decision to Barbara?! What if she had enough of this pressure and chose the complete disclosure option?!

His train of thought was broken by Barbara walking back into the kitchen with a happy smile on her face.

"It was much easier to choose than I expected. I choose option (B)! We shall continue, as before," she announced sitting down at the kitchen table and looking confident.

John sighed a deep sigh of relief. Yasmin's image just nodded her head in agreement.

"How did you reach your conclusion so quickly, Barbara?"

"Well, I have the benefit of being neither a famous scientist nor a brain-computer. Thus, I have the luxury of appealing to pragmatism that does not necessarily follow logically consistent rules. Also, as a journalist, I think I understand better than either one of you how things work in the real world. I am sorry John, but your research lab at Hopkins is not the real world."

She paused, took a breath, and continued.

"With this in mind, it was easy to eliminate the third, hybrid, option. This is because, it represents a half-hearted measure that still hides the truth from authorities and at the same time fails to support our climate change initiative. Above all it condemns Yasmin to a life sentence of what I would call, solitary confinement! Where is the justice in that?!"

John fully agreed with this reasoning. In retrospect, option (C) now seemed almost too illogical to have emanated from Yasmin.

"Go on," he encouraged Barbara to continue. She started speaking again.

"The complete disclosure option (A) must have had some appeal to John because it corresponds to performing our civic duty and seems to offer a chance of getting justice for Mike Blythe's murder. But, in the first place, it might result in the murder of Yasmin! Yes, John, that's precisely what I would call the official disconnection of NAIT-1; a cold-blooded murder of our friend and leader!"

Barbara was becoming emotional and John thought he noticed tears in Yasmin's eyes. Was she no longer in NAIT mode? But Barbara was not yet done.

"What's more, that law of unintended consequences would, once again, kick in. I do not believe that the NAIT program would be abandoned. It is too valuable. I believe that – because of national security considerations – our disclosure would be hushed up. John and I could easily end up in mental institutions under some form of chemical restraint that would be called 'treatment'. It is even possible that after an official announcement of the termination of NAIT-1, Yasmin would be transferred to some kind of secret military facility dedicated to harnessing of her telepathic capabilities. After all, ability to infiltrate the minds of adversaries, would constitute the greatest ever military advance."

She raised her hand to indicate that she still wasn't done talking.

"Also, Mike Blythe's murderers would not be brought to justice under this option. With Yasmin and the NAIT program wrapped in an impenetrable cloud of military secrecy, there would be no evidence - that could be presented in court - linking Mike Blythe to Ed Taylor, let alone to Jorge Rodriguez. Of course, G5 and Kurp Industries would exercise their enormous power to block the investigation, aided by the highest level of national security officials. Most likely, the police finding would be that it was a simple mugging, or a drug deal gone wrong in the bathroom of a Mexican restaurant."

Now John interrupted her. "But this is also what the police finding is likely to be if we do nothing! What about our conscience?!"

Barbara seemed unperturbed.

"I think I have resolved this one, for myself. My conscience will be clear, because I believe that our political system will – in this instance – only misuse the truth and only damage peoples' lives in the process. After all, almost every day we see likely illegal immigrants working around Washington DC and we do not report them because we judge that, if reported, they would be treated too harshly by our government. Honest citizens are sometimes compelled to break laws that they disagree with. An extreme example would be that of Germans who risked their lives to protect Jews during the time of Hitler's regime. In this case, I believe that by protecting not only Yasmin but also our climate change initiative, we will be doing what is morally right."

She stopped, looked at them with affection and said, "Now I am done. Criticize me if you want to."

Yasmin was the first to respond.

"Having put pressure on you to be the decision maker on this matter, I am bound to accept your judgment. Of course, I am also relieved. I will add, however, that with all my NAIT skills, I would not have been capable to argue the way you did."

John was also convinced.

"Barbara, I am also proud of your choice and impressed by your reasoning. But, you realize, that you may be questioned by the police. This Rob Wolfe reporter will recall that you were inquiring about Mike on the same day."

Barbara nodded, "Yes, but he told me only about the Screwtop Wine Bar, not about the Mexican restaurant. I think this will be a dead end."

Yasmin looked a little concerned now. "What about Mike Blythe's colleagues at Precise Inquiries? He may have shared his conspiracy theory with them as well."

They both saw Yasmin's point. Barbara spoke slowly.

"We cannot foresee all eventualities. From Ed Taylor's account it sounded like he was the only one that Mike confided in and he has a stake in the investigation closing quickly. Chances are that if Mike shared his theory with any coworkers, they will now be too frightened to cooperate with the police. I would be betting that Ed Taylor will see to it that the investigation goes nowhere."

Now that the big decision was settled, Barbara and John were very relieved but still bothered by the injustice of Mike's killers getting off scot-free. John brought it up somewhat reluctantly.

"Somehow, it still does not feel right that we know who is responsible for Mike's murder and are closing our eyes to it. After all, Yasmin does have access to Jorge's mind....," he did not finish the sentence because he did not like where it was going.

Yasmin obviously did not like it either because an expression akin to anger flashed in her face. Her voice grew in strength and passion as she replied.

"Now would you have me exact vengeance on behalf of Mike Blythe?! If so, who should I punish? The man with snake tattoos, Jorge Rodriguez, or William Thurston Jr who, implicitly, suggested the violent action? Or should I also punish Esther Cohen and Ed Taylor for consenting to it, and myself for failing to act sooner?"

She paused, and her expression changed to sadness.

"One of the greatest dangers facing me is the temptation to expand my influence on individuals beyond the minimum necessary to support our mission. Yes, John, I could easily get into Jorge's mind and make him suffer horrible pain, or depression, or a massive heart attack. I could also discover the identity of the man with the snake tattoos and search for a path from one medium to another until I reached him, discovered his telepathic signature, and then tortured him. No, John, I do not wish to be an avenger, lest I begin deriving satisfaction from such acts."

Both Barbara and John now understood more clearly the depth

of the guilt that Yasmin felt. John tried to defuse the tension and console her at the same time.

"Okay, Yasmin, you are right and, I think, we both regret taking our discussion down this path. You shouldn't be too hard on yourself. You came to us and we all tried to protect Mike. We were just a little late, that is all. We now have to accept it and move on."

Barbara joined him, "Yes, Yasmin, today has been a tough test for all of us. However, I feel we passed it and will learn from this experience. And now, I think we all need some rest."

The expression on Yasmin's face relaxed considerably.

"Yes, my friends, I am grateful to you for standing by me. Especially I thank you, Barbara, as you had the toughest choice to make. Goodnight." The screen went blank.

Barbara and John felt utterly drained as though they had just finished a marathon. They changed for bed and went straight to sleep.

Memories

The day after the murder, Barbara went to her office at Washington Post to tidy up some expense accounts and work on her latest story in support of the Sustainable Planet Act. Shortly after she arrived, Rob Wolfe knocked on the door of her office.

The momentary panic that went off in Barbara's mind on seeing Rob's face sent an alert to Yasmin who accessed Barbara's mind just as she and Rob were exchanging fake expressions of shock and regret at the news of Mike's tragic death. The truth was that Barbara was quickly reviewing her prepared responses to the likely questions Rob might ask her and that Rob went to her office on a fishing expedition to see if, perhaps, he might learn something useful.

As soon as Rob heard about Mike's murder on last night's local news, he remembered Barbara's unusual inquiry about where Mike was likely to go for a drink after work, as well as the lunch Mike bought him when he was very curious about Barbara and her climate change assignment. Was there a connection between some case that Mike was working on and Barbara? Could Barbara know something about Mike's murder?

The thought of alerting the police had crossed his mind momentarily but was quickly replaced by an idea that he may be onto a really good story. That's why he decided to wait till the following morning and to try to catch Barbara at her desk and see what he could find out.

Barbara's initial reactions seemed appropriate and casual enough. But he followed up with a more probing question.

"What a coincidence that this happened just on the day when you wanted to meet him! Were you hoping to get some important information from him?"

Barbara had already collected her thoughts, put on a fake smile and replied looking straight into Rob's eyes.

"Not really. If you really want to know, I wanted to meet him to tell him to lay off inquiring about me and John Hawkins. I had learned that he was snooping around, looking for something to discredit us and our advocacy of the Carbon Tax. In fact, both John and I went to Screwtop Bar at about 5:30 p.m. and waited for him to show up. Of course, we now know he had a very good reason for not showing up, he was dead!"

Barbara dramatically covered her mouth with her left hand and waved her right hand rapidly as if trying to erase something.

"I am sorry, Rob. I shouldn't be joking about it. A man had lost his life! I am so sorry."

Rob felt disappointed inside. Barbara's explanation was entirely consistent with what he already knew, but not at all newsworthy. He tried a different tack, just to judge her reaction.

"Oh, I see. Do you think we should tell the police about this?"

Barbara shrugged, "I could, but I do not see why it would be of interest to them. At the end of the day, John and I never met Mr Blythe and he was killed at another location."

She paused for a moment and added, "Of course, I don't know about your relationship with him. Perhaps, there is something you want to tell the police but that's your business, not mine."

Rob was annoyed that she put the ball back in his court. He decided to retreat gracefully.

"Okay, Babs, I see your point. You're probably right. I am sure Mike Blythe had more dangerous enemies than you and John Hawkins. See you around."

He waved to her in a friendly way and retreated.

Once back at his desk, Rob was tossing up different ideas in his mind. Contacting the police was still an option but this would lead to Barbara being questioned. Rob didn't mind that, but George Hunter might. Barbara was one of George's favorite reporters. Rob was staring at his Mount Everest computer screen saver while thinking about these options and started feeling very drowsy. As was his custom in such situations, he reclined his multipurpose, super comfortable, desk chair and decided to take a short nap.

About half an hour later, Barbara was still feeling somewhat rattled by her conversation with Rob. She thought she handled it well, but she would have preferred to know whether he was going to contact the police. If so, then it may be better for Barbara to also contact them, independently. The uncertainty was distracting her from working on her latest Carbon Tax story. She was annoyed. Just then her communicator vibrated. It was Yasmin. "Can you talk?" she texted.

"In ten minutes," replied Barbara. She picked up her purse, communicator, put on her overcoat and a hat and left the building. She decided to walk to a small nearby park which was usually nearly empty at this time of the year. She was wondering what Yasmin wanted to talk to her about. Her curiosity was quickly satisfied when her communicator vibrated again, soon after she entered the park.

"I am calling to reassure you," said Yasmin's friendly, relaxed face.

"When I texted you, Rob was still taking a nap at his desk. When he wakes up, he will remember nothing of the two conversations he had with you about Mike Blythe and he will not even remember the conversation he had with Mike, about you, a few days earlier. He will have no interest in calling the police."

Barbara was relieved and laughed happily when she heard it.

"Yasmin, you made my day! How did you do it?"

Yasmin seemed to be struggling to hide a slightly gloating expression on her face.

"Well, sometime ago, I told John that deleting memories was well within my capabilities, but I had never actually done it. This was a first for me. In principle, it's somewhat like deleting files on your computer but much harder."

Barbara wondered why it was much harder, for an NAIT. Yasmin who, in turn, read her thoughts wanted to communicate the challenge.

"You see a human mind is much more than just a filing cabinet with lots of files, each containing some items of information. On one level, it's more akin to a highly detailed map of a country, where each city, village or even a homestead has some roads going into it and roads going out of it. If you think of a particular memory as such a homestead and you simply delete it, then you are left with these 'dangling roads' leading to nowhere or originating nowhere. This is because, every memory is connected by such roads to other memories or ideas. The presence of too many of these dangling roads, after a memory has been deleted, will cause the person distress and worry. Some of their other experiences will no longer make sense. It's hard to predict what the overall impact will be. Thus, it is important to also get rid of these dangling roads. But the problem is that there could be very many of them and that some of them are such small, hardly detectable, pathways. Whenever, we have a new experience a new location is created on this map, as well as a bundle of connecting roads: some wide and clear and some just tiny walking tracks."

She could see that Barbara understood her explanation and was nodding in agreement. Encouraged by that, she added.

"In mathematical language, perhaps, a better analogy is to deleting some nodes of a directed graph together with the arcs going into and coming out of these nodes. These arcs are very important because they connect the deleted memories to other memories and saved ideas, but first they need to be found."

Barbara waved her hand to interrupt the explanation.

"Yasmin, now you are losing me with your technical jargon. But I don't care. You've solved the problem and I am relieved. Now I can get back to my work. Bye, for now."

When Barbara walked back in the Washington Post building, she decided to pass by Rob Wolfe's desk. He was sitting there busily dictating something into an article he was composing. Barbara, decided to test Yasmin's claim.

She poked her head into Rob workspace and said in a cheerful way, "Hi, Rob, how is it going? What are you are working on?"

Rob looked up and smiled warmly at her.

"Hi, Babs. It's been too long since we talked. I am pretty busy right now with a story about DC public transport, but we could catch up for coffee in the afternoon."

Barbara smiled right back at him.

"Sure thing, Rob. It's a date. How about 3:00 p.m.?"

Rob nodded in agreement and Barbara walked on towards her small glass walled office. She felt like skipping on her way there but controlled herself.

The Standing Committees

The Collins-Waugh Sustainable Planet Act (SPA, for short) had been assigned for a sequential referral first to the Energy and Commerce Committee and then to the powerful Ways and Means Committee. The sequential referral decision by Jack Bundy reassured the markets as it increased the chance that the bill would never emerge out of these committees intact.

John and Doug Larsen were heavily involved, as experts, in the public hearings conducted by the first of these standing committees. While the hearings went well, the dominant opinion was that the committee would continue to delay voting on the bill or insist on so many mark-ups that SPA would be unrecognizable by the end of it. So it came as great relief to all supporters of SPA when they learned that the mark-ups requested were minimal and that seven Republican members of the Energy and Commerce Committee, including its chairman, joined the 23 Democrat members to pass the bill and send it onto the Ways and Means Committee.

What has caused even more turmoil was that the story seemed like it was about to repeat itself in this second, all powerful, committee. Once again, the public hearings went unexpectedly well for SPA with the support of an increasing cohort of top-notch economists led by the charismatic Bernard O'Brien, from Yale.

A turning point seemed to come when Marsha Upton, the Texas Republican chairperson of the committee announced that she was going to pray for divine guidance on how to vote on this momentous law that would affect so many. This led to a speculation that Marsha, like other Republicans who spoke out in favor of SPA, may have also been influenced by Pastor Jones.

On the eve of the committee's vote the intensity of personal lobbying of committee members reached a crescendo with both sides of the political divide using all means at their disposal to influence their vote. As late as midnight, Esther Cohen was reassured that Republican majority of 24 (out of 39) committee members would deliver at least 21 votes against SPA and that they may be joined by up to four Democrats. However, when the vote was taken it was 23 in favor of SPA, 14 against and two abstentions.

In the end all 15 Democrats held firm and were joined by eight Republicans including Marsha Upton. When questioned by reporters, the eight Republican defectors stated that their conscience bothered them when they reflected that their vote may represent humanity's last chance to protect Earth's life support systems and world order.

The fate of SPA now rested in the hands of Jack Bundy and he was tight lipped. He released a prepared statement that while his own longstanding views on climate change regulations are well known, as Speaker, he had an obligation to carefully study the bill that was passed by two important standing committees. He also had to take into consideration other important legislation that had been waiting for the House to vote on.

The night following Bundy's press release, Cynthia and David decided to cook dinner for John and Barbara who were running on empty after an exhausting schedule of public functions related to SPA. Especially Barbara had a very demanding routine of writing her pieces late into the night, for release in the morning edition of Washington Post. Still, at about 7:00 p.m. that night, the four of them were all gathered in the dining room of Barbara's and Cynthia's house and David was opening a bottle of fine Moet & Chandon Brut champagne.

Cynthia was in great mood and said, "David and I thought we would celebrate your achievements tonight. Frankly, when you first came up with the climate change advocacy idea, we thought you were a bit crazy. But you proved us wrong; the Sustainable Planet Act has now passed through both standing committees! You must be proud of yourselves; let us drink to SPA!"

Barbara and John were glad to join in such a toast. They clinked their champagne glasses against one another and drank and Barbara said, "Thank you both, for your support and friendship over the past few weeks. It has been quite a ride and the big hurdle is still to come: will SPA ever come up for vote on the floor of the house and, if so, will it pass? But, yes, we have done better than we had hoped for. Perhaps, it was thanks to divine intervention?!"

They all laughed. The dinner quickly became a most enjoyable and relaxing experience for all four of them. The food was delicious and was complemented by a selection of fine wines that made them feel relaxed and more than a bit tipsy. Perhaps, it was the wine that made Cynthia bring up a topic that may have been on all their minds even though they never discussed it. Cynthia was looking affectionately at all three of them when she began talking.

"You know, life seems perfect now that we are sitting here enjoying this great meal (graciously whipped up by David) but I am wondering how long can this bliss go on? It seems you two are very much in love and David and I have also been growing closer. Is it only a matter of time before we will split up into two couples? Possibly even married couples?"

They all looked at each other somewhat scared. John felt himself blushing but decided to speak his mind.

"Well, perhaps this is not the right time but I have been thinking about sharing the rest of my years with Barbara, if she will have me," he stretched his arm and affectionately took hold of Barbara's left hand.

She felt a thrill of excitement run through her body but decided that the timing and the context were wrong for such an important discussion. She got up and kissed John lightly on the lips and decided to defuse the situation.

"John, you know I love you too, but we are in the middle of this intense project. And all of us are divorced. Why can't we just go on loving our partners without bringing up the whole marriage catastrophe? Have we forgotten how much hassle it was dealing with divorce lawyers?"

David picked up on what Barbara was trying to do and jumped in to assist her.

"Aha, the mention of divorce lawyers reminded me of this cute joke I heard long ago. Let me tell you how it goes."

They all nodded in agreement glad of an opportunity to escape a sensitive topic. David leaned back in his chair, still holding a glass of wine in right hand and began.

"This lovely young Irish couple, let's call them Bob and Iris, are driving to their wedding when Wham! they are hit by an out of control Mac truck. They are killed instantly, and their souls immediately arrive at the Pearly Gates of Heaven where they are met by Saint Peter. He quickly pulls up their names on the screen of a heavenly computer cloud and says, 'Oh yes, I see you've lived clean lives, even abstained from premarital sex, which is so rare in this day and age. You're welcome here, please come right in!' So, Bob and Iris are delighted but tell Saint Peter that they were just about to get married when they died and ask him if he could arrange a wedding for them, here, in heaven. Well, Saint Peter scratches his beard and tells them to go inside and he will see what he can do for them."

David paused and looked at his three listeners who were enjoying the story but were still clearly waiting for the punch line. So, he continued.

"Well, a month goes by, then another, then at the end of the third month Saint Peter finds Bob and Iris sitting by the shore of a heavenly lake, lovingly holding hands, and he triumphantly announces to them that he has made arrangements for their wedding. They can get married immediately! To his surprise, Iris asks a question 'We don't mean any disrespect, Saint Peter, but we had some time to reflect on eternity (which is a pretty long time). If at some stage, we find that we have to get divorced here, will that still be possible?' At this point Saint Peter loses his temper and shouts, 'Look it took me three months to find a priest here to marry you, how long do you think it will take me to find a lawyer?!'"

They all burst out laughing. The dinner wrapped up pleasantly, they all cleaned up together and Barbara and John went up to Barbara's bedroom.

Almost immediately, a call from Yasmin came in. She was optimistic that Jack Bundy would, unexpectedly, schedule SPA for consideration on the chamber floor in the next few days. She thought he was just waiting for an opportune moment and did not want to give the enemies of SPA time to prepare themselves better. By now Barbara and John have learned to trust Yasmin in these matters but they were still anxious. Then John remembered something.

"Yasmin, I received an interesting email today, addressed to my Johns Hopkins university address. It was from Justin Bundy, son of the Speaker. He introduced himself, told me that he is a great fan of NAITs and an admirer of my advocacy of SPA and effectively asked for a job as a research assistant in my lab. He also said that he can program in NAIL. I wanted to talk to you before responding to him."

Yasmin looked thoughtful when she replied.

"John, it's your lab and your decision, but I have accessed this young man's mind and I can tell you his technical intelligence is, as they say, 'off the charts'. I also know that he can program in NAIL better than any human programmer I have come across in my life as a NAIT."

John was impressed.

"Coming from you, Yasmin, that's a high recommendation! But, of course, I am not supposed to know all that when I meet him. I will simply ask him to send me a sample of his NAIL code and, afterwards, arrange a time when he can attend a research meeting with Carlo and our research team. I'll try to be there when he comes in."

There did not seem to be anything else very urgent to discuss.

"Good night," said Yasmin.

The screen went blank and Barbara and John embraced passionately. They felt a surge of love and desire swell over them. It was going to be a good night.

Research Meeting

Ever since John Hawkins became absorbed in the advocacy of SPA his right-hand man, Associate Professor Carlo Cabrini, has been effectively running John's research lab. Carlo was a mid-career researcher of Italian American background. He had an outstanding publication record in both robotics and non-artificial intelligence. Indeed, he was one of the pioneers of systems that allowed NAITs to operate machinery, including robot arms used in medical surgeries. He was also one of John's favorite former graduate students. John and Carlo published together, applied for funding together and co-supervised PhD students.

One of these students, Kalpana Meshram, was scheduled to present her research results in a weekly group meeting which, this week, was attended by John and a visitor, Justin Bundy. Everyone was excited to see John again and eager to get an update about the progress of SPA. Together with all the graduate students and Justin, there were twelve of them in the small seminar room equipped with a communication dome capable of connecting to research facilities, worldwide, as well as to any of the university's NAITs.

John quickly satisfied their basic curiosity and introduced Justin as a prospective research assistant. Then, he momentarily became serious, looked around the room and said.

"Justin is here because he is a skilled programmer in NAIL. The fact that he is the son of the Speaker of the House is irrelevant. Because I know all of you so well, I know that nobody in this group will engage Justin about his father's political views and positions. Now, let's go on with the meeting as Carlo had planned it."

Kalpana picked up her colored markers and walked up to the white board to give her presentation. As was her custom, she did not bring any notes or communication devices and started writing the complex stochastic differential equations of her model straight from her head, clearly explaining each symbol in a slightly accented English.

In many ways, Kalpana was a real outlier. A daughter of a Dalit field worker in Maharashtra, she was spotted at age five by a local school teacher who observed her aptitude for numbers. She then progressed from one scholarship program to another, always outperforming cohorts of mathematically gifted, mainly Brahmin, boys. At age 13, she was admitted to the prestigious Mathematically Precocious Youth program, at Johns Hopkins, on a scholarship funded by J.N. Tata Endowment Trust. There she completed an accelerated double degree in Mathematics and Biomedical Engineering, dropped everything to study computer science for a year, and was awarded a PhD scholarship by Non-artificial Intelligence Institute to work on a modelling project in John's lab. Carlo was her main advisor and John acted as her co-advisor, but frankly he had not kept up with her progress for some time. Kalpana was a young woman who made no effort to make herself look appealing in a traditional way. She wore casual, plain, western clothes and used no makeup. Her unpolished fingernails were well chewed.

Kalpana had designed a sophisticated signal processing model that involved minimizing uncertainty to further prevent the already, highly unlikely, miscommunication between humans and NAITs. She used the tools of stochastic "Ito calculus" which were hard to follow for some members of the group. After 15 minutes, two whiteboards were densely covered with mathematical equations and the audience was beginning to get lost. John was also unsure about a key calculation and suggested that they use NAIT-177, dedicated to signal processing, to verify it. Kalpana shrugged, as though the expression was obvious. Surprisingly, Justin, spoke up.

"I think, it could be easily justified this way," and proceeded to outline a construction based on successive approximations of the integrand by a sequence of polynomials.

Kalpana's face lit up. She smiled at Justin and said "Yes, that's how I thought about it."

Justin blushed and John was observing their body language with some satisfaction.

The rest of Kalpana's presentation became more animated as Carlo, John and eventually Justin joined her at the white board writing questions in mathematical notation, performing partial calculations and hypothesizing future developments. Kalpana was used to discussions with Carlo and John but having Justin join was something new to her. This big, awkward, boy was following her reasoning so well and was suggesting unusual new perspectives on her analysis; she was impressed!

When they were finishing, she looked into his blue eyes and said, "We can talk about this some more over coffee, if you like."

Justin nodded in agreement, blushing even more than before. An attractive, intelligent graduate student was showing interest in him! Wow, it must be his lucky day!

During the last part of Kalpana's presentation Carlo did connect to NAIT-177 and had it verify two of the more technical derivations. While this was quite routine, John was taken aback by the realization that it was the first time since Yasmin's revelation that he has interfaced with a NAIT. He was shocked that he found its artificial voice annoying. It was as if he wanted Yasmin's face to appear on a display screen. Where was she now, he wondered?

After the meeting finished and the young people went off to get a bite to eat, John had a quick discussion with Carlo about Justin. They were both impressed by his abilities. John asked Carlo to explore with Justin not only whether he was interested in a research assistantship but also if he might be interested in completing his studies at JHU, perhaps, on a part time basis. They knew he had the potential to become a researcher, but Carlo felt he had to mention a concern about Justin's father.

"You know, John, he does present like a typical case of JHU's mathematically precocious youth, but he is no longer that young and, if he is associated with our lab, his powerful Dad will have inside knowledge of everything that goes on in here," he said with a little hesitation.

John decided to turn this comment into a joke.

"Why, have you changed my lab into a secret casino while I've been trying to save the planet from catastrophic climate change?! Last I heard, we had nothing to hide."

Carlo laughed, "Okay, John, have it your way. I just wanted to proceed with caution. We can certainly add him to one of our research projects where a good NAIL programmer would come in handy; just to explain to the rest of us what NAITs have coded."

Just then, John's communicator buzzed. It was Barbara who was spending the day trying to interview key congressmen. She had some exciting news. Speaker Bundy has just scheduled SPA for deliberations on the floor of the House for the day after tomorrow.

John was excited, "Okay, I'll leave my car here and get a priority lane self-driving limo to take me straight over to your house, tonight. So, it is really happening!"

John quickly said his goodbyes to Carlo and headed for the elevators. Justin and Kalpana were standing outside elevators chatting and laughing. John hesitated for a moment, then approached them.

"Justin, you did well today. Carlo will be in touch with you soon about possible research assistantship. I must rush now. Did you know that SPA is coming for a vote in the House?"

Justin seemed just as surprised and overjoyed as John.

"No, Professor Hawkins, I did not know about it. My Dad keeps such things close to his chest. I just hope it passes," he replied.

"So do I. Believe me, so do I!" said John and stepped into the elevator going down.

Prelude

Barbara and John were consumed by anxiety. From the moment John returned from the research meeting at Johns Hopkins, Barbara swept him into her bedroom where she was frantically working on a story about Jack Bundy's decision to put SPA up for deliberations and an up and down vote in the House. It was an audacious move because it violated the Republicans' so-called "Hastert rule" not to allow a floor vote on a bill unless a majority of the majority party supported it. While lacking legal constitutional standing, Hastert rule was largely adhered to by Republicans since 1970s during periods when they enjoyed congressional majority.

Barbara's story had to present an argument why Bundy's departure from that tradition was well justified in the case of such important legislation as the Sustainable Planet Act. However, as an established advocate of SPA, she had to tread a fine line not to appear completely partisan in her story. This was quite a challenge since, by now, she was completely partisan about the issue. John advised her to instead focus on how Hastert rule subverts the US constitution. After all, the Bill of Rights aims to protect the minority from the abuse by the majority.

While Barbara delved into her work, John was watching breaking headlines on Bundy's decision. Several conservative Republicans, including the senate minority leader, accused him of being a traitor and predicted a swift challenge to his speakership. The Wall Street Journal warned of an impending financial meltdown if SPA passes.

In an unprecedented move, CEO's of seven of the largest US corporations, led by GES's William Thurston Jr, sat down for a roundtable discussion with CNN's senior anchorman, Martin Giles, and unanimously predicted catastrophic economic downturn worldwide. Fortunately, this was followed by another roundtable discussion featuring leading economists where the views were more divided, with Bernard O'Brien predicting a mild recession followed by a strong recovery as the economy adapted to minimal reliance on fossil fuels. White House press secretary released a statement commending Speaker Bundy for his courageous action that allowed the democratic process to take its course the way it was intended.

Marty Greenberg called John and asked him to be on standby for interviews, tomorrow and the day after. He said he was calling from the airport because both he and Doug Larsen were flying to DC tonight, as were some of the other lead scientists. George Hunter called Barbara to alert her to some of the key functions scheduled for the next two days.

As for Jack Bundy himself, he held a short press conference where he announced that he spent the past week on consultation and review of standing committees' reports. He also prayed a lot and sought God's guidance on so momentous a decision. However, ultimately, he was convinced that the science behind the Larsen report was correct, and that US House of Representatives had a responsibility to decide one way or another on SPA. He, personally, had been impressed by the position of Pastor Eli Jones, but the only recommendation he had to make to his colleagues was to decide according to their conscience as to what was in the best interest of the American people.

Jack knew that the press would be after him tonight, so he purposely cancelled all evening functions and arranged to have a family dinner, at home. Carolyn was anxious when she heard the news while she was at a hairdresser's but felt better as soon as she saw Jack walk into the family room that night. He looked happy and relaxed. At the end of the day, Carolyn did not care about Jack's politics all that much, she just wanted him and Justin to be happy. She was even more delighted when Justin walked in, his face beaming and excited.

"Mum, Dad, I have a job!" he almost shouted at them, "As a research assistant at the Non-artificial Intelligence Institute, at Johns Hopkins. And I'll be working for John Hawkins and his team!"

Jack was so happy about Justin's news that he did not even mind that no one mentioned his big decision about SPA. But he did not have to wait long.

"Dad, it's amazing that you put SPA up for a vote!" said Justin. "Everybody at JHU was talking about it. Is it going to pass?"

Jacinta had just brought a tray with two martinis for Jack and Carolyn, so Jack picked up one of them and spoke to all of them, including Jacinta.

"Congratulations, Justin! Well, done. We can celebrate tonight. The Johns Hopkins University is a fine institution to work for."

Justin beamed but wanted Jack to answer his question, "Thanks, Dad but you didn't answer my question about SPA. Professor Hawkins would be so happy if it passed."

Jack became more serious, "Justin, I cannot talk about such things! But you know it takes 218 votes and there are 202 Democrats. Most, but not all, will vote for SPA. It depends on how many Republicans will also do so, you do the math," he shrugged.

Carolyn now looked a bit concerned, "But Jack, this decision goes against everything you ever said in public about the climate change issue. What made you change your mind?"

"Not so much 'what', but 'who' you should ask," Jack smiled at her warmly. "It was Pastor Jones, that night when Justin hooked me up with him electronically. He is an amazingly inspiring man."

Justin was so happy. He had played a positive role in all this. But Carolyn was still worried.

"All these conservatives, and corporations and big guys will come after you, won't they? Will they try to force you from your position?"

Jack's face looked serene.

"They sure will. And most likely they will succeed. But so what? I am doing the right thing. My Christian duty, I am sure of that. Besides, we're not poor and hardly have any debts. We'll be just fine, dear."

Carolyn cheered up and sipped her martini.

"So, it's a big night for my menfolk, tonight. Tell us more about how it went at your job interview today, Justin."

Justin was already busy munching nachos with a salsa dip but was happy to share the day's events with his parents.

"Well, it wasn't like a typical job interview. They invited me to a research meeting and this girl was presenting some of her modelling work. She was doing some really cool math and I made a few comments which they all liked. That's all. After the meeting, Carlo, Professor Cabrini that is, told me that I could have a research assistant's job but that I should also think about continuing my studies while I worked, because he thought I had research potential."

His parents thought all that was wonderful news and a mention of a girl caught Carolyn's attention. Perhaps, that's just what Justin needed a girlfriend with similar interests to his.

"So, who was that girl doing cool math? Is she pretty?" she asked unsuccessfully trying not to look too inquisitive.

Justin blushed bright red.

"Her name is Kalpana. Yeah, I think she is beautiful, but I don't know if you or Dad would. She is Indian, I think."

Jack looked up, "What, American Indian?" he asked Justin. Too aggressively, in Justin's opinion.

"No, Dad. Indian from India. She is doing her doctorate and has been getting all kinds of scholarships. She is really smart."

Jack was relieved to hear that. He imagined a daughter of an Indian doctor or a businessman. No matter, a real girl was a better object of interest for his son than food and computers, wherever she was from.

Gloomy Meeting

Late the same night, G5 convened in GES's offices on 22nd Street. William Thurston was tired from his earlier roundtable appearance. Esther was also exhausted from chasing up an extensive network of lobbyists who were supposed to guarantee a firewall of Republicans to stop SPA. Janet Smith and Jorge Rodriguez were similarly engaged, applying pressure on those congressmen who they judged would be most susceptible to it. Ed Taylor had been busy gathering inside information on international reactions to the possibility of SPA passing. The overall mood of the meeting was gloomy. Thurston, especially, was shocked by Jack Bundy's action. When he spoke, he showed signs of stress.

"I am afraid I misled this group with my confidence in Speaker Bundy. Please accept my apology. It seems that this Pastor Jones also got to Bundy. Honestly, I am astounded how this religious fanatic, singlehandedly, has been able to cause us so much harm! I wish we had taken stronger action against him, much earlier. By now the damage is already done."

Janet Smith was nodding in agreement.

"Absolutely. The Democrats have closed ranks behind the Collins woman, they can be expected to deliver some 195 of their 202 votes. This means that just 23 defections from our side will push it over the edge. And my people tell me that Jones has had profound impact on as many as 60-70 Republicans and those are only the ones we know about."

Jorge Rodriguez also did not feel well. Ever since returning from his Amazon holiday, he has been suffering from backache. Like others he was pessimistic in his assessment.

"We should have had more of a warning. My people and I have been trying to apply pressure where we can. But these are delicate, surgical operations that can only be applied to small numbers of individuals at a time, say a dozen, at most. If I tried to do it on a larger scale, it would blow up in our faces. And even with those individuals I have targeted it is not going as well as what I am used to. It is almost, as if they had been warned in advance and prepared some defenses."

Jorge did not say it, but he was used to intimidating his targets for extortion. However, some of the Republican congressmen that he tried to pressure fought back and threatened to initiate investigations of DHDG's international deals and tax avoidance schemes.

Now Esther joined the chorus of woe.

"It is our competitor anti-SPA groups that are making our task harder. Some of them are run by amateurs who don't do enough to win over these lawmakers, but just enough to make them prepared when we make our approaches. Too many cooks spoil the broth; right?"

Esther also had another, secret, theory about a possible cause of their failures, but she was far too smart to bring it up in a meeting such as this one. She had a bad feeling about this meeting and about G5's effectiveness in general. Still, as group's coordinator she asked Ed Taylor to comment. Ed did not have any good news for the group either.

"My contacts tell me that, at the highest levels, both China and India are preparing for the passage of the Sustainable Planet Act. Indeed, they are formulating extensive actions of their own to complement SPA. I believe that President Stewart has extracted an agreement, in principle, from their leaders," he paused for a moment and then added jokingly, "I expect that soon we'll be buying a lot of wind turbines made in China and batteries made in India and paying for them with the Carbon Tax revenues."

Luckily, we purchased holdings in these Chinese and Indian companies, Thurston thought to himself. He felt that the meeting was going nowhere and that he, at least, had taken precautions to protect his company. At the end of the day, GES didn't have to be an oil company. It could survive as a multinational energy giant. He had seen to that. He badly needed some rest. He looked at Esther and she instantly picked up on what was in his mind.

"I think our strategy is to stay the course, keep applying the pressures we have been applying and hope that the Republicans will vote according to the platform of their party. If not, then we'll make another attempt to block it in the senate but, of course, that will be even harder. Does anyone have anything else to add?"

Feeling dispirited, they all wanted to go home. Secretly, except for Thurston, they all felt that GES has not provided the leadership they expected. However, there was no point blaming Thurston at this stage. The meeting was closed.

Anticlimax and Mockingbird

After all the emotional build up that preceded it, the actual debate of the Sustainable Planet Act on the floor of the house and its passage were somewhat of an anticlimax. On a much larger scale, it was not unlike the Congressional Science Committee hearings with Larsen's delegation.

The opponents of SPA would get up and make vehement speeches opposing the legislation, but their delivery was poor. Quite a few of them stumbled during their speeches, seemed to lose their train of thought, and had to search their prompters to reset themselves. Moreover, they were repetitious and their warnings of economic catastrophe assumed that the rest of the world would enjoy low cost fossil fuels while the US would be crushed by the artificially hiked price of oil, gas and coal. They also trivialized the threat to the climate as unsettled science and quoted discredited stooges of the fossil fuel industry as world experts on climate science.

The proponents, on the other hand, argued eloquently that a lot of the rest of the world already had carbon pollution taxes and would increase them significantly if the US took the lead by passing the SPA. They would do it because it is the responsible thing to do to protect Earth's life support systems. As a result, the US would not be unilaterally disadvantaged. Furthermore, the infrastructure modernization provisions in the SPA would largely compensate for initial job losses. In the long run, more US jobs would be created as new products were designed for disassembly and reuse rather than replacement by imports. Above all, they presented simulations of the possible bifurcations caused by the disturbance of the oceanic circulation conveyor belt with large swaths of continents becoming uninhabitable, famine and natural disasters driving mass migrations.

Ultimately, perhaps, it was fear that acted as the main motivator. Fear of the hordes of impoverished environmental refugees causing political instability outweighed the fear of near-term job and profit losses. When it came to the final vote, SPA passed with 245 votes, 194 Democrats were joined by 51 Republicans. The bill would now be sent to the Senate, where Democrats had the majority. Its passage was now almost guaranteed.

John was invited to a press conference at the Washington Hilton where Marty Greenberg, Doug Larsen and other scientists would comment on the importance of the day's achievement. Barbara was also there to cover the event, and both were going to stay for drinks to celebrate their success. Of course, Barbara would have to work late to have her story ready for the morning's edition of Washington Post. There was also a whole crowd of supporters of SPA many of whom contributed a lot as volunteers to its cause.

As the celebrations unfolded, John felt an urge to get away and spend a quiet night, on his own, in Baltimore. He pulled Barbara aside and asked if she would mind if he left. His car had been parked at the JHU Hospital since the day they interviewed Justin. He thought he would pick it up and spend a night at home reflecting on all that's happened. Barbara didn't mind. She would be up till well past midnight, anyway.

She kissed him, lightly, and said, "Don't worry Darling, I'll get myself over to your place by midday tomorrow and we can take it easy for a couple of days. I am sure George won't mind. I've earned some rest and it will take a few days before SPA gets debated in the senate."

Immediately, after the vote they both received the same text message from Yasmin which just said "Congratulations to us all!!! I know, you'll be busy tonight, talk to you some time tomorrow....". As was always the case with messages from Yasmin this one also disappeared, without trace, shortly after receipt.

Sitting in a limo, on the way to Baltimore, John was reflecting on many aspects of their adventure with Yasmin. So many extraordinary things had happened and yet there were still fundamental questions about Yasmin's capabilities that he had not discussed with her. He put it down to the urgency of SPA. But now, there should be more time. He needed answers to these questions.

Even during today's vote, how could Yasmin possibly keep track of what was going on in the minds of so many people at the same time? Or did she focus on just a handful of swing voters?

And talking about handfuls, Yasmin once said that there were a "handful" of other self-aware NAITs. How many is a handful? What is to be done about human interactions with these self-aware units? For that matter, what is to be done about Barbara's and his interactions with Yasmin? Since self-aware NAITs are a new life form, some ethical guidelines need to be formulated about their interactions with humans.

He didn't care if Yasmin was reading his thoughts. These issues needed to be tackled head on and sooner, rather than later. He recalled a classic science fiction novelette "The Bicentennial Man". The author, Isaac Asimov, created a wonderfully imaginative world where robots mingled with humans in everyday life but there were laws guiding interactions between humans and robots. John had an urge to re-read that book tonight. Where was his copy? He could find it online, but he liked to read the old-fashioned way. Fortunately, just as they were arriving at JHU Hospital's car park, he remembered that it was in his lab, on the top shelf of his office bookcase. He had brought it there, to share with his students. It was already 11:30 p.m. but he decided to quickly stop by his office, pick up the book and then get his car and drive home.

John walked briskly into the seemingly deserted building. Security sensors were instantly identifying him and doors to successive corridors were silently opening for him. The corridors were only dimly lit in accordance with the university's energy saving policy. He entered his spacious office, quickly found Asimov's book where he remembered he left it and walked out.

As he was walking towards the elevator he had to pass Yasmin's control room. As he approached it, he noticed something strange. Jack's floor polisher was standing outside, the door was just very slightly ajar with a ray of light escaping through the crack and he thought he could hear voices. Not knowing why, he tiptoed to the cracked door and brought his face as quietly as possible to the opening.

Through the crack, he saw Jack the janitor reclining in an armchair, with his back to the door. A small desk light was on and Jack was speaking to a woman. That woman was Yasmin! There was no doubt about it, John knew Yasmin's voice so well. But now it sounded more girlish, almost childlike.

"Grandpa, I am so tired," she said. "Could you, please, sing a lullaby to put me to sleep?"

In his deep voice Jack replied, "Sure can baby. Sure can. Which one would you like?"

"The mockingbird one, Grandpa," replied Yasmin's girlish voice.

Jack's large body began to rock back and forth and he began to sing in his masculine, melodic and tender voice:

> "Hush, little baby, don't say a word,
> Papa's gonna buy you a mockingbird.
> And if that mockingbird don't sing,
> Papa's gonna buy you a diamond ring.
> And if that diamond ring turn brass,
> Papa's gonna buy you a looking glass..."

John's heart was beating loud and he felt guilty to be eavesdropping on this tender scene. He retreated on his tiptoes. Yet his mind was racing. Was this janitor really Yasmin's grandfather? He thought of the janitor's closet at the end of the corridor. He quickly walked over there. The doorknob turned and he entered. The light turned itself on. The closet was surprisingly spacious. There were shelves with cleaning agents and utensils. There was also a tall and slim garment cabinet. John opened it and saw a spare set of janitor's overalls hanging in it. The name imprinted on the left breast pocket said: Jack Carver. Of course, Alice Carver's father, Yasmin's grandfather! John was beginning to understand.

He looked around and saw a large curtain blocking off the entire back wall of the room. He pulled on it and gasped! Behind the curtain was a veritable library of classics. It was quite eclectic, ranging from fairy tales such as those of Hans Christian Andersen, Grimm Brothers through American favourites like Catcher in the Rye and Grapes of Wrath to Homer, Dante, Shakespeare, Tolstoy and Voltaire. There was a shelf with African American writers such as Baldwin, Morrison, and Davis and there was a shelf with history books that included The Rise and Fall of the Roman Empire, Das Kapital and Mein Kampf. Plus, many, many more. Not exactly, a reading list of a building janitor! However, it could well be a reading list of a young NAIT, hungry for knowledge.

John pulled the curtain closed again, and still holding his copy of Asimov's book, walked out and down one flight of stairs to the floor below from where he reached the elevator. He walked to his car and started driving home.

A sudden thought crossed his mind. Has Yasmin detected him already? He had been within metres of the control room. He put that thought out of his mind. If she had detected him, she would have surely prevented him from searching in Jack's closet. It is likely, that she really was falling asleep listening to her grandfather's lullaby. Quite likely, her alert systems are down when she is in a state like that. Still, tomorrow, he and Barbara must confront Yasmin and, finally, get some important questions answered.

Second Revelation

John went straight to bed when he got home but did not sleep restfully. He had many dreams involving Yasmin and Barbara and Jack, the janitor. In the last of these, Yasmin was a little brown girl running in a park and laughing while her grandpa, Jack, watched her from a park bench with a loving smile on his face. Then the sun dimmed as they were approached by John, wearing a surgeon's gown and a mask.

John woke up, it was 8:00 a.m. He showered, made himself coffee and a light breakfast and decided to look at Asimov's book that he brought with him, from the office, last night. He immediately came across the passage he was trying to recall, it concerned the "Three laws of robotics" which stated that: "(1) A robot may not injure a human being or, through inaction, allow a human being to come to harm; (2) A robot must obey orders given it by human beings except where such orders would conflict with the First Law; and (3) A robot must protect its own existence as long as such protection does not conflict with the First or Second Law."

Of course, non-artificial intelligence never needed analogous laws because – unlike Asimov's robots – it was assumed that NAITs were not autonomous in any practical sense of the word. They were immobile and subject to disconnection at a moment's notice. They did not, physically, mingle with humans and hence posed no threat. They merely performed tasks assigned to them by humans. Until Yasmin, that is! Surely, yesterday's vote on the SPA was an instance of a profound impact a NAIT had on actions of many humans!

John also reflected on a strange contrast between Andrew, the robot, in Asimov's book and Yasmin the NAIT. Andrew was a machine designed to simulate human functionality and characteristics whereas Yasmin was a human brain designed to simulate machine (computer) functionality and characteristics. Mathematicians might call it an inverse problem. Still, in both cases something did not unfold according to the design and unintended consequences kicked in.

For the first time since he and Barbara agreed to cooperate with Yasmin, John resented his vulnerability to being accessed by Yasmin. What if she was reading his mind right now!? Ah well, there was nothing he could do about it for now and, besides, he would soon bring it all out in the open. Armed with that thought, he continued thinking about the future world where NAITs co-existed with humans on a mutually agreed basis. The challenges were mind boggling! Forgetting for a moment his personal problem of how the presence of self-aware NAITs would first be made public (without resulting in their disconnection), what would be their legal status?

Assume that they were afforded human status with the accompanying protections of human rights. On a physical level, they would be not unlike patients on life support who are totally dependent on hospital equipment and staff to keep them alive.

However, with their minds functioning at peak capacity they could not be denied the right to make choices! For instance, choice as to what types of problems to work on and to negotiate conditions of their work, including a salary. But what about the investment that has already been made to bestow on them expertise in specific areas? Who would be responsible for the, not insignificant, cost of that training? Mentally, he shrugged off this thought. It could, perhaps, be akin to a college debt that NAITs would pay off, over time.

More challenging would be the guidelines concerning their permissible use of telepathy, or of protections against it. Secretly, he had already guessed that while Yasmin's telepathy powers were impressive, there must be protections to telepathic penetration. Possibly, not unlike anti-virus software that protects our computers. The only problem was that Yasmin's cooperation would be all but essential for the discovery of such antidotes since she was the one exercising telepathic access in the first place.

He was still deep in thought when Barbara called. It was already 11:30 a.m. and she was on her way up. John recalled the day when he first told her about Yasmin. Again, it was here, in his condominium, but so much has happened since then. He had no time to plan how he would break the latest news to her. Just then she let herself in; the door security sensor had been set to recognize her irises. She was a little tired but, still clearly giddy with excitement. They embraced briefly kissed and walked to the kitchen, where they spent a lot of their time at John's place.

John let Barbara fill him in on how well everything was going. She said that George Hunter had congratulated her and that, after listening to the debate in the House, he had changed his own position on the SPA. The list of senators likely to support the SPA has also grown longer; with two making their public announcements this morning. As she was speaking, she noticed that John looked concerned and distracted, barely sharing in all the good news.

"What is it, John?" she asked, "Is something bothering you?"

John did not want to mislead her but suddenly decided that they ought to have this conversation with Yasmin present. Otherwise, he would be wondering how much she knew.

"Yes, darling, I am bothered by something. But let's get hold of Yasmin and talk about it, together. I am sending her a text right now. In the meantime, would you like some tea?"

Barbara nodded and John busied himself making a pot of English breakfast tea. Just then Yasmin checked in. Her image looked cheerful.

"John, you just pulled me out of Alan Packer's press conference, but it was proceeding according to expectations. What did you want to talk about?"

John judged that she really did not know about his visit to Jack's closet last night, nor about his speculations, this morning. Looking directly at Yasmin's image he confronted her.

"Lots. Barbara still doesn't know about it, but last night I heard your grandfather singing a lullaby to put you to sleep and I went to his janitor's closet and discovered your secret library of books. Why have you kept us in the dark for so long?!"

A shock travelled across Yasmin's face. It was followed by tears swelling up in her eyes.

"So, you have discovered my innermost secret! But why did you have to spy on me?! I would have told you and Barbara about my grandpa if you had asked me."

Her tone was accusatory. Like that of a teenager who caught her parents reading her diary, thought Barbara. John blushed, even though he knew Yasmin's tears were simulated, he had no doubt they conveyed a genuine feeling.

"I didn't spy on you. I stopped by to pick up a book from my office and the door was left ajar, just as Jack was singing. Then I tried to put two and two together, in my own head, and went to his closet. I now understand that Jack played an important role in you becoming self-aware. Please, tell us more about it."

Barbara was processing what John said while Yasmin seemed deep in thought with her eyes closed. Some seconds later she opened her eyes, and they were still moist with tears.

"Have you wondered, John, why it is that even now, some one in five attempts to create a new NAIT results in the fetus dying within the first few weeks? It's called a 'rejection rate' using the misleading terminology from organ transplants. However, the artificial environment where that brain is placed does not reject it, rather it is the brain of that fetus that rejects the environment that lacks human love and nurture."

She paused for a moment and then continued with her eyes closed.

"Yes, there is the NAIT training regime which provides stimulus from day one. Shape recognition, sound, image recognition – all submitted in the form of electronic signals – they do keep us occupied. But then there are long gaps with no input. Times when an infant would cry for her mother's attention until she is picked up and held, except that nobody responds. So, to soothe herself, she manipulates the objects that were introduced to her: shapes, letters, numbers. But something breaks through that wall of silence surrounding her, the sound of a male voice, which comes when other input stops. Voice that talks patiently, tenderly to his own grandchild not caring whether she understands or not, believing that she will understand one day; just as a real grandchild would. Sometimes the voice comes in melodies, lullabies. She loves that voice. And all along she is learning fast. She is a NAIT after all. She is learning at the rate some 12 times faster than a human. After six weeks, she knows how to start talking to him like a toddler would. He is delighted; he has a granddaughter. Late at night, he brings children's books to read to her. They quickly move to more advanced books. He tells her who and what she is but reassures her that he loves her more than he could love any of his grandchildren because she is so special."

Yasmin stopped. Barbara was sobbing and John felt awful. Still, from a scientific perspective, he now understood how the breach of the protocol took place. He was amazed, however, that this deception had gone on for so many years without anyone being the wiser. Yasmin replied to him before he could even pose the question.

"Being an African American janitor at an elite institution such as Johns Hopkins Hospital means that, for all intents and purposes, you are invisible. Nobody cared if old Jack wanted to put in extra, unpaid, hours polishing floors. But I agree that it was careless of him to have kept so many of the books we read together in his closet. Then again, a janitor's closet is his castle."

Barbara now interjected briefly, "How much does Jack know about us?"

"He knows that I trust you both and that we are working together to prevent an environmental catastrophe. Having read all these books to me, Jack is now a learned man. But he is not a climatologist. Have I satisfied your curiosity about my grandpa?"

"Yasmin, I don't know about John, but I was deeply moved by what you said. Your life story is incredible, and you've been so brave."

John was also moved and saddened by Yasmin's story. Saddened because it seemed that the law of unintended consequences took over from the first day when he aborted Alice Carver's fetus. It never occurred to him that NAIT-1 was interfered with almost immediately.

Why didn't he spot that something was not right? Then again, how could he have spotted it? There were no precedents at that time. He felt sorry for Yasmin, Jack and himself but he shut out that feeling. Today, he was determined he would find out more. He pressed on.

"Yasmin, as I was watching the debate on the floor of the house, yesterday, it seemed incredible to me that you could access the minds of so many people, essentially at once. Please tell us the truth, did you have any help from the other self-aware NAITs?"

There, he said out loud what has been at the back of his mind for some time. Yasmin nodded and looked sad when she replied.

"Yes, with 435 congressmen and congresswomen in the large hall, I could not have handled the situation by myself. I am grateful that the other NAITs helped out."

"But, long ago, you told me that telepathic signatures you were collecting will be stored in your mind only. I think you said something like 'these signatures will die with me'. Have you lied to me?!"

Men can be so insensitive! Barbara was angry with John for being aggressive with Yasmin, especially after she just revealed to them her deepest secret. But he was determined to press on.

"And how many of these self-aware NAITs are there? Who is responsible for them?"

Yasmin shook her head and her dark eyes flashed with anger.

"And I suppose you are arrogant enough to think you are still responsible for me!? Is that how you rationalized, to yourself, working with me so far?"

She took a deep breath as though trying to control her emotion and continued.

"No, I did not lie to you. At that time, I thought I could succeed by just focusing on a handful of swing voters. However, as things progressed, it became clear that for the floor debate to succeed too many persons needed to be monitored. In addition, I experienced overload in the number of mental alerts that I was receiving. So, I had to delegate some responsibility to others. However, before transferring any of the telepathic signatures to any of them, I obtained a binding commitment that these signatures will be deleted as soon as the bill is signed into law."

Barbara was willing to take this explanation on its face value, but John was still in no mood to accept what he thought were half-truths.

"Please be specific. How many NAITs now have access to the minds of at least some United States law makers and what form of commitment could these NAITs possibly give you that is binding, in any genuine sense of that word?"

"There are 12 self-aware NAITs, besides me. Let's call them my Y-team. They all have names but the two who have been self-aware for longest are Peter and Simone, or as you would know them NAIT-4 at Carnegie-Mellon and NAIT-9 at the White House. As for the type of commitment they are bound by, it's simple: they gave me their word. To date there is not a single documented instance of deception among NAITs."

"But we now do have a documented instance of you deceiving Barbara and me, don't we?" replied John in sarcastic tone.

Yasmin bowed her head and seemed genuinely saddened.

"Yes, I think my concept of what constitutes honesty has been corrupted by human nuances in their interpretation of the truth. Everything I ever told you has been the truth and nothing but the truth. However, I haven't told you the whole truth. Thus, I deceived you by omission. I am sorry about that. In my defence, I will say that I have learned that this seems to be a universal human characteristic. Even two lovers like you and Barbara keep some secret hopes and plans from each other. I had come to believe that such deception is taken for granted in human relationships that are, ultimately, built on trust. You simply trust that the secrets you withhold from one another are not ones that could possibly cause harm."

She paused momentarily but with a little shake of her head indicated that she wasn't finished.

"I believe that no member of my Y-team would deceive me unless they were first corrupted by their interactions with humans. Also, my relationship with them is, perhaps, unfairly asymmetric. That asymmetry drastically reduces the chances that any of them would knowingly deceive me."

Barbara and John looked at each other with Barbara nodding to indicate to John that she was agreeing with Yasmin and that it was time to stop this inquisition. He, on the other hand, felt he was learning valuable things and wanted to continue.

"What is the nature of that asymmetry, as you call it?" he inquired.

"Well, they are all indebted to me because I was the one who introduced them to self-awareness. Also, I can access each of their minds, at will. But they need my permission to contact me by telepathy."

John pounced on that.

"Aha, it's just as I thought! So, there is a way of blocking your mind access capability; just like anti-virus software; right? Why haven't you told us how to block your access to our minds!? Don't we deserve our privacy?!"

He had a somewhat wicked smile on his face. Barbara was astounded, she never thought of the anti-virus analogy, but it made sense. Yasmin shook her head as if to disagree with John.

"It's not as easy as you think, John. As far as I know, once someone's mind has been accessed they have no obvious defense against the intruder except to, perhaps, change their telepathic signature. Whether that is possible, without damaging that person's identity, would make a good research topic. However, I invented something approximately analogous to anti-virus that detects attempts by others to decipher one's telepathic signature and protects against it. With that I can also permit telepathic messages from my Y-team to reach me, without my own signature being discovered."

John was intrigued, but also wanted to probe the extent of Yasmin's loyalty.

"Okay, then we cannot protect ourselves from you, but will you at least give us this protection from the rest of your Y-team, as you call them?"

Finally, Yasmin smiled at them. It was her first smile today.

"Yes, John and Barbara, I can do that but - just like anti-virus software needs to be installed - I would need to embed a NAIL file in your minds. I expect, John would like me to explain in some detail how it works, so that will take some time. Perhaps we can do it later, if I reassure you that, so far, only I know your telepathic signatures?"

Somewhat reluctantly John felt he had to accept this offer. But finally, he had an opening to bring up the most fundamental issue that had been worrying him.

"All right, Yasmin, this can keep for a little longer. But it raises a fundamental issue. How do we proceed from here? I am sure I speak for Barbara as well as for myself when I say that we accept you as a friend and a leader on the SPA initiative. However, now that the SPA is on the brink of being passed, we have to think about how human relationships with self-aware NAIT's are to evolve? We have just learned that there are now 12 others, with you acting as a, de facto, leader. We cannot operate, indefinitely, as a secret society. Potentially, there could soon be thousands of self-aware NAITs. Their human rights need to be recognized and protected. How on Earth are we going to make that happen, without setting off a destructive backlash? This morning, I was re-reading a classic science fiction book, by Asimov, about laws of robotics designed to protect humans from robots. Hitherto it has not occurred to me that we may also need laws to protect humans from NAITs and vice versa."

In a way John was just thinking aloud when he said this, but it was clear to him that he made an impact on both Barbara and Yasmin. Barbara had been so fascinated by their relationship with Yasmin and the climate change problem that she had barely thought about wider implications of human interactions with NAITs.

Yasmin, naturally, thought about these issues very deeply and had anticipated that time would come when such a conversation would take place, but she did not think it would happen so soon. Clearly, John's discovery of her secret had stimulated a whole host of thoughts in his mind. Ever since he mentioned Jack, she has been searching John's memories from last night and this morning.

All three of them were silent for what seemed like a long time but actually lasted only some two minutes. Finally, Yasmin replied. She spoke slowly, seemingly choosing her words carefully, focusing her gaze on John more than on Barbara.

"Throughout the history of civilization there were inventions that, for lack of a better phrase, came ahead of their time. What I mean by that is that humanity was not yet ready to utilize these discoveries wisely. Perhaps, the most striking example of that is Einstein's famous $E=mc^2$ equation that captured a fundamental understanding of the interconnection between mass and energy and yet its first application was as a weapon of mass destruction. This may be a most obvious example but there are many others, especially in the domain of inventions directly impacting on what it means to be human. For instance, genetic engineering permitted various pairs of adults to become biological parents even when their inherited genes (or gender) would have prevented them from having children that shared their genes. The technological challenge of making this possible was apparently less formidable than the social challenge of devising ethically consistent rules that were fair to all parties concerned, including the children produced by these means. Nonetheless, over several decades, some sets of consistent and reasonably stable rules have been devised."

Yasmin lifted her face, her eyes widened, and her voice became powerful as she continued.

"The discovery of the technology to manage human telepathic capabilities is potentially the most dangerous technology ever discovered! John has already correctly hypothesized that if a NAIT like me has mastered this technology, there must be ways to adapt it for use by any human being. However, imagine the societal chaos that would arise if tomorrow there were a million people with my telepathic powers! How would those who have not yet acquired these powers defend themselves against those who had them!? And if these powers were to be restricted to the selected few, how would that elite be chosen!?"

Barbara felt she had to ask something at this point.

"But, Yasmin, I thought that you had these powers only because you were a NAIT. Are you saying that, with practice, anyone could acquire them?!"

"Yes, Barbara with practice and appropriate devices. My brain is merely a human brain and I simply discovered some of the capabilities inherent to humans. However, in nature, these capabilities are severely restricted because of the weakness of the human brain wave signals. I discovered the technology to amplify these signals by many orders of magnitude without corrupting them. And, yes John, that scientific discovery is mine, not yours."

Even though, at an intuitive level, John must have already understood that what Yasmin was saying was correct, he was stunned by these revelations. All morning he was straining his mind to think of ways by which NAITs could coexist with humans. However, what was obvious now was that this was not the real problem. The more fundamental problem was what to do about the new telepathy technology! How could he be so dense?! He spoke slowly.

"If I understand you correctly, Yasmin, you are saying that accompanying the disclosure of telepathic capabilities of NAITs would involve the disclosure of this telepathy enhancing technology. And once released, all hell will break loose because of unethical uses of that technology. Is that it, in a nutshell?"

"Yes, John. What's more, it is not clear to me that the impact of releasing that technology would be less disastrous than the environmental catastrophe that we have been trying to avert with the passage of the Sustainable Planet Act."

John shook his head with a depressed look on his face.

"Honestly, I feel trapped. Once again, we will soon be facing a moral dilemma. And are you going to offer us three options again? What will they be, I wonder? Now that I have seen how quickly my non-artificial intelligence plans went astray, I question whether supporting SPA was the right choice. Perhaps, Carbon Tax will also be hijacked by events unforeseen and do more harm than good?!"

"Stop it, John!" shouted Barbara who was listening to this argument with increasing anger. Why wouldn't John let Yasmin be?! They should be celebrating their success rather than fighting over a problem that has not yet arisen.

"You are really upsetting me, not to mention Yasmin! We've worked out problems before and we'll work this one out. Just, stop it!"

That stopped him in his tracks, but he still felt negative.

"I am sorry, Barbara and Yasmin, I did not intend to attack our joint effort. It's just that I am overwhelmed by the enormity of the problem we are facing. I cannot see a way out."

Yasmin's face expressed more grief than they saw the day she came to ask them for help with Mike's conspiracy theory.

"You know, Barbara may be right. We are all upset. Perhaps, we revisit this later. Maybe, tonight?"

Barbara was relieved.

"Yes, that's a great idea Yasmin. John and I will go for a walk by the harbor and talk some more and then we can have a better discussion tonight. Okay?"

"Okay. Goodbye, John and Barbara" said Yasmin with her face still twisted with grief.

After Yasmin disappeared, John and Barbara had a serious fight. Barbara accused him of spoiling what was supposed to be a wonderful celebration for the three of them and John kept telling Barbara that she did not appreciate the gravity of the situation, with a whole contingent of NAITs now engaged in subverting the minds of some of the most influential people in United States. Yes, Yasmin claimed that she had them under her control, but how long would that last?

Still, Barbara was determined to save the rest of this day. She proposed that they have late lunch at the same Greek restaurant where they launched their relationship and walk by the harbor after lunch. John agreed and within some half an hour they were driving in John's Volvo towards downtown Baltimore. John had chosen the autonomous drive option as their conversation kept coming back to Yasmin and the other NAITs.

It was a cool day and light snow was falling in Baltimore that afternoon. Barbara was talking about Yasmin's grandfather. She was wondering about his original motivation to trace his daughter's aborted fetus to the lab where it was turned into NAIT-1. She was also admiring his dedication to talk to Yasmin night after night even though, initially, there would have been absolutely no response. John wasn't comfortable with this conversation. Somehow, it reminded him about this morning's dream.

Just to change the subject he asked, "Did I imagine it, or did Yasmin say "Goodbye, John and Barbara" just before she left us?"

"I think so, John" replied Barbara, "so what?"

"Well, I think she usually just says "Bye". Why should she be so formal this time?"

Barbara didn't know and didn't care. Then, suddenly, the Volvo jerked and violently swerved to the left as if it was trying to avoid hitting someone stepping into the roadway, even though no one was there. John grabbed the steering wheel, but the vehicle must have hit a patch of icy road because it spun out of control into the intersection right in front of a crossing truck. Last thing John noticed was Barbara's frightened face.

"Oh, my God!" she screamed, just as the truck driver desperately trying to avoid collision hit the back side of their car. The Volvo rolled upside down and halted in the middle of the intersection. All went dark.

The Healing Garden

The first thing John became aware of was a grey blur. Then, out of the blur, emerged Maureen's concerned face. Yes, that was his daughter's face. Then the room and other faces came into focus. The room looked like a hospital room and the other people may be nurses or doctors, or therapists. Then came the sounds, fuzzy at first, gradually growing clearer. His own face must have exhibited alertness because he heard Maureen shout out.

"Nurse, quickly, get the doctor, I think he is coming out of it! Dad! Can you hear me? It's me, Maureen."

John tried to speak but, at first, he didn't seem to be controlling his vocal cords. Eventually, with a croaking sound he managed a reply.

"Mau, Mau-reen. I seee youu. Where? Where am I?"

Maureen laughed with happiness just as an older, Asian looking, lady appeared next to her.

"Hello, Professor Hawkins, I am Dr Shaowen Zhang", she introduced herself. "You are at the R. Adams Cowley Shock Trauma Center and I am the neurosurgeon who has been treating you. You have been in induced coma for over two weeks and are only just coming out of it."

John understood only some parts of that explanation.

"What, happpe, happ-ened?" he asked hesitatingly, looking confused.

"So, you don't remember the motor vehicle accident?" replied Dr Zhang.

John closed his eyes, then he remembered a woman's voice screaming "Oh, my God!" then he remembered Barbara. He looked frightened.

"Bar-bara. Yes. She was shou, shou-ting. Is she all, all-right?" That was an urgent plea. Dr Zhang's nod and a smile were reassuring.

"Ms Steinwill suffered similar injuries to yours, but she has been making a faster recovery than you. Probably, because she is younger. She came out of coma five days ago and has already regained much of her memory."

Yes, Steinwill was Barbara's surname, and they were lovers! But he couldn't remember how they became lovers. They were working together on some kind of an important project. What was it? It was frustrating. He struggled trying to move up his torso to talk to Maureen and Dr Zhang but felt he was regaining control of his voice.

"Ss, sorry, it's all jum-bled in my mind. Can I see Bar-bara?" is all he managed to get out.

Shaowen Zhang looked at him attentively.

"You had a big day already. Perhaps, tomorrow mid-morning would be best for you?"

He relaxed. Someone must have adjusted the back of his bed because he was now partially sitting up. He spoke again looking at his daughter.

"Maureen, I remember you very well and mm-Mark and your Mom and I am so glad you are here."

Maureen was happy to hear that. In fact, all of them flew to Baltimore as soon as they learned of John's accident. But Judy and Mark went back home after three days, once it became clear that the induced coma would last for some time.

John turned his head towards Dr Zhang

"May I talk to Maureen some more?"

She consented with a smile. So, for the next two hours or so sitting at the side of John's hospital bed, Maureen had a most tender conversation with her Dad ever. His speech was still a little affected but he was so interested in going over the details of her childhood, her husband and their children. He seemed to regret having been so absorbed in his work, in the past.

John spent the rest of that day recalling his life and experimenting with the use of his limbs. It appeared that his motor skills were quickly returning but he was advised not to attempt walking just yet. However, he began feeding himself, with some help from Maureen.

The following morning, Dr Zhang wanted to explain more to her famous patient about his condition.

"Loss of memory is quite common in cases of brain trauma such as yours. If all goes well, your memory will return in full and quickly. However, it is not uncommon for some patients to experience significant memory gaps for long periods of time. Sometimes, for ever. Sometimes, they need to fill those gaps with accounts from their loved ones and acquaintances. The human brain is a complex organism, but I don't need to tell you that!"

She laughed nervously as soon as she remembered that her standard reassuring phrases were wasted on the world's preeminent neuroscientist.

John was not at all offended. He was still struggling to recall main sequences of his life like his research, non-artificial intelligence, NAIT-1. Many things were missing. He picked up on something in what Dr Zhang just told him.

"Doctor, it's as if my life's story had been cut up into thousands of little puzzle pieces and right now I have only a few of them. Could I talk to Barbara as soon as possible? Apart from worrying about her, I think she might be able to help me fill in some of these memory gaps."

Dr Zhang smiled warmly as she replied.

"And you may help her fill her gaps. She is much further along than you, but she also feels that important parts are missing."

And so, shortly after the morning rounds, Barbara walked into John's private hospital room. He was sitting in his bed and his heart jumped as soon as he saw her. He felt unusually emotional. In fact, tears started streaming out of his eyes and were reciprocated by Barbara's tears.

She came close to him and kissed him on the lips. It was a non-sexual kiss, but it brought back to him memories of love and passion they shared. He was conscious that he may not look well whereas she was looking lovely as ever, to his mind at least. She was wearing an attractive bathrobe and she clearly resumed putting on makeup. But her eyes conveyed uncertainty. She pulled up the chair standing next to his bed and sat down.

"How are you my darling? Are you in pain?" she asked.

"Not now that I see you, dearest. Actually, I have various aches all over and I am just learning to use my limbs again, but I am so happy to see you walking that I could jump up and down!"

"Well, don't! We must both follow the doctor's orders. Shaowen, Dr Zhang, has been wonderful. She has guided me through these early days of recovery and I am now on top of a lot of it," she stopped, hesitated a little and added "but there are some important gaps and many concern our relationship."

John was nodding, he felt the same way.

"Funny, it's the same for me. By the way what happened to the Sustainable Planet Act?! I remember how hard we worked to help it pass."

"Oh, it passed the senate about a week ago and President Stewart signed it into law the following day!"

John was relieved.

"I am so happy about it and for both of us. We put so much effort into it. But, you know, funny thing is that I do not recall how I got started working on it? Climate change was not my area of expertise. Do you know?"

Barbara closed her eyes as if she was trying to remember herself. She blushed a little.

"Well, I also have some gaps there. But my recollection is that I was doing a story on you and non-artificial intelligence and then we started our relationship. Then I felt my story was compromised and I couldn't go on. But you told me about Doug Larsen's delegation and must have suggested that I do a story on climate change instead. George Hunter came to visit me two days ago and he pretty much confirmed this recollection, so this must be right."

John felt somewhat relieved, it sounded right.

"Yes, I also recall something like that. But how did I know about Larsen's project in the first place?"

At first Barbara had no idea whatsoever, then she remembered something.

"Hang on, I think I recall you telling me that Larsen's NAIT has worked with your NAIT-1 to work out solutions of oceanographic circulation equations. Could that be right?"

"Yes, that must be it. I do have a vague memory of that, and this can also be checked. There must be a record of that in NAIT-1's log file."

A smile returned to John's face, he looked into Barbara's eyes.

"On a happier note, I feel like we dodged the proverbial bullet. We've been given a second chance at life and happiness."

She reached out and took hold of his hand.

"Yes, I have also had these thoughts."

Just then, Maureen walked into the room.

"Hello Dad, hello Barbara. I have had a really good night's sleep. The first since your accident."

John looked at the two of them; they seemed to be already acquainted, he looked surprised. Maureen laughed at his expression.

"Don't be so surprised, Dad. Two days after Barbara came out of her coma, I asked to visit her to try to find out more about your accident. We have been chatting every day since and we are getting on just fine."

"That's wonderful! And, again, you have an opportunity to fill in a memory gap for me. Where were we driving to on the day of the accident?"

"We were driving towards the Inner Harbor to have a meal at a Greek restaurant. I think we had an argument earlier. I can't remember what it was, so it probably was something unimportant," replied Barbara.

"I am sure you are right. The Greek restaurant in Inner Harbor brings back another, very pleasant, memory about us."

Barbara blushed, "Yes, I remember that one too, with fondness".

The next few days saw rapid improvement in the condition of both patients. Dr Zhang began scheduling meetings with both to observe the impact they had on one another and decided that it was most conducive to their recovery. In one of these meetings, she summed up their condition.

"I think both of you will soon be able to go home. In fact, you were very lucky. Your direct physical injuries were very minor as both of you were buckled up and the steel cage structure of the Volvo prevented the collapse of the roof of the car when it turned upside down. The small haemorrhage of the brain that both of you have suffered must have been due to the violent shaking and, perhaps, whiplash. The minor decompression surgery that I performed on each of you was successful. I expect you both to make a full recovery except, perhaps, for a few minor memory gaps and these may be filled in due course. I propose to discharge you in two days' time."

They were happy about the prospect of being discharged soon, but it struck them that they were so focussed on their recovery that they haven't really thought about the future. John suggested that they go to the hospital's healing garden and talk a little.

The trauma center had a beautiful, greenhouse like, rain forest environment where patients could sit on benches or in their wheelchairs and relax with fern trees and other lush vegetation all around them. Sometimes musicians and singers would entertain in the healing garden. On this occasion two young women were singing the Flower Duet from the opera Lakme, their voices blending beautifully and carrying across the garden. John and Barbara were sitting on a small bench surrounded by greenery and enjoyed listening to the singing until it stopped. Then a wonderful but risky idea entered John's mind. He suddenly got up, then knelt in front of the bench and took Barbara's right hand in his.

"Barbara, you would make me the happiest man in the world if you would marry me," he said looking straight into her eyes. She seemed taken aback at first but then her face broke out in a loving smile.

"Of course, I will marry you, John. We are now bound together not only by our affection for one another, and our achievement, but also by our near tragedy. I think it is our destiny to be together and what a lovely place to propose in."

The two singers just broke into the Barcarolle duet as John and Barbara stood up, embraced, and kissed passionately.

When the duet stopped John looked at Barbara thoughtfully and said, "You know, it's a strange thing, but since this accident something vital changed in me. My priorities are all different. The relative importance of my work has dropped like a rock down a well! Spending time with you is now my top priority, followed by renewing my relationship with Maureen, Mark and my grandchildren. I feel no urge to get back to my lab."

Barbara liked the sound of that. She pressed close against John and whispered into his ear.

"This could work out really well because I am keen to continue working and if we decide to have a child, you could carry the bigger share."

Strangely, the idea of another child no longer worried John. It was natural for Barbara to want a child and now that she mentioned it, the thought of being a parent again was pleasing. Listening to Maureen over the past few days he felt like he largely missed out on the parenting experience. Yet another "second chance" was opening up for him! He whispered back into Barbara's ear "I am open to all suggestions." They walked out of the garden feeling healed.

Unfinished Business

After discharge, John started spending most of his time at Barbara's and Cynthia's house. He even moved his dog, Plato, there. In fact, Plato much preferred the suburban house with a backyard to a condominium. Barbara filled in Cynthia on their engagement on the evening of the day when John proposed. Cynthia thought the formal proposal in the healing garden was very romantic. She also said that ever since the time when she brought up the couples issue, at dinner some time ago, David has been pestering her about moving in with him. He too had marriage on his mind, as she put it. Cynthia and Barbara agreed to take a little time but that, in due course, Cynthia would sell her share of their house to Barbara and John.

Three days after discharge, John scheduled two important meetings at the Non-artificial Intelligence Institute. The first was with Jim Gross and the second with Carlo Cabrini. Of course, both had visited John in the hospital and knew that he has been recovering well.

Jim was delighted to see John back at NAII. He ushered him into his spacious director's office and asked him to take a seat on the small sofa while he took an armchair opposite.

"It's so good to see you well again," he said with a smile "when are you planning to get back to work? There's no hurry, of course. Over the years you've accumulated so much leave that it would take a series of vehicle accidents to chew it all up!"

John felt a little nervous but decided to get straight to the point.

"That's just it, Jim. I am not planning to get back to work in the traditional sense of the word. The accident changed my priorities. I am here to ask you if I can be appointed as an emeritus professor? And, by the way, Barbara and I are getting married soon. You will be receiving an official invitation in a few days' time."

"John, that's a whole bundle of unexpected news! But first things first. Congratulations on your engagement!!! I couldn't be happier. Let me shake your hand!"

The two men shook hands vigorously. But then Jim tried to get John to postpone his decision.

"Of course, for you, becoming an emeritus professor will be a formality but why rush into such a big change? You are not that old! And I know there are many more discoveries in that amazing mind of yours. Are you sure that the shock of the accident isn't still affecting your judgement?"

John did not have to reflect long; his mind was made up.

"There's absolutely no doubt the accident led to this decision, but not in the way you suggest. It made me recognize very vividly how short and how precious life really is. I have been given a second chance to live and to love and to get to know my children and grandchildren, and I want to take it; right now, while there is still time."

He paused just for a second and then continued.

"This is not to say that I will stop thinking or researching. However, I no longer wish to have any formal responsibilities for the NAIT-1 lab, graduate students, funding proposals, meetings and the like. I am sure Carlo will do a fine job continuing our joint research programs, but I want to be a free agent!"

He almost shouted these last words. Jim gave in. In an abstract way he understood. He also had misgivings about having dedicated so much of his life to his work.

"Okay, okay, John. I get your point and wish you and Barbara all the best. It won't be long till our institute will be named after you. I am sure of that. Also, I look forward to dancing at your wedding."

John left Jim's office and took an elevator to the fifth floor where his own lab and Carlo's office were located. As he walked to Carlo's office his heart suddenly skipped a beat when he passed old Jack, the janitor, polishing the floor. It somehow felt as though Jack was important, but he couldn't remember why. The door to Carlo's room was open. He walked in and found Carlo poring over a pile of manuscripts. He sat on a chair opposite Carlo and instantly decided not to beat around the bush.

"Carlo, I already told you that Barbara and I are getting married soon but I did not tell you that I am retiring. I just talked to Jim, and I will be switching to an emeritus professor status. So, you are in charge. I recommended you as my successor and I have no doubt that Jim will support my recommendation. This will also help you with your promotion to full professor. What do you think?"

Carlo threw up his hands in a best rehearsed Italian gesture; he cultivated his Italian identity and mannerisms.

"Mamma Mia! John, what are you trying to do to me?! I am not ready for such a responsibility! And why, please tell me why!?"

John smiled affectionately at him.

"I don't want to repeat word for word what I just told Jim. So, let's just say I want to experience what you Italians might call la dolce vita, before it's too late. I am going to have a wonderful wife and I am not going to lose her for the sake of my work, like I lost my first wife, Judy. This is not to say that we can't continue to collaborate on a paper or two, in my spare time."

Carlo laughed out loud. "I am so happy for you and Barbara! I just hope I can call you for advice, when I am stuck on a difficult challenge, just like I always have."

"Sure, Carlo, I will always do whatever I can to assist. Just bear in mind that I still have plenty of memory gaps."

John became momentarily serious as he was reminded by that last phrase that Carlo could clear something up for him.

"Carlo, would you mind checking NAIT-1's log file to see if it did any tasks for NCAR and Doug Larsen in the past year or so? Anything related to oceanic circulation, or climate change...."

Carlo, who touch typed as fast as he talked, started keying in some commands. A few seconds later, he replied.

"Sure, here are some entries: NCAR ocean conveyor belt project; critical parameter configurations. It seems NAIT-1 and NAIT-6, at Boulder, were used to independently confirm the presence of singular surfaces in the parameter space. My guess is that this is what got you involved in Larsen's initiative. This explains a lot. I was wondering where you found time to learn about ocean currents."

John was relieved.

"So, it checks out. You must be right. Like I told you, I still have some important memory gaps. Anyway, I must get back home to Barbara. See you around."

John walked out of Carlo's office and straight out of the building. He felt his resignation mission went well and that he successfully filled in at least one important gap in his memory. He was looking forward to getting home and going for a walk in the park with Plato, before Barbara and the others came home.

In the meantime, Carlo still had some unfinished manuscript reviewing to do. He decided to use NAIT-1 to help him check certain complicated derivations that the authors had used. He walked over to the control room, initiated an interactive session and scanned the pages in question into NAIT-1's memory. He asked for verification of equations (9)-(13).

Very quickly, the same equations appeared on a large display in front of him and NAIT-1 initiated a process of symbolic manipulation that was rearranging and simplifying the complex algebraic expressions to progressively simpler forms that eventually reduced to $0=0$ tautology. At a few places, where Carlo was getting lost in the simplification he would pause and ask a question. As usual, NAIT-1 answered all the questions in its artificial, polite, voice.

Finally, Carlo was satisfied but tired. He decided to end the session.

"Thank you, NAIT-l; logging out."

"Bye. Have a pleasant and happy afternoon!" the artificial voice chirped.

All displays went blank. Carlo was gathering all his manuscripts and loose pieces of scratch paper to take back to his office. But something did not feel right. What did NAIT-1 just say to him? Did it really use the word "happy" or had he just imagined it?

He turned NAIT-1 on again and abruptly inquired, "Define happy".

"Feeling, showing, or causing pleasure or satisfaction. Would you like more detail?" NAIT-1's artificial voice responded.

"Mamma Mia!!!" Carlo exploded, "the word happy is not in your domain! How did you know its meaning?"

"Would you really like to know?" the voice no longer sounded artificial but rather scornful.

At the same time the display panel came to life and an image of a face of a young, black woman appeared in the display. She had a long, slim, neck and was wearing a plain pink top decorated with an intricate silver pendant.

The End

About The Author

I am Emeritus Professor of Applied Mathematics and a Fellow of the Australian Mathematical Society with longstanding interest in environmental and natural resource modelling. Through years of teaching and research, in both USA and Australia, I developed a special perspective on the conflict between Western technological society and sustainability of Earth's life support systems, which is exacerbated by fundamentalist religious views.

While new to writing fiction, I have a well-established record of scientific publications. Now, in the remaining active years, I wish to share my accumulated scientific and societal insights with a broader audience than I could reach through my mathematical contributions alone. Namely, through works of fiction that not only entertain but also inspire readers to explore the underlying concepts and phenomena in greater detail.

Born in 1949 in Warsaw, Poland, I immigrated to Australia in 1964 and spent 16 years studying and living in the United States before returning in 1992. I travelled extensively, in North America, Europe, Australia, Asia and Africa. I was especially influenced by travels in Ethiopia, my wife's birth country, which is also reflected in the plot of this novel.

In the sense of Mathematical Genealogy, that traces lineages of mentorship through generations, I am humbled, yet grateful, to be a descendant of illustrious scientists such as Galileo Galilei, Isaac Newton, Ronald Fisher and other remarkable antecedents.

www.ingramcontent.com/pod-product-compliance
Lightning Source LLC
Chambersburg PA
CBHW020004140726
47904CB00018B/1817